Time: The Present

Time: The Present
Selected Stories of Tess Slesinger

Introduction by Vivian Gornick
Afterword by Paula Rabinowitz

RECOVERED BOOKS
BOILER HOUSE PRESS

Contents

Introduction

by Vivian Gornick

The great Rosa Luxemburg, radical extraordinaire, possessed a rich appreciation of life in all its varied manifestations. While the potential for socialist revolution was her core passion, she was sensually engaged by love and literature, flowers and music, sunlight and philosophy. She had, as well, an ardent interest in replacing the theory-driven jargon that dominated the speech and writing of her fellow socialists with the lucid plain-speak that alone could stir the hearts as well as the minds of the rank and file. She wanted working men and women to feel the beauty of Marxism as she felt it.

Luxemburg also loved a man who was her polar opposite: Leo Jogiches, a rigid Marxist whose temperament was as angry, brooding, and remote as Rosa's was warm, open, and immediate. Jogiches subscribed wholly to the credo of the Russian radical, Mikhail Bakunin, which famously declared the true revolutionary "a man who has no interests of his own, no cause of his own, no feelings, no habits, no belongings, not even a name. Everything in him is absorbed by a single, exclusive interest, a single thought, a single passion—the revolution." This made Rosa crazy. As she and Leo hardly ever lived in the same town at the same time, their correspondence was vast and on Rosa's end often despairing. She once wrote him, "When I open your letters and see six sheets covered with debates about the Polish Socialist party, and not a single word about ordinary life, I feel faint."

Tess Slesinger is the prodigiously talented, left-leaning writer of the 1930s whose fiction was often grounded in social realism but dipped in a modernist irony that Luxemburg might well have envied. The situation that Slesinger repeatedly nailed would have been mother's milk to Rosa: a marriage wherein the wife tries to convince the husband that personal happiness and the struggle for social justice need not, indeed must not, be mutually exclusive. Implicit in this view is the conviction that if people give up sex and art while making the revolution, they will produce a world more heartless than the one they are setting out to replace.

***

Tess Slesinger was born in 1905 in New York City into a well-to-do Jewish family of European extraction. She was educated at the Ethical Culture school in Manhattan, then Swarthmore College and the Columbia School of Journalism. In 1928 she married Herbert Solow, an intellectually rigorous man on the left associated with the Menorah Journal, a leading Jewish-American magazine of the 20s and 30s, among whose editors and contributors could be counted Elliot Cohen who, years later, became the first editor of Commentary and Lionel Trilling who, years later, became, well, Lionel Trilling.

Around these people swirled a group of marvelously neurotic literary and political intellectuals devoted, one and all, to the idea if not the reality of socialist revolution. It was among them that Slesinger experienced the kind of sensory deprivation that triggered her gift for criticizing intellectualism bereft of emotional intelligence.

In 1932 Slesinger divorced Solow, and within two years had published a novel and a collection of stories; thereafter she seems to have written almost no fiction. In 1935 she made her way to Hollywood where she embarked on a remarkably successful career as a screenwriter. Here, on a movie set, she met an assistant director named Frank Davis who, in 1936, became her second husband. With Davis she had two children and teamed up to write the screenplay for a number of films, among them *The Good Earth* and *A Tree Grows in Brooklyn*. In 1945, her life was cut short by cancer. She was meaning of *Time: The Present* resides in the stories that illustrate the shocking strangeness of sexual intimacy, especially among people for whom marriage has been a rude awakening. It is here, with this subject, and mainly through her perfected use of the internal monologue, that Slesinger's mind shines, and her talent reaches far.

In the story called "On Being Told That Her Second Husband Has Taken His First Lover", we have a woman talking to herself as she lies in bed in the arms of her husband who has just confessed to an infidelity and is anxious to know that he will be forgiven. He obviously thinks this is the first she will have even imagined his cheating on her, but she has in fact long suspected it. "So it's nice my dear" she is saying to herself, "that you are always so clever; and sad my dear that you always need to be. Time was when a thing like this was a shock that fell heavily in the pit of your stomach and gave you indigestion all at once. But you can only feel a thing like this in its entirety the first time...."

The narrator sees the fear in her husband's face and she despises him for it, at the same time that she is gripped by her own fear that he might leave her. Then the ineluctability of the situation hits her full force: "For you see it all suddenly, you see it there in his face, reluctant as he is to hurt you," he is not going to end his affair. In fact, "He will be lost to you the minute he walks out of your sight; he will be back, of course, but this time and forever after you will know that he has been away, clean away, on his own. You see it in his face, and your heart which had sunk to the lowest bottom, suddenly sinks lower." To this day these lines chill my heart.

Of course, not a word of these thoughts is ever spoken. In the course of this monologue we come to feel viscerally the treacherous undertow that pulls at a marriage in which the burden of disastrously mixed feelings conspires with what is said and what is not said to, ultimately, make each partner feel trapped in an alliance with a stranger posing as an intimate.

In one version or another, this same wife and husband appear in the stories "Mother to Dinner", "For Better, For Worse" and "Missis Flinders". In all of them a woman, young or initiated, puzzles over the inescapable feeling that, essentially, the man she calls her husband is "other." He is the man to whom she is married, yes. The man with whom she lies down every night, yes. The man whose disapproval makes her heart shrivel, yes. But what does all that mean? Who, after all, is he? She will never have the answers to these questions, but marriage is the school she attends in order to learn who she is.

In "Mother to Dinner" we are invited into the mind of Katharine, a 22 year old bride of eleven months who has been out shopping for a dinner she plans to make that evening for her husband and her parents. While shopping, Katharine has been delighted to watch herself imitating her mother's life—the pleasure she's taken in choosing this cut of meat, that firm tomato.

However, the scorn of Katharine's husband, a man of severe intellectual standards who holds her bourgeois mother in contempt, keeps breaking into her daydream. She recalls his often having taunted her with the prediction that because she had no serious work and thinks so much of little things (like shopping for dinner), it will not be long before she becomes her mother. Would that really be so bad, Katharine thinks resentfully. As she walks home, she feels herself already frowning across the table at her keenly intelligent husband "politely insulting" her clueless mother.

More than frowning: agonizing. She thinks of all the women she'd seen shopping, and wonders if they had been aware of "the uprooting, the transplanting, the bleeding involved in their calmly leaving their homes to go live with strangers." Suddenly, she is attacked by loneliness and feels a strong desire to call her husband but she knows she'll only get his firm, business-like voice asking 'What do you want, dear?' and that stops her cold. "Probably Gerald (the husband) was right, she thought wearily—for he was so often 'right' in a logical, meaningless way"—that thinking, as she did, about every small thing was "an imbecilic waste of time," .an irrelevance. Yet she can't help also thinking, "[B]etween two people who lived together, why should anything be irrelevant?"

On the other hand—and she has no reason to not want there to be another hand—she's been shocked to realize that she herself has something to answer for. If she's honest with herself, she must admit that much as she loves and admires Gerald she had expected to regard him as her mother regarded her father—"with a maternal tolerance touched by affectionate irony"—and this had put him on his guard. He was right when he said to her, "You resent me because you have a pre-conceived idea of the role to which all husbands are rel-egated by their wives; you'd like to laugh me out of any important existence."

This last sentence is the key to many Slesinger stories in which we have a husband bent on devoting himself to large, world-making concerns while his wife wishes to "trap" him in the insignificance of domestic happiness. Interestingly, when Slesinger allows the husband to speak for himself, his position is not without merit. While the dominating point of view belongs to the woman, it often seems that Slesinger wishes to mete out some measure of sympathy to the man as well; nailing him is not really what she's up to. Even in "Missis Flinders", the most sav-age and the most woman-centered of the internal mon-ologues, a ragged vein of pity for both the wife and the husband runs just beneath the story line.

"Missis Flinders" was published in 1932 in *Story Magazine* and made a tremendous stir because it openly used abortion as the issue at stake in a marriage that is failing for the reason most marriages fail: emotional good will, if it ever existed between this husband and this wife, is now draining steadily away...and the world

10

inside the mind of each is beginning to look surreal.

Margaret Flinders, one half of a radically left couple, stands on the steps of a maternity hospital watching her husband, Miles, running about in the street, trying frantically to hail a taxi so they can get home to face the alienating consequences of the decision they'd taken to abort the child she had only days before been carrying. Margaret had wanted this baby badly, but Miles had persuaded her that nothing was more important than insuring their economic (and therefore intellectual) freedom. "We'd go soft," he had said, if they started having children. "We'd go bourgeois."

Yes, she repeats to herself, with the taste of iron in her mouth, they'd go soft, "they might slump and start liking people, they might weaken and forgive stupidity, they might yawn and forget to hate." Having a baby meant "the end of independent thought and turning everything into a scheme for making money...why, in a time like this...to have a baby would be suicide—goodbye to our plans, goodbye to our working out schemes for each other and the world—our courage would die, our hopes concentrate on the sordid business of keeping three people alive, one of whom would be a burden and an expense for twenty years...."

She had begun to see Miles as "a dried-up intellectual husk: sterile, empty, as hollow" as she now feels herself, driven to mask his personal anxieties behind the political rhetoric of their times. And then comes

11

an implicating thought. Perhaps it was really that one needed to believe in oneself in order to welcome parenthood—and neither she nor Miles did. Perhaps, after all, parenthood meant having the courage to risk seeing oneself replicated in another human being—and neither of them did. After which comes an even greater piece of suspicion: "Afraid to perpetuate themselves, were they? Afraid of anything that might loom so large in their personal lives.... Afraid, maybe, of a personal life."

***

Slesinger was often compared to Mary McCarthy, a writer who was also given to irony and irreverence. But McCarthy's irony always carried the sting of one who takes no prisoners, whereas Slesinger, no matter how mocking, leaves her readers feeling that courage and cowardice in her characters are dealt out indiscriminately (Ah, Rosa! Ah, Leo!) The deeper story in Slesinger is always that of people trapped together in levels of anxiety that approach the existential. For this reason her satire stops short of murder, and her feeling for life's unavoidable sorrow remains haunting. *Time: The Present* strikes a note of human watchfulness that often gives up the stereotypic for the tragic.

Time: The Present

Selected Stories of Tess Slesinger

Memoirs of an Ex-Flapper

Vanity Fair, December 1934

In those days there was time and money for everything. The panic of 1905 had died as we were being born and our parents brought us up to feel that, so far as "nice" people were concerned, everything was immutably in its place. The century was young when we were young, the "nice" people lived where there were plenty of parks and private schools, the poor people knew their place and went about properly in rags; the only thing to fear (in those days of the Hendrik Hudson Centennial, 1909, which we witnessed from the roof of our eight-story sky-scraper apartment) was an occasional drunk rolling out of a pre-prohibition swinging door—and of course the Public School Children. And though we were New Yorkers, born and bred, though we grew up in the sound of grinding street-cars and played among the skirmishes of passing trucks, though we knew blue-birds chiefly by hearsay and had to take crocuses for granted, still we were not so badly off—for Riverside Drive and Central Park, where our nurses took us skating after school, the empty lots (which our mothers in vain pronounced Treacherous), even the forbidden streets where the poor people lived, with their Public School Children, were as dear and familiar and safe as the back-yards which we were born without.

In the morning there was the "I cash clo'es" man groaning down the street and at evening there were the men bearing ladders and lighting our city by gas; in winter there was Private School and in summer Vacation, either the Mountains or the Seashore (to which our Papas commuted) and returning in the late fall to find our enemies, the Public School Children, already back at work, as pale and tough as we had left them in the spring. We who attended Private Schools were both proud and ashamed, down on Riverside Drive, of our Fraüleins sitting in rows upon the benches, and, secretly, we envied and feared the Public School Children, invading our park at three o'clock with their oil-cloth-covered books slung by a strap across one shoulder. Sometimes a playmate was segregated with "Whooping Cough" on a placard on his back; and, from our sandpile or the playground swings, we waved, and the quarantined one would whoop back lonesomely over the hill.

There is no telling exactly when the change began to take place, nor how it first manifested itself in our ten-year-old minds; but it is certain that that first decade of our lives was the only peaceful one we've ever known. It must have happened gradually, that our Mamas forgot to listen sometimes, that our Papas occasionally grew cross, that war stepped out of our history books and took possession of our street. Our friend the Elevator Man read the papers all day long, riding up and down from the first floor to the eighth; the maids hanging out washing on the roof quoted their fellows' opinions. All up and down the block the little girls playing hopscotch began to murmur between twosies and threesies, *Who're you for, Sister, who's your Papa for? My Papa's for the Germans, my Papa's for the French, my Mama's neutral—it's your turn, your turn, Leona! you've got to do twosies again!* Until at School we learned to say Liberty Measles, the Public School Children all took up French; our Mamas said to eat every scrap of food on account of the Belgian children who had none, and our Fraüleins grew pale over their letters from home; until everybody on our block but the janitor's half-witted daughter had learned to shout *The Allies! the Allies! my Papa says we CAN'T be neutral any more!* and down on Riverside Drive our youngest brothers joined the Public School Children in turning the summer-houses into forts.

The Fraüleins disappear somewhere, the Bohemian cooks drop their German fellows; the Elevator Man departs in two-rooms-and-kitchenette—respectable couples went to bed, for lack of space, on the divans in their sitting-rooms; quite "nice" people, for a brief spell during the housing shortage, had their kitchens in their bathrooms; and all this with no Greenwich Villager's delight. The coal-shortage left our houses cold, so that for one winter the only comfortable room in our house was the dining-room, in which we took turns dressing. We still had respectable addresses, but, actually, we were living little better than the Public School Children in their slums on Amsterdam Avenue.

In short, our Private School world was shot to hell.

Our homes were no longer the pleasant, leisurely open-houses that they had been; it was no fun to invite one's class-mates to the room where one's parents slept; the cooks despised their "families", turned snobs and misers, and were less ready to bake cakes impulsively. And beside all that, there was an air of worry in our homes that it was nicer to escape. So we took to the streets in a body, and upper Broadway was our Street. Flashy delicatessen-restaurants had sprung to life, and Chinese eating-places one flight up. Cheap jewelry shops, hosiery shops, souvenir stores, seven-dollar-dresses lent a transient, tourist air to what had been our slowly growing small town.

And so we who had never been to war emerged from it, and into a hard-boiled adolescence. We banded together; like our brothers in the army, we adopted a uniform. Like them we had our codes and traditions—and, God knows, a language of our own no sensible adult over seventeen could fathom. In short, we organized. We became Flappers and Collegiates. We still went to School (high-school now) in tam-o'-shanters, middies, and leather coats; our families saw to that. But after school we donned our native costumes and assumed the curious characteristics of our tribe. Dresses to our knees, our coats thrown open, stockings rolled, and striped scarves flying, galoshes (no matter what the weather) loose and flapping round our ankles; bright weird hats with sporting feathers, our faces painted and powdered in the nearest telephone booth, beyond our mothers' sight or recognition. The object was to keep moving and to stay away from home as long as possible.

Our gait was necessarily slow, because of galoshes and the "college walk"; we marched arm in arm, Leona and I (when we weren't at the movies), with a drawling slow-motion, sliding as near to the sidewalk as we could manage, our flat bellies thrust out before us, our backs arched as for a swan-dive; we almost broke our necks with the effort to hang our felt-lidded heads like blasé flowers. Our conversation, at fourteen, was divided between basketball and sex. We passed friends from other Private Schools and made scathing comments on their costumes, which were identical with our own.

***

"Frances! she was a wall-flower three times at the Horace Mann Christmas dance," Leona would confide; "spent most of her time in the ladies' room." Frances was prettier than any of us, as I remembered her, but she was "tame"; she didn't have a "line"; she wore taffeta instead of jersey to the dances and she was always wanting to be a "sister" to the boys. Discussion of the Charleston; Gilda Grey and the Shimmy; how the Japanese Gardens (wedged in between a theater and a vaudeville-house) was the darkest movie on Broadway; here we would stop off and listen to records—*Kalua, Everybody Step, The Sheik, Japanese Sandman* on one side of a record, with *Avalon* on the other. We discussed, further, how some really "nice" boys did go to Public High; how high-hat Charlie had grown since he went away to Exeter; how probably our parents did pet in their day but were never honest enough to admit it; how F. Scott Fitzgerald was the greatest writer that ever lived. "But do you really think—" I start to ask Leona; and she hushes me, for she has spied our boy-friends down the block.

This is the high point of the afternoon. The boys weave toward us with the same slow-motion, their bodies slouched, their shoulders hunched, their trouser cuffs half-in, half outside the open galoshes. Like us, their open coats reveal flying scarves, their flat hats repose drunkenly over the right eye; under their scarves their four-button jackets close nearly to their ties.

Leona and I talk, with a kind of laconic animation,

our eyes, as we approach the boys, turned away like parallel pairs of headlights; without looking we know that the boys turn their eyes away too, bending them toward the curb. It is only when we are almost abreast that we allow ourselves to give the tribal start of surprise and flip our felts at our class-mates. The boys, humming "What'll I Do," float past us, eyeing us infinitesimally beneath weary lowered lids, offering us a mockery of the collegiate salute, their hands too weary to more than touch their hats; Leona and I lift our brows a notch higher in bored salutation and can scarcely wait to draw out mirrors and see how we look at the big moment. "Morty's wonderful," I breathe. "Collegiate," Leona returns more correctly. When Leona and I dreamed about Morty, we did not dream about his magnificent basketball muscles exposed to us daily; we dreamed about the collegiate slant of Morty's hat, the look of the dope-fiend assumed in his collegiate sixteen-year-old-eyes.

In the Spring of 1920 we all became Shifters. To be a Shifter one merely wore an ordinary paper-clip in the lapel, hat-brim, or other conspicuous spot. The initiation consisted simply of carrying out any demand levied by a Shifter-member of the other sex. Ted, for instance, made Leona telephone a lady, picked at random from the phonebook, and inform her that her husband had just dropped dead at his office; Leona hung up in triumph on a woman distracted by sobs, and received her Shifter-clip.

But we were growing restless—we had a public now, and our public demanded something of us. We read about ourselves constantly in newspapers and magazines; we were eyed like some curious brand of expatriate and questioned as though we had dropped from Mars; by the world disapproved and of that world disapproving, we learned that we were a wild crowd, and we had to make good our legend. Life began at fourteen. We became acquainted with the interiors of taxi-cabs, and in the whirling little rooms we learned to drink like acrobats —on the wing, straight out of the flask. We discovered tea-dancing to fill our afternoons—we went more times than we were allowed (dressed in our jerseys and outlandish felts, our bright red mouths and flat-heeled shoes) to the Plaza, the Commodore, the Biltmore; we felt our power as we crashed place after place and captured it by making it unendurable to the older generation—and then when we had taken a place by storm, we coldly abandoned it and caused the rush to some place else. We began to crash the night-clubs too, and, pretty soon, there was no place in town where our parents were ashamed to be seen that we youngsters didn't know. We still adored basketball, we still got sick from bad whiskey, we still suffered pangs from our Private School conscience—but we had, by God, learned not to expose such weaknesses before the adults. We had made good our threats at last: we were as wild as our parents had feared, and more scared and more lost than any of them knew.

I suppose that the effect upon the rest of us was, as it was intended to be, on the whole good. It must have taught us well-bred little boys and girls at the least the untruth of the common slander that Negroes have an unpleasant odor; for certainly none of the Wilsons and Whites and Washingtons in our school ever smelt of anything but soap. And we were brought up, through weekly ethics lessons and the influence of the inevitable elderly lady teacher who had never got Harriet Beecher Stowe out of her mind, to the axiom that all men were created equal.

The few scattered colored children in clean clothes, then, contributed practically to our liberal education. But what effect we, in our more than clean, our often luxurious clothes and with our pink and white faces, had in turn upon them, it is impossible for one of us to judge. Although I can tell you today what has happened since to a number of my old schoolmates, even to those in whom I have long ceased to be interested, and although I run every year across gossip concerning still others, none of us has any idea what happened to our colored classmates. Some of them left school before the high-school years were over; some of them were graduated and stood at our elbows with their rolled-up diplomas; but all of them have equally dropped out of our common knowledge since. Where are they now? Did they drift back to Harlem, those Wilsons and Washingtons and Whites? How do they look back upon their ten years' interlude with white children? I cannot imagine. But I remember vividly the school careers of the two who were in my class.

***

The Wilsons, brother and sister, joined us in the sixth grade. Paul was exquisitely made, his face chiselled and without fault; a pair of delicately dilated nostrils at the end of a short fine nose, and an aureole of dim black curls. Elizabeth was bigger, coarser, more negroid; darker, her lips were thick, her nose less perfect; but still she was a beautiful child, luxuriously made, and promising to develop into a type of the voluptuous Negro woman at her best. Elizabeth was older than Paul; but her brain, like her nose, was less sharp, and both were put into the same class.

For the first week or two our kind teachers paid them the surplus attention which was always extended to Negro, or crippled, or poverty-stricken children. They suggested that Paul be chosen when the boys were choosing up sides; they asked the girls to take Elizabeth as partner. The children stood off from them no more than they stood off from any newcomers. We were not adultly snobbish; we merely glared at all newcomers in our world until they should prove themselves worthy. But by the end of the month, there was no longer any question of choosing Paul: Paul himself was the chooser and the permanently chosen; likewise Elizabeth was besieged with requests for the seats on either side of her in assembly, and it became an honor to have a seat in the same row; and the teachers turned round, and were given rather to suppressing the colored Wilsons than to bringing them out.

For after a certain natural humility had worn off, Paul and Elizabeth were not merely taken into the group; they took over the group. Including the faculty. They were a smashing success. For one thing, they feared nothing; furthermore, they proved marvelous athletes; and they were born leaders. Electing Paul to the captaincy of the basketball team was a mere formality; even if he hadn't richly deserved it, he would have permitted no one else to hold it. Elizabeth was as strong as a horse, less skilful, less graceful than he, but easily outshining, by her animal strength and fearlessness, all the white girls in the class. Beside their athletic prowess, which alone would have won them popularity in a class of eleven-year-olds, both of them were gifted with an over-powering jubilancy and a triumphant bullying wit, which inevitably made them czars.

They ruled the class with a rod of iron, chose their intimates, played with them, dropped them, and patronized the teachers. Their power spread to politics; by the end of the first year Paul was president of the class, and Elizabeth, who could not spell, secretary. Their class-meetings were masterpieces of irreverent wit

and bedlam, subtly dominated by the tacitly authoritative Paul. The teachers turned over to them the difficult
business of controlling the class after recess, and Paul,
in his double capacity of legal president and illegal czar,
easily succeeded where they had long failed. Even his
sister, who was no small power among the girls, feared
and adored him. If her authority was for one moment
questioned, she had only to say, "I'll call Paul. . . ."

I remember myself—and probably not a few others
of the dazzled little white girls did the same in secret—
going home to dream about marrying Paul and taking
Elizabeth to live with us. I remember a moment of certainly unprecedented and of almost unsurpassed voluptuous pleasure on an occasion when Paul, twisting
his wiry body into one of those marvelous knots from
which he unrolled himself to shoot a basket, stretched
so far that his shirt left his trousers and revealed a few
inches of coffee-colored skin glistening with sweat,
which caused me to gasp with delight. We girls chose
to play against the boys of the class rather than among
our-selves, and I was surely not the only girl who had
voted favorably for the pure delight of being tossed on
the ground and swung round the hips by the jubilant
Paul, who had, beside his lovely body and fierce little
nostrils, not the slightest inhibition.

For two years the noisy Wilsons demoralized the
entire class into a raucous group that was never tired
of wrestling, playing basketball, shouting jokes, and

merrily defying the teachers. Not even the famous Seventh Grade Trouble, which involved the Wilsons as central figures, subdued them. Not even the visit, upon that terrifying occasion, of their mother. All of us made a point of walking past the principal's office to view Mrs. Wilson, who sat there, dressed in black and with her face held low and ashamed as though she were the culprit herself. We whispered afterward, among ourselves, of what a lady Mrs. Wilson was; we had never before seen a colored lady.

The high-school years loomed ahead. We were to be joined by another section of the same grade, and we were determined to maintain our solidarity with Paul at our head. Our reputation as a champion class had preceded us; but with it, we soon noticed, a reputation for rowdiness. Paul was instantly elected captain of the basketball team. But he was just nosed out of the presidency by a white boy belonging to the other section, who must have gained some treacherous votes from among our own. Although the other boy occupied the chair, Paul managed, for half a year, to bully even the new section into slowly waning submission to the last echoes of his power.

Elizabeth's popularity remained limited to the girls in our own old section. The others adopted her at first as a novelty, but they had not been trained to her loud hearty jokes and her powerful wrestling, and soon tired of her and left her to her old companions. These dwindled slowly, as we girls gained consciousness of our status as girls and wished to dissociate ourselves from anything rowdy. Of course it was our fault—we could have pushed Elizabeth forward and remained loyal to her—but we had so many things to think of in those days. And I think something of the sort was bound to happen to Elizabeth anyway; she did not have the native personality to warrant and sustain the unlimited popularity which had fallen on her partly because of her strength and partly because she was her brother's sister. There was a quiet girl in our class, less mature than the rest of us—who were, in that first year of high-school, more fiercely mature than some of us are today, which is ten years later. This girl, Diana, fastened upon Elizabeth as a chum, and from now on the curious pair were inseparable.

I remember the early days when it became the thing for the boys to take the girls to the corner soda-store after basketball games, and for each boy to treat one girl to a fudge sundae. We couldn't help noticing that the boys, so eager to rough-house with Elizabeth in the classroom, hesitated among themselves as to which should treat her, and that the same one never treated her twice. We noticed too, that the soda-clerk stared at the dark blemish in our small white group. Elizabeth never seemed to notice anything; she developed a habit of kidding the soda-clerk in a loud professional voice, and soon our indignation was shifted to her, and we told her to lower her voice and not fool around with soda-clerks. Toward the end of the year Diana and Elizabeth dissociated themselves from our group, and began to occupy a little table by themselves in a corner. Here they would sit and pretend to be alone, and we could hear them giggling and whispering happily. Paul, of course, was still too young and too "manly" ever to join these parties.

**

In the course of that first year in high-school many things beside the soda-parties happened to us. Wrestling between boys and girls was outlawed, the girls began to loop their hair in buns over the ears, and the boys began to appear in navy-blue long trousers.

I remember Paul in his first longies. Instead of navy-blue, he appeared in a sleek suit of light Broadway tan, nicely nipped in at the waist, which harmonized with his clear mocha skin and showed off his dapper little figure to perfection. But it didn't quite fit in our school. I noticed that day, standing in line behind him to buy lunch tickets, that he wore brand new shoes: they were long and very pointed, and polished a brilliant ochre; they were button shoes, with cloth tops; they squeaked like nothing else in the world. I remember staring at them, and wondering where I had seen shoes like those before: was it in the elevator at home?

We were so grown-up that year that instead of shooting baskets in the twenty-minute recess that followed lunch, we got one girl to play the piano and the rest of us danced. Only about half of the boys were bold enough to dance; Paul still belonged to the group which stood in a corner and laughed and imitated their bolder friends, waiting for younger girls to be imported into the high-school department next year. With one boy to every pair of girls, it was not surprising that Elizabeth danced more than half of her dances with her friend Diana. The rest of us paired off with our girl-friends equally often.

But for no reason that anyone could see, Elizabeth's friends still diminished week by week. She had occasional spurts of her old popularity, but these were chiefly occasioned by reaction against some more stable idol, who would soon be restored to her post. Elizabeth's one permanent friend was Diana, the quiet little blonde girl who had no other friends. As far as I know, Diana was the only girl who ever invited Elizabeth to her house, and it was rumored that Diana was the only one who had seen the inside of the Wilson house, but Diana could be made neither to say whether it was true, nor what it was like if she had seen it. As for the rest of us, we were a little uncomfortable about omitting Elizabeth at afternoon parties at our homes; but somebody's mother settled it for us by saying that she thought it would be an unkindness to the little colored girl to invite her to a home where there would be none of her own people.

That year evening dances broke out among us. For the sake of girls who might never be asked, there was a rule that everyone must come unescorted and unescorting. It was easy enough, of course, to break the rule. Most of the girls came regularly attended by boys from the upper classes. Elizabeth came the first few times with her brother, which was as good as coming unattended. Paul stood in a corner with the stags; Elizabeth sat with the other girls who had come unattended or attended by brothers, looking very dark and strange in her short-sleeved light dresses, and accepted gratefully her few opportunities to dance.

There began to be whispers among us of what we would do if Paul asked one of us to come to a dance with him, or offered a treat to a soda. We admitted to feeling uncomfortable at the thought of being seen on the street with him. At the same time we realized that what we were contemplating was horribly unfair. But Evelyn—Evelyn, who led our class in social matters because at fourteen she wore rouge and baby French heels—said, "School is school; it's not the World; it's not our Real Lives," and we let it go at that. As we had tacitly adopted policies toward Elizabeth, we now officially adopted one toward Paul; we were to be extra nice to him, but not in the way that one treats a boy; and we were to dance with him when he asked us, but very kindly refuse his invitations to escort us anywhere outside the school walls. Fortunately for our peace of mind, ethics lessons were that year changed to weekly lessons in elocution for the girls, and public speaking for the boys.

But none of us was given the chance to refuse him. So far as I know, he never asked a girl to go anywhere with him, never left the stag-line at our Friday night dances, and after the first half-dozen, he never even came with Elizabeth. He scrupulously avoided even the careless physical contacts in the elevator, of which the other boys took modest advantage. Also, when we followed our policy of being nice to him in school, we found ourselves politely ignored. Paul grew increasingly sullen, even occasionally rude, and one girl reported that he had passed her on the street and pretended not to see her, neglecting to lift his elegant tan felt hat.

In the middle of that year Elizabeth's friend Diana was withdrawn from the school by her parents and sent to a boarding-school in the South, rumor said to get her away from the black girl and teach her a proper sense of color.

With her friend gone, Elizabeth picked up smaller fry and dazzled them, because, unlike Paul, she seemed to want never to be alone. But even with these she learned to disappear at the school door, or at most to walk no further with a white classmate than the end of the school block. There, making some excuse about having to hurry, or going in another direction, she would dash away with a good-humored smile. I remember watching her running away from us once and wondering to what strange world she disappeared every day after school.

Of course, not one of the nice girls in our school would have dreamed of hurting Elizabeth's feelings by suggesting that she leave us on the street, but there must have been some hesitating on the corner before Elizabeth so effectively learned that her position with her white schoolmates ended with the school door. Or could it have been that dark lady, who had sat in the principal's office with her head lowered as though she were the culprit, that time of the Seventh Grade Trouble? But no matter, we were in our third year of high-school now, and had forgotten the seventh grade as we had forgotten the famous trouble, and were used now to seeing our dark classmate hurry off after school and run down the long block, leaving us standing on the corner, discussing our this and that, which was so awfully important to us. . . .

In the third year of high-school, Paul simply did not appear. We were, I suppose, faintly relieved, in so far as we thought about him at all. He removed, after all, such uncomfortable questions as playing other schools with a Negro on our first team. And our own old section, our merry, rowdy section, of which Paul had once been undisputed king, had imperceptibly melted away, the boundary line was wavery, our old loyalty vague, a thing of the past; Paul, so far as he was anything in our minds, was a memory belonging to our lost section. When we asked Elizabeth what had happened to him, she told us he was going to another school because he didn't like girls and considered our private school sissy. She carried it off rather well, I think. One or two of us suggested that he might have been fired, because we all knew that his work had gone off badly in that last year.

Elizabeth herself, in those last two years, toned down considerably. Her prowess in studies had never been great, and she seemed now to be devoting more time to them. Her athletic ability had not lived up to its promise, because she had been after all primarily interested in rough-neck play, and seemed unable or unwilling to tame her strength and spirits into rules and skill. She abandoned the bright colors she had worn as a child, and came to school in neat and modest dresses. She dropped without reluctance into the common order of students, learned to toady as she had once been toadied to, and managed to keep up a decent sober reputation which ensured her a mild amount of companionship, restricted, of course, to within the school walls. On committees Elizabeth volunteered for unpleasant jobs and carried them out cheerfully and efficiently. She grew generous and sweet-tempered, and a little like a servant; and like a servant, she was thanked for her services and forgotten.

Paul had dropped out of our existence.

***

The last time I saw either of them was at our graduation dance. Elizabeth had long ago given up coming alone

40

to our dances, but she came, of course, to this one, looking rather too burly and black in the prescribed white dress, with bare arms which hung like bones from her ungainly shoulders. She was the whole of the committee on refreshments, and all during the first part of the evening she stood behind a table with her diploma tucked on a rack over her head—nobody from her family had come to see her be graduated—and cheerfully dispensed sandwiches and ice-cream.

Everybody was mingling proudly in the big assembly room, waiting for the chairs to be removed for dancing; everybody was very nice to Elizabeth and even took down her address as a matter of form, but in the rush of taking addresses that really meant something and comparing notes about future colleges, she was forgotten, and if it hadn't been for a teacher who came to her rescue, she might have been completely alone. When the dancing began, the teacher led her away from the buffet table with her arm around her, to bring her to the row of chairs where girls sat waiting for partners.

Some of us must have had compunctions—I know I did—floating by her in our partners' arms, for on that night the least popular girl had achieved a faithful escort, if only by importing boys from classes below who felt it an honor to be there at all. But none of us felt badly enough to urge our partners to leave us and dance with Elizabeth. Later one or two boys danced a waltz with her, because a waltz was the least difficult thing to sacrifice. She sat all evening and talked cheerfully to the teacher. She looked uncomplaining, as though she had quietly learned her place. She even seemed to enjoy watching the rest of us dance.

The evening broke up on a high-note of "See you again," "Don't forget," and "Oh, the most marvelous time!" and I remember emerging from the dance-room in a fever of happiness, walking on winged feet. I pushed my way through the gay crowd outside the door. Somebody tapped me on the arm: "Miss!" I turned and saw, for the first time in three years, Paul Wilson, the king of our old section! I smiled eagerly, delighted to see him again. "Why Paul!" I exclaimed, holding out my hand.

He was as beautiful as he had been three years before, but his face was different, hardened perhaps, so that the dapper tan clothes he wore made him cheap and flashy. He still wore pointed button shoes with cloth tops. He was standing by the wall with his hat pulled down over his eyes. "Why, Paul!" I said.

He looked up, caught my eye, and shifted his away as though he had failed to recognize me. He looked down at the floor and spoke in a low voice. "Miss, would you mind finding my sister Elizabeth Wilson inside and say her brother is waiting for her?" He stuck his hands suddenly into his pockets with something of his old sullen gesture.

I remember turning from him with an overpowering sense of guilt to spare him embarrassment, and going back with tears burning my eyes to find Elizabeth. I left him standing there against the wall, with his hat over his eyes, snubbing his former classmates, while they passed their former god and leader, some of them too happy to distinguish his features under that hat, others no doubt turning from him to prevent his embarrassment, and even, on that happy night, to spare themselves. . . . This should have been his graduation.

Brother to the Happy
Pagany, Fall/Winter 1932

The body becomes a sieve through which life streams and no one no vessel to catch it to take hold and give it form to receive it as a present for no one wanted it— this is what it is to be old, to be old she thought, and petty things grow paramount in the brain: sugar the celery because Gladys and damned if I'll be Grandma to a book of poems too nasty to read in the bath-tub— and never a word to a soul for whom could you tell it to anyway what was he these days and for how many years past, oh Lord! but an old man who if you woke him in the night had no teeth in his head.

Why where's Dennis where's Dennis she cried out when her daughter oh what a tall clean lovely girl came into the room so different from when with a school-bag.

Yes where's the boyfriend where's the boyfriend he quavered too but meaning it so stupid that she turned on him Oh put in your teeth old man she said impatiently and had to turn it into a joke because of that lovely clean girl who was and couldn't help it, his daughter

Oh gosh Sally said, didn't I tell you I thought we told you

Don't tell me he's not—she said and could feel the blood stifling in her temples like when one of her flushes

There's a poetry meeting tonight, gosh mother I'm sorry I thought we told you, I surely thought

Resentful woman that she was and hating it bitterly when her son-in-law relegated her to "Grandma" producing nothing but a book of poems to justify the stigma what does she do but cry out in a voice that rang sharp and false as a counterfeit coin But what a shame, a shame! and here I am with his favorite his very favorite—for a coward she was too afraid to face him without his very favorite

The boyfriend won't be here you say, the boyfriend won't be here said the old man and he could leave his teeth out for all of her the poor old man

If it isn't my bitch of a sister he cried bounding into the room and no eyes for anyone but her, a big clean fine-looking man only Gladys was letting him get fat, and there they stood in the middle of the room wrestling pinching sniffing made for each other that brother and sister where could they have found mates so fitting and God knows they never had. My bitch of a sister he cried, and where's the *dichter* he said coolly while his nose thrust forward like a rodent's made little glances as if he would smell out Dennis from his hiding-place, and the mother watched how his eager face smirking made circles around his sister's neck while she stood there grim like a tree fighting him fighting didn't she know she wanted him the prim prudish tall clean lovely young thing with the shape of her face exactly like his

Don't you see your mother bad boy don't you see your mother? she cried merrily oh these scenes between brother and sister they made you drunk made you merry. If it isn't my Old Lady he said and bounding over picked her up and kissed her with loud smacking sounds over the cheeks and mouth but it was different it was different, you can't fool me my boy. And your father. . . . My liege, he bowed, distaste in his mouth for the old man who was like a shrivelled cocoanut like a dried up monkey and the old man was he ashamed did he feel obscene that something so big had come out of him away back in his young days the old man grinned and turned away his head

And what do you think, he said, your rival, he said to his sister, isn't coming, Gladys isn't coming. Have you been a good enough Old Lady, he said to his mother, all week to deserve such luck? Oh I'm sorry, oh why not, she said and genuinely sorry almost for an absent

Gladys was a sweet thing a simple thing and it is highly probable that sugaring celery is the very best thing you can do with it and she would like to tell Gladys—Oh why isn't she coming I'm so sorry

What, what? they all cried as the old man toothless and mouthless gesticulated and mumbled some joke getting the best of him in his old age, oh dear oh dear what life was full of jokes that can't be beat, who would have thought who would have thought eh, eh, that's a good one ...

What is it Pop? can't you spit it out? would the boy never forgive his Pop for being old

Open your mouth old man, she said sharply, speak plainly for heaven's sake.

I only said I only said it's so funny what's-her-name isn't coming and the boyfriend ain't coming and I only said how funny because

(Really isn't the dichter coming?)

And what's funny about that you silly old

I only said how funny because that means it means that just the family only the family

As if Gladys and Dennis weren't in the family you old fool more in it that you or I you stupid

Hot dog he shouted to his sister, do you mean he really isn't coming you mean, hot dog he shouted, Pop's right, it's the old family circle without any chaperones

And half-way across the room to his sister he stopped he stopped short and she stood there like a young maiden with morals

Supper, supper, she cried for she could feel that something was wrong now the old man with his silliness perhaps

Do you remember he said how I used to twist your thumb to make you walk faster to school? How he was looking at her at his sister as if please forgive me but after all

Eh what kids you were, what kids you were mumbled the old man

Do you remember how I sneaked you into the boys' lab because you wanted to see standing-up toilets

Into the what, into the what murmured the old man not daring to believe could something so rich so tremendous! right here in his own family, Wild Indians they were

Do you remember how I let you carry my heaviest books and made you think it a special honor oh you little dumb-bell what a little dumb-bell you were

Dennis has the most amusing that is they are also heart-breaking

Do you remember I told you that every man you saw on the street had done it even the tailor, not *Gerald* you said not my own *cousin!* and I said yes even Gerald everybody but your wonderful big brother

Poor Dennis—she was speaking to her mother with eyebrows raised please listen, please listen,—they sent him to boardingschool when he was so young poor dear

49

and he wasn't the type oh he wasn't the type at all

Oh the hell with Dennis tonight he cried smirking

Tell us, tell us Sally, she said, oh oh once a mother-inlaw always a maybe he wasn't here the poet but she could feel his accusing eyes just the same You're not paying enough attention to me—tell us, tell us

You see it was a very religious place

and for that I have to pay my daughter has to pay, just because his mother didn't want him around the house and sent him off to a religious place and now we have to pay he has to be a poet

Oh it was awfully strict and he must have been such a pathetic adorable little boy

For Christ's sake he threw at his sister, can't he outgrow it, can't you leave him home this once now we're all together again

I should say, I should say so, just like the olden times, the old man cackled with pride in the phrase

Shut up old man with your nonsense she cried and looked anxious at her daughter sitting there so stiff what's the matter with you little girl don't you like it any more when your brother

Did the boy get married first mamma, the old man asked, I always forget, did the boy

Your daughter, he said pointing at his sister, she was the one, she did it

But how is Gladys's *teaching*, Sally cried as much as to say oh that Gladys oh that teaching is there anything interests me so much? like a teacher herself raising her eyebrows for you must remember you must remember

Good Lord, I suppose she I suppose it's

Sa-ay, sa-ay, I can remember you two the old man was mumbling sly and shy, bits of celery hanging down out of his mouth like a dog he had grown like a toothless old dog, but it was too much for him suddenly what was he but an old man wrinkled dry like a raisin like an old woman, Eh what a pair you were

Of course her curriculum must be pretty well confined but still I thought, Dennis and I thought, Sally said oh so sprightly oh so interested and alive oh so exact in how she clipped out her words blinked her eyes why my dear you can't imagine how Dennis (the dear boy) how we just put our heads together and as for Gladys a sister a dear sister dear old Gladys

Regular wild Indians, wild Indians I used to call you

Shut up old man, who cares about that now, she said bitterly, they've grown up you fool can't you see, they've got husbands and wives of their own now

I'm sorry, I'm sorry the old man mumbled

Oh what the hell Pop, where's your spirit, he cried but his own spirit was dead dead in his eyes and he kept them down on his plate and wouldn't look again at his sister so smug so upright so married so happily married at the other end of the table from him.

Well mother he said, and he looked forty and dull the kind of man you wouldn't believe being a mother to, well mother, and how do you like the quiet family party for a change eh

Why it's nice, it's nice, she purred oh stupid stupid do they think I'm blind do they think I'm dumb quiet family party my eye, more like a dynamite party I'd call it—only of course I miss the others they're part of the family too just as much every bit as dear

Used to ride horseback, horseback on the parlor floor brought out the old man noble, emphatic, as though he sensed denial in the air as though he would face them with the facts face them with the facts for the fine clear moment that he remembered them

My father is pleased to serve us word-salad said the son after a moment in which they had let the facts fall into their plates and watched them lie there and tried to stir them into the pudding

Your father is growing old, she said feeling a dignity like a flowing of new life in her veins for she too like the old man could face for a moment his facts, and you must not

My little girl is busy missing Dennis, she said kindly, and what hate flashed at her out of her daughter's eyes as her face a guilty red looks down again at her plate.

And what makes my *brother* so quiet said Sally in her smarty-thought-he'd-have-a-party voice

Why nothing, he answered her politely, the rejected the hurt the aging brother, brother to the happily married

Like the olden times, the olden times, ah yes wild Indians, that was a good one, a good one—the old man let fall to nobody for he had retired decently into his old man's world

If you'll excuse me, the son said rising

Take care of yourself, sport, he said clapping the old man on the shoulder, you're the only Old Man we've got, remember sir! Be good to yourself mother—, must run off I'm sorry I promised to call for Gladys—seven years married and the name still like an unexpected sour apple in his mouth

Regards won't you, he said politely to his sister, to your to Dennis.

Where is he going, where is he going asked the old man coming bewildered out of his world

Leave him alone, he must call for his wife

He should bring her back here, tell him he should bring her back

Why I'm afraid Pop

Of course, of course, she soothed him, he doesn't know what he's talking about, run along my son and give her my love son tell her how sorry we were how sorry we all were

Tell her, Sally began, I want to speak to her about

Well toodle-oo, he said turning at the door and whose fault was it that his eyes were a second too slow to meet his sister's.

So they sat there as though it were a stadium which crowds of people had just emptied and the stillness and the loneliness sat on their heads while the hour uncoiled itself out of a gigantic spool and she thought how her own aging body was the personal medium for time

Well daughter

Well mother

Like flies they drifted caught beyond struggling in the heavy syrup of time

How is Dennis's work Sally?

Wild Indians the old man breathed and she thought how time made an exception for him he was no fly he hopped like a bird into the past if he wanted to and for this reason he was no longer alive

He has a new poem he thinks you will love he said, Grandma will love this one.

Why the dear, did he really say that

Flies caught with a leg each in the thickness of time

Damn it mother why do you never believe when I say something nice about Dennis? of course he said it, he definitely said when he gave it to me to read. Here's one Grandma will love—and why you can't believe me.

The darling, she said, he really said that eh

Oh my poor, she said suddenly to the old man seeing with pain how he was living himself twenty years back, how bad your teeth must feel, take them out my dear, let mamma clean them for you. Your father, she said to her daughter, is growing old, old.

The Old Lady Counts Her Injuries

Vanity Fair, October 1934

For the third time the old lady walked up to the information booth, approaching with the question on her
trembling face that she was ashamed to put into words
again. For the third time the clerk shook his head before
she quite arrived, carrying his chin to a precise spot
above his right shoulder and quivering it like a doctor
pronouncing a bad diagnosis against his will. A kind of
professional sympathy spread into his face, when he per-
ceived her age again. "If you could tell me what he looks
like?" he suggested, his jaw swinging back to center.

The old lady stood there, feeling a silly, fatuous
smile crawling on her lips. He is a darling little boy,
she wanted to say, in a sailor-suit and a big hat with a
navy-blue band; his hair is cut Buster Brown over his

eyes, his upper front teeth are missing and the lower two just coming in; we think his teeth are not coming in quite straight, she thought of saying. For a moment she stood there, as little able to control the smile as to stop the slight, inquiring waver of her head that age had brought her. And all at once her face grew rigid, for she could suddenly not picture her son as he must look today. "Never mind. Thank you," she said, carving out the words to make them perfect.

***

She turned and walked primly out of the clerk's cold sight. I am an old lady, she thought indignantly; he has no right to keep me waiting so. I am an old lady and still he is as inconsiderate as he was when he was a child; he is an ungrateful son. She walked, distraught, about the station; sat down at last upon the edge of a bench, denying herself what comfort it might have given her. I am an old lady and I am very nervous and sitting about stations makes me sick and he knows it, she thought, whipping herself up to a frenzy of nerves that played in her tired muscles until they ached. I feel faint, she thought angrily; what if I should topple over on this bench and die, just as he comes swanking into the station, supercilious and fine, coming too late to meet his old mother. . . .

The thought gave her sustenance and she let herself sway on the bench with one hand to her forehead, pleased

to imagine that she attracted interest from some pas-
sers-by. Why, yes, we saw her, they would tell him, she *did*
look ill, your mother, was she? She pictured Harry kneel-
ing by her side; and then in spite of herself she pictured
him rushing to a telephone booth—*Evelyn* mustn't worry!

Evelyn! In the presence of her daughter-in-law, the
old lady always felt a mild disdain, flying to do her bidding nevertheless—to keep the peace with Harry, she
told herself. Those awful week-ends in Evelyn's house!
the old lady would keep up a steady stream of silent
abuse against her daughter-in-law as meekly, and yet
sarcastically, she put down the child if Evelyn said to, or
stopped brushing her hair because Evelyn said it would
take out the curl. Very many things had the old lady sub-
mitted to, and found only petty revenge in the righteous
silent diatribe, or in an occasional furtive glance at her
son. When she thought of Evelyn she thought again of
the cruel day they had sprung through a door at her,
Harry and Evelyn, to attack her with their news; to stand
there grinning, hand-in-hand, as though to emphasize
her age and loneliness; and to this day she could call
back to her face the grimace she had made when Evelyn
slyly called her "Mother." That Harry had not bothered
to tell her by himself had been the first symbol of his
handing together with Evelyn, that day and forever. The
old lady felt a moisture gathering in her eyes.

***

Inconsiderate he had always been, but this was the worst—and the last, she told herself grimly. They had already missed the two-seventeen. But she would wait for him—oh yes; she would wait only to tell him what she thought of him, of him and his fine Evelyn. She would not come down to their country place and be told how to treat her own grandchild, neither this week-end nor ever any other. That was over. She had learnt her lesson, she said brokenly to him in her mind; Evelyn has taken you from me, she sobbed, and I may be old but I am not a fool. Your father would tell you a thing or two he were alive, young man, she wept, and she wept for the image of his father whom she saw vividly now as he had been in the '90's, when Harry was a child. But at once the image grew blurred and foreign, as though she herself, even at the age of seventy, had outgrown it, just as she had outlived the young man with the sweeping black moustache who had been Harry's proud young father. She found as little comfort in the memory as one would find in a daguerreotype—he had died and she had gone on, and now Harry was all that was left to her.

She would hold out to Harry, reproachfully, the gift she had bought for her grandchild, that she had bought with a fleeting nostalgic pain and felt was really for her son. Here, she would say, bitter and ungracious, take it, take it to my grandchild, I am not coming with you, not today and not ever again. Once and for all let us have it out between us, she would tell him I don't like Evelyn and she poisons your mind against me; I'll not have any stranger-woman's child calling me Mother like that, telling me what I may and may not do with my own grandchild, my own son's child. That is over, Harry, she told him firmly in her mind, and suddenly stared about the station with the blackest apprehension in her bones.

***

She was a nasty, cruel, selfish old lady, not fit to be a mother, she tormented herself now—for what if something had happened to Harry! Now her hand flew in genuine pain to her heart, and her heartbeats came like the knocking of hail upon a window-pane. She remembered the day they had brought him from school with a broken leg; the wild, hot night she had spent on a train going up to the Adirondacks because they had telephoned something about an appendix; she felt again the black horror of apprehension that she had suffered every time her boy was not home by ten minutes past six for his supper. She saw him groaning on his little bed as they tenderly slipped his sailor-suit off his wounded leg; she felt her own hand again on his little stomach that was so white compared to his sun-burned legs as he lay, sheepishly glad to see her when she climbed the wooden steps to his tent—in a tent they had kept her little boy, while his appendix nearly burst within him! She saw herself pressed to the interminable nursery window, peering down the winter-darkened street, her heart in her throat until she saw him round the corner, carelessly swinging his baseball bat. . . .

He was coming, and what he carried in his hand, instead of a bat, was a brand-new bag of golf-clubs. Relief was so quick that it sickened her, apprehension turned to gall in her month. The mist in the old lady's eyes was drawn back instantly, leaving them bright and hard. That, her son? Her little boy in a sailor-suit? That stout and aging man, carrying his belly like a portent before him, looking like a thousand other middle-aged commuters who had been beautiful babies back in the '90's when their papas' moustaches bent to tickle them? She felt bitter and cold, and she shook with an unhappy kind of laughter at the grim revenge which time had played on her little boy.

She could see him advance in a straight line a little way, then veer sharply, looking about the station. He put down his bag of golf-clubs and she could see him ridiculously scratch his ear; and then he stood, middle-aged and childish, looking for his mother. At once she rose and started toward him, in an agony of fear lest he have a moment's worry.

To her delight it was she who surprised him, she who had the foolish pleasure of saying first, "Oh there you are!" when she stole deliberately up behind him. Beautiful was his smile when he bent in relief to kiss her, beautiful his voice as he greeted her with joy. "Mother! we missed a train, I'm sorry, I rushed so I didn't even stop for lunch. We can just make the next one if we fly!"

He darted ahead of her, golf bag and all, and she tottered after him, worried to death about his having no lunch. "You ought to know better," she gasped; "running around like that on an empty stomach, you could catch anything, I think that's awful." Her words were drowned in his joyful exclamation tossed back over his shoulder: "We've got half a minute—are you with me, Mom?" Happier than she ever remembered feeling in her life before, she ran on, panting luxuriously: "There's nothing more important—eating regularly—I've always told you that—" "Had to stop," he threw back over his shoulder, "and get these new clubs for Evelyn, wouldn't dare face her if I hadn't—" But the old lady didn't hear his words with any part of herself that mattered, for they were running past the information booth now and she caught the clerk's eye and nodded violently, pointing ahead with pride to the fine haunches of her little boy romping before her, see, see, he *did* come, and isn't he a darling? We had his teeth straightened, his father and I, she wanted to shout at the clerk with his commiserating chin, and she felt fine and strong again even though she sensed that silly smile crawling fatuous and triumphant across her trembling lips.

The Lonelier Eve

The New Yorker, April 1934

Going to the movies alone is a lonely, morbid thing; one goes, perhaps, deliberately to intensify the mood. One glances selfconsciously down the dark rows, sees strangers only—come, perhaps, for the same lonely reason—and seats oneself, full of self-pity, alone at last in the friendless dark. I had gone in this way one afternoon and found myself in a smoking loge, alongside a woman of no age, of no particular description, of no personality whatsoever.

The newsreel started. "Fine face he has," whispered my characterless companion when President Roosevelt shuddered on the screen. I looked to the right of her, I looked to the left of myself; no, we were, as I had thought, alone. I said nothing, steeled my face, and steeled my ears. "Quite right, quite right," muttered the woman when Mrs. Roosevelt said she hated war. "They stop at nothing," she said when the ski-jumpers hurled themselves over cliffs of snow. "I don't care for her type," she observed when the healthiest girl in Idaho blinked through a nest of curls. "They talk of peace, and then look what,"' she said angrily when ten million dollars spent on tanks and bigger cannons appeared before our eyes. I continued to say nothing. I drew myself back into my own seat and thought bitterly that I had come to indulge my own loneliness, not to alleviate a stranger's.

***

The comedy began. I learned from my neighbor that it was cheap, that it was slapstick, that it is a crime to feed the public ugliness, that, on the other hand, if the public demands such ugliness, what could the movie-producers do? I sat in bitter silence, I wriggled, I moved my hand from the chair-arm we shared between us. And at last I grunted in assent. I grunted partly because I was sorry for her, partly because she made me feel, somehow, responsible.

The main picture came on. "Oh, I do like Cagney," she said impulsively, and, leaning forward, clasped her hands beneath her nondescript chin. "Yes, he is amusing," I whispered back, relenting, even warming a little to her fellow-loneliness, her simple joy. She glanced my way for a sharp, brief instant; then gave me her negligible profile again, faintly lit with love for Jimmy Cagney. "This gangster stuff—not a good influence," she murmured, worried. I grunted again, a noncommittal grunt. "Still, I guess it's what the public wants,' she countered. "Hmm," I said politely. I wondered if movies and chance acquaintances in the audience were all the social life the poor creature had. "Oh, how he treats the women!" she breathed with pleasure as Cagney dragged a beauty by the hair. "And yet so unreal," she said next, bridling. "Still," I ventured, "it's harmless enough." She turned in my direction again, in surprise. "I beg your pardon?" she said coldly. "I said it's not lifelike at all, but as you say, it's what the public wants," I stammered, feeling apologetic, as if I had erred in some way. She said nothing for a moment, examining me rather superciliously, and then turned her face determinedly to the screen again. We were silent for fully five minutes, during which I felt relieved, yet guilty. "Blondell—she's not my type," she said at last, and I felt myself forgiven.

"Plot isn't much," she murmured next. I hastened to agree. I observed she bridled a little and moved in her seat. "Still, it doesn't really matter," I said conciliatingly. "There was a second silence between us. I felt it as keenly, as guiltily, as though I were this woman's hostess, as though I had invited her here, and now must see that she enjoyed herself. I couldn't bear her silence. "I mean, as long as the *continuity*, as long as the *acting...*"

the morning for which Mr. Marvell's Christmas speech had been announced (Mr. Marvell being the 'M' in 'M & J'), Joey Andrews, No. 191-23, 167B, who had been till three weeks before without a number in the army of the unemployed, wrote his name and number on the top line of Mrs. Summers' fresh page at exactly eight-eleven. Mrs. Summers asked Mr. Andrews if he had fallen out of bed; she said it was nice to see some face beside Mr. Keasbey's so early in the morning; and she said she had sat up in the bathroom all night (not to wake *Mister* S) going over her records and trying to make them tally.... And Mrs. Summers, who limped before nine and immediately after five-thirty because there was not, she said, very much sitting on her job, limped off with the salesbooks for the hat-girls who were also part of her section.

Once more as Joey Andrews looked down from the mezzanine onto the great sleeping main floor below he felt in his stomach the dull ball of fear which a lover experiences when he recalls how nearly he missed going out on that particular Tuesday on which he met his love. But propping the biography of Dostoievsky against the *Memoirs of a Grand Duchess* on his own table of History and Biography, Joey Andrews felt that any recollection of his eight-months' nightmare among the unhired was unworthy of No. 191-23, 167B of a great department store. And wondering to what table *Jane Eyre* belonged (for surely it was not a biography?), "I must forget about the Washington Square gang," he scolded himself, "I

68

don't belong with them any more"; and went to lay *Jane Eyre* tentatively on Miss Bodkin's table of Classics.

Downstairs the perfume girls were drifting in; the floor-walkers adjusting their button-holes and their smiles, moved here and there with dignity. Having arranged his own table, Joey Andrews looked about his beloved book department for some way to be helpful, some way to live up to the Christmas spirit of M & J. He didn't quite dare to fix Miss Bodkin's table; and he was just pulling the long white nightgown off Mr. Keasbey's New Fiction when Mr. Keasbey himself walked in—it was the dot of eight-fifteen—and, forewarned by the section-book violated, bearing another's name before his own, gave Joey a haughty, suspicious look and began flying around his table making kissing sounds until his fingers came safely to rest on the handle of his very own duster.

Now the cosmetic girls were mounting stacks of cold cream on their counters while near the doors the cheap stockings stretched coyly over amputated limbs. On the mezzanine behind the book department the hat girls in their drab black dresses and exquisitely sheer-hosed legs began clapping the hats on stalks like flowers. Mrs. White who kept the lending library at the back came next; the Hierarchy permitted Mrs. White and Mr. Keasbey to bow with formal recognition of mutual virtue—Mrs. White had been with M & J a noble twelve years to Mr. Keasbey's noble fifteen—before Mr. Keasbey hurried to return *Rebecca of Sunnybrook Farm*, which he borrowed every night that it had not been taken by a customer, for his mother who was eighty and had stopped sleeping. Mrs. White began driving the hairpins into the pretzel high on her head; and when Mr. Keasbey laid Rebecca on the table before her, pointed her mouth like a pencil and made a check-mark with her head: down—one, two; hold; up—one, two—and Mrs. White and Mr. Keasbey part for the day.

Miss Paley of the Modern Library and movie-editions, to whom the Hierarchy does not permit Mr. Keasbey to bow, mounts the mezzanine stairs with a look of resigned bewilderment on her melancholy face. Two decades of teaching school have left her permanently surprised at finding herself daily entering the Commercial World (and how had she ever, in the teeth of Mr. Neely the Principal's disapproval, made the Change!)—and also there have been rumors breathed by Miss Bodkin that Miss Paley's life in the Commercial World is to be very brief indeed, and it may be that some of these rumors have even reached Miss Paley. Yet here she is, daily from nine to five-thirty, not selling children's books, as surely, she complains to Joey Andrews who rushes forth to help her with her jungle of cheap editions, as surely she had, after two decades of teaching little children, every reason to expect? had she not, as Mr. Neely (who put things so well!) had put it, a gift for understanding children? But Mr. Neely warned me, she whispers through her closed white mask, that the Commercial World was something else again . . . and drawing out the handkerchief (given her by the bestspeller's mother) from her place in the Modern Library copy of *The Old Wives' Tale* which she reads at idle moments in the day, Miss Paley dismisses Joey with a kindly, authoritative nod as though he were the first-grade pupil who had just collected the rulers. And Joey, rather glad to get away, for ever since Miss Bodkin breathed the rumor, Miss Paley has been touched for him with some infectious germ, takes up his stand by his table of History and Biography.

Miss Willows the buyer trips over to her desk and lays her hat in the bottom drawer. But as yet no Miss Bodkin. Miss Willows bites at her pearls as she makes a hasty survey of the book department, arranges Christmas calendars with her head on one side like a bird. Still no Miss Bodkin (Joey Andrews hates to think of no Miss Bodkin.) "Heavens knows," murmurs Miss Paley to Mrs. Summers on the subject of varicose veins in which they both specialize; and Miss Bodkin's chum Miss Rees slips in on the stroke of eight-twenty, the deadline, and carelessly pulls the cover off *The Young Girls* Series for which Miss Paley would cheerfully trade her miniature set of Proust; and "*I* know as well as Heaven," returns Mrs. Summers humorously, and she has forty minutes more of the luxury of limping. Beautiful Miss Fern Stacy who is so dumb (according to Miss Bodkin) that she can hardly make change, takes her place behind the stationery counter—Mr. Keasbey had fought bitterly against its ignoble presence in the book department, even for the Christmas rush week. Mr. Keasbey stands with his arms folded, his head lifted; a fit citizen in the world of M & J, fit door-man to the gate of Heaven: perhaps one day Mr. Marvell will pause and glance at his noble mien, his professorial posture, and will think to himself, What a man! what a faithful employee. . . . And there suddenly is Miss Bodkin, having signed in fraudulently in the space left blank by her good friend Miss Rees, a Miss Bodkin defying a gullible world to imagine that she was not present at least as early as Mr. Keasbey, and that she does not every Saturday of her life make off with a first edition hidden away under one of Mrs. White's lending library covers. . . . Joey Andrews feels waves of purple sliding shamefully down his spine at the sight of Miss Bodkin's goose-berry breasts squeezed tight under her black satin dress; he remembers that it has been a long time since he has dared to ask a girl for a date, and that tonight is Christmas Eve.

Eight-thirty; and Mr. Keasbey, for the fifteenth annual successive time, leads his class as though he were the monitor, down the mezzanine stairs for Mr. Marvell's Christmas speech.

***

"and Mr. Marvell who needs no introduction has come all the way from White Plains at this early hour to give us one and all his Christmas message." (Mr. Sawyer of the Personnel speaking—O thank you, thank you for nothing, murmured Miss Bodkin, her small face expressing sarcastic devotion; Mr. Keasbey delivered a withering glance; and Joey Andrews, though sick with admiration for her goose-berry breasts, moved away from her contaminating influence, for Joey, having had a Job for only three weeks was still more in love with the job than he was with Miss Bodkin.)

Beyond where the shoe-clerks were gathered a white-haired man rose and bowed. "What a fine face," whispered Miss Paley; "he has Mr. Neely's eyebrows exactly." Faint applause, led by smart clapping of department heads, while the great man smiled dreamily.

"My friends. (Mister God in person, murmured Miss Bodkin mouthlessly; and Joey Andrews stared for comfort at the graveyard of boils on the back of Mr. Keasbey's neck.) I only wish it were possible to know each and every to shake each and every to wish each and every but—the. femilay. of. M & J. is. too. large. (Laughter, the lingerie girls throwing themselves in fake passion against their shrouded counters; under cover of the polite sounds Miss Willows the buyer leaned across Joey Andrews and hissed Miss Bodkin kindly stop that talking. The white hairs in Mr. Keasbey's ears bristled sexagenarian triumph.) My friends, a spaycial responsibility toward your country, your fellow-men the femilay of M & J have you ever stopped to think how the department stores contribute to the good cheer of this heppy holiday come rich and poor alike gifts for his loved ones differences forgotten all men are equal at Christmas and who has the honor the privilege the blessing (Bring on the castor oil, groaned Miss Bodkin.)

"Who. but. you. my friends. And this year in especial when so many renegades and complainers of course a bad year but take the good with the bad life wouldn't be moch fon if we didn't have our ups and downs like our good friends the ladies of the elevators here—and our slogan is down with the complainers friends, we don't want 'em here why up at Princeton we used to wash out their mouths with soap maybe we ought to enlist the parfume gehls to do the same thing here. (Haw haw roared the shoe-clerks remembering public school but the book department merely smiled condescendingly, such humor was beneath them and they knew was meant to be.) Bear in mind my good friends a job for every good man or woman in this countray if you don't like this countray you can go to another if you don't like your job here you can leave it always plenty only glad step in shoes.

"One word in closing to the new friends taken on to help us in this merry busy season. We wish we could permanently retain each and every make a permanent member of the femilay of M & J each and every but let me say to each and every WE will do OUR BAIST if YOU will do YOUR baist . . . and this is YOUR big chance to prove yourselves invaluable to US, on this last day of the Christmas rush when SOME of our friends unfortunately MUST BE DROPPED (the book department glances briefly and guiltily at Miss Paley, who continues to stand with her hands clasped as though Mr. Marvell were the Principal leading assembly.) And I say this not merely to our new but it applies also to our old this is the day for EACH and EVERY.

"In conclusion it is good-will that counts good cheer is the baist policy the spirit of Christmas all year round is our slogan we are one big femilay and we spread our good cheer our customers expect it demand it PAY for it and now my friends I wish each and every a merry and profitable Christmas KEEP ON YOUR TOES ALL DAY OUR PROFIT IS YOUR PROFIT IT MAY BE THAT YOU CAN WIN YOURSELF A PERMANENT POSITION my friends I thank you each and every one."

Smatter of applause, Mr. Keasbey clapping on and on like an old Italian listening to the opera, while the section managers turned back toward their sections; but a thin man in a striped tie (Gadowsky who edited the monthly M & J Banner) leaped to a counter and cried: "Just one moment, friends. Let's give Mr. Marvell a hearty send-off to show our appreciation—altogether now, M and J 'Tis of Thee. . . ." The song straggled out across the floor; heads craned for a last glimpse of Mr.

Marvell, but Mr. Marvell was on his way back to White Plains; the song died.

***

O God, if the gang could see me now, thought Joey, taking his place for this day of days before his careful table of History and Biography. (Y'oughta forget that bunch, y'don't belong with them any more. And look around, look around, Jesus it's like heaven to be working.) Now there steals over the book department, the hat department, the entire floor below, a period of hurried hush, of calm excitement; a poised expectancy, denoting the birth of the Store for this great day. Now the aisles lie flat and virgin, waiting, breathless and coy, for merry and profitable defilement. (Remember Pete . . . passed his examinations for the bar . . . in between starving he handed out grocers' handbills . . . and Dopy Simpson, turned down a job for $11 . . . said he wouldn't stay straight under $25 per.) Now you can hear Miss Bodkin whispering with Miss Rees about the rumored romances of Miss Fern Stacy the stationery girl: "when she said *three* I knew she was lying, there aren't three men in the city fool enough to propose to a girl a depression year like this." (Remember Rounds . . . been a scholarship boy at a swell prep-school until the Depression cut down the scholarship fund . . . went around saying over Latin verbs to himself. . . . Dad said

I'd meet swell fellows in New York, but he didn't think I'd find 'em on a park bench.) Now the large clock over the entrance doors jumps to eight-fifty-three; Miss Paley stands sweet and serious like a school-teacher—and God, it's as safe as being in school again, thinks Joey, coming here every day, nice and warm, watch-ing the clock jump like that on its way to nine. . . . Mrs. Summers, her eyebrows dancing like harassed ghosts, limps like a nervous shepherd among her flock; only seven minutes more of that limping, Mrs. Summers! M & J expects courtesy health good cheer of its employees, the customers expect it demand it pay for it. . . .

Now Miss Paley closes *The Old Wives' Tale* with the best-speller's handkerchief in her place, and stands lifting her melancholy mask like a lamp waiting to be lighted. Behind her you can see tucked over a row of books her pocketbook, another of her many crumpled handkerchiefs, a pocket-comb; for Miss Paley has moved in (despite the rumors), Miss Paley has settled in (she has not heard the rumors), among the cheap books, as she had for two decades in her class-room, this is YOUR day, Miss Paley, to prove yourself invaluable, and YOURS too, Joey Andrews, and YOURS and YOURS and YOURS, each and every. . . . (Remember Jonesy, a real bum, Jonesy . . . turned Christian and left the gang, went and hung about with the Christers on the Y bread-lines . . . pan-handling and spending his pennies on Sterno, which he converted into alcohol by filtering it through his handkerchief at the horse-trough at the end of the Bowery . . . in his Sterno he thought or pretended he thought he was Jesus. But Rounds who had been a scholarship boy said he'd go Red before he'd stand on a breadline or sing Onward Christian Soldiers like Jonesy.) Now you can hear Miss Bodkin: "I hate this God-damn place, they fix the quotas high so nobody can possibly make a commission except the week before Christmas." Foolish Miss Bodkin! a daughter of the femilay of M & J: doesn't she know when she's well off? take care, Miss Bodkin, this is YOUR day too. (Remember fumbling in the ash-can for a paper before turning in—those nights you hadn't the wherewithal for a flop—turning in on the grassy center of Washington Square, surrounded by those beautiful houses . . . dreaming and planning with Rounds the One Perfect Hold-up—can Mrs. Summers read the mind . . . ? remembering, because you couldn't sleep, how long it had been since you had had a girl . . . remembering, because you couldn't sleep for the drunks singing at the other end of the park, *If you've said your prayers Joey my son no harm can come to you.*) Now Mr. Keasbey stands at the top of the mezzanine stairs with a dignity like the dignity of a Painless Dentist, his arms folded, threatening and somber, as he turns and prepares for his victims. Miss Willows herself descends from her desk and takes a position in the middle of the floor sucking her beads, a debutante hostess waiting, leaning forward from the hips, to greet the crowds that must be stamping outside in the Christmas cold. Now the outside entrance doors are thrown open and you can see the waiting customers pour into the vestibule sliding and coming to a stop like beads in a box. Now the big clock jumps to eight-fifty-eight; Mrs. Summers can limp for two minutes more, and she limps from clerk to clerk, her eyebrows dancing, begging everybody to remember the Christmas spirit, and that extra pencils will be under each cash register.

(*You can get anywhere in this country with an education my son* said his father . . . oh gee pop, you were right, if you could only see me now! *I want you to have a high-school diploma son.*) Now the aisles below lie flat and smooth like roads, and the customers stamping in the lobby are a frenzied herd of cattle. "Watch the customers sharply," said Miss Willows; "and remember there are plenty of store detectives in disguise all over the store *watching every move you make.*" Remember there are plenty of detectives, remember this is YOUR day, remember the Christmas spirit . . . remember they stood on a corner of fourteenth street where a young man promised them a bad Winter and Rounds said "I'd sooner go Red than stand on a breadline," and Joey Andrews shook in his thin-soled shoes for he knew he'd starve sooner than stand on a breadline and he felt he'd stand on a breadline sooner than go Red . . . remember KEEP ON YOUR TOES ALL DAY THERE WILL BE DETECTIVES WATCHING EVERY MOVE YOU MAKE

"Move over." It is Jonesy the Christer, lit on Sterno. "If you believe, believe, believe on the Lord. . . ." "Smart Aleck, dirty sucker, hanging around the Y . . . mamma's boy. . . ." *Papa can anybody in the country be the president?*

Three drunks sitting on the bench too happy to go to bed (sitting in the lobby of their swell hotel, drinking, guzzling, gossiping.) "Yesh shir, the mosht turrible thing in thish country is the bootlegger liquor . . . all the lovely young college boys going to their raksh and ruinsh. . . ." "If you believe, believe, believe. . . ." *Yes my son and remember Abraham Lincoln was born in a log cabin and Our Lord was born in a Manger.* "In the war we had such nice warm mud. . . ." "Shut up, Bug-Eye, what'd it get you?" "In the war we had such nice warm blood. . . ." "If I wash preshident of the United Statesh, firsht thing I'd do I'd forbid the lovely young college boys. . . ." *Just close your eyes Joey if you've said your prayers nothing can happen to you.* "Such nice warm mud. . . ." "Sometimes I think Bug-Eye's just plain nuts." "I lost my leg in Avalon. . . ." "Onward Chris-tian so-o-oldiers. . . ." "When we ask them for something to e-a-t. . . ." Rounds came back from the toilet: "I can't remember a deponent verb, I hate to forget all that." "If you believe, believe, believe. . . ." *Do I have to eat spinach mamma? Yes Joey think of the little Belgian boys who haven't any—and it will make you big and strong.* "Work and pray, live on hay, there'll be jobs in the sky by and by." Rounds said all the comfort stations in the world wouldn't bring him comfort and controlled by the competent motions of well-trained officers, who reason, who separate, who mollify and implore. Still mad, but under direction at last, the crowd settles around counters screaming to be fed.

The mezzanine grows tense with desire for invasion.

The first customer toys with one foot on the stairs; pinches her pocket-book and climbs laboriously upward. Miss Bodkin's short, smart legs run to capture; but over Miss Bodkin's black banged head Mr. Keasbey has already made a dignified assignation; like one hypnotized the customer makes her way surely and pointedly toward those grave commanding eyes. Miss Bodkin turns back in anger; meets Joey Andrews' admiring eye, and irresponsibly sticks out her tongue. Joey Andrews feels his confidence in No. 191-23, 167B slip a little as he sees with a pang Miss Bodkin guessing he is absolutely no good with girls.

"Mrs Summerssss sssign please!" Miss Bodkin bags the day's next sale.

Surely these determined ladies and gentlemen (or are all the gentlemen detectives?) are not the same race as those tentative unhurried customers who loitered and weighed two weeks ago. Now they hurried fiercely, became insane people at indecision, rapidly bought two if they could not decide upon one. After favoring her customer with a cheap *Lorna Doone* from her classics table, Miss Bodkin with malice and caution sells her the latest detective story right off Mr. Keasbey's beautifully stacked table, right under Mr. Keasbey's bristling but dignified nose. Mr. Keasbey bending his stately professorial back takes out his feather-duster and gives his books where Miss Bodkin has ravaged them a quick indignant flick. Miss Bodkin retires with the slyness of a nun to her own table.

A lady grazing close to Joey Andrews is captured by Mr Keasbey two strides ahead of Miss Bodkin who retires viciously blowing her bang off her eyes, and in passing murmurs, "If I printed what I thought about the sixty-year-old teacher's pet, it would make a book too awful even for my own Classics table." But all the lady wanted, and she said so too frankly, was a ninety-five cent copy of *Robinson Crusoe* for the kids and when Mr. Keasbey lost out trying to explain the value of the three-fifty illustrated issue on his own table, he turned her over in haste to Miss Paley; because Christmas is here, and Miss Paley's cheap editions are petty game at this season to an old hunter like Mr. Keasbey. . . . But Miss Paley receives the gift gratefully and looking at Mr. Keasbey's dignified face, who knows but she forgets for a minute Mr. Neely. Now Joey Andrews has his day's first customer, and he will never forget her kind eyes and brown fur coat as she stands eagerly waiting for him to wrap her package with the Christmas twine. Miss Paley on her knees hunting and hunting for *Robinson Crusoe* which is hard to find because it is exactly the color and size of *The Romance of Leonardo da Vinci*, lifts a face modestly benign with the joy of laboring to catch her breath, for Miss Paley knows from her last decade's experience that if she rises too quickly she is likely to get the least little bit of swimming in the head.

The invisible electric wire carried rumors from clerk to clerk. Free lunch would be served in the basement; twenty minutes to eat. A hat-girl had been arrested for stealing change. A shop-lifter had been caught downstairs. The man in the gray felt hat was a Store detective. The Store had already done one-eighth more business than it had done by eleven-thirty of last year's Christmas Eve. Miss Bodkin's sales were higher than Mr. Keasbey's. Miss Stacy had run out of Christmas stickers three times. Mrs. White had sent down a twenty-dollar bill to be changed (no clerk was permitted to make change of anything higher than a ten out of his cash register) and the bill had not come back, after thirty minutes.

The first batch went to the free lunch at eleven-forty-five. They came back. They talked. They conquered. There was no second batch, except Miss Paley who went for a cup of tea. Miss Bodkin said the lunch was made of pieces of wrapping paper from returned purchases of 1929.

Mrs. Summers asked Joey Andrews if he thought he could make out without any lunch. Joey Andrews said sure and dashed off to his next customer.

Joey Andrews was drunk. If for a moment he found himself without a customer he ran up to one lady after another like a lost child seeking its mother.

Miss Willows forgot that for the last two years she had been buyer for the book department; the fire of selling caught in her veins again; she sold passionately. Let Miss Bodkin take the credit down in her salesbook, let Mr. Keasbey receive the commission—but let Miss Willows sell again! Her pearls caught on the edge of a table; scattered underfoot—Miss Willows laughed; turned to a customer and kicked the pearls recklessly out of her way. Miss Willows too was drunk.

Miss Bodkin whispered that her sales had reached $150.

Miss Willows greeting customers at the top of the stairs had lost her debutante coolness and become a barker for a three-ring circus.

Mr. Keasbey broke down a reserve of years and squeezed Joey's arm as he pushed him out of his way.

Miss Paley, weak from no lunch, brushed her hand across her eyes and smiled until her whole head ached.

So it went on, and Mrs. Summers passed among them, conspicuous for her white head, for her customer-like lined face, and in the back of her distracted eyes lurked worry like guilt.

Who shall say that even Mr. Keasbey was actively, consciously motivated by the few cents' commission he was piling up? Each one was simply part of a great selling team, schooled and trained to perfection, each part functioned perfectly. All the time the crowd was changing, but imperceptibly; the stream which fed it must be flowing as fast as the stream which ebbed away. Now one was handing fifty-seven cents change to a gentleman with a green tie, now one was looking through the crowd for the lady with the feather.

In all his life Joey Andrews had never been so happy. His day was measured by customers, not by sales. He was mad with the delight of being necessary to so many people at once, with being efficient for his great team, with knowing exactly what part he had to play.

Miss Willows' voice grew hoarse, strangely naked she looked without her beads too—this way for calendars, this way for the latest fiction—Miss Willows was selling herself and was lost in passion.

But worry was growing out of Mrs. Summers' eyes. She hovered for a brief second about Miss Paley as she stung open the drawer of her cash register. The invisible wires hummed again: Has Miss Paley, maybe Miss Paley, it looks as if Miss Paley. . . . But Miss Paley, blind and dazed and cheerful, still flies among her cheap editions, still makes her way mildly in the Commercial World.

Still the crowd filled the aisles, covered the floor. Only now the incoming stream was heavier than the out-going, complemented by clerks and secretaries from Brooklyn to the Bronx. There was no slack, no shading. Even as there was no telling how the crowd melted and swelled again, there was no telling whether one's feet hurt or did not hurt; not only did no one attend to bodily functions, it was as if they had ceased to exist.

To get to your cash register now meant a hand-to-hand battle. The little bells rang as clerks shot out their drawers, counted rapidly, slammed them shut again. Joey Andrews clicked his open; good God, the bills under the weight were rising mountainously. He wasted a second of M & J's time: he felt with his finger the soft resistant pad of bills.

Mrs. Summers with her kind and tortured smile, her worried eyes, her dancing brows, hovered briefly about Joey Andrews' cash register. Mr. Andrews. . . . Mr. Andrews. . . . Joey Andrews gave her a bright child's look with eyes which looked swiftly away, beyond her, in liaison with his next customer.

Feet were like rubber tires now. Bodies were conveyors of books. Minds were adding machines. Fleeting glimpses of strained and happy faces—it might be Christmas, it might be the warm contact of body with body, of air made of the mingling of human breaths, it might be the happy exchange of one human tribe with another, the excitement, the warmth, the continuous roar of sound. . .

There was a slight lull, as there is sometimes a lull in a storm. Joey Andrews, running like a mountain goat, caught Miss Bodkin's round black eyes, caught Mrs. Summer's level worried look . . . and then he found the eye of a lady with a scar on her throat, who was holding out a book to him, begging, begging for the kindness of his service. . . . And then there was a flurry of ladies with anxious faces and Boy Scout nephews in small towns; Miss Rees had a sudden success with her Green Mountain Boys and Joey Andrews deserted History and Biography to take on her overflow. And the human storm was loose again, wrapping them all together in an efficient human mass. . . . Mrs. Summers stands like a bird of ill omen hovering over Miss Paley's cash register.

The invisible electric wires are humming again. Six hat-girls are going to be dropped, three of them old employees, three of them just taken on for the Christmas rush. They don't tell them, says Miss Bodkin viciously, until the last minute—so they'll keep on selling to the end. Miss Bodkin knows everything before anyone else. Paley's going to get hers, too, I know it, says Miss Bodkin—and Joey Andrews wonders what Miss Bodkin is doing tonight, on Christmas Eve, he wonders if he might have the nerve. . . .

Five-twenty-five. Joey Andrews flew to his cash register, back to the customer with the scar on her throat, back to his beloved cash register. "Well," says Miss Paley to Mrs. Summers, "it can't be helped and it can't be helped." It has happened. Miss Paley's got the sack. They've told Miss Paley they're letting her go. This is Miss Paley's last day. What do you think, Paley's just been fired. Jesus, poor old Paley. . . . Joey Andrews has a customer who wants something in green to match her library curtains. "Heaven knows," Miss Paley said, "I cannot understand, cannot comprehend . . ." and everybody knows that Miss Paley is using big words to keep from crying, and to show that she was a teacher for twenty years. Joey Andrews' customer would prefer something a shade darker; maybe that Oscar Wilde. Mrs. Summers with her eyebrows going like an orchestra leader's baton: "I just feel terrible about this, Miss Paley, just terrible, I knew it last night and I couldn't sleep, they don't let us tell you till the last minute." Joey Andrews' customer doesn't see why they don't put out a Shakespeare in green suede—or even a dictionary.

Someone wants to buy Miss Paley's copy of *The Old Wives' Tale.* Such a nice lady, Miss Paley would like to tell her how much she loves that book. "Next to my Jane Austen," she almost says, holding her side as she graciously hands over the book. "The Commercial World," says Miss Paley, reaching over for the wrapping paper. "My principal told me," Miss Paley said. "A natural teacher. Born, not made. He told me in so many words. . . ."

The clock jumps to five-twenty-seven. Three minutes more in the Commercial World, Miss Paley. Three minutes more of non-limping, Mrs. Summers. Three minutes more of being a human being, Miss Willows!

Mr. Keasbey is smiling like a boy. Christmas Eve—he hasn't missed one in sixty years with his mother; bought her a shawl, he had, on the third floor, got the employees' discount; had it for her in his locker. Good cook, the old lady, probably'd spend the whole day getting up his Christmas dinner. "My principal told me," Miss Paley said; "he is a man who never minces words. Myra Paley, he told me. . . ." Joey Andrews flies back to his cash register, he does not like to look at Miss Paley any more, Mrs. Summers is standing tentatively: "Mr. Andrews, oh Mr. Andrews." Joey Andrews eyes her with his bright-eyed look, punching at the buttons which make the drawer slide out and tap him gently in the stomach: "Mr. Andrews—I see you are too busy now." "My job at the school," Miss Paley says, "is gone; it's gone, my principal told me." Mrs. Summers is off again, non-limping her last two minutes, like an unwilling bird of ill-omen off with her little mes-sages—the hat-girls now.

And at last the closing bell rang and customers clung where they had been indifferent before and sales-clerks turned cold who had been themselves leeches ten seconds earlier, and customers would not, could not, tear themselves away until *Stars Fell on Alabama* was sent to Arkansas and *The Moving Picture Girls* to Far Rockaway and until they had made ab-so-lutely sure that the price was erased from the Grosset and Dunlap edition of *The Bridge of San Luis Rey*—and Joey Andrews, making out a final sales-check, catches Miss Bodkin's eye on him at last, kindly at last, friendly at last, as if at last she were perceiving him, and Joey Andrews' heart leaps with the thought of Christmas Eve and the chance, the bare chance, that Miss Bodkin, with her gay little bobbing breasts. . . .

"My principal told me," says Miss Paley, not sitting as she had last night, on a counter and girlishly swinging her legs as she added up her sales—but standing off a little, apart from them, as the great store empties, as the people whom the em-ployees of M & J have served all day go home and leave the Store to the clerks, to whom it properly belongs, Miss Paley stands all by herself, while Mrs. Summers (avoiding her now, for Miss Paley is dead) moves like a plague from hat-girl to hat-girl, infecting them, six of them, with the poison from headquarters that has killed Miss Paley. Miss Bodkin, although she has higher sales than anyone else with the possible exception of Mr. Keasbey (who bends his hand over his salesbook as though he fears someone might copy his sums) subdues her joy in her sales as a man uncovers his head for a passing funeral—and there is no doubt about it now at all, Miss Bodkin is definitely smiling at Joey Andrews as if she liked him.

They handed Miss Paley her handkerchiefs and pencils in silence. For all they were kind to her, and patted her shoulders, they were really hurrying her a little, too, hurrying her out of their lives—Miss Paley was bad luck. "Maybe your next job will be a sitting-down one, honey," said Mrs. Summers, limping at last. They all wished Miss Paley would hurry. It is not nice to see someone dead. "Goodbye, all," Miss Paley said, and with a last bewildered look set her feet on the stairs to make her exit from the Commercial World. And they watched Miss Paley float out with her handkerchiefs, her pencils, and her varicose legs, and all of them knew they would never see her again—and Joey Andrews, turning back with relief to his salesbook, gathered courage to return Miss Bodkin's smile.

Mrs. Summers is bearing down upon Joey, smiling too, suddenly everyone is smiling at Joey, Joey Andrews is a good boy and everyone is smiling very kindly at him and Joey happily smiles back. "different with you, you are young," Mrs. Summers is saying. Young, yes, Joey Andrews is young as hell, and Miss Bodkin evidently thinks she has smiled at him too boldly, for now she lowers her eyes to her salesbook again. "You are young and life holds many opportunities," Mrs. Summers says, smiling and smiling. "They don't let us tell them till the last minute, I tried to tell you but you were so busy, you were so happy, but it's different with you, you're so young," says Mrs Summers, smiling pleading for forgiveness. Of course I am young, thinks Joey Andrews, impatient with the old, with the white-haired Mrs. Summers—and he tries to catch Miss Bodkin's eye again and signal her, We're both young, tonight's Christmas Eve—but the old will never have done talking to the young, and Mrs. Summers goes on: "and so if you will leave your things tonight on my desk, and come for your paycheck next Thursday. . . ." Nobody is smiling at Joey Andrews now, everybody is looking down very conscientiously at his own salesbook, he feels without knowing quite why that they are anxious to have him go, he hurries through counting the sales he scored for M

& J, he stands apart a little as Miss Paley had, and when Miss Bodkin, not smiling any more now, comes and asks him in a low voice if he would like to come to her party tonight, just a few friends, just Miss Rees and herself and a few of the fellows, Joey Andrews says stiffly, "Thanks very much, I have a date," for Joey Andrews knows now why Miss Bodkin took to smiling at him so suddenly, Miss Bodkin knows everything ahead of everyone else—and Joey Andrews is not going to hang around people and be bad luck.

for Miss Mildred, it is not ladylike to have a job and Annie wants Miss Mildred to know that she knows it. . . . Mrs. Friedman's place at the head of the table is still empty; behind it the goldfish swim from one end of their bowl to the other: will it be one of her sick days, so that for company all day long Annie will have her high voice talking into the telephone, Well you know, it comes and goes, it gets better and worse. . . .

Annie wipes the sweat that rolls down her face. New York in Summer is hot and lonely. In the big rooms beyond the kitchen the furniture is covered with flowery cotton, the pictures are heavily veiled, the curtains camphored and rolled away in the closets—the Friedmans' old Elsa, bringing her baby spent two Spring days in helping. The rugs are gone; Mrs. Friedman's weary, hurrying footsteps (when she is well) can be heard all over the house, sharply tapping the bare floors. It seems that everyone except the Friedmans is away for the Summer; the dumbwaiter shaft is almost silent now. The Allens' Bertha, that wild one, sent a post card from the Seashore; the Goodkinds' Elsa is in the Mountains; almost the only one left is that Greenhorn, the Golds' Lisa, who cries down the shaft from the fourteenth floor because she is homesick. Annie is ashamed that the Friedmans are not going away; she is ashamed of what people must be saying, the milkman, and the Allens, and the Allens' Bertha. And it is all Miss Mildred's fault: a job she has to have, like any common person! Annie has heard Mrs.

Friedman sighing to her sister, Mrs. Rosen-bloom; Mrs. Rosenbloom always snaps back, She don't get it from *our* side of the family! Yes, it is lonely without the Allens' Bertha, she misses her jolly *Achtung!* Annie! have you given Mrs. F. her orders for the day . . . ?

But today is Thursday! On Thursdays Annie's hair is in curlers from Wednesday night; she does her work all day long with her hair tied up in a bandana which presses the little bumps against her head and reminds her constantly of Thursday night and Joe. For on Thursday nights the Friedmans eat early and Annie, in a fine black dress that once belonged to Mrs. Friedman, goes with Joe to Trommer's beer garden in Brooklyn. That Joe! if only he would not be always after her about getting married . . . with his forty dollars (hardly the price of a coat! Mrs. Friedman says) every Saturday. . . .

Mister Robert was ready. Annie snatched the bacon and glided into the dining-room, passing the swinging-door from her shoulder to her elbow so that it would swing quietly back to its place. Last night Mister Robert came into the kitchen with his tuxedo jacket over his pajamas and knocked things about in the ice-box until Annie came out with a coat thrown over her nightgown and made coffee for him while he teased her about Joe Schmidt and said, A plumber always sleeps with his tools and an extra toilet lid under his pillow, and, When you lived on a farm, Annie, how could you tell which was you and which was the cow; Annie had giggled till she could hardly talk, Mister Robert was a jolly one, not like Miss Mildred. (That boy has never given me a moment's trouble, Mrs. Friedman used to say to her sister Mrs. Rosenbloom.) But today he had forgotten, and when Annie accidentally grazed his sleeve with her hand he drew his arm back sharply, and with his eyes still fastened on the newspaper began blindly chasing the bacon on his plate.

Ya, it is lonely in the Summer, thinks Annie, back on her side of the swinging-door, and it will be a long time before evening and Joe. But tonight will come and Joe will come, and after he has stopped being angry about getting married, they will drink beer and be jolly under the trees at Trommer's.

Mr. Friedman picks his watch off the table and without looking at his children sticks his paper under his arm—and comes briskly toward the kitchen. Annie stands modestly waiting, with one hand on her hip, her behind stuck out a little, like Mrs. Friedman—she is no Greenhorn any more to stand with her hands dangling and her feet far enough apart for a milking-stool between them!

Well, Annie, said Mr. Friedman cheerfully, and she knew it was something unusual—generally he called her Elsa or What's-your-name—looks like another hot day, what? Annie blushed and swayed her shoulders, Mr. Friedman was nice and jolly like Mister Robert. Mrs. Friedman's going to stay in bed today, Annie, and

I know I can count on you to take good care of her. Oh yes, Mr. Friedman, I'll do everything. Yes, I know you will, Annie, you're a good girl, you take care of all of us. Oh, and by the way, Annie. . . . He looked at her helplessly. His eyes shot up toward her Thursday bandana and glanced away again. Of course I know, Annie. . . . He was silent, twisting his watch-chain. Of course, Mr. Friedman said, looking out of the window, I know today is Thursday, but you could have Sunday although it's not your Sunday—you see there'll be some people dropping in to see her tonight—I mean—I hate to ask it, Annie. . . . Don't worry yourself, Mr. Friedman. I'll stay in, said Annie.

Mr. Friedman stood there smiling and blinking, Oh thank you, Annie, that's mighty nice, that's—*mighty* nice; suddenly he held out a dollar bill, tickling her hand; Buy—buy yourself something, he said. Oh no, Mr. Friedman, no thank you—Annie put her hands behind her back. Then Mr. Friedman was in a great hurry, he put the bill back in his pocket (Annie wondered if it meant one of Mrs. Friedman's hats—maybe that black satin one with the rose—instead!) and said, Well what you say goes, you're the boss around here, Annie! and started to go out.

Annie stood there suddenly frightened, thinking how mad Joe would be—with his What do they think you are anyway, a horse, do they think they own you?—but Mr. Friedman was waiting for her to laugh at his joke, so she laughed and flapped her dishcloth at him coyly and he rushed out with a Yes, sir, you're the boss, Annie! and Annie was left alone with a long day before her and no Joe at the end, and really, she thought, maybe it would be better if I just marry Joe right away . . . but Ach! look at me standing here dreaming like a Greenhorn with Mrs. Friedman sick. . . .

* * *

Annie set the breakfast tray gently on the table in Mrs. Friedman's bedroom, for halfway down the hall she had heard her high voice at the telephone, Well, it comes and goes. . . . As she silently straightened brushes and little boxes on the dressing table, she watched in the mirror Mrs. Friedman propped on one elbow, with her free hand smoothing the long lacy skirts of the telephone doll. Do you mean to tell me, Mrs. Friedman said, Am I in my senses, Mrs. Friedman said, and she rolled her eyes to the ceiling with that look of pain she used to have when Annie was a Greenhorn and wasted time heating soup-plates or forgot, the last thing at night, to turn down the covers on the Friedmans' beds; Well, Mrs. Friedman said, shaking her head at the telephone, if that isn't the limit, and she expected you to believe it, say, people don't starve as easy as all that, no such luck—and then she gave the little groans and oh my's and don't tell *me's* that Annie loved to hear.

Annie hovered about the dresser hoping Mrs. Friedman would talk to her and at last, when she hung up the receiver and replaced the doll, she turned to Annie with a sigh. Annie, did you ever hear such a thing! Remember that devil Katie from the Swedish Agency, that took such advantage my sister had to turn her out without a character? She's been bothering my sister all Summer to take her back, says she can't find another place without a character. (Of course she can't, but it would be a crime to give her one.) Well! this morning that devil has the crust to come back pretending she's *starving* and faint right outside my sister's door! Not that I believe she really fainted . . . have you ever heard of such cheek? And the idea! as if anybody could starve in a big city like this—my goodness, this is 1930, not the year 1!

Annie stood with the duster in her hand and rolled her eyes shyly to the ceiling. Such cheek, she murmured as she gave an elegant little flip of the duster along the foot of Mrs. Friedman's bed. Oh, it just discourages you, said Mrs. Friedman sighing deeply, such treatment in return for every kindness; it was different when I was young I can tell you that, Annie, you girls today have it mighty easy; my mother's girl got up at five and worked all day and *never* had a night off, and you wouldn't believe what they paid her! A girl knew her place in those days—and there was no *starving* either! Well get back to work now, Annie, you'd chatter all day if I didn't stop you . . . no use your wasting time just because I'm flat on my back. . . .

Annie went singing down the long hall, singing inside of herself of course, because only a Greenhorn sings out loud anywhere but the kitchen or her own room, and Annie had come a long way from being a Greenhorn like that foolish Katie . . . from the days when Mrs. Friedman didn't trust her to open the Linen Closet and had to keep telling and telling her, remember this, remember that . . . those awful first nights when there seemed to be a hundred Friedmans instead of only four, and her serving-cap, shaking like a bug in her hair, threatened to fall off and splash in the gravy . . . the first time the Friedmans had Company . . . how the other girls laughed at her up on the roof on wash-day because she was afraid to go near the edge . . . how everyone said Greenhorn, Greenhorn . . . how stupid she had been when she had murmured *Leider*, I am sorry, that first morning when Mrs. Friedman told her And no small children, think of that: *Leider*, the Green-horn said! No, Annie could hardly believe she had been so dumb—crying for home in her little room at night . . . praying . . . writing letters to her mother . . . dreaming all the time how she would sail back in the First Class with her pockets filled with money . . . actually longing, just imagine, for the days when she was nothing but an ignorant country girl, leading a cow through the village street and chewing a blade of grass. . . .

There goes Mrs. Friedman's telephone again. . . . *Oh yes, my dear, it's got the better of me again. . . .* How nice

102

to have Mrs. Friedman sick and in the house all day. . . . *It comes and goes. . . .* Annie lifted the statue of the lovely lady with a dress falling off one shoulder and dusted the table under it (Don't neglect what you can't see!)—such a fine piece! could she and Joe ever have a thing like that in their house?

No, Annie was no Greenhorn any more and she didn't like it when Joe or the Allens' Bertha teased her about those days; sometimes Joe puffed out his cheeks and rubbed them red, That's how you used to look Annie! and Bertha would say, Will I ever forget your face Annie the first time you saw a nigger—it was only poor old Albert, but you sure thought he was a devil out of hell. . . . Ach, so long ago, can't you forget? I didn't know any better, Annie would tell them—and she no longer asked her mother in letters what was doing on Saturday nights at home . . . those Greenhorn dances, imagine, jumping up and down, swing to the left, swing to the right . . . how hard it was to find anything to write her mother about, after all how could that old-fashioned old German woman in her wooden shoes, who had never even seen a subway or a movie, understand this smart new Annie who powdered her face . . . who had a fine room to herself with curtains crossed like the curtains in Mrs. Friedman's own bedroom, a clean little room, papered with pink roses like the inside of a cardboard box for ladies' handkerchiefs . . . who was trusted every day to polish the grand silver that stood in rows on the sideboard. . . . Catch Annie going back to Germany! no, sir, not even in the First Class, not even with her pockets filled with money, no, no, Annie is an American now, she will never milk a cow again, New York is her home and she wears high heels even with her uniform, makes over Mrs. Friedman's old hats for herself and knows about saving money in the bank and buying bargains and keeping a fellow waiting like any American girl, and when she goes out on Thursday nights and alternate Sundays she looks more like a lady than Miss Mildred who leaves her crêpe de chines hanging in the closet and goes to work in old sweaters with glasses sliding down her nose!

Oh, but she was smart, that Annie! You couldn't fool her, she knew how to do things right—how to dress, how to work, how to save her money. Na, that stupid old bear of a Joe, with his Let's get married tomorrow, Annie. . . .

***

Mrs. Friedman, did you ring? Yes, Annie, I was thinking you might as well go over my room. It won't bother you, Mrs. Friedman? Well yes, of course, but I don't want anything neglected just because I'm flat on my back, I'm not one to let my own suffering interfere, just work quietly Annie and don't chatter, I'll lay still and rest. . . . Yes, sir, what do you think of that devil Katie? Starving's out of date, I told Mrs. Rosenbloom to tell her. Some of these

104

ignorant girls just don't know when they've got it good, a place in a liberal American family, every advantage. . . . O that telephone, your friends don't do you any favor calling up when you're sick, no I'll answer, Annie . . . ! Hello, hello, oh Mamie, I was wondering why I didn't hear from you, well, you know, it gets better and worse . . . I can't complain . . . it comes and it goes ... if I'm alive Mamie!

Mrs. Friedman sighed; Annie, Annie, it's a relief to have you around the house instead of some Greenhorn *schlemiel*—I've taught you a good German word, na, Annie? and don't forget I've taught you everything else you know, don't you be in a hurry with that young man of yours! you know a good berth when you see one, don't you Annie; you're nobody's fool; you know what side your bread is buttered on, don't you, Annie. . . . And rolling her eyes to the ceiling she said in a low voice as if to somebody else, Nobody knows what I suffer, not even the doctors. . . .

And Annie felt proud that Mrs. Friedman made jokes with her, and wasn't she a smart American girl to know which side of her bread was buttered, and she felt terribly sorry for Mrs. Friedman's sufferings—Mrs. Friedman said it was something ladies her age get; Annie couldn't remember her mother ever having it, but she knew it must be something terrible; Mrs. Rosenbloom had it, too, and when she came with Mr. Rosenbloom for a visit in the evening the two Ladies would lie back and talk about it together, and Mr. Friedman and Mr. Rosenbloom would pick up their handkerchiefs and

Mrs. Friedman was in bed, directing things with a hand to her side like a sick queen, Don't forget under things, Annie; I hope Mr. Papenmeyer is prompt with that meat; be careful with those flowers, Annie; my, they certainly look real, everybody wants to know where I got them, but I'd be ashamed to tell 'em they were so cheap—and Annie forgot about Joe and got down on her knees and scrubbed till her face was purple.

And at the end of the morning she brought Mrs. Friedman a jelly omelet and blushed all over when Mrs. Friedman said, Oh, Annie, you're a treasure, what would I do without you! and wished Joe could have heard her being praised like that. Then Mrs. Friedman said, Hasn't that devil sent the meat yet, Annie? and Annie said, Not yet, and Mrs. Friedman said, Isn't that the limit, just when I'm flat on my back, and Annie said shyly, It's the most terrible thing I ever heard, and together they rolled their eyes to the ceiling, Mrs. Friedman with her head leaning back against the pillow and Annie standing over the foot of the bed with Mrs. Friedman's jelly omelet on a large tray in her hands.

***

But now the morning was over and Mrs. Friedman was asleep with one arm over her face, and the dirty lunch dishes were piled in the sink and the kitchen was far away from the bedroom and very empty and the long afternoon was beginning just as it did every day, only when Mrs. Friedman was well she came into the kitchen in a fine black coat, gave a quick look around and walked smartly out, slamming the door behind her—but whether Mrs. Friedman was sick or well, it was always lonely in the afternoons.

The dining-room looked gloomy and dead through the window in the swinging-door. When there was no longer work to be done in those big rooms beyond the kitchen, they seemed too strange to enter alone. . . . It didn't seem right, after the nice busy morning together, Mrs. Friedman falling asleep at the other end of the house . . . now there was nothing left awake except those silly goldfish swimming from one end of their bowl to the other . . . if it was Winter Annie would rap on the dumbwaiter for a little company with the Allens' Bertha.

Oh yes, the afternoons were lonely, and it was too bad that she wouldn't be going out tonight with Joe to Trommer's (after all it *was* her night out) and what was she to do this long afternoon by herself before Mr. Papenmeyer sent the meat and vegetables? A letter from her mother lay on the chiffonier in her room, but it would only make her sadder because everything at home was bad and her mother always wrote if Annie was so grand now, why couldn't she send them more money? So Annie put the letter away in a drawer and got out the bedjacket she was making for Mrs. Friedman's birthday present—nobody crocheted like Annie,

Mrs. Friedman said—but it didn't do at all, and at last she gave it up and sat down with a sigh on her bed . . . *I wish I was married.*

Yes, it would be nice to have your own house with Joe and to save up for a radio and to have babies (two, like Mrs. Friedman, not thirteen like her mother in the old country)—oh yes, it would be fine to have Joe all the time in the same house, the same room, at night in the same bed. Twenty-eight she was, and at home if a girl was not married at twenty-eight the children followed her down the road singing songs and laughing—and a girl's mother was after her all the time. But what did they know there, Annie thought,—in America everything is different, why the Allens' Bertha said it wasn't so bad in America if you never got married, the only thing is to have enough money, she said, and have a good time. . . . Well, that was all right for Bertha—she hated babies and she said all men were alike and she'd like to see the one worth tying up with. . . . But it was different with Annie, Annie wanted to get married all right—some day—and Joe was a good man . . . maybe he was right when he said Annie got these stuck-up ideas about forty dollars from Mrs. Friedman and when he said Mrs. Friedman took advantage of her (after all, Thursday *was* her night out!) and God knows there were nights when Annie couldn't sleep for wanting Joe.

Yes, these afternoons were lonely, and Annie sat on that white bed for a long time without moving, and then she looked up at the trunk (filled with things she was saving for her trousseau) that hung on a shelf over her head and suddenly she remembered what that queer one, Miss Mildred, had said to her once. Miss Mildred had marched into Annie's kitchen one day, I've never seen your room Annie, would you mind letting me see it? She looked around without touching anything. So this is what they give you, well, well, like a palace only a little more like a coffin with your toilet in a closet and your trunk hanging over your head on a shelf, isn't that just too lovely; did you ever stop to think, Annie, that that trunk might fall down on you some day and it would be nobody's fault but your own? And suddenly Miss Mildred looked at her with her shiny glasses, Why don't you get married, Annie? Believe me, if I could find a man who'd take me out of this house and not put me in another just like it, I wouldn't be here another night! You mustn't talk like that behind your mother's back, Annie began, but Miss Mildred stalked out of the room. Now Annie sat and looked up at that trunk above her head and shuddered . . . and then she had a feeling that she just wanted to lie down and cry.

But no—only a Greenhorn like the Golds' Lisa cried!— her eyes would be red while she was waiting on the table and Mr. Friedman would come out with one of his jokes about Somebody—Somebody's Sweetheart hasn't been around lately, or Somebody looks like the Niagara—and Mister Robert would scream with laughter. . . .

But how mad Joe would be tonight! Nowadays, he was mad at so many things, at Annie and the Fried-mans and his job and America, that sometimes Annie was scared of him, he was so changed. So jolly he had been when she first met him, at a dance hall that the Allens' Bertha and her sailor-friend had taken her to, always so cheerful, always talking America this, America that: he clapped his hand over her mouth when she spoke in German. You are finished with all that, he said, you must become a real American, and he walked with an American newspaper and a little dictionary in his pocket. They went to the movies in those days, American movies and American down-town dance halls, never to Trommer's, never to any place that reminded them of Germany. Annie was ashamed because Joe was so much more American than she was, she cut off her hair, she bought herself silk stockings, she asked the Allens' Bertha to buy her powder and gloves. But nowa-days he said if he could make forty dollars a week he'd just as soon live in Germany, he said America's not such a grand country after all, there's a lot of Jews and rich people here the same as any other country and the peo-ple that have the money keep it. . . .

As crazy as Miss Mildred he sounded sometimes, thought Annie, like the time she had stalked into the kitchen with her hat and coat still on and said to Annie, Well, Annie, where do you think I've been today? and Annie said, I don't know, Miss Mildred, where? Miss

Mrs. Friedman felt and when Annie said, Better, she threw up her hands and said Thank God in a big deep voice, and then she frowned, If she's so much better she had no right to send for me, God knows I don't feel too good myself and nobody would believe how upset I was when that Katie—a girl ought to be put in prison for scaring a person out of their wits! I gave her a cup of coffee too, I'm too soft-hearted, I should have sent her about her business at once. I never would have come today if my sister hadn't phoned—leaving my *schlemiel* to spoil the dinner. Ah, Annie, I wish there were two of you!

Annie was happier in the kitchen now. She picked up Mrs. Friedman's bed-jacket again and started to crochet briskly. It was nice thinking of the two Ladies chatting in the bedroom about their sickness; Mrs. Rosenbloom would take off her shoes and lie down on Mr. Friedman's bed and the two Ladies would lie there side by side, shaking their heads and sighing, Oh yes, it comes and goes, and then they would talk about that devil Katie for a little while and Mrs. Friedman would say how she didn't know what would become of Miss Mildred and Mrs. Rosenbloom would say . . . and then they would lie there shaking their heads because nobody knew how sick they were. . . .

Sick! Joe said (Joe had it in for Mrs. Friedman) she's a big strong woman and she makes *me* sick, that's the only thing that's the matter with her. No Annie, you can't expect a man to wait forever, he said, and he called Mrs.

113

Friedman such bad names that Annie had to tell him to just take his hat off of her clean white sink and get, but it wasn't her sink Joe would say, it was Mrs. Friedman's and what was she but a goddam Jew no more American than they were—and sometimes he would take his hat and go and Annie would be afraid he had left for good. But Mrs. Friedman always laughed. Don't worry, Annie, he'll be back, and if he isn't there's plenty of fish in the sea for a smart girl like you—and sure enough (Mrs. Friedman was a wonder!) he always came back on her next evening off.

Joe was wrong to talk against Mrs. Friedman. Didn't she stick up for Joe herself? Didn't Mrs. Friedman say he was better than the other fellows she had had because he spoke good English and she wasn't going to have her kitchen filled with rough foreigners who were taxi-drivers and what-not, and they didn't mean any good to Annie either, You can bet your last red cent on that, you don't hear Italian fellows talking about getting married, do you? Annie had had an Italian fellow once, and she certainly didn't hear him talk about getting married, she didn't hear him talk about anything because it was when Annie was new and they couldn't understand each other's English so they just met in the park and made love—Mrs. Friedman put an end to that when the dirty dago telephoned and asked for Annie Friedman, Annie said it must be her cousin from Newark and Mrs. Friedman said, Oh, and he talks with an Italian accent, does he? and went back to the phone and gave that fellow a piece of her mind. . . . No, I know what's best for you, Annie, keep Joe as a steady and be engaged to him and then when he's made enough money. . . .

What with Joe coming, and everything to worry about and Joe sure to be angry all over again—thank goodness the Ladies were inside, lying side by side, peacefully talking about this and that, shaking their heads and sighing. . . . She would surprise them! She would bring them a tray of tea and buttered toast before Mrs. Friedman thought of asking. She carried the tray briskly down the long hall while the Ladies' voices got louder and louder, and then, when she stood in the doorway they suddenly stopped (they must have been talking about Miss Mildred again!) and Mrs. Friedman said quickly Ah here's Annie with tea, Annie you're an angel! And when she was halfway down the hall again with empty hands she heard them start all over again, and she hated to hurry away from the friendly buzz of their voices which died down so that when she stood again in the doorway of the lonely kitchen there was no sound except the hum of the frigidaire, and it was lonely and there was nothing to do but to think again of Joe.

That Joe! a girl couldn't get him out of her head— Maybe he was right—it wasn't fair, it wasn't natural, to keep a man waiting. . . .

But whenever she went to Mrs. Friedman with her mind half made up Mrs. Friedman shook her head and sighed, Annie, Annie, you don't know when you're well off; an independent girl like you earning good money and having plenty of freedom and what do you want to do but throw it all away just because a man lifts his finger; I don't say Joe isn't a good boy he is, God forbid I should keep anybody from doing what they want, but I'm just giving you the best advice I can; after all you are a young girl and your mother isn't here; now come, come now, Annie, what would the Ladies say Saturday afternoon if they didn't find Annie's cookies, and look at Elsa, Annie . . . but don't think I couldn't get another girl tomorrow and cheaper, too, so just let me know when you're going; well, what do you say? Well what could Annie say when Mrs. Friedman was ready to hurry her right out of the house tomorrow and get in some new girl, some Greenhorn that would burn the vegetables and forget to baste the meat, so Annie said she didn't mean right away, she meant maybe in a couple of months maybe in the Fall or something like that. And Mrs. Friedman said, angrily, Look here, Annie, you can't run off and leave me in the lurch like that; I'm surprised, Annie, after all I've done for you; have you no sense of gratitude I took you in when you were absolutely *green* . . . ?

Now Mrs. Rosenbloom was going, Annie heard her call out Goodbye, goodbye, and she hurried out to open the door for her. Mrs. Rosenbloom held her cape around her throat and said, Annie compared to what I feel my

sister is in Paradise, don't tell her, I wouldn't have anybody worry for worlds, but if Mr. Rosenbloom knew what
I went through he'd send for a million big doctors from
Germany. . . . Well I'm coming back after dinner . . . if I'm
alive . . . nobody should worry about me. . . .

And now the vegetables had come and there were
the butter-balls to roll and Annie began to feel a pleasant hurry in her bones, for dinner was coming and the
Friedmans were coming and everything must be perfect
because everybody counted on Annie. As for Joe. . . .

***

It was nice waiting on them at dinner without Mrs.
Friedman there, Annie felt that she was taking Mrs.
Friedman's place because she cut up the meat in the
dining room and served it herself, and Mr. Friedman
said, What's for dessert, so I should know how much to
eat? and when Annie said Ice-box cake, Mr. Friedman
and Mister Robert opened their mouths and patted
their bellies like little boys. Miss Mildred, of course,
sat there as glum as ever, picking at her food as though
nothing was good enough for her!

While she was cutting up the meat on the sideboard
for seconds, Annie heard Mister Robert say, Gee I forgot
about mother's being sick, I made a date tonight, who's
going to stay in? and Mr. Friedman said, What's-her-
name said she'd stay, and Miss Mildred butted in, Why

do you make her stay in on her one night out, that isn't fair, father, and Mr. Friedman said, Oh, for heaven's sake, Mildred, if the girl doesn't mind why should you? and Miss Mildred said in her disagreeable way That's just it, she *ought* to mind, and Mister Robert screamed Socialist! and threw a piece of bread at her and Annie felt like laughing when it splashed into her plate. Come, come, Robert, said Mr. Friedman, is that a way for a man to treat his sister, and then he made a funny noise as if he were choking and wiped his eyes with his napkin and Annie could see he was laughing himself, and she couldn't help laughing too. Fools! said Miss Mildred and didn't eat another thing, just sat there with her glasses shining like crazy and looking as disagreeable as she possibly could.

Mr. Friedman and Mister Robert got very jolly after that, kidding Annie every time she handed them anything, and Mr. Friedman said, Oooooo look at Somebody's hair tonight and Mister Robert roared, Do I have to? Annie just shook with laughter! Then Mr. Friedman put out his hand and pulled the ends of her apron so it came off and dragged on the floor while she was passing the coffee, and Mister Robert said, Papa, papa, I'll tell on you, undressing young women when your wife's sick in bed, and Annie escaped through the swinging-door with the apron crumpled in her hand, laughing and blushing like sixty!

So by the time Annie had cleared the dining-room and brought Mrs. Friedman her supper on a tray (Mister

Robert and Mr. Friedman sat on the edge of her bed handing her things and being very quiet while she sat up and held her side and said she really couldn't complain, except for that pain in her side and a little difficulty in breathing and an appetite like a bird—Miss Mildred stood in the window with her back to everybody and played with the cord of the shade) she was feeling so jolly and important that she hardly cared what Joe said when he came. After all, Mrs. Friedman knew best. No, sir, the Friedmans' Annie is no Greenhorn, she knows how to treat a fellow the same as any American girl!

So when the kitchen door-bell rang she stuck out her behind defiantly and opened the door.

***

Joe came in with a big smile on his face that slowly got smaller and smaller. Hello, he said, pulling at her apron, what's the big idea, going to a masquerade? Joe, said Annie crossly, can't you find time to shave before calling on a lady? Oh, I'm calling on a lady, are I, said Joe throwing his hat on the kitchen table; well, leave me tell you you don't look like one, not in that rig; what's the big idea? Now Joe, said Annie, grabbing his hat off the table and hanging it neatly on a nail, how many times have I got to tell you . . . And by the way, Joe (Annie rubbed the nails of one hand on the inside of the other, as she had seen Mrs. Friedman do), I won't be able to go

119

out with you tonight, Mrs. Friedman's sick.

Sick is she, growled Joe, tapping his pipe so the burnt tobacco flew all over the floor, what's the matter with the old hag? Now you know perfectly well Joe Schmidt, she's not at all strong and she's not so young, and she's got something the matter with her ladies of her age get. . . . Say, who're you fooling, said Joe, I knew plenty of dames in the old country that age and they weren't too sick to milk cows every day, and he laughed nasty and said I suppose only Ladies get it? So Annie said very snappy, Well, they get it in this country, that's all.

Joe stood there stuffing his pipe angrily. At last he spoke in German. Annie I've had enough of this, he said, it's Mrs. Friedman this and Mrs. Friedman that and I'm sick of it—listen, Annie, she's a big, strong woman, she can have less rooms and do her own dirty work—you don't have to spend your life taking care of other people's houses. Annie said, How can you be so common, Joe, this is my home and I do my share in it just like Mrs. Friedman does hers, and what do you want, do you want her to stop entertaining . . . ? Look here, Annie, I'm not going to wait around until Mrs. Friedman dies and then you'll think you have to cook for that fat-headed son of hers. . . . Now, Joe, do we have to go over all this again; you don't know how nice Mrs. Friedman is to me; why she told me only today I'm like one of the family. . . . The one that does the work, Joe said; aaaaaaah, the old hag, she makes me sick. . . .

Excuse me, Joe, that's Mrs. Friedman's bell, she wants her tea; I'll be right back. . . . Annie, you listen to me, do you hear . . . ? Now, Joe, shut up a minute and don't drop your ashes on my nice clean floor, I'm going to give Mrs. F. her tea; and Joe said, Well, pour it down her neck, the dirty old Jew.

When she came back Joe was sitting on the kitchen table with his feet on a chair, smoking his pipe. Thanks, I'm making myself right at home, he said, I'm just crazy about this wonderful sofa you have in your lovely parlor. If you think, he said, kicking the chair, that I'm going to get out of here just because they asked you to stay in tonight . . . I'm going to stay right here in this goddam kitchen and talk to you; things can't go on like this, do you hear, Annie, I'm not going to be a monkey any more.

Sssshh Joe, don't shout like that in my kitchen. *Your* kitchen! he roared, that's a hot one, that is. He spoke more quietly. All right, Annie, I won't shout, only let's talk it over; are you listening to me, Annie, and will you please, for God's sake, stop washing those dishes while I talk?

Joe, I might as well get them out of the way, it don't look nice. . . .

Oh, don't it look nice, Joe mimicked her angrily with his little fingers crooked. Pfui, you sound just like Mrs. Friedman!

Joe. . . .

If you don't listen to me, I'll shout like hell, I'll shout so everybody can hear, I don't give a damn for your lousy

121

Friedmans. . . . But he sat down quietly. Oh, Annie, he said, you ought to marry me pretty soon, it isn't natural for a man, Annie. . . . *Are they calling you again? What do they think you are, a horse?*

Annie was too frightened to move; she thought Mrs. Friedman would get right out of bed and come down the hall and say, Now march, young feller, the way she had to the delivery boy who got fresh when Annie was new and hadn't learned to say Knock your block off. I'll be right back, Joe, she said soothingly, I guess she wants a hot-water bottle before the Company comes, and she ran down the hall and felt awful when Mrs. Friedman said, What's your hurry, Annie, the outside of this bottle is all wet, and if Joe can't talk more quietly he'll have to go, where does he think he is anyway, and then she ran back to the kitchen.

Annie, can't you see, it just makes me sick, Annie, to see you running around waiting on a lot of people instead of getting married to me, Joe said; listen, Annie, don't you like me any more? Annie put her arms around his neck. Of course, silly, you're my boy. Joe began kissing her, but all the while she kept one eye open to stare through the window in the swinging-door. Annie, Annie, Joe whispered, we'll be married soon, ya Annie? we'll have a little house of our own, ya, please, Annie? There was a loud ring and Annie jumped away and smoothed her skirt. Joe grabbed her, but Annie pulled herself away, Excuse me Joe, that's my bell, and ran out to open the door and let in Mr. and Mrs. Rosenbloom, who whispered, How is she, Annie? oh my poor sister, if she knew how I was feeling myself!

Joe was standing in the kitchen with his hat in his hand and he said, I'm going, Annie, that's all there is to it, this is the end; every time I get started talking you run away and do something for those people, I'm sick of it, I'm *through.* . . . He put on his hat and buttoned up his coat and tapped his pipe as if each thing was the last, but Annie knew what to do. She reached up and started to tickle him under the arms and he kept trying to push her off and keep from laughing. And then all of a sudden he was kissing her again and saying she must marry him right away. See, Annie, I can't wait for you any more, sweetie; that's what it is, I've waited nearly four years and it makes a man sick; ow, stop tickling, Annie. . . . Then he wasn't able to speak any more. He reached up under her skirt with one hand and Annie felt his hand playing with her garter, and she got excited. But all the time her ears were straining for the sound of bells, and she giggled nervously. . . .

Then a bell rang, very sharply. Annie pushed him away and bent down with trembling hands to fasten her garter, and Joe asked in a dazed voice, What was that? My doorbell, of course, Annie answered in a shaky voice, and as she stood up Joe put his hands around her neck and said, I dare you not to answer, until suddenly the bell rang again and Joe let her go.

***

It was the Mandelbaums and the Steins who had met in the elevator and they all came in pointing their fingers at one another and saying, No *we* caught *you*, and as soon as they got inside they were very quiet and the two Ladies said, How is she, Annie? and Mrs. Stein stayed in back of Mrs. Mandelbaum on purpose to smile at Annie and say, I'd like to steal you Annie, but I guess I haven't got a chance, have I? Annie ducked her head to hide how red her face was, but she felt very pleased and she stood there swaying her shoulders modestly until she heard Mr. Friedman kissing Mrs. Mandelbaum and saying, Aha, look what the cat dragged in, what did you bring your husband for, Mamie? and then she went slowly back to the kitchen.

She found Joe sitting and staring ahead of him angrily and she wished suddenly that he would go home, she was tired of seeing him there and fighting with him and going through everything all over again and the Company inside laughing and scraping chairs excited her and she wanted to watch them through the swinging-door.

I'm sick of this, Annie, Joe started all over again. You listen to me, Annie. . . .

You listen to me, Joe Schmidt, said Annie, tossing her head, what do you think I am anyway, a Greenhorn, that I should get married just because a man lifts his finger, look at me, independent, making my own money, I should throw it all away just because. . . .

All right, Mrs. Friedman, Joe said, very nasty. Ach, be

124

yourself, Annie. You didn't use to talk like that. What's the matter with me anyway, why shouldn't we get married? Now, Joe, we've been over all this; you know very well we want to wait until we have enough money to do everything nice. . . . But we won't starve on forty dollars. . . . Mrs. Friedman says times are hard, and you might lose your job . . . and you'd be satisfied to make forty dollars the rest of your life. . . . Why not? forty dollars is a lot of money, it's more than your father in the old country ever heard of or mine either; you get these crazy ideas from your Lady, I tell you; I don't want to live like them, I don't want to marry a Mrs. Friedman. . . . But Joe, look at Elsa, what a hard time she had. . . . What do you mean hard time? She ain't starving and she's got a nice fat baby, and she doesn't have to live in somebody else's house. . . . But she hasn't any other hat to wear, Winter and Summer, but the one Mrs. Friedman gave her three years ago. . . . Christ, Annie, it's not so long ago that you never heard of anything but a handkerchief to cover your head. . . . Shut up, I'm no Greenhorn any more. . . . And I tell you I wish you were, you were a lot nicer to me in those days. . . .

Annie could hardly sit still she was so impatient and she began to listen for the men's voices in the parlor. It sounded like the beginning of a card game, very jolly and friendly. She wished she had thought of making cookies to surprise Mrs. Friedman . . . and she itched to be at the window of the swinging-door. . . .

Don't you see, Annie, you've got ideas in your head? why my God, have sense. . . . Oh, for Christ's sake, Annie, let's get out of this damn house tonight, we'll get married in the morning—oh, for Christ's sake, Annie, can't you see what a fool you are, can't you see Mrs. Friedman don't give a damn for you . . . ? I can see you have no manners, Mr. Schmidt, and I wish you'd go home, I'm sick and tired—what do you think I am, anyway, you must think I'm crazy; how could I leave Mrs. Friedman in the lurch . . . ?

Mr. Friedman called loudly Elsa, Annie, What's-your-name, are you going to let us all starve?

Joe swore and pounded his fist on the top of the washing-sink. Annie got up without looking at him and filled three large trays with glasses and plates and napkins and ginger ale and carried them one at a time through the swinging-door. She set a glass of ginger ale before Joe, and he threw it in the sink. She didn't look at him. She hurried in to Mr. Friedman and the gentlemen who were sitting around the green card table waiting for her.

Annie always fed the gentlemen first, she knew the ladies could wait, and it was fun passing them things that they took with the wrong hands because all rules were off when the ladies were not in the room, and Annie didn't bother about left shoulders or anything—and fat Mr. Mandelbaum winked at her and said he was winning all Mr. Friedman's money, and Mr. Friedman roared and said Elsa's too smart to believe that, Moses! Then she carried the last tray in to the ladies and was helping them daintily when suddenly she remembered Joe sitting angry alone in the kitchen and she got so frightened— maybe he might get really mad and leave once for all and she'd never—and she began to tremble and hurry. . . . But Mrs. Rosenbloom stopped her to ask the recipe of her ice-box cake, Maybe my *schlemiel* can learn to make it, she said, and Annie had to stand in the doorway and tell it to her three times before she could get away.

Well, did you feed the pigs? Joe said as soon as she got back to the kitchen. Annie are you going to spend the rest of your life feeding the pigs? Oh, but Annie was sick and tired of the whole thing. She rolled her eyes to the ceiling like Mrs. Friedman: You talk like an ignorant foreigner, and please remember this is Mrs. Friedman's kitchen.

That's something I never forget, said Joe savagely. And I tell you what, Annie Schlemmer, I'm sick of this business, I'm not going to hang around any more, I'll get another girl, a nice girl that thinks forty dollars is a lot of money. . . .

Aaaaach, you and your other girls! So go and get one, a fine girl you'll get, one that's too dumb to want a decent coat to her back—

You make me sick with your coats! he shouted, what the hell do I care . . .? In America a fellow wants his girl to have a nice coat, said Annie tossing her head, a decent fellow would be ashamed. . . . Well, I'm not that kind of a fellow, Joe said. I'm the kind that's ashamed to hell to have my girl cooking for a lousy Jewish outfit and eating what's left over and saying thank you every time they step on her neck, that's what. . . . Annie held her head in the air and tapped one foot on the floor as Mrs. Friedman did when she was scolding a delivery boy. Any decent fellow, she murmured, any gentleman—

Pfui! said Joe, shut up, you make me sick, you do, talking like Mrs. Friedman and getting so stuck up and ladylike; I'm through with you, see, I'm through. I'm not going to be a monkey all my life—a fellow can't make love to his girl because a couple of fat old Jews want a glass of ginger ale! Pfui! I'm through, I swear to God I'm through, and I'm never coming back. . . .

Well, just let me know when you're going, said Annie, still tapping her foot, I don't have to worry, I can get someone else easy. . . .

All right, I *will* go! shouted Joe. He stood up and slapped his hat on the back of his head just as he used to, before Annie taught him better. So long, he said carelessly. Annie stood there dully without saying anything. Goodbye, I said! Joe said loudly. Annie stood there without looking at him. Goodbye, Annie, Joe said in a fierce voice, aren't you even going to kiss me goodbye? Annie didn't move. All right, don't! said Joe. Annie heard the doorknob rattle. But when she turned round, there was Joe standing at the door looking at her and twisting the knob with a hand behind his back. Go already, she said, and she gave him a little push with her hand. The door closed behind him.

Annie went into her own room and kicked off her shoes and sat down on the bed. She felt like crying—but she was no Greenhorn to go crying her eyes out after a man. . . . Anyway he'd come back. . . . But suddenly she put her head in the pillow and cried like any Greenhorn.

***

Outside they were saying goodbye. Miss Mildred had brought the company to the door and Mr. Stein was saying, Well, Mildred, it's pretty late for us working-men, isn't it, and Mrs. Stein said, Try and tear you away from a card game though and then she said, Did I tell you my son sent his regards, Mildred? and Mrs. Mandelbaum said, You won't be working long, Mildred, before you know it you'll be getting married, and Mrs. Rosenbloom said, Married! and then her troubles begin; come on, Al, I can't stand here talking all night; goodnight, Mildred, you don't look well, dear, and take care of your poor, poor mother—Al, come along, can't you see I'm dying on my feet?

Annie thought she'd better go to Mrs. Friedman and see if she wanted anything; it would be nice just to say a word to somebody before she went to bed. Outside the bedroom door she heard Mrs. Friedman and Miss Mildred talking in loud voices. For my sake, then, Mrs. Friedman was saying angrily, what's the matter with you; you're twenty-three years old; three times she said her son asked for you; would it have hurt you. . . . Annie stepped into the room and Mrs. Friedman said sharply, And what's the matter with you, Annie, with that sour face, are you going to worry me, too? Oh, it's nothing, Mrs. Friedman, Annie said sniffling, only Joe—he went away again. And he'll come back again! said Mrs. Friedman; my God, don't air your troubles; what do you want me to do about it? Miss Mildred looked at them with her eyes very bright behind her glasses. Why don't you advise Annie to get married mother, you don't even have to find a man for her! Mrs. Friedman said bitterly, Do you compare yourself with Annie? Oh no, certainly not, said Miss Mildred laughing in a nasty way, I should say not; oh my goodness, no, why Annie's *pretty*—and she's five years older!

That'll do now, Mildred! Annie I'll have to have a hot water bottle, nobody knows what I'm suffering. Wait a minute—I almost forgot, Mildred will you get that black hat of mine out of the closet? That's a pretty cheap trick, said Miss Mildred, a pretty. . . . Mildred, will you do as I say? said Mrs. Friedman. No! you can do your own dirty work! said Miss Mildred and stalked out of the room. Annie felt ashamed that she had brought her troubles to Mrs. Friedman when God knows she had troubles of her own with that crazy one! Just help yourself to that hat Annie, said Mrs. Friedman pathetically, it's in the corner there . . . and my hot water bottle please. Nobody knows. . . .

There was sobbing behind the closed door of Miss Mildred's room and Annie hurried with her new hat past the parlor in which Mr. Friedman was yawning and folding up the card table. In the kitchen she turned her new hat round and round in one hand, while the water for Mrs. Friedman's hot water bottle splashed into the sink, and the hat looked funny to her. After a while, she saw what was funny about it. It was Mrs. Friedman's old black hat all right, but there were a couple of loose black threads on the side where the flower had been . . . still, it was a fine hat all the same. . . .

Ben Grader Makes a Call

Vanity Fair, January 1935

Ben Grader came out on the street, a free man—and wondered just how he would tell Millicent that he had lost his job.

It was mid-afternoon, and, from being unaccustomed to freedom except on Sundays, he stood for a moment in surprise, as though he were a stranger in town; which he was, this time of day. When it became perfectly clear that Mr. Turpin was not running downstairs after him to say it was a mistake, or a practical joke, or that they were testing him for promotion (instead of making it necessary for him to explain this untimely liberty to Millicent), Ben Grader started briskly down the street, a little self-conscious, like a wallflower heading determinedly for the ladies' room.

The crossing was an embarrassment, for there were now several directions to walk. He dug into his pockets and found no answer: only his watch and four ticket-stubs—he was proud suddenly that he and Millicent had taken the Atkinsons to the theater last night. And so he consulted his watch: three-thirty it said, and as though it lent him a certain sanction, he wheeled about and continued his walk downtown. By the second crossing he had learned to keep going, and scarcely touching his friend, the watch, he gained the next corner and considered himself safely launched. Warm for April, he told himself politely; oh yes, generally cooler this time of year, he answered amiably. Streets quite empty for a Thursday, aren't they? Yes, yes indeed, odd day, odd hour, to be about, just about, like this (without so much as a briefcase under the arm). . . . Strolling, are you? he asked himself carelessly. Why, that's about the size of it. Any place special, may I ask? he badgered himself. Say, mind your own business, old man, he told himself irritably. What the devil, Ben Grader, he said, you're stalling. . . . (You were afraid of Turpin, now you're ashamed before your wife.)

What do you do if you meet someone else out strolling—or out stalling—this odd hour of day (and without so much as a brief-case!), he wondered. Out strolling, old man? he asked hypothetically. *Why, yes,* answered, hypothetically, his fellow stroller, *the trouble with this country is that the people don't stroll enough.* I thought

134

maybe you looked kind of seedy? Ben Grader asked quizzically. *Well, I've been strolling around some time now; almost six months.* Is that so? (Ben Grader felt superior.) I've just begun; this afternoon; at three o'clock. *Well, see you at the Battery some time, old man, I've got to run. I'm doing the museums this week.* So long, old man— say (Ben Grader put it to him squarely), do you by any chance go in for *stalling* too? The hypothesis snorted. *Of course! The trouble with this country is the people don't stall enough; so long, old man.*

***

Pretty soft, wandering like this with your hands in your pockets. The Battery, eh? Quite a lark to stop in and stare at the old fish again; good old fish. You could go there weekdays and really make a study of it, an intelligent study, and on Sundays take Millicent, astound her with your knowledge. *My God, don't you get bored, Ben darling, hanging around the Aquarium all day?* Bored! He wheeled on Millicent indignantly. Bored? I should say not, why, a man could spend his time a good deal worse than just studying those old fish; now take the morays, for instance. He nodded sagely to himself. Then, of course, there were the museums, the libraries, all free. There were also the parks (later on, when one was more accustomed, perhaps). Next week you could take in the zoo. *Isn't that lovely, darling?* he could hear Millicent say dubiously, wondering if perhaps he had gone mad. My dear, the trouble with you is, he told her sadly, that you work in that ivory tower of an office and you've lost your sense of leisure. I've always said the trouble with Americans is. . . . Listen, Millicent, working in that damned place is making you smug, you're in a rut. . . .

Of course, I could have told Turpin to go to hell. Still, what would it have got me? Or him either—stuffed shirt of a personnel manager. I suppose he couldn't help it. Be out on his ear himself one of these bright sunshiny April days—out for a stroll. But aren't we all (all except Millicent—and Richard Atkinson). All *what?* Oh—*we* are the ru-lers of the king's na-vee. Say, singing out in the streets is at least a month ahead of your act, big boy. Why not? Trouble with this country is the people don't sing enough. Cut out this stalling, Ben Grader said sharply to himself; where do you think you're going?

Listen, Turpentine, I said to the old fool, the reason I don't slit your throat from ear to ear is I know you haven't anything to do with it. You're a cipher in the economic machine. And the machine is collapsing; Turp, I said, you better get out from under yourself. You think I'm sour just because I've been fired from this lousy capitalist office? No sir, that's just where you're mistaken, Turp old fool. (*Now aren't you the big brave wolf?* said Millicent, hissing in his ear.) Listen, Turp, I said, do you know what? The boys in the office laugh like hell at you behind your back, the way you waggle your hips walking, just like a woman, you ought to see them imitating you. . . . (*My hero,* said Millicent, rolling her eyes.)

Listen, Millicent, do you know what I really said to him (I won't tell you). I said, Mr. Turpin, I'll certainly be mighty sorry to leave this office and all the good friends I've made here, including you, Mr. Turpin. Oh sure, Mr. Turpin, I understand, gosh if you didn't drop some of the staff where would you be this fiscal year, oh sure. . . .

Oh Millicent, Millicent darling, I don't know why I said that, only when a man gets low he wants to he kicked lower, it's as if he lost his manhood somehow, when he's fired from a job. Do you mind, Millicent, for a little while—that *you* will be paying the rent? *Of course not, sweetheart, please don't, worry, I don't care at all.* Oh, you don't, don't you? Well, let me tell you you don't know how a man feels—or maybe you don't think I'm a man any more, is that it, now that I. . . . *Oh Ben darling, don't be so stupid.* . . . Listen, Millicent, it's all very well for you to talk, but let me tell you, working in that office is making you smug as hell, why Harriet Atkinson said only last night that you had changed. . . .

***

All this time Ben Grader's steps took him unfalteringly south and west. They carried him down blocks of avenue and veered into shaded side-streets; they never stopped for book-shops, automobiles or even well-loved speakeasies. The Battery was still ahead; there were more speakeasies; there was a library, a post-office, a church—also there was home. But what was home in the late afternoon without Millicent there? (And Millicent would be working in that smug office for at least two hours more.) No, obviously he was not going home. However, there was no use discussing it with himself yet; time enough—his feet might pause in the corner drugstore and after he had bought cigarettes, they might carry him back to the home side of Fifth Avenue again. Never let your left foot, he told himself coyly, know where your right foot is taking you.

My dear Millicent, he said impatiently, of course I still love you! but science—why, they've tried the experiment with monkeys time and time again. *Darling! Monkeys?* Yes dear, you know, he said impatiently, how they changed females from one cage to another—I mean, proving that variety, proving that infidelity. . . . *Darling! are we monkeys?* My dear Millicent, that peculiar feminine logic of yours! A man is different from a woman, my dear, and besides you've grown smug, working up there all day in that big ivory capitalist office, I mean you're so busy doing unimportant things you've got into something of a rut, my dear. *But Ben darling, if you love me, if I'm still attractive to you. . . .*

My dear Millicent, he said angrily, just because you work in a lousy office, just because you happen to be . . . well, don't think you can order my life, just because for a while you're paying the rent, I mean, don't forget I'm still the man of the family, Millicent. Besides, the trouble with this country is there's too little infidelity. . . .

No, I don't mean for you to go and do likewise, he shouted at her. One trick like that, my little woman, and we're through!

He was trembling with anger against her as his steps landed him on the familiar drug-store corner. Her unreasonable female logic challenged him; he grew defiant as he stood there arguing with her. What do you want me to do, hang around the Aquarium and the museums and the zoo? he said to her. But after all it's absolutely none of your business! he said and bought a package of cigarettes that were definitely not her brand, and resolutely continued west.

My God, the way women hound one! he said, as though Millicent were pottering after him on determined feet. He veered sharply. Ass! it's only four o'clock. All women looked like her from the back. Terrible how one's conscience turned all women into one's wife. Terrible too how a man had occasionally to take his manhood out of camphor and brush it up a bit. . . .

Ah, here we are, he said cheerfully to himself at Number 47, much as one says Ah! nice doggie, I've got a little dog like you at home! on encountering a formidable beast on a lonely country road. Ah, exactly four o'clock! he said, glancing at his friend the watch. Oh, I just thought I would drop in, he practiced airily:

why not? (No.) I've been wanting to see you alone for a long time (better, much better), why should that surprise you? Say, you haven't got an inferiority complex have you, just because you don't work all day in a lousy sunny capitalist office? What? who, Millicent? *of course* she wouldn't mind, she's the most sensible girl in the world. We have the *completest* understanding . . . she's the loveliest, sweetest, grandest wife a man ever had, she knows, my Millicent does, that the theory of the new leisure class is to kill time somehow, that infidelity is an occupational disease of the unoccupied . . . my Millicent, my darling Millicent. . . .

Altogether it was a brave and lonely Ben Grader who turned his back on all the Millicents that sadly were not in the street behind him, a brave and lonely Ben Grader who eventually took off his hat as he stood ringing Harriet Atkinson's doorbell at an hour when he was pretty certain that his friend Richard Atkinson (working smugly in a lousy office) would not he at home.

Missis Flinders

Story, December 1932

"Home you go!" Miss Kane, nodding, in her white
nurse's dress, stood for a moment—she would catch
a breath of air—in the hospital door; "and thank you
again for the stockings, you needn't have bothered"—
drew a sharp breath and turning, dismissed Missis
Flinders from the hospital, smiling, dismissed her forever from her mind.

So Margaret Flinders stood next to her basket of
fruit on the hospital steps; both of them waiting, a little
shame-faced in the sudden sunshine, and in no hurry
to leave the hospital—no hurry at all. It would be nicer
to be alone, Margaret thought, glancing at the basket
of fruit which stood respectable and a little silly on
the stone step (the candy-bright apples were blushing

caricatures of Miles: Miles' comfort, not hers). Flowers she could have left behind (for the nurses, in the room across the hall where they made tea at night); books she could have slipped into her suit-case; but fruit—Miles' gift, Miles' guilt, man's tribute to the Missis in the hospital—must be eaten; a half-eaten basket of fruit (she had tried to leave it: Missis Butter won't you . . . Missis Wiggam wouldn't you like. . . . But Missis Butter had aplenty of her own thank you, and Missis Wiggam said she couldn't hold acids after a baby)—a half-eaten basket of fruit, in times like these, cannot be left to rot.

Down the street Miles was running, running, after a taxi. He was going after the taxi for her; it was for her sake he ran; yet this minute that his back was turned he stole for his relief and spent in running away, his shoulders crying guilt. And don't hurry, don't hurry, she said to them; I too am better off alone.

The street stretched in a long white line very finally away from the hospital, the hospital where Margaret Flinders (called there so solemnly Missis) had been lucky enough to spend only three nights. It would be four days before Missis Wiggam would be going home to Mister Wiggam with a baby; and ten possibly—the doctors were uncertain, Miss Kane prevaricated—before Missis Butter would be going home to Mister Butter without one. Zigzagging the street went the children; their cries and the sudden grinding of their skates she had listened to upstairs beside Missis Butter for three days. Some such child had she been—for the styles in children had not changed—a lean child gliding solemnly on skates and grinding them viciously at the nervous feet of grown-ups. Smile at these children she would not or could not; yet she felt on her face that smile, fixed, painful and frozen, that she had put there, on waking from ether three days back, to greet Miles. The smile spoke to the retreating shoulders of Miles: I don't need you; the smile spoke formally to life: thanks, I'm not having any. Not so the child putting the heels of his skates together Charlie Chaplin-wise and describing a scornful circle on the widest part of the sidewalk. Not so a certain little girl (twenty years back) skating past the wheels of autos, pursuing life in the form of a ball so red! so gay! better death than to turn one's back and smile over one's shoulder at life!

Upstairs Missis Butter must still be writhing with her poor caked breasts. The bed that had been hers beside Missis Butter's was empty now; Miss Kane would be stripping it and Joe would come in bringing fresh sheets. Whom would they put in beside Missis Butter, to whom would she moan and boast all night about the milk in her breasts that was turning, she said, into cheese?

Now Miles was coming back, jogging sheepishly on the running-board of a taxi, he had run away to the end of his rope and now was returning penitent, his eyes dog-like searching her out where she stood on the hospital steps (did they rest with complacence on

143

the basket of fruit, his gift?), pleading with her, Didn't I get the taxi fast? like an anxious little boy. She stood with that smile on her face that hurt like too much ice-cream. Smile and smile; for she felt like a fool, she had walked open-eyed smiling into the trap *(Don't wriggle, Missis, I might injure you for life, Miss Kane had said cheerfully)* and felt the spring only when it was too late, when she waked from ether and knew like the thrust of a knife what she had ignored before. *Whatever did you do it for, Missis Flinders, Missis Butter was always saying; if there's nothing the matter with your insides—doesn't your husband . . . and Won't you have some fruit, Missis Butter, her calm reply: meaning, My husband gave me this fruit so what right have you to doubt that my husband. . . .* Her husband who now stumbled up the steps to meet her; his eyes he had sent ahead, but something in him wanted not to come, tripped his foot as he hurried up the steps.

"Take my arm, Margaret," he said. "Walk slowly," he said. The bitter pill of taking help, of feeling weakly grateful, stuck in her throat. Miles' face behind his glasses was tense like the face of an amateur actor in the role of a strike-leader. That he was inadequate for the part he seemed to know. And if he felt shame, shame in his own eyes, she could forgive him; but if it was only guilt felt manlike in her presence, a guilt which he could drop off like a damp shirt, if he was putting it all off on her for being a woman! "The fruit, Miles!" she said; "you've forgotten the fruit." "The fruit can wait," he said bitterly.

He handed her into the taxi as though she were a package marked glass—something, she thought, not merely troublesomely womanly, but ladylike. "Put your legs up on the seat," he said. "I don't want to, Miles." *Goodbye Missis* Butter Put your legs up on the seat. I don't want to—*Better luck next time Missis Butter* Put your legs *I can't make out our window, Missis Butter* Put your "All right, it will be nice and uncomfortable." (She put her legs up on the seat.) *Goodbye Missis But.* . . . "Nothing I say is right," he said. "It's good with the legs up," she said brightly.

Then he was up the steps agile and sure after the fruit. And down again, the basket swinging with affected carelessness, arming him, till he relinquished it modestly to her outstretched hands. Then he seated himself on the little seat, the better to watch his woman and his woman's fruit; and screwing his head round on his neck said irritably to the man who had been all his life on the wrong side of the glass pane: "Charles street!"

"Hadn't you better ask him to please drive slowly?" Margaret said.

"I was just going to," he said bitterly.

"And drive slowly," he shouted over his shoulder.

The driver's name was Carl C. Strite. She could see Carl Strite glance cannily back at the hospital: Greenway Maternity Home; pull his lever with extreme delicacy as though he were stroking the neck of a horse. There was a small roar—and the hospital glided backward: its windows ran together like the windows of a

145

moving train; a spurt—watch out for those children on skates!—and the car was fairly started down the street.

Goodbye Missis Butter I hope you get a nice roommate in my place, I hope you won't find that Mister B let the ice-pan flow over again—and give my love to the babies when Miss Kane stops them in the door for you to wave at—good-bye Missis Butter, really goodbye.

Carl Strite (was he thinking maybe of his mother, an immigrant German woman she would have been, come over with a shawl on her head and worked herself to skin and bone so the kids could go to school and turn out good Americans—and what had it come to, here he was a taxi-driver, and what taxi-drivers didn't know! what in the course of their lackeys' lives they didn't put up with, fall in with! well, there was one decent thing left in Carl Strite, he knew how to carry a woman home from a maternity hospital) drove softly along the curb . . . and the eyes of his honest puzzled gangster's snout photo-graphed as "Your Driver" looked dimmed as though the glory of woman were too much for them, in a moment the weak cruel baby's mouth might blubber. Awful to lean forward and tell Mr. Strite he was laboring under a mistake. *Missis Wiggam's freckled face when she heard that Missis Butter's roommate . . . maybe Missis Butter's baby had been born dead but anyway she had had a baby . . . whatever did you do it for Missis Flind. . . .*

"Well, patient," Miles began, tentative, nervous (bored? perturbed? behind his glasses?).

"How does it feel, Maggie?" he said in a new, small voice.

Hurt and hurt this man, a feeling told her. He is a man, he could have made you a woman. "What's a D and C between friends?" she said. "Nobody at the hospital gave a damn about my little illegality."

"Well, but I do," he protested like a short man trying to be tall.

She turned on her smile; the bright silly smile that was eating up her face.

Missis Butter would be alone now with no one to boast to about her pains except Joe who cleaned the corridors and emptied bed-pans—and thought Missis Butter was better than an angel because although she had incredible golden hair she could wise-crack like any brunette. Later in the day the eight-day mothers wobbling down the corridors for their pre-nursing constitutional would look in and talk to her; for wasn't Missis Butter their symbol and their pride, the one who had given up her baby that they might have theirs (for a little superstition is inevitable in new mothers, and it was generally felt that there must be one dead baby in a week's batch at any decent hospital) for whom they demanded homage from their visiting husbands? for whose health they asked the nurses each morning second only to asking for their own babies? That roommate of yours was a funny one, Missis Wiggam would say. Missis Wiggam was the woman who said big breasts weren't any good: here she was with a seven-pound baby and not a drop for it (here she would open the negligée Mister Wiggam had given her not to shame them before the nurses, and poke contemptuously at the floppy parts of herself within) while there was Missis Butter with no baby but a dead baby and her small breasts caking because there was so much milk in them for nothing but a. . . . Yes, that Missis Flinders was sure a funny one, Missis Butter would agree.

"Funny ones," she and Miles, riding home with numb faces and a basket of fruit between them—past a park, past a museum, past elevated pillars—intellectuals they were, bastards, changelings . . . giving up a baby for economic freedom which meant that two of them would work in offices instead of one of them only, giving up a baby for intellectual freedom which meant that they smoked their cigarettes bitterly and looked out of the windows of a taxi onto streets and people and stores and hated them all. "We'd go soft," Miles had finally said, "we'd go bourgeois." Yes, with diapers drying on the radiators, bottles wrapped in flannel, the grocer getting to know one too well—yes, they would go soft, they might slump and start liking people, they might weaken and forgive stupidity, they might yawn and forget to hate. "Funny ones," class-straddlers, intellectuals, tight-rope-walking somewhere in the middle (how long could they hang on without falling to one side or the other? one more war? one more depression?); intellectuals, with habits generated from the right and tastes inclined to the left. Afraid to perpetuate themselves, were they? Afraid of anything that might loom so large in their personal lives as to outweigh other considerations? Afraid, maybe, of a personal life?

"Oh give me another cigarette," she said.

And still the taxi, with its burden of intellectuals and their inarticulate fruit-basket, its motherly, gangsterly, inarticulate driver, its license plates and its photographs all so very official, jogged on; past Harlem now; past fire-escapes loaded with flower-pots and flapping clothes; dingy windows opening to the soot-laden air blown in by the elevated roaring down its tracks. Past Harlem and through 125th street: stores and wisecracks, Painless Dentists, cheap florists; Eighth Avenue, boarded and plastered, concealing the subway that was reaching its laborious birth beneath. But Eighth Avenue was too jouncy for Mr. Strite's precious burden of womanhood (who was reaching passionately for a cigarette); he cut through the park, and they drove past quiet walks on which the sun had brought out babies as the Fall rains give birth to worms.

"But ought you to smoke so much, so soon after—so soon?" Miles said, not liking to say so soon after what. His hand held the cigarettes out to her, back from her.

"They do say smoking's bad for child-birth," she said calmly, and with her finger-tips drew a cigarette from his reluctant hand.

And tapping down the tobacco on the handle of the

149

fruit-basket she said, "But we've got the joke on them there, we have." (Hurt and hurt this man, her feeling told her; he is a man and could have made you a woman.)

"It was your own decision too," he said harshly, striking and striking at the box with his match.

"This damn taxi's shaking you too much," he said suddenly, bitter and contrite.

But Mr. Strite was driving like an angel. He handled his car as though it were a baby-carriage. Did he think maybe it had turned out with her the way it had with Missis Butter? I could have stood it better, Missis Butter said, if they hadn't told me it was a boy. And me with my fourth little girl, Missis Wiggam had groaned (but proudly, proudly); why I didn't even want to see it when they told me. But Missis Butter stood it very well, and so did Missis Wiggam. They were a couple of good bitches; and what if Missis Butter had produced nothing but a dead baby this year, and what if Missis Wiggam would bring nothing to Mister Wiggam but a fourth little girl this year—why there was next year and the year after, there was the certain little world from grocery-store to kitchen, there were still Mister Butter and Mister Wiggam who were both (Missis Wiggam and Missis Butter vied with each other) just *crazy* about babies. Well, Mister Flinders is different, she had lain there thinking (he cares as much for his unborn gods as I for my unborn babies); and wished she could have the firm assurance they had in "husbands," coming as they did year after year away from them for a couple of weeks, just long enough to bear them babies either dead-ones or girl-ones . . . good bitches they were: there was something lustful besides smug in their pride in being "Missis." Let Missis Flinders so much as let out a groan because a sudden pain grew too big for her groins, let her so much as murmur because the sheets were hot beneath her—and Missis Butter and Missis Wiggam in the security of their maternity-fraternity exchanged glances of amusement: SHE don't know what pain is, look at what's talking about PAIN. . . .

"Mr. Strite flatters us," she whispered, her eyes smiling straight and hard at Miles. (Hurt and hurt. . . .)

"And why does that give you so much pleasure?" He dragged the words as though he were pounding them out with two fingers on the typewriter.

The name without the pain—she thought to say; and did not say. All at once she lost her desire to punish him; she no more wanted to "hurt this man" for he was no more man than she was woman. She would not do him the honor of hurting him. She must reduce him as she felt herself reduced. She must cut out from him what made him a man, as she had let be cut out from her what would have made her a woman. He was no man: he was a dried-up intellectual husk; he was sterile; empty and hollow as she was.

Missis Butter lying up on her pillow would count over to Missis Wiggam the fine points of her tragedy: how she had waited two days to be delivered of a dead baby; how it wouldn't have been so bad if the doctor hadn't said it was a beautiful baby with platinum-blond hair exactly like hers (and hers bleached unbelievably, but never mind, Missis Wiggam had come to believe in it like Joe and Mister Butter, another day and Missis Flinders herself, intellectual sceptic though she was, might have been convinced); and how they would pay the last instalment on—what a baby-carriage, Missis Wiggam, you'd never believe me!—and sell it second-hand for half its worth. I know when I was caught with my first, Missis Wiggam would take up the story her mouth had been open for. And that Missis Flinders was sure a funny one. . . .

But I am not such a funny one, Margaret wanted, beneath her bright and silly smile, behind her cloud of cigarette smoke (for Miles had given in; the whole package sat gloomily on Margaret's lap) to say to them; even though in my "crowd" the girls keep the names they were born with, even though some of us sleep for a little variety with one another's husbands, even though I forget as often as Miles—Mister Flinders to you—to empty the pan under the ice-box. Still I too have known my breasts to swell and harden, I too have been unable to sleep on them for their tenderness to weight and touch, I too have known what it is to undress slowly and imagine myself growing night to night. . . . I knew this for two months, my dear Missis Wiggam; I had this strange joy for two months, my dear Missis Butter. But there was a night last week, my good ladies, on coming home from a party, which Mister Flinders and I spent in talk—and damn fine talk, if you want to know, talk of which I am proud, and talk not one word of which you, with your grocery-and-baby minds, could have understood; in a regime like this, Miles said, it is a terrible thing to have a baby—it means the end of independent thought and the turning of everything into a scheme for making money; and there must be institutions such as there are in Russia, I said, for taking care of the babies and their mothers; why in a time like this, we both said, to have a baby would be suicide—goodbye to our plans, goodbye to our working out schemes for each other and the world—our courage would die, our hopes concentrate on the sordid business of keeping three people alive, one of whom would be a burden and an expense for twenty years. . . . And then we grew drunk for a minute making up the silliest names that we could call it if we had it, we would call it Daniel if it were a boy, call it for my mother if it were a girl—and what a tough little thing it is, I said, look, look, how it hangs on in spite of its loving mother jumping off tables and broiling herself in hot water . . . until Miles, frightened at himself, washed his hands of it: we mustn't waste any more time, the sooner these things are done the better. And I as though the ether cap had already been clapped to my nose, agreed offhandedly. That night I did not pass my hands contentedly over my hard breasts; that night I gave no thought

Strite; he kept his car going at a slow and steady roll, its nose poked blunt ahead, following the straight and narrow—Mr. Strite knew what it was to carry a woman home from the hospital.

But what in their past had warranted this? She could remember a small girl going from dolls to books, from books with colored pictures to books with frequent conversations; from such books to the books at last that one borrowed from libraries, books built up of solemn text from which you took notes; books which were gray to begin with, but which opened out to your eyes subtle layers of gently shaded colors. (And where in these texts did it say that one should turn one's back on life? Had the coolness of the stone library at college made one afraid? Had the ivy nodding in at the open dormitory windows taught one too much to curl and squat looking out?) And Miles? What book, what professor, what strange idea, had taught him to hunch his shoulders and stay indoors, had taught him to hide behind his glasses? Whence the fear that made him put, in cold block letters, implacably above his desk, the sign announcing him "Not at Home" to life?

Missis Flinders, my husband scaled the hospital wall at four o'clock in the morning, frantic I tell you. . . . But I just don't understand you, Missis Flinders (if there's really nothing the matter with your insides), do you understand her, Missis Wiggam, would your husband . . . ? Why goodness, no, Mister Wiggam would sooner . . .

155

! And there he was, and they asked him, Shall we try an operation, Mister Butter? scaled the wall . . . shall we try an operation? (Well, you see, we are making some sort of protest, my husband Miles and I; sometimes I forget just what.) If there's any risk to Shirley, he said, there mustn't be any risk to Shirley. . . . Missis Wiggam's petulant, childish face, with its sly contentment veiled by what she must have thought a grown-up expression: Mister Wiggam bought me this negligée new, surprised me with it, you know—and generally a saving man, Mister Wiggam, not tight, but with three children—four now! Hetty, he says, I'm not going to have you disgracing us at the hospital this year, he says. Why the nurses will all remember that flannel thing you had Mabel and Suzy and Antoinette in, they'll talk about us behind our backs. (It wasn't that I couldn't make the flannel do again, Missis Butter, it wasn't that at all.) But he says, Hetty, you'll just have a new one this year, he says, and maybe it'll bring us luck, he says—you know, he was thinking maybe this time we'd have a boy. . . . Well, I just have to laugh at you, Missis Flinders, not *wanting* one, why my sister went to doctors for five years and spent her good money just *trying* to have one. . . . Well, poor Mister Wiggam, so the negligée didn't work, I brought him another little girl—but he didn't say boo to me, though I could see he was disappointed. Hetty, he says, we'll just have another try! oh I thought I'd die, with Miss Kane standing right there you know (though they do say these nurses. . . .); but that's Mister Wiggam all over, he wouldn't stop a joke for a policeman. . . . No, I just can't get over you, Missis Flinders, if Gawd was willing to let you have a baby—and there really isn't anything wrong with your insides?

Miles' basket of fruit standing on the bed-table, trying its level inadequate best, poor pathetic inarticulate intellectual basket of fruit, to comfort, to bloom, to take the place of Miles himself who would come in later with Sam Butter for visiting hour. Miles' too-big basket of fruit standing there, embarrassed. Won't you have a peach, Missis Wiggam (I'm sure they have less acid)? Just try an apple, Missis Butter? Weigh Miles' basket of fruit against Mister Wiggam's negligée for luck, against Mister Butter scaling the wall at four in the morning for the mother of his dead baby. *Please* have a pear, Miss Kane; a banana, Joe? How they spat the seeds from Miles' fruit! How it hurt her when, unknowing, Missis Butter cut away the brown bruised cheek of Miles' bright-eyed, weeping apple! Miles! they scorn me, these ladies. They laugh at me, dear, almost as though I had no "husband," as though I were a "fallen woman." Miles, would you buy me a new negligée if I bore you three daughters? Miles, would you scale the wall if I bore you a dead baby . . . ? Miles, I have an inferiority complex because I am an intellectual. . . . But a peach, Missis Wiggam! can't I possibly tempt you?

To be driving like this at mid-day through New York; with Miles bobbing like an empty ghost (for she could see he was unhappy, as miserable as she, he too had had an abortion) on the side-seat; with a taxi-driver, solicitous, respectful to an ideal, in front; was this the logical end of that little girl she remembered, of that girl swinging hatless across a campus as though that campus were the top of the earth? And was this all they could give birth to, she and Miles, who had closed up their books one day and kissed each other on the lips and decided to marry?

And now Mr. Strite, with his hand out, was making a gentle righthand turn. Back to Fifth Avenue they would go, gently rolling, in Mr. Strite's considerate charge. Down Fourteenth Street they would go, past the stores unlike any stores in the world: packed to the windows with imitation gold and imitation embroidery, with imitation men and women coming to stand in the doorways and beckon with imitation smiles; while on the sidewalks streamed the people unlike any other people in the world, drawn from every country, from every stratum, carrying babies (the real thing, with pinched anemic faces) and parcels (imitation finery priced low in the glittering stores). There goes a woman, with a flat fat face, will produce five others just like herself, to dine off one-fifth the inadequate quantity her Mister earns today. These are the people not afraid to perpetuate themselves (forbidden to stop, indeed) and they will go on and on until the bottom of the world is filled with them; and suddenly there will be enough of them to combine their wild-eyed notions and take over the world to suit themselves. While I, while I and my Miles, with our good clear heads will one day go spinning out of the world and leave nothing behind . . . only diplomas crumbling in the museums. . . .

The mad street ended with Fifth Avenue; was left behind.

They were nearing home. Mr. Strite, who had never seen them before (who would never again, in all likelihood, for his territory was far uptown) was seeing them politely to the door. As they came near home all of Margaret's fear and pain gathered in a knot in her stomach. There would be nothing new in their house; there was nothing to expect; yet she wanted to find something there that she knew she could not find, and surely the house (once so gay, with copies of old paintings, with books which lined the walls from floor to ceiling, with papers and cushions and typewriters) would be suddenly empty and dead, suddenly, for the first time, a group of rooms unalive as rooms with "For Rent" still pasted on the windows. And Miles? did he know he was coming home to a place which had suffered no change, but which would be different forever afterward? Miles had taken off his glasses; passed his hand tiredly across his eyes; was sucking now as though he expected relief, some answer, on the tortoise-shell curve which wound around his ear.

Mr. Strite would not allow his cab to cease motion with a jerk. Mr. Strite allowed his cab to slow down even at the corner (where was the delicatessen that sold the only loose ripe olives in the Village), so they rolled softly past No. 14; on past the tenement which would eventually be razed to give place to modem three-room apartments with In-a-Dor beds; and then slowly, so slowly that Mr. Strite must surely be an artist as well as a man who had had a mother, drew up and slid to a full stop before No. 60, where two people named Mister and Missis Flinders rented themselves a place to hide from life (both life of the Fifth Avenue variety, and life of the common, or Fourteenth Street, variety: in short, life).

So Miles, with his glasses on his nose once more, descended; held out his hand; Mr. Strite held the door open and his face most modestly averted; and Margaret Flinders painfully and carefully swung her legs down again from the seat and alighted, step by step, with care and confusion. The house was before them; it must be entered. Into the house they must go, say farewell to the streets, to Mr. Strite who had guided them through a tour of the city, to life itself; into the house they must go and hide. It was a fact that Mister Flinders (was he reluctant to come home?) had forgotten his key; that Missis Flinders must delve under the white clothes in her suitcase and find hers; that Mr. Strite, not yet satisfied that his charges were safe, sat watchful and waiting in the front seat of his cab. Then the door gave. Then Miles, bracing it with his foot, held out his hand to Margaret. Then Mr. Strite came rushing up the steps (something had told him his help would be needed again!), rushing up the steps with the basket of fruit hanging on his arm, held out from his body as though what was the likes of him doing holding a woman's basket just home from the hospital.

"You've forgotten your fruit, Missis!"

Weakly they glared at the fruit come to pursue them; come to follow them up the stairs to their empty rooms; but that was not fair: come, after all, to comfort them. "You must have a peach," Margaret said.

No, Mr. Strite had never cared for peaches; the skin got in his teeth.

"You must have an apple," Margaret said.

Well, no, he must be getting on uptown. A cigarette (he waved it, deprecated the smoke it blew in the lady's face) was good enough for him.

"But a pear, just a pear," said Margaret passionately.

Mr. Strite wavered, standing on one foot. "Maybe he doesn't want any fruit," said Miles harshly.

"Not want any *fruit!*" cried Margaret gayly, indignantly. Not want any fruit?—ridiculous! Not want the fruit my poor Miles bought for his wife in the hospital? Three days I spent in the hospital, in a Maternity Home, and I produced, with the help of my husband, one basket of fruit (tied with ribbon, pink—for boys). Not want any of our fruit? I couldn't bear it, I couldn't bear it. . . .

Mr. Strite leaned over; put out a hand and gingerly selected a pear—"For luck," he said, managing an excellent American smile. They watched him trot down the

161

steps to his cab, all the time holding his pear as though it were something he would put in a memory book. And still they stayed, because Margaret said foolishly, "Let's see him off"; because she was ashamed, suddenly, before Miles; as though she had cut her hair unbecomingly, as though she had wounded herself in some unsightly way—as though (summing up her thoughts as precisely, as decisively as though it had been done on an adding-machine) she had stripped and revealed herself not as a woman at all, but as a creature who would not be a woman and could not be a man. And then they turned (for there was nothing else to stay for, and on the street and in the sun before Missis Salvemini's fluttering window-curtains they were ashamed as though they had been naked or dead)—and went in the door and heard it swing to, pause on its rubbery hinge, and finally click behind them.

Kleine Frau

Modern Youth, March 1933

The sun had reached the low point in the sky where it caught the copper side of the mountain over-hanging the lake and everybody knew it would not last much longer. Away off in the distance a hazy line of hills took on a faintly glowing pink; the snow on the Austrian Alps was reflecting the last of the sun. The village's one street which bordered the lake breathed quietly, getting ready for night; the man who ran the Store was closing up, and the couple who ran the café were shaking out checkered cloths, preparing to open. The very mature girl of eleven who untied her mother's row-boats when tourists wanted to hire them, was drawing the last of them onto the little beach beside the dock; when she was finished she put on her wooden clogs again and went to stand with her mother and half a dozen villagers who were scattered on the dock and the edge of the shore, shading their eyes and looking out over the lake. Somewhere beyond the middle four row-boats were standing, close together, not moving; in two of them were the dark silhouettes of men; two were empty.

***

The half-dozen peasants had grown to ten by the time Pauline and her husband, wandering down from the big hotel on the afternoon of their thirtieth day of honeymoon, sighted them. Dick jumped down the little bank and held out his hand to Pauline; picking up the skirt of her native *dirndl*, she scrambled after him. They approached the group, but stood a little apart, feeling rather out of touch with the peasants, whose drawling *Steyerish* dialect made their German almost unintelligible even to Richard, who was way ahead of Pauline. Pauline stood there feeling very slim and American in the pink and blue costume whose bodice lay in loose inadequacy over her small American breasts; she smoothed the blue apron and looked down at her high-heeled black slippers to see how the dust had treated them.

This day was one of the last in August; although it was only six o'clock the sun was so low, the coming twilight so mistily gray, that they could not make out what was going on. Half way to the other shore the four

164

row-boats stood on the still lake as though painted. The peasants' faces gazed outward unmoved. "Speaking of Indians," Richard whispered, "these birds' poker faces can't be beat—those who have their backs turned even seem to have poker backs." He indicated the back of a fat woman, dressed in the pink and blue *dirndl* of the village, standing stolidly on the extreme edge of the dock. "Is someone drowning, or are they merely out to watch the sun set?" Dick whispered again, a moment later. The peasants were standing now in little groups, mostly men with men, and women with women or children. Two tiny girls, dressed in minute replicas of their mother's dress, pulled at the skirt of the fat woman, whose back faced them, stolid and secretive; they looked like full-grown pygmies, mature on some fairy scale.

"We'll find out soon enough," said Pauline.

She wanted to go on, though, without finding out; she really wished they had stayed up there on the broad terrace with the funny Germans (how they loved her American stupidity, unable to distinguish Austrians from Germans!) who called her *Kleine Frau,* drinking tea and eating too much *Schlagobers.* She didn't really like the peasants—oh they were all right to look at because they were picturesque, and sometimes it was exciting to try and talk to them, but when you came closer, their faces were so stupid: stupid and yet lowering, like the faces of bulls considering a charge. . . . And she felt something funny about this; something she didn't like. "Instinct" made her take Dick's arm and squeeze it; but she didn't say anything, she had been married four weeks and already she had a motherly tolerance for Richard's stopping at anything that looked queer and waiting till he had solved it and could explain it to her.

The man who had closed up the Store came down now and joined a little knot of peasants. They said something to him, all talking at once. The store-keeper nodded, turned to look at the sun, and moved up by himself, looking like the rest toward where the four boats were standing: two of them empty.

Richard drew his arm from Pauline's and approaching the store-keeper, who was least like a peasant, asked what was happening out there on the lake. Pauline could always understand Dick's German: it sounded just like English. She wondered why the store-keeper, who was always so polite, did not turn round and bow to her; she saw him point to the boats, to the sun, and back to the boats again; she heard his answer, without understanding a word. But the minute Dick told her, she felt that she had known it "instinctively" all along: someone had gone down. "They've only got ten minutes more to find him," Dick said, "before the sun sets."

Dick did not come back to Pauline; she half expected him to come back and take her hand; she found herself shivering. The water was so still. But "the calmest lake is treacherous," Pauline's mother always said. Pauline shuddered, with her shoulders drawn up to her ears, looking at the "treacherous" water, in which, only that afternoon, she had swum the "Australian crawl" in her low-backed bathing suit. . . . She could almost hear her mother saying in a cheerful, determined voice, "Well, our presence here is useless; since we can do nothing to help, it would be just morbid to stay." Pauline wanted to say that to Dick. But she didn't dare. He was so withdrawn from her. It was something like the time he had played poker with the men on the boat and hadn't wanted to stop even to light her cigarette. Men were not really very sensitive. . . .

The mature eleven-year-old girl who had rented them a boat the day before; had become a child again with excitement; she kept bouncing up and down and pointing, and Pauline could see her mother trying to keep her still. She never turned round to look at Pauline—little hypocrite, she thought, remembering how yesterday the child had tapped her teeth delightedly to see if they were real (even a pretty peasant girl had such disgusting, rotten teeth!); for that matter, nobody else was paying any attention to her, the store-keeper who *küssed die hand* five times a day when they went in for American cigarettes at three schillings a stale package had not even bowed, the cheerful old couple who ran the café stood right beside her and never nodded. Treacherous, like the lake, she thought; one minute all smiles, and the next. . . .

The fat woman with her back to them turned round; her children turned with her. The fat woman's broad face was as expressionless as her back had been. But she seemed to have some authority; for a moment the peasants took their eyes off the four boats and listened to the woman who talked rapidly and with many meaningless gestures. Pauline was enraged because she could not understand a word. She looked at the woman standing there with her back to the lake, a little girl reaching to her bulging hips flanking her on either side. She thought the woman looked like all the Annas and Theresas she had ever seen waiting on tables in America. Funny how you never noticed them there, while here, in their own country—even funnier, for that matter, to think of them having a country!—while here Dick was always saying "What a fine build," "What a splendid peasant type" about people who looked like the fat woman. Pauline always agreed; she remembered Saturday afternoons in art galleries off Fifth Avenue. But to herself she thought, It's all right if you like it—and secretly felt that nobody did. Imagine them in evening dress! And that was, after all, the true test of a woman's beauty. She looked down now at the flat bodice of her own *dirndl* under which her own small breasts moved and pointed like pencils when she walked. . . . The fat woman turned round to the lake again; Pauline saw her look first at the sun, like someone consulting a clock, and then shade her eyes to look out across the water.

***

She hated Richard's standing apart from her; he looked as though he had forgotten her, and would not like to be reminded. If they had to stand up and wait for a peasant to drown, she thought facetiously, at least they could stand together. She couldn't help thinking how nice it would be if they had stayed quietly and had more tea on the terrace. But men were so restless. . . . She felt very lonely and unprotected, but somehow she was ashamed to turn her eyes up toward the big friendly hotel at the other end of the lake.

Suddenly Dick turned to her. His face, in that rosily graying air, looked white. "It's someone belonging to the woman on the edge of the dock."

The man drowning belonged to the stolid woman who looked calmly at the sun as though it were a clock: as though she had left something at home to boil and wondered whether her husband would drown fast enough. . . . But she looked like servants—she looked like all the Theresas Pauline's mother had ever had—how queer to think of her with a husband, and those two children pulling at her apron. Why didn't she cry and scream, why didn't she pray, why didn't she *do* something? was she too stupid to know how to behave when her husband was drowning?

***

The bottom rim of the sun began to slide slowly down behind the mountain. From now on Pauline knew that it would seem to go faster. The peasants turned their heads oftener now to look at it. As if they were watching a race, Pauline thought impatiently. My God, have they no thought of what is happening, a man is drowning, and they stand and wait, using the sun for a clock! She looked at the watch on her wrist: ten minutes past six, there would be no time to get into the full-dress *dirndl* of red and black that nobody at the hotel had seen, that they would laugh at and love (the *Kleine Frau* looks more American than ever in her costume, they always said admiringly). Had Dick forgotten, she thought resentfully, that this was Saturday night and. . . . She was stricken with horror of herself. I must be hys-terical, she thought pleasantly, and crossed the ends of her *dirndl* shawl higher over her throat.

If only someone would talk to her, if only Richard— but Richard stood with his white face turned to the lake and the peasants stood like wooden figures with their backs to her and on the lake the four boats sat without moving. If only someone would move. The fat woman on the edge of the dock, if she would weep, if she would have the decency to wring her hands—Pauline had a moment's mad vision of herself comforting the woman, patting the weeping, orphaned children, the nice Austri-ans on the terrace murmuring about the kindness of the *Kleine Frau*. . . . But nobody paid any attention to her. The old couple of the café—how they bowed and beamed when Pauline came there for a glass of beer; and had the little girl with the clogs forgotten how only yesterday. . . .

Yesterday! Yesterday she had been a baby, protected by her mother, courted by Richard; yesterday she had been on her honeymoon. But the world had changed at sun-set; stood still; it seemed that the boats out there would never move again, that the people on the shore would never lower their hands from their eyes, that the whole graying scene would never change. Why doesn't someone take care of me? Perhaps she would faint: then would the fat woman forget her husband and her children and the sun that she used like a clock, and remember her place, and come with water, with comfort. . . .

The sun was squashed on the hills; only a puddle of gold was left.

Richard was talking again with the store-keeper. He turned, his face grim with horror: "It's a child, a four-year-old child, that woman's youngest." And he walked as though in a trance, away from her, away from the storekeeper, and only stopped when the water at the shore-edge came in little ripples up over the toes of his shoes. Pauline's heart went sick inside her. *Ein kind!* But I adore children. "I adore kids," she had said to Dick on the boat, and she had read to a group of them one night in a corner of the salon. "I adore kids," she had said to him as they watched little Lord Fauntleroys sailing boats in Kensington Gardens. "I adore kids," she had said as far back as Central Park, at home, when they had passed a row of them, playing before their nurses. I adore. . . . *Ein kind!* One of those little things, with long braids if it were a girl, shaved head if it were a boy. She must know if it were a boy or a girl. A child was drowning . . . terrible . . . but: was it a boy or a girl? She felt herself smiling. "I must hang on to myself," she thought, "I am becoming hysterical."

***

The evening wind blew, like a draft from an open grave.

Why didn't the stolid woman weep? Too stupid, she must be incredibly stupid, women like that belonged in kitchens in America. Pauline was intolerably impatient, as though a time were being cut out of her life, as though a time were slowly dragging itself out in which she had no existence. And Richard stood by and let it happen, let the damp evening breeze coldly extinguish the light of their honeymoon; let her stand there alone while a crowd of peasants stood with their backs to her.

One by one the peasants lowered their hands from their eyes; there was no longer need to shade their eyes, for there was no longer light to shade them from.

Now the evening air blew colder, the smooth lake lay glistening with shadows and cold pearl lights, a sheet of ice, on which sat four boats, unable to move. The figures of the watchers on shore grew hazy, immersed, jelled, in inertia. And half an hour back, tea on a terrace . . . would it happen again, just like that? No, the smallest detail of this graying scene was so implacably printed on Pauline's mind that she felt she must live in it forever, apart from Richard, a Richard who stood with white face and eyes straining out over a cold, still lake, with feet dipping deeper, as the slight tide rose, into innocent wavelets on the edge of the shore. She remembered her mother shielding her with her skirt from the sight of an accident on the street, hurrying her away. Men were insensitive. She wanted someone to call her *Kleine Frau* in a hurry.

***

There was an absent-minded air about the boats that was maddening. The terrible primitiveness of their telling the time by the sun was maddening too, but it made her want to smile. And if it were a child drowning up at the hotel? She could imagine the guests, crowding to the edge of the terrace, the ladies with their husbands behind them, holding their hands. Women would become hysterical, their husbands would comfort them. Servants would bring tea and smelling salts. But here, in the growing dark, they could think of nothing but the sun; and in a moment when its reflected light died, there would be nothing. . . .

She was so cold, so lonely, so frightened. Dick had no right to forget her like that. She wanted to call him, she had every right to tell him indignantly to take her home; but men were so frightening when they were not thinking about women—as though they were in another world. She felt that he would not hear her voice, nor feel her touch, he might look at her without seeing her.

She felt worse than alone with all these strange, stupid people about her—they were like the shabbily dressed people whom she had had to pass one night on a poorly-lighted street in New York; it seemed as though all poor people (except servants, who were neat and kind) had mean, stupid faces, they all looked inhuman and foreign and sly, hostile. It was funny how they changed when they became servants. I suppose contact with nice people, she thought. The fat woman on the edge of the dock, watching her child drown—what a comfortable servant she would have made, if only she had the sense to know it.

It was almost as black as night. Already three stars pricked the sky. That was the way it was here, in this little village surrounded by mountains; as soon as the sun dipped behind them, there was no more light; it was night at once.

The eleven-year-old girl who untied boats prevailed upon her mother to take her home. Someone gave the stolid servant-woman on the edge of the dock, whose child was drowning, a box to sit on; she looked perfectly square with her bottom bulging below the tight pink apron-string. The little children with her shifted from one leg to the other; probably they wanted to go home and have supper; they were tired of waiting for their little brother (or sister) to drown.

***

It was so dark now that the four boats had merged into one mysterious shadow far out on the lake, barely standing out from the dimness of the opposite shore. Three or four peasant women gathered their skirts in their hands and clambered slowly up the little bank to the street, turning for a last look as though they expected some miracle to have happened in those twenty seconds, while their backs had been bent forward, their eyes climbing the tiny bank ahead of their feet. Then they went slowly down the road. The little groups of men made one group now, shaking their heads and looking out over the lake and shaking their heads again. Only Richard still stood by himself, and Pauline could see the side of his face, whiter than ever in this dark, staring out, not moving, the eager little waves spitting about his heels.

One row-boat broke loose from the others, took on a dim, moving shape, and headed slowly toward the dock. Pauline thought she would never forget the slight grazing noise it made as it slid past the dock onto the little beach. Three men climbed out, breathing hard; they shook their heads and spoke briefly. One of them was gleaming with water, only a coat thrown over him hiding his wet nakedness; his eyes were blood-shot, distended. The woman on the box sat perfectly still, her back as impassive as ever. Pauline drew back in fright as the swimmer, panting, brushed past her, before he threw himself down to rest.

Two more boats broke loose and rowed for shore. Only one was left. Pauline could see that there was just one man in it. Slowly the two dark shapes rowed for shore. Nearer and larger they came. On the shore's edge was a moment of suspense; why did one boat remain out there alone? The boats docked silently. No need to ask questions. A rower spoke briefly to the woman seated on the box. Her senses heightened, Pauline made out the meaning of his words: "The father—*dein mann*—will stay out there—all night—to wait—he will not come in."

The woman stood. She put up her hand to shade her eyes from habit, or perhaps from hope that there would suddenly be light to shade them from, and took a last look at the solitary boat. Then she motioned to her two little girls, made her way between the staring peasants, and clambered heavily up the bank. On the street she, too, turned for a last backward look mopping her face with a large, red man's ban-danna. Then Pauline saw her big back jogging slowly down the street, a small replica of herself trotting on either side. One child would not come home for supper, not tonight nor any night; but there were still two trotting beside her and these two must be fed.

The store-keeper crossed himself, shook his head mutely at the mute lake, and led the way up the bank.

The remaining loiterers turned to go, all crossing themselves silently. None of them had seemed to give a thought to God during the struggle with him; but now that God had conquered, they remembered, and before wandering to their homes and eating, they seemed impelled to acknowledge his power with a quick salute. Only out on the lake the dumb patient shape of the father waited, who had not yet admitted to himself that God had beaten him in open battle.

But what *was* ailing Richard? He stood there with his back to her and his toes dug into the sand as though he had taken root. Pauline stood behind him, afraid somehow to touch him, while the cold breeze reached up under her *dirndl* skirt and froze her bare legs. At last she spoke, in the sort of vague, timid voice that one half hopes will be indistinguishable from air.

"We might as well go now."

"We might as well go," he echoed, as though he punctiliously caught the words out of the air and put them in a shape.

He followed her up the bank and down the little street and she could see he was biting on something bitter, but for the life of her she couldn't guess what. She felt so lonely, so very sorry for the *Kleine Frau* that she saw bobbing so gallantly down the dark street.

"It's cold," she said plaintively.

He glanced at her as though he couldn't quite place her in his memory.

"I'm goose-flesh all the way up to the knees," she said loudly, like a person rapping for the last time on a closed door before turning away. "What a tragedy, Richard!"

From behind the door she heard his voice: "Oh yes, it gets cold here as soon as the sun—"

They walked in silence down the street which had gone to bed, toward the hotel. The outside lights had come on up there, and were strung merrily across the terrace. She thought of the child's game of prisoners' base, and the hotel became the post which one touched crying "Home Free!" and if only she could reach the steps before this terrible loneliness engulfed her altogether. . . .

"I can hardly believe it's the end of August," he started politely; and suddenly gripped her arm tight with his fingers and blubbered. "You didn't think I was afraid, did you Pauline? You don't think it was fear? Those God-damn inefficient idiots, monkeying around with rowboats . . . Pauline, you didn't think I was afraid?"

"Richard—afraid? But afraid—what are you talking about?" Oh, but she had put up with enough for one day!

"You know I'm a crack swimmer, you know I've won cups . . . and you don't know what I'm talking about?" he said furiously; but he didn't let go her arm. He held it as though he hated it, but as though it were the only real thing he could find.

We must get back to the hotel, to what we understand, Pauline told her feet.

"Pauline, every minute I thought I would help. And

178

every minute I couldn't, something stopped me. It felt like embarrassment. How can anyone feel embarrassed about saving a child? My God, it feels like insanity. They were so stupid. I could have helped. But I felt like a tourist. You wouldn't bring electric lights into a church lighted by candles. Would you? I couldn't seem to show off my smart American system. . . ."

"I think you're crazy," she said harshly. "Don't you think you could spare me this? I'm shivering, I'm ready to scream. Don't you think you might have some consideration?"

He pulled away his arm and drew back. "You frighten me," he said. "Who are you anyway? I don't know you."

But they had come to the foot of the narrow, winding stairs which led up to the lighted terrace, to civilization. The hotel loomed above them. Inexplicably Pauline felt warm and happy again, in the sudden, inexplicable certainty of being happy soon. Men were funny. Of course. It was what you had to expect. They were simply children, and prone like children to sudden selfishness, to blind spots. You had to point the way, to soothe; and before it was too late, before they slipped out of your grasp, you simply had to put your foot down.

"We are both in a state of nerves, dear," she said kindly. "And no wonder! after what we've been through. Now come along like a good boy before we catch our death of cold."

For a minute he stood there, his mouth open

waiting for words, wavering between hating and following her. Pauline seized his arm firmly until, dazed and submissive, he had put his foot on the first step. Up and up, toward the nice Germans (Austrians?) who ate with such bad manners yet were gentlemen through and through; she would stare out over the "treacherous" lake and the fringed ends of her shawl would shiver in the breeze. *Kleine Frau*, do not take it so to heart, *Kleine Frau*, undoubtedly she has so many *kinder* she does not know yet which is lost. . . . And before the evening was over Richard must be made to apologize for his unreasonableness.

Mother to Dinner

The Menorah Journal, March 1930

Katherine Benjamin, who had been Katherine Jastrow for something less than a year, said Goodafternoon to the groceryman and, stooping to the counter, gathered two large and unwieldy packages close to her body, balancing one elbow on her hip so that the hand, crawling to the top, could hold sternly separate the bottle of milk from the package of Best Eggs. The thin, one-eyed errand boy who sprawled on an empty packing-box near the door leaped to his feet and opened it with a flourish and a "hot, isn't it?" And sliding past him, curving her body to make a nest for the projecting bundle, she heard the screen door swing lightly closed behind her, flutter against the wood frame in a series of gently diminishing taps.

Why did one say Goodafternoon instead of Goodbye

to tradesmen and teachers, she wondered, following her packages as they bobbed evenly down the street before her, recalling (as she adjusted her gait to her burden) countless times when she had waited, in middies and broad sailor hats, for her mother's comforting "Good-*morning,* Mr. Schmidt," and Mr. Schmidt's answering "*Good*morning, Mrs. Benjamin, *good*morning I'm sure." And now Katherine, no longer in middies or accompanied by her mother but modestly wearing a ring on her left hand, heard herself kindly bidding Mr. Papenmeyer Goodafternoon, and feeling, as she said it, very close to her mother, feeling almost, as she nodded firmly to him, that she was her mother. (Gerald predicted with scorn that it would not be long before Katherine would speak of Mr. Papenmeyer as "my Mr. Papenmeyer" and he suspected that she would even add, in time, "he never disappoints"; but she was not to suppose, he said, that he would glance benignly over his *Saturday Evening Post* as her father did, and listen.)

Katherine hugged her packages like babies; in them lay, wrapped in glossy wax paper, in brown paper bags, in patent boxes, the dinner to which Katherine's mother and father were coming as guests. . . . The dinner over which Katherine would frown at Gerald politely insulting Mrs. Benjamin; over which Mr. Benjamin would cough and insist on the worst cuts of everything. . . . She hoped nervously that Gerald would not be insolent and argumentative, that her mother would not be stupid. . . .

She must protect them both. . . . And she began to dread the strangeness which always oppressed her on beholding her mother in a house which was her home and not her mother's. . . . Ridiculous, she said brightly, I'm not going to let *that* happen again. . . .

The spire of the church on the corner raised itself in the form of a huge salt-shaker against the mild, colorless sky. The sun, a blurred yellow lamp, glimmered palely behind veils of soiled cloud; it might rain, for the air was sodden, the leaves on the tree before the church hovered on the air with a peculiar waiting indifference, like dead fish turned over on their backs and floating in still water.

And for years to come she, "Mrs. Gerald Jastrow," would walk, heavily laden with her thoughts and her packages, in Fall, in Winter, and in Spring, from Mr. Papenmeyer's meat-and-grocery store through these same streets, past the church with its salt-shaker spire, past the row of low brick houses, past the tall india-rubber apartment with the liveried doorman shuffling his feet under the awning, stretched like a hollow wrinkled caterpillar to the curb, to her own home, which she shared with Gerald, of whom she had never heard two years before. . . .

***

Katherine's fingers, tapping the sagging bundles, reviewed their contents. Meat—Mr. Papenmeyer's recommended cut for four—bread, milk, corn, tomatoes—without her asking, the clerk had passionately assured her they were firm—two large packages it amounted to, one small slippery one under her elbow, and her purse. By a minute flexing of her left hand she could feel the key tucked neatly in her glove to save her trouble when she reached her door. An absurd ritual, that, said Gerald; one which in the sum total could not save her much trouble. You've picked up all these damn habits, he said, from your mother: they're a waste of time, they take more time to remember than simply to leave out; be careful, Katherine, before you know it you will be keeping a platinum-framed market-list. But these little rituals made doing the things fun, Katherine argued; when she remembered, at the grocer's before picking up her packages, to tuck the key in her glove, a horde of vague recollections, almost recollections of recollections, unravelled pleasantly in her mind. They gave meaning to what would otherwise be just marketing; they formed a link not only with yesterday and tomorrow, but with other women squinting at scales and selecting dinners for strange men to whom they found them-selves married; with, if you like, her mother, who had been doing these things every day for thirty years. You may say pooh Gerald, she said, but there are many things which you, who are after all a man, cannot be expected to know; why two years ago you didn't even know me. . . .

Were the flat faces she had left haggling over green peas and punching cantaloupes aware of the waiting uncertainties, the uprooting, the transplanting, the bleeding, involved in their calmly leaving their homes to go to live with strangers? Strangers—husbands—Gerald A. Jastrow—I met a boy named Gerald A. Jastrow at a party, he asked to take me home—I am sorry, I am seeing a boy named Gerald Jastrow, he has a cowlick which trembles when he argues—but mother I am seeing Gerald tonight—Gerald says, Gerald thinks—I am going to be married—his name? (*whose* name?—oh, the Stranger's)—his name is Jastrow, Gerald Jastrow—I've been married for eleven months—my husband's name is Gerald Jastrow, no I don't know him, he's a Stranger to me, but I put away his male-smelling underwear. . . . Katherine reached the sidewalk just in time to avoid a cab which sped down the street in front of her house.

She smiled brightly at the elevator man, an expert, busy, kindly smile; she felt again like her mother. "Wouldn't be surprised if a storm blew up," Albert said to her shrewdly, resting his hand in a friendly way on the lever. (A storm, she didn't want a storm, Katherine thought, suddenly frightened; Gerald might say what he liked about the risk of motoring being greater than that of flying, and the chance of being murdered in sleep greater than that of being struck by lightning: she *wouldn't* fly, and she cowered before thunder and lightning.) "Oh do you think so?" said Mrs. Gerald Jastrow, and she looked in awe at the elevator man, as if it was all in his hands whether a storm came or not. "Oh I hope

What nonsense, she said crisply, amazingly comforted by a slant of faint sunlight which quivered through the gloom. Look, she said, it is my own house. . . . Reassured, she dropped her packages on the kitchen table. But someone should be there to greet her, she felt, to rise from one of those friendly chairs and say to her: What did you buy? How was Mr. Papenmeyer the butcher? Was the one-eyed errand boy there today? Come in, take off your hat and gloves, I am glad you are home. . . . A year ago she would have stood at the door and shouted *Moth-er,* where *are* you? And if Mrs. Benjamin had not come in haste at her call, a white- aproned German maid (Mrs. Benjamin chaperoned their love-affairs so successfully that they generally stayed with her for years, like obedient nuns) would have come and said, Oh Miss Katy, your mother said to tell you she went over to your Aunt Sarah, your uncle's not feeling just right.

But she would call *up* her mother, she thought gleefully, running to the telephone: Hel*lo,* mother, what do you think I bought for supper? The butcher said. . . . Do you think there will be a storm, mother . . . ? As she lifted the receiver from its hook she thought she heard faint steps behind her; Gerald, she thought in a flash, and slid the receiver back to its place. Of course it wasn't Gerald, at four o'clock in the afternoon, of course it wasn't anybody; but suppose he had come upon her tele-phoning her mother: she could hear him say, as he had said last Sunday, catching her at the telephone (and of course one

187

and untouched. But with her mother, these moments grew into comfortable hours, never forgotten, linking one with another, remaining always, a steady undercurrent, ready to rise and fill them at the lightest touch.

And sliding the bread into the shining modern breadbox she felt a strong nostalgia for the worn-out tin that had stood for years on her mother's shelf. This cold affair of shelves and sliding doors, glittering knobs and antiseptic lettering suggested too much newness, too little use and familiarity; her mother's loomed in contrast, a symbol of security, almost a refuge from storm. And yet Mrs. Benjamin, with the vision of that old, battered, loyal thing in the back of her mind, had come with Katherine graciously, gayly even, to buy this tawdry substitute. (My little girl, she had said to the clerk, smiling ironically at him and drawing him into her sympathy, would like that Modern Breadbox. It was as if she had said, My little girl has tired of her old mother, she wants the latest thing in young men, one that can scientifically explain away the fear of lightning.) Feeling warmly bound to her mother, she caught herself opening and slamming the little door a second, unnecessary time, an old nervous habit of her mother's. For a moment she felt purified, intensely loyal, as if by this gesture she had renounced the new for the old. She walked from the kitchen with her mother's tired, elastic step, the step of a stout woman who has shopped all day, whose weary body will neither submit to rest nor important ones. Gerald's words: but true, true.) But Gerald himself had so *little* concern for the small things she did all day that she refrained from telling him anecdotes which she passionately feared might bore him, but which, nevertheless, she collected like bouquets of precious flowers to lay before him if she dared. Looking about the empty room, Gerald's desk standing solidly in one corner reproved her; she became irritated that her mind flew so often to thoughts of her mother. . . .

Like a human shuttle she wove her way between these two, between Gerald and her mother, the two opposites who supported her web. (Why couldn't they both leave her alone?) When she was with her mother she could not rest, for she thought continually of the beacon of Gerald's intelligence, which must be protected from her mother's sullying incomprehension. And when she was with Gerald her heart ached for her deserted mother, she longed for her large enveloping sympathy in which to hide away from Gerald's too-clear gaze. From sheer hopelessness and irritation, tears filled her eyes. . . .

She was glad to escape from the kitchen, for she had begun to hate Mr. Papenmeyer's excellent foods, which would merge artfully and serve as the camouflage of a family battle. As long as the dinner lasted, she knew the conversation could be kept meager and on a safely mediocre level. But Katherine, sitting between her mother and father, and eyeing her husband with apprehension, would know that around her own table, consuming food she herself had prepared, a victim would be fattened for slaughter, a victor strengthened for battle. And whoever won, Katherine lost. . . . Oh come, she told herself, exasperated, this isn't the Last Supper. . . .

***

But that wasn't furniture moving, she told herself grimly, crouching on the window-sill and regarding the street which was lying quietly in its place before her house—not twice, she said, that's Albert's thunder. It rumbled from a great distance, as though it were in hiding.

Certainly, she thought, her mind returning, like a dog worrying a bone, she lived with Gerald on a higher plane—if her misery was sometimes more acute, her pleasure, in proportion, was more poignant. While they had felt nothing deeply, Katherine and her mother, as they had built up, over tea-tables, simple patterns of thought, simplified ways of looking at things. What if Katherine had had to stoop her mind so that they might stay together? at least they could talk, at least they kept each other company. (Gerald said their talk was no more than gossip; he said that Katherine and her mother had shut themselves up in a hot-house, talking and com-forting each other for griefs that could never come to them while they remained in their lethargic half-life.) But in a world like this, thought Katherine,

192

where thunder-storms can creep on one ruthlessly, why shouldn't two people who love each other hide away and give one another comfort?

Thunder rumbled more constantly now. Katherine, suspicious of it, in spite of its distance, detected in its muffled rolling a growing concentration, as if it were slowly gathering its strength, as if it were winding itself up for a tremendous spring. Should she telephone Gerald?—*no.*

The thought of Gerald frightened her. He led such a curious existence apart from her every day from nine till six. Katherine and her mother had always known exactly what the other was doing, at almost every hour in the day. It was a comfort to stop suddenly, look at one's watch, and think "Mother's at the dentist's now" or "I should think mother would be on the way home now." But there were times when Gerald was in the room with her, sitting beside her, lying beside her in bed, when she didn't know exactly where he was. . . .

Gerald said—and with some justice, she admitted to herself—that she and her mother had lived like two spoiled wives in a harem kept by a simple old gentleman who demanded nothing of them beyond their presence and the privilege of supporting them. But because of his docility one could not take seriously a possible injustice to him. Beside his work downtown, Mr. Benjamin mailed their letters, called for their purchases, or did any of the little errands which they had spent the day in pleasantly avoiding. If he entered the room where Katherine and her mother were talking, it had seemed quite natural for Mrs. Benjamin to say, "Dear, we are talking"; it seemed natural because of the peaceful expression with which Mr. Benjamin picked up his *Saturday Evening Post* on the way out of the room. All Katherine's uncles were disposed of in the same way by her aunts.

Gerald referred to the Benjamin men as "poor devils," as "emasculated boobs." You resent me, he said to Katherine, because you have a preconceived idea of the role to which all husbands are relegated by their wives; you'd like to laugh me out of any important existence. (Indeed, it was only at moments when he was away and when she was performing, in his absence, some intimate service for him, that she could look upon Gerald as her mother looked upon her father; with ease, with possession, with a maternal tolerance touched by affectionate irony. Here were things of which she could be certain: that he rolled his underwear into a ball and dropped it on the floor, that he left his shoes to lie where they fell, that he draped yesterday's tie around the back of a chair. But she could never achieve this intimacy in his presence: when Gerald was with her, when she *thought* about Gerald, it faded; there was more strangeness.) Gerald again! She was aware of a wish to sink Gerald into the bottom of her mind: she was too much aware of him; when she read, when she visited, when she noticed things, it was always with the desire to re-port back to Gerald: nothing was complete until Gerald had been told.

She and her mother had discussed and reported everything. But she could no longer be alone with her mother, for it seemed as though Gerald sat in taunting effigy between them, forcing Katherine for her mother's sake to deprecate him, for his sake to protect him, from obscurity, from misrepresentation, from neglect. . . .

His presence, even now, while she was alone, sat heavily, reproachfully, in the empty rooms, forbidding her to call him up, forbidding her to recall comfortably past days she had spent with her mother. This was not living, Gerald said, to spend one's hours in introspective analysis, to brood over the past. Katherine's flights he called "a worthless luxury, like the visits of the rich to Palm Beach or Paris." But it was living, Katherine knew unhappily; she was living most acutely.

***

The room darkened suddenly. Something of the tension which would be upon her later, as it always was when her mother and Gerald were in the same room, came upon her now, as she sat straining for the sound of thunder, watching shades of gloom silently lay themselves in the hot room. Katherine held her breath waiting for thunder, for rain, anything. Voices of children floated reassuringly up from the street, and in a moment the sunlight reappeared, tentative, tempting one to believe in it for all its faintness. The thunder sounded like the chopping of wood in a far-off field. Katherine longed for her mother. She wished she were not so near the heart of the storm.

She hated herself for thinking of her mother. But not to think of her demanded a complete uprooting, demanded a final shoving off from a safe dock into unknown waters. Besides, she felt guilty toward her mother, she brooded over her as one does over a victim, pitying him, resenting him and utterly unable to forget him.

For against her mother Katherine felt that she had committed a crime. She had abandoned that elderly lady for a young man who, from her mother's point of view, had been merely one of several who had taken her to dances, to dinner, who had kissed her in the parlor, with whom finally, inexplicably, she had come to have more dates than with any other. She had abandoned her mother, left her sitting at home with no more evening gowns to "take in," no one to sit up for, no young men to laugh about in the bathroom at four o'clock in the morning when Katherine came home. She had left her to sit opposite an old man at dinner every evening, she had imposed upon her the tragedy of being a guest in her own daughter's house; she had reduced her to a stranger.

But a little bit her mother had the advantage. She had seen Gerald, after all, in the absurd rig of tuxedo and stiff shirt, calling upon her daughter with flowers, with books, leaping to his feet when she (Mrs. Benjamin) entered the room. She had watched Gerald for a year politely talking parlor politics with Katherine's father, posturing

196

ridiculously when he held Katherine's coat, becoming perforce friendly with the elevator boys in the Benjamin apartment, slinking shamefacedly before a doorman who had seen him too often. Nothing, Katherine reflected, could be more unreal, more unconvincing, than a young man in the act of courting. She could never forgive Gerald for having let her mother observe him in that role. (Equally she could never forgive her mother, blameless as she was, for having seen him.) Her mother could never take seriously, surely, a marriage which had grown from love-making in taxi-cabs which had been reported to her with amusement by Katherine, brushing her teeth in the bathroom. She had not shared with her mother the tortuous transition which had left her no longer an amused observer, but a help-less, suffering participant. All the indication Mrs. Benjamin had had of Katherine's growing need of Gerald was a burst of hysteria and a state of nervous irritability which had succeeded the usual calm of Katherine's disposition—before suddenly one evening, preparing her charity report in a black lace dress, she was confronted by two embarrassed young people who declared their ridiculous intention to marry.

This, Katherine felt, she should have spared her mother. She should not have caused her, so heart-breakingly, to drop her charity report on the marble table and to look suddenly at her daughter with reproachful eyes, saying, half-humorously, What, daughter, tired of your old mother already?

She had left her parents for no reason, they had given her no cause to leave them, she had left them for no better reason than that when Gerald said to her that he would never again ask her to marry him, she had been seized with panic lest he meant it.

Gerald, who two years before had not existed. Whereas her father and mother had fed her porridge, given her blackboards, measured her growth against a door, for a long period of twenty years during which Gerald had never heard of her. She was unsafe, she cried internally. She was living with a stranger in a strange land where storms evolved closely about one. She was living with a stranger who had no knowledge of the first twenty years of her life, the major portion of her life. She was living in a strange land where her childhood had no existence. It was unreal, it was unsafe, it was terrifying. Gerald liked to hear her tell stories of her childhood; but it was as if, when she told him little things she remembered, she and he were together contemplating the childhood of a stranger. She held tightly to the arms of her chair, but the slippery wood was repelling. Suddenly everything was reduced to an absurdity. It was, to Gerald, as though she had not begun to exist until he had noticed her two years before, at a party, and asked to take her home; but suppose she had not come to the party—she had come only out of boredom; or suppose, to make it more ridiculous, she had not worn the particular blue dress which had caught Gerald's eye? and he hadn't asked to take her home? Their life together seemed no more than the result of a series of insignif-icant accidents. Could it be real? Could she share the rest of her life with a stranger whose eye had casually fallen on a blue dress? With someone who had known her for only two years out of her twenty-two?

Katherine felt herself to be struggling somewhere in the middle, between two harbors, unable to decide whether to swim backward or forward, tempted almost to close her eyes and quietly drown where she was. Shut-tle, shuttle, she murmured to herself, miserably, exas-perated at her weakness, her helplessness.

***

Smoking in the yellow room, she waited with unhappy certainty for Albert's storm which would surely come now. The air was oppressive, sullenly pregnant. It was as if an evil thing crouched in the room, waiting for birth. Dark was gathering in shades, permitting still a faint yellowish gloom. Wind was dead. Katherine, fearing and hating the coming storm, nevertheless feared and hated the moments of waiting even more. A clock on the mantel slowly ticked off the moments she would have to wait; it was in league with the coming storm. Her body was chill in the midst of heat.

She was weary already with the nervous effort she would make to bring Gerald and her mother close to each other, with her own struggle to remain equally close to both of them, simultaneous with her desperate attempt to conceal from each the af-fection she felt for the other. Gerald and her mother sitting and eating in this room, which now was the home of the storm, would be a cat and mouse, quietly stalking each other under cover. (Was this true? or did their struggle for supremacy take place merely in her own mind? Because she must know, she must know.) Katherine would twist herself this way and that to keep the evening characterless and blessedly dull, rather than immerse them all in the horror of an argument, in which their superficial sides would represent symbolically their eternal, fundamental resentment. Katherine must take no sides, Katherine must flit nervously from one side to the other, breaching gaps with hysterical giggles, throwing herself into outbursts of hysterical affection, making a clown of herself in order to distract these two who fought silently for her. She was loathsome to herself.

Her mind struggled with a remote memory. Something—perhaps the slumbering quality of the air which sheltered the coming storm so that its pent-up evil would suddenly roll forth and smother the world— reminded her of a thing which seemed to have happened when she was a child. Frowning, she gazed into herself to recall. And it came back to her. She had cried one day for her mother and they had told her that Mrs. Benjamin had gone to Atlantic City for two days and that this young lady would take care of Katherine while her mother was away. Katherine kicked and screamed, but Miss Anna proved so entertaining—she showed her how to make a whole family of paper dolls live through a day's work and play—that she forgot her mother and was surprised to hear the next day that she would be home in an hour. Suddenly she hated Miss Anna, and when Mrs. Benjamin came home she found her daughter crying angrily, Miss Anna bewildered, murmuring, But she seemed so happy, she seemed perfectly happy. . . . I was not happy for a minute, Katherine screamed, I was waiting the whole time for my mother to come back.

Enraged with herself, she wondered whether she retained somewhere the idea that because her life had begun with her mother, it would end with her, whether some childish part of her could not accept their parting as final and looked upon her life with Gerald as no more than an interlude. Oh Gerald, Gerald, she sobbed, I am worse than unfaithful to you. . . . I hate my mother, she is a venomous old woman who tries to keep me from you. . . . The injustice to her mother overwhelmed her. She hated herself. She felt like the child of divorced parents, driven from one to the other and unable with either to make a home.

***

I have been married during every month except June, she thought, lifting her head and quietly looking, as if to remember, about the room. She was comforted by

Gerald's desk, which had been with her during eleven months. Thunder, blasting the earth in a distant place, filled the room. She had been married for eleven months and had never told her mother anything but house-keeping troubles. Why? A second roll of thunder sounded.

She was surrounded, she could not escape. She was suspended, she could take refuge with neither Gerald nor her mother, she was caught fairly by the thunder....

Deception had begun with her engagement. One had to keep one's eyes constantly glowing, however ter-rifiedly they looked at the approaching cliff, one's words constantly gay and effervescent, lest one's mother look searchingly at the prospective bride and say, But are you sure, Darling, absolutely *sure?* Of course one was not sure. One was suspended, even as now, with thunders rolling in from all sides. (I ought to start the dinner, I ought to start the dinner: I *can't,* I can't.)

During a wedding trip one was awakened to innu-merable things, most of them delightful, all of them ter-rifying. A longing had filled Katherine intermittently to be back from this trip of surprises: she pictured herself talking to her mother all day for many days, sharing with her, not details, but the contemplation, of intimacies. It seemed to her the most delicious part of the trip, that she would return and talk about it to her mother. Ger-ald's jealous allusions to her mother she had accepted with a tolerant smile; his analyses—for it was then that he had violently expounded his harem theory—meant nothing to her, they seemed to have no connection with reality. "Dearest mother," she had written, "all the things I have to tell you! I can hardly wait to see you. . . . So many things have happened. And of course, Gerald being a man. . . ." (Was that lightning, or was it the mere lifting of the curtain by the wind? The dinner, the dinner was waiting to be cooked: I won't *touch* it.)

The awful farce at the station, where Mr. and Mrs. Benjamin had come to meet them, came to her vividly now. Mr. Benjamin, having screwed his courage to the point of making Katherine remember his presence long enough to kiss him, retiring to help Gerald, competently wasting time with the luggage in the background, mother and daughter swaying in a series of embraces—Katherine was suddenly lost, locked, imprisoned, in the body of a stout, fashionable stranger. Why doesn't she look at me? she thought, all she wants is to hold me, to squeeze me, to choke me to death, it never occurs to her to look in my face. Sweeping her daughter to one side, Mrs. Benjamin sprang forth to smother Gerald. She had no right to, cried Katherine wildly to herself, as she turned from her father's vague embrace, and all the things which Gerald had said of her mother came back to her and they seemed true. And at the same time she felt passionately that Mrs. Benjamin must not expose herself to Gerald's unsympathetic eye; horrible embarrassment arose in her, when, thank God, she saw that Mrs. Benjamin in her eagerness had missed her aim; her kiss floated on past Gerald's never undo the thing that was between them, for it was Gerald who stood between her mother and herself, just as her mother stood between herself and Gerald.

Well, *was* Albert's storm coming or wasn't it, she thought impatiently, and beat out her cigarette on the window-sill, dropped the dead stub and watched it hurtle past awnings and window-boxes and land haphazardly in the gutter. (And what about the dinner?)

A clap of thunder brought her trembling to her feet. It had traveled with treacherous silence from a great distance to burst like a shell in her ear. And now lightning quivered across the pewter sky in a blinding streak. Katherine, trembling, holding to the mantel, felt all the elements of storm gathering closely about her. The intense heat and stillness in the room vibrated with suppressed force. She had a sense of something evil, something unhealthy, waiting beneath the table to be born. The room was alive, awake, crouching before the storm, waiting in every sense for its approach.

She laughed aloud, nervously, when the thunder sounded next, meek and far-off; it rumbled for a few seconds, then it rolled toward her with increasing force until something cut it off sharply in the height of its passion. The storm was playing with her; it was here, but it played at hiding, it retreated and advanced so that she could never be sure of it.

What was she to do, what was she to do? Should she, could she telephone?—*no.*

Thunder shook the house. Malicious streaks of lightning drew themselves across the sky, lighting up the gloom until the day shone for a second like steel. Suddenly night came. Winds came alive and tore drunkenly down the street. Another long re-verberating crash of thunder, incredibly near and ear-splitting. There was a moment of suspension, while only the wind moved. And then the sky retched and large cold drops of rain like stones pelted the windowpanes. . . .

***

Panic seized Katherine. She rushed to the window to escape. She was afraid of the room. It rocked with unhappy speculation. She stood at the window facing in, and saw how the storm was fed from within her room. The lightning lit it like quick fire, the thunder sounded in it long after it had died outside.

The thunder bounced about the room, striking at corners, rolling over furniture, shaking the walls, groveling derisively at her feet.

It seemed to her that before the next clap of thunder she must have reached a decision or she would die. But what decision, she cried, striking her fist against the window? What decision? about what? The problem was obscure. (She imagined her mother struck by lightning, her stout body collapsing with dignity under a tree, she heard herself telling Gerald with triumph as an overtone to her grief, My mother is dead, I have only you now.) And if the problem was obscure, how much more obscure the solution. (She imagined Gerald struck by lightning, a look of hurt surprise in his eyes as he fell beneath a tree, murmuring something about scientific chance, she heard herself telling her mother, strange relief mingling with her sorrow, Gerald is gone, mother, I shall have to come back to you.) And the next thunder rolled down a hill, louder and louder, faster and nearer, and fell to the bottom, bursting into cannon balls, exploding with insane crashes, and in a thousand voices splitting the earth in its center. Katherine burst into passionate tears.

Now everything was the storm. The storm, which had circled about the room, wished for closer nucleus, and entered her body. The lightning pierced her stomach, the thunder shook her limbs, and retreated, growling, to its home in her bowels. There was no escape for her; she was no longer imprisoned in the storm: the storm was imprisoned in her.

She stood in a shaking lethargy, she had no will, no feeling. She was frozen; she was a shell in which storm raged without her will. All the world had entered the room. . . .

It came to her slowly that there was a new sound in the air, a sharp metallic ring that repeated itself at intervals. She had no idea how long she might have been hearing it in the back of her head before she took notice of it. Now it rang again, sharply, there seemed to be fright in it, or anger, she could not tell which. On stiff

But in the same moment Esther's body became tenderly reminiscent of its new experience. It had been good to feel hands of new desire upon her body again. Good to feel hands which were strange grow familiar, and yet, exploring out curves and recesses, remain strange, stranger's hands. As her lover was a new lover, her body became a new body. She was conscious of it, she breathed through it, she felt with it, as she had not for a year, not since her first shy ecstatic contacts with Mark, her husband. There was no happiness in this strange embrace: there was hunger in it, sharp, delicious suspense, a reminder of that lost virgin ecstasy, a hint of that old sense of luxurious defilement. . . . There came over her body with the memory an expanding surge of voluptuousness, of freedom, of abandonment, a yearning to open itself wider than it had dared, in its timidity, to do last night to David. Esther wished he were with her now, lying cramped in this small berth, she could almost feel his hand as it had stolen for the first time, so painfully, under her dress. . . . And she felt suddenly defiant toward Mark: Mark who with his superior knowledge had initiated her into the ways of men and women, Mark who had been so long for her the only man. Now she was his equal. Now, after a year of half-resentful submission, she had proved by one act that she was not dependent upon Mark for fulfillment, she had made herself once more separate and whole. And when she thought of those past days filled with futile resenting, it was with the incredulous amusement that one feels on treading in daylight the path that was so impassable the night before.

For when Esther, a night's journey from Mark, raised her face in a strange moonlight unlike that which fell upon her home, and saw above her the strange face of David lit by its own light of desire, she made no move to check the answering radiance of her own body. And when she felt, later, his kisses, now upon her neck, her throat, and finally sharply on her lips, the inside of her body broke into a thousand pieces, beating for escape against suddenly rigid limbs. When one of those strange hands, after exploring, caressed, Esther's only movement was one of acquiescence.

Esther made no decision. Yet she felt her mind, as she felt her body, joyfully sinking, deeper and deeper, into trembling abysses. He ceased to be David. He ceased to be any man; he took on the multiple identity of Stranger. In this capacity she loved him, she desired him.

Then David was sobbing upon her breast. She hushed him, he must not become David to her, he must remain Stranger. Hush, she said. Let us sleep, she said. Obediently, with his head still on her breast, he slept.

Mark was far off. Mark was conquered. She could feel, aloofly, pity for Mark. Her body was strong, freed of dependence. Her mind congratulated it.

For a few moments she slept. She awakened suddenly, as if she had been shaken, finding a body stirring on her own. At once she knew that this was not Mark, who was moving from her, turning his head to sleep more deeply. A man lay asleep beside her, a strange man, bathed in foreign moonlight. She dared to put out a hand and gently touch his bare shoulder. It was cold. Carefully she covered it, for it belonged to her lover. She laughed within the cavern of her stomach at how little he meant to her. She had released her body from her husband by lending it to another man, and now it belonged neither to her husband nor to the other man, but only to herself, as it had when she was a child, before anyone had touched it. (She could keep her body or she could lend it where she would, in strange beds, to strange bodies she had never seen.)

And here lay a man sleeping. In the morning he would wonder. He would wonder if he was the first, beside her husband, to hold her in passion. Perhaps he would pride himself, as men do, upon having seduced her; and this was a joke that tickled her deeply. Perhaps he would fall in love with her; but this she did not desire, for if he loved her he would too nearly become Mark.

The back of his head looked, where the hair swirled around a cowlick, like a small boy's. Mark's head looked like this, too, when it was turned from her in sleep. In this same way she had lain beside Mark, musing while he slept. In this same way countless women lay musing, beside countless sleeping men: husbands, or lovers. In a half-dream she felt an immense pitying tenderness, a vague maternal superiority, for Mark and David, suddenly become as one, playing at being men, then turning from her and falling, exhausted, into childish slumber. Babies clutching frantically at the mother's breast, greedy, aggressive, passionate, sucking at it in engrossed selfishness, then turning their tender heads, appeased, to sleep, their sated little mouths open, with little drops of milk. . . .

She shook David gently. You must go back to your own room, it will soon be morning. He arose, ashamed in the common light of morning, of his nakedness. He stumbled, he blinked his eyes, a child awakened in the middle of night to change beds. Alone, she laughed herself softly to sleep.

Her body vividly retained and relived every sensation. But in her mind, as she flew over shining tracks, away from David, back to Mark, remained only the knowledge of her release; the event was lost in its significance.

And now in the train it was in a few hours that she would see Mark. Their meeting was so impossible to conceive that Esther felt that her life would end as the train entered the station. It might be that seven days lived apart had made them strangers. It might be that Mark, coming to her after a stranger had come to her, would himself take on the quality of a stranger, and love her in a new, strange way; and this she both wanted and did not want. All her feelings about Mark left her puzzled.

She saw him in the station before he saw her, when

he was stepping about, puzzled, in his gray suit, looking about for her. She sat on her bench, with her bag at her feet, her book under her arm, like anybody else, like everybody else, unable to rise and greet him. She watched him. There was nothing in him of the stranger, his gray suit was even more familiar than his face. Mark appeared a familiar figure in a familiar world; she herself seemed a creature in a dream, unable to join him. She felt that if she were to speak to him, he would not feel: he would go on, blindly, regardless of words, regardless of her touch, looking about that station for the real Esther.

But as he turned in her direction, his face changed with recognition. He came toward her from a great distance, smiling, but with little accelerated pace. It came to her that perhaps Mark also was puzzled.

So many things occurred to her as he was coming toward her in his gray suit. Many circles separated her from him. Yet, unknowing, he walked calmly across them, a straight line penetrating the rims of many circles, yet coming no nearer. Eddies of sensation swept him now toward her, now backward, away from her. His figure was now large and clear, the only real thing in a cardboard station, and now dim and blurred, one of many in a big room. Suddenly he was upon her, and she felt her legs shakily obeying her, she felt herself rising mechanically to greet him.

Esther. . . .

Kisses in a station mean nothing; they show to indifferent spectators nothing, except that two people are related, by blood, marriage, or friendship.

Conversation in a street-car equally means nothing. One's husband says that you look well, that you are very sunburned. You reply that you hope he, poor thing, hasn't been overworking in all this city heat. There is a terrible embarrassment. . . . Together you imply that conversation, real conversation, is postponed until you reach privacy. Esther was frightened by the prospect of this approaching privacy; she wanted the street-car to continue forever, and yet she was impatient in it, restless. The reality of the street-car, the homeliness of it, the stuffy yellow smell of it, brought back to Esther more than the sight of Mark; the commonplaceness of their act in entering it gave her an odd sense of returning to life, of life going on, unimportantly, unchanged. Where then was the magic in her night with David? If fifty hours later one could enter a street-car and smell it and feel it no differently from before?

The sudden privacy of their home, the sudden rising on all sides of them of four known walls, was terrible. In the station, in the street-car, their intimacy had been to some extent apparent, in contrast to the indifferent passengers struggling with bags and children; because they had been unable to exchange anything more significant, they were unable to exchange glances of sympathy, of understanding, holding a promise of future

215

release. They had no longer any excuse; here was respon-sibility; their home, their being enclosed alone by four walls imposed upon them the convention of intimacy. Because there were no strange eyes upon them, their separateness from one another became more definite. Two people have lived together for a year, have been apart for the first time. Letters which said nothing have passed between them. Seven days have passed, which neither shared, nor can ever share, with the other.

They no longer know each other.

Here Mark can take off his coat; here Esther can fling aside her hat, casting eyes that recognize and appraise around a room she has not seen for a week. Here they can sprawl and light cigarettes. But they look at each other, helpless. They are embarrassed. It is not like returning to one whom one has known all one's life, it is not returning to a home in which one has lived all one's life. Before, they had felt this room to be a refuge from their old, separate homes, it had a newness, a novelty; because they had not lived here always, it seemed a wel-come temporary shelter. Before, they felt themselves to be engaging in a flight together: that they ate together, slept together, walked together, seemed remarkable, rather than habitual.

But it is returning to a place which makes it a home. Now suddenly the permanence of their room, the perma-nence of each other, are enhanced because one of them has been away, because she has come back. They do not know each other as habitual partners, they are frightened.

But Mark goes to Esther and puts his arms round her and kisses her many times, without looking at her. Between kisses he is able to say, never looking directly at her: Esther, you are home. You are home. Dear Esther, I missed you.

Esther said: *But what have you been doing, Mark?* Your letters said so little. For after all he too had had a kind of life, while she had been away, while she had been unfaithful to him.

They sat down to a breakfast which Mark had clumsily prepared. This touched her, and as she ate, she praised everything extravagantly. Mark's gratitude, his embarrassment, laid a tender responsibility on her. She wanted to comfort him, to warm him, to raise him. His deprecation, as he outlined the events of his week alone, hurt her. She smiled eagerly at him, pretending interest, while she tried to focus her attention. . . . And Saturday I had dinner with the Harrises and we talked so late they asked me to spend the night. Sunday we all took a ferry ride. I went to a theater with Alfred. . . .

Incredible, thought Esther: these events did not compose life. And yet, when he asked her in turn to describe her week, she said things like: We went for an all-day picnic. We climbed the highest mountain in the State. I had a huge appetite. I wrote you, didn't I? about the Barn Dance.

Of course, when she said all-day picnic, a thousand

pictures rose in her mind to make the words meaningful: David holding her in the air to be the highest person in the State. But when he said dinner with the Harrises, it was incredible, it was incredible that he and their friends had continued to exist while she was away. She tried to picture him there. She remembered the room in which the Harrises lived. But when she tried to imagine Mark sitting and talking with them far into the night, she saw herself inevitably sitting on the sofa laughing with Julia Harris. And yet these things had happened to him and she was not there.

Suddenly they talked more fluently. It seemed that the night Mark spent with the Harrises was more than a night spent with friends; for they had talked until morning, and in the course of their conversation Mark had had glimpses of features in the Harrises' relationship, a relationship which had often piqued him and Esther. This interested them both and drew them together. And then it developed that the mountain climb Esther had mentioned had more to it than a mere mountain climb; for it was topped by an Aurora Borealis, of a most remarkable sort: the lights were seen at first in a compact ball, closed like a fist in the middle of the sky, coloured in streaks like a ball of clay, and then the fist opened suddenly while they all watched and poured its contents on all sides of them, like an umbrella, David had said (who was David?), like an umbrella with multi-coloured ribs. And this reminded Mark . . . and that reminded Esther . . . until they spoke eagerly, remembering countless small things, interrupting each other more and more, until, laughing, they decided to take turns in telling.

And Esther, watching his eager face, comparing it with David's which she could scarcely remember, found in herself a certain reluctance to tell him things. She could not detect the point at which she began, resentfully, to feel herself slipping into old grooves; but suddenly she was aware of pouring herself into Mark till there was nothing left for herself. She had expected everything, nourished by the secret of her night with David, to be different, new. But everything was the same. Only that Esther was tortured by the impossibility of picturing, of believing in, Mark's life during those seven days in which she had been away. She was unreasoningly jealous that he had continued to eat, to sleep, to live, without her. But the present grew so substantial, so enduring, so much like a thing which had always gone on and always would, just so, without any changes, that sometimes Esther wondered if she *had* been away. And then, forcibly conjuring up her secret night in which to take refuge from this every-dayness, this complacency, she wondered if she had ever come back.

Mark, with his feet on a chair, was feeling the first of these, that she had never been away. His surprise at seeing her had worn off. He listened to her as one does to a story, rather than to an intimate journal; he selected the events which most amused him and laughed joyously, so that these became the most amusing also to Esther. She hated this: she hated the pressure of his guiding hand, she hated this turning herself inside out to please him. She dug out of herself the buried memory of her night with David. She wrapped herself away from Mark in her secret and became silent.

He said: Say there, none of that, you're back now, you've got to amuse me, that's what I keep you for.

She hated his matter-of-fact humour. But also she was seized by her old, fearful desire to please him. She told him how the girls had taken David Wood's enormous shoes and flung them far out on the water, how enraged they were when the big things calmly floated on the surface. At the mention of David, she felt a malicious pleasure, although she could scarcely picture his face.

She was silent again, staring out of the window, trying to recall the face of David, with whom she had slept, trying to escape from the intimacy that grew and entangled her in the room, which seemed suddenly small and close. Mark imposed on her silence. Or he spoke, demanding an answer. She answered quickly, her mind rebelling, the image of David becoming faded and dim, like the faces in old daguerreotypes.

Then Mark read aloud from an article he had found in the paper and put aside to read to her. His scorn, curling round the article, breaking his voice, extended to her because she could not share it in equal measure.

She struggled vainly for a vision of David.

She had built with David a small house. Then she had turned him out of it, because she wanted to live in it alone, she wanted to take refuge in it from Mark. But when she retired into it, when she bolted its doors, it collapsed, it fell about her feet; Mark looked through its walls and she was as naked as though it had never been built. The house did not exist because Mark did not see it. . . .

And here is Mark, coming toward her, invading her secret, her invisible world, as though it did not exist: Mark with desire in his eyes. His coming now is different from his coming to her in the station. Now he comes firmly, with assurance. different from David's: it is unclouded by doubt. Resentful, yet relenting beneath his hand, she puts her fingers in his hair, on the back of his solid neck; he kisses her deeply at once, he needs no preliminary. He carries her to the bed and undresses her, a happy child unwrapping a gift.

Again, again, it is happening. His desire, stealing into her blood, robs her of secrecy, awakens her own ardor. What he feels, she must come to feel. Sweet, sweet, to submit. . . . But this must not happen again—David, Stranger, where are you, help me!—and unwillingly she rouses herself out of the pleasant languor into which she is sinking.

Stop, stop, I must speak to you first, I have something to tell you.

She was answered by his frightened look, his immediate attention.

She spoke it all in one breath. At the Farm . . . David . . . I let him. . . . We slept together.

She felt her body cower beneath his uncomprehending stare. She saw the knowledge of what she had told him pass through his ears and into his eyes. And with the telling she saw that she had destroyed her only secret; she had let him into the very house she had built against him.

His eyes were rapidly and curiously surveying her body. His look seemed to her the acme of curiosity, disembodied from emotion. Yet here was a man looking upon the body of his wife and imagining it perhaps in the embrace of a stranger. His gaze was endless, insatiable. She wished she could swallow her words.

It doesn't seem to mean anything, he said to her. It doesn't make sense, he said.

He touched her body curiously with his fingers, a child investigating a dropped toy, discovering to its amazement that it is intact. He smiled. Esther saw his eyes withdraw from her body, she saw come into them an intentness which meant that he was looking into himself.

Esther, he said, puzzled, I don't seem to feel anything. Esther, it's as though it hadn't happened. You see, I wasn't there. I can't believe, Esther, he said as he smiled, I can't believe that it really happened. I wasn't there, don't you see, Esther: it has nothing to do with me.

It had only to do with him, thought Esther ruefully; David was nothing, David was an academic memory, an empty symbol. The night with David was remote. The night with David had never been. There was only Mark: there was fighting against Mark, and there was being with Mark: but there was nobody else.

My Esther, said Mark, and he took her two hands, and his words and his look and his gesture shut out unreality from them and warmed and lighted the house in which they lived together. Let us not allow irrelevancies to come between us. I want you.

She was lost, she had come back to him, she had never been away. She was as a river brushed by the wind . . . but on the shore an imp of consciousness stood and mocked, and then was lost to sight. That imp, she knew, would meet her and torture her again . . . but later, later, later.

The Times So Unsettled Are

Redbook, March 1935

The little Austrian girl Mariedel, sitting numbly in her deck-chair (they were passing Ellis Island now and soon would dock), had not cried for twenty years, since she was ten. Then they had brought home the body of her brother, killed on the Italian front, and Mariedel and her mother had wept unceasingly for three days. Her mother had virtually never stopped; meals and sleep and occasional bursts of gayety were merely interludes for Mariedel's mother, for her real life had been given over for almost twenty years to weeping. But Mariedel had never had a tear again—not for her father, horribly wounded toward the end of the War, nor for her second brother dead of some mysterious disease in the trenches; not even for her sweetheart Heinrich who had died two months ago, shot down on the parapets of the Karl Marx Workers' Home which he had always predicted would some day serve as barricades. Heinrich is dead, they said to her very gently—her weeping mother, her crippled father, her friends—Heinrich has been killed, Mariedel, don't you understand, don't you hear us? Yes, said Mariedel over and over again; I understand; Heinrich is dead—and I am going to America; the *Amerikaners,* Richard and *die schöne* Mahli, they always asked us to come, but now Heinrich is dead and so I am going alone; excuse me, but I cannot weep. For she had cried herself out in 1914, and no tears were left for Heinrich, whom she loved the most.

What had died really for Mariedel was Vienna, her beloved city. It was not the Vienna her parents had known, of course—all her life she heard them tell sadly of the music now withdrawn from the cafés, of the balls and excursions and military splendor that were gone forever. But that was not Mariedel's Vienna. Mariedel's *Wien* was a tortured little city with the bravest and saddest and oldest young people in the world. Night after night they sat in the cafés, Mariedel and Heinrich and their contemporaries, and talked of Vienna's future, so bound up with their own—and most of them looked to Socialism as their parents had to God. Five of their number had killed themselves—one apparently for love, the others for vaguer reasons; yet no one was particularly shocked, reasons were not sought for long;

they all understood, the rest of them, meeting again to drink coffee in the *Herrenhof,* that Karl or Mitzi or Hans had been pushed just so much farther than he or she could endure, and that at any moment it might happen to one of the surviving coffee--drinkers. The times are so unsettled, they said, explaining to themselves, and to the childishly emotional Richard and Mahli from *Amerika;* and nodded much as their elders did, and went on drinking their coffee.

They had gone in, too, their little band, for resolutions to leave Vienna, to strike out for Berlin which they hated, or America which they feared. There things always seemed to go better; one could have a job that might lead somewhere; one might marry and raise children; one might take part in a government less deadlocked than their own—there might perhaps be a future more vital than drinking coffee in the same *Café-Haus* every night. But none of them ever left. And when the *Amerikaners, die schöne* Molly (who signed her letters "Mahli" when she wrote to Mariedel, because that was Mariedel's way of saying it) and Richard, came and were taken into their midst for the brief and lovely month of their honeymoon, and begged them all to come to America and start life over again, they had all of them laughed and shrugged their shoulders and said *"vielleicht"* and known very well that they would never leave Vienna. Richard and Mahli had laughed too, and said that when they came to celebrate their golden wedding, they would undoubtedly find their old friends in the same *Café-Haus,* at the same round table in the corner, the men with long white beards—all laughing and promising to come to America and ordering another cup of coffee: with *Schlagobers* when they could afford it.

Richard and Mahli had been particular friends of Heinrich and Mariedel, even though Heinrich was never gay and always distrustful of strangers, especially tourists, especially Americans, of anyone who was not a Socialist, in short. But they were so warming, Richard and Mahli, so happy together, and so much in love that everybody fell in love with the pair of them—just as they fell in love with everyone they met and the whole little city of Vienna, which they never tired of comparing with their own New York. They talked German so badly, especially Mahli, and so eagerly—it was so funny to hear them addressing each other as *"sie"* because they could not learn the ramifications of the personal pronoun. And they looked so hopelessly, so ridiculously American—Mahli like a tall American chorus girl in the pink and blue peasant *dirndl* which she wore about their rooms, with her boyish hair-cut and her tiny American breasts which scarcely bulged above the apron; and Richard, attempting on Sundays to resemble his Viennese comrades on their *Ausflüge,* continued to look like a cartoon of an American in his baggy knickers and shoes with saddles, and his horn-rimmed glasses through which his eyes looked so straight and pleasantly clear.

The most disillusioned of their little band had fallen in love with these Americans, even Heinrich, bitten with distrust and worse (for Heinrich had stopped believing in God more suddenly than was good for him)—even Heinrich had let the Americans laugh at him and tease him, and sometimes he was almost able to joke back, just like Mariedel.

The Americans had chosen Heinrich and Mariedel for their particular friends because they saw that they too were in love. But Mariedel knew that theirs was a different sort of love; they had been brought up, Mariedel and Heinrich, in too much poverty and change, and their love was more of a refuge than a source of gayety to them, it was a necessity as bitter as the need for bread. They loved each other in the way that sole survivors on a ship must love—and they did not doubt each other, but they doubted themselves and everything about them. For in a shipwreck such as theirs, where brothers turned on brothers and fathers against their sons, how could they be sure even of their love enduring? And Heinrich was so bitter that he even doubted love— in his mind, that is; in his bitter mind; for his heart (which Heinrich believed as poor a word as God) had really never failed her. No, Heinrich, snatched from the University and forced to earn a living for his widowed mother and his sisters, who hated him for supporting them and hated him for being a Socialist, starving and living in wretched, disease-ridden quarters, could not allow himself to be happy in the "unsettled times." He could enjoy nothing that was not whole and lasting, could trust nothing that was not severe.

He had been an ardent Socialist; but when the Socialists took over Vienna, had Heinrich permitted himself to be really happy? to rejoice? Not for long. There were his Socialists, doing all the things he had wanted them to do; they taxed the rich; they housed the poor—but Heinrich was never satisfied: they must tax the rich ever harder, they must house the poor better and faster, they must carry on the fight in the country outside Vienna, or Heinrich predicted their downfall. Mariedel and Heinrich would wander arm in arm through the fine courts of the Workers' Houses, where the poor were quickly learning the cleanliness and healthful habits of the rich, they would look into the community stores lining the streets below, they would visit the charming practical apartments where sunlight and plenty of heat entered every room—and Mariedel had felt happy, happy as she had been in her childhood before the War, when everything was good and gay and plentiful. Look, Heinrich, look at the little children wading in the community fountain— two months ago they would not have known what it is to have a bath. Look, Heinrich, the mothers, so proud of their new homes, their clean children; how well they care for the gardens, they who a short time before saw only a potted flower now and then. Look, Heinrich, at the new building going up over the hill, how fast it rises, the workmen love what they are building, the bricks fly into place as though they loved it too. Everyone, everything, working together, Heinrich, for the poor, at last, for the majority, the real people, look, Heinrich, is it not beautiful and gay? But the lean look never went from Heinrich's eyes, not altogether; yes, there would be pride in them as he saw how swiftly building after building mounted the old streets, how each house was better than the last—but he would run his hand along the parapets above the courtyards where the children played: "Some day these all will be barricades, Mariedel, it cannot be done through peace, we must have more blood-shed, Mariedel, before the rich will permit such houses to stand for the poor." His eyes would sweep the dingy sections of old Vienna, spread below them. "All that must be wiped out and built over, Mariedel, work must be done faster, we must be stronger, more inexorable, like the Communists—too many of our Socialists are dreamers, and these houses, they are so few, Mariedel, they are built on dreams instead of power." He would not take transient happiness; in the same way he would not really take her love. Perhaps he was waiting till the world too should be wiped out and built over, a fit thing to house their love.

"But you poor silly children," the happy Mahli had cried, out of her own joy and love; "you are in love, you live together when you can, why don't you get married and do it properly?" Mariedel and Heinrich laughed and shrugged their shoulders; naturally Mariedel would have married Heinrich any time he said, but in her heart she knew it was wrong as long as either of them had a reservation. She too longed for a whole country that could live and eat in peace and security, a world which could wipe out the memory of a brother brought home dead from the Italian front and causing a little sister to shed the last of her tears. "Oh, Mahli," she had said often in her faulty English, "the times here so unsettled are." And Richard and Mahli had laughed at her English and hugged each other and hugged Mariedel and Heinrich, and sung over and over again, "Oh Mahli, the times so unsettled are."

"But you ought to come back with us!" Richard and Mahli had cried together. "We'll find jobs for you somehow, Richard, your father, darrling—you could live right next door to us, we'd find them a place, wouldn't we, darrling—you bet we would, beloved—and then you could be married and live the way we do, the way you ought to. Vienna is lovely for a honeymoon (thank you, Richard darrling) but for young people starting out it's dead from the neck down, isn't it, beloved? Of course it is, darrling. So do come back with us," they cried together, "Mariedel and Heinrich, won't you, couldn't you really now?"

Mariedel had smiled softly across the table to Heinrich. To tell him that if he went to America of course she would come too; to tell him that if he stayed behind in Vienna and spent the rest of his life fighting and being underfed, she would stay with him anyway; to tell him that she loved him. Heinrich had always the same answer to make in his precise, cold, studied English—but smiling, for he loved these Americans and their contentment was infectious: "If Vienna is dead, then Mariedel and I are dead too, Vienna is our city. We will live with it or die with it. If we do not marry, it is because we do not believe in marriage; marriage does not stop a husband from being killed in war or revolution, it does not stop a wife from having too little to feed her children, it does not even ensure love. Yes, we would like to be married, if it would mean that we could live as we believe people should. But, for us in Vienna, we must fight and keep on fighting. . . ." And Mariedel, loving him and aching for him, painfully wishing to be loyal and to be thought loyal in the eyes of the Americans, would look across at Mahli and try to make her understand by making her laugh: "With us, it is so different, Mahli—the times so unsettled are."

In the end, of course, everything that Heinrich said was proven right. The Socialists had not lasted, their dreams had been put down by blood-shed, blood-shed in which Heinrich himself, who loved peace and wanted peace more than anything in life, more even perhaps than he wanted Mariedel, in whom he sought it, had voluntarily taken part. And he was right too, it was as well to be still young and to lose one's life-long lover as it would have been to lose a husband; however it was,

Mariedel, on hearing her father and her mother and all her friends murmur gently, Mariedel, Heinrich has been killed, can't you understand?—Mariedel could not weep. It was as if she had wept for the death of Heinrich almost twenty years before, when she wept for the death of her brother. The old folks went on weeping when once they got started—Mariedel's mother had never left off again; but Mariedel was still of that younger stock, that had shed their last tears with their first, and Mariedel could not weep, she must go on living somehow. Almost at once the memory of Mahli and Richard had come back to her like a little island of safety in the middle of all the chaos. She would go to America. They would revive that little month in which she and Heinrich had been so nearly happy with their American friends; and in any case, Mariedel would find something to shock her from this numbness. And so she had written to Mahli, saying that Heinrich was dead; saying to forgive her for not writing in nearly three years but that the times so *very* unsettled had been that there had seemed somehow little use; and that now Mariedel would like to come along to America—since the Socialists were finished, and many of her friends now dead or scattered, and *Wien,* as Heinrich had prophesied, as the lieber Richard had said too, was dead as well. Mahli's cablegram had been prompt, the first thing after Heinrich's death that meant anything to Mariedel: "Come soon as you can arrange so sorry about Heinrich visit me as long as you like love Mahli." She had even remembered to sign her name "Mahli"!

So it was all over with Heinrich and Vienna and the Socialists, thought Mariedel, sitting numbly in her steamer-chair when they told her they would be landing in thirty minutes now. She thought she would never go back, unless it were to die. And she remembered that last sight of the crumbling Workers' Home—which would now, her old father said, be turned over to the rich to do anything with they liked, while the poor would be thrown out on the streets again—where Heinrich had met his death. Broken glass and legs of furniture lay scattered on the ramparts; there were blood-stains on the parapets which Heinrich had rightfully seen as barricades. She had stood there, as numb as she was now in her steamer-chair, with twenty-years-old tears frozen in her throat. They had all hoped that the sight of the ruined Home where Heinrich had died would make Mariedel weep again; they wanted her to weep, to weep as she had when she was a child, because they thought that was nature's way of healing. Mariedel had wanted to weep too. But she could only stand there, wondering if Heinrich had been right—that the Socialists should have trained an army and fought with the weapons of their enemies, even though their end was peace; and wondering too if Heinrich had been right about that other thing that he always so passionately declared, that there was no God, that the sooner people knew it the better it would be for them.

For Heinrich, of course, with all the unhappy youths of his age, had been a violent atheist. Mariedel herself never went to church, not since they had been to the funeral of her second brother; and she knew that her mother went only to find another place in which to weep and remember, and weep more hotly. No, Mariedel did not believe in any sort of church-God; and yet she never brought herself to curse the thought, as Heinrich had. It was as if Heinrich, expecting things from some King of Kings, turned his disappointment to denial that that King had ever existed. Mariedel expected very little, except perhaps Heinrich's love—and perhaps that was it, for her, perhaps that was why in the inner parts of her brain, or her heart (which Heinrich never let her talk about, because it sounded synonymous with God) she nevertheless held some sort of belief in something. If it had been Mariedel who had been killed, she felt now, instead of Heinrich, then Heinrich would have seen in her death still further proof that there was no God; but Mariedel, not even able to weep for Heinrich, knew that there had been *something* between them, which no chemical could account for and no revolution wipe out—something in their hearts which not even Heinrich's death could end. She had it still, she had his love for her and her love for him, and sitting there in her deck-chair, not speaking to a soul on board, remembering numbly how her city and her lover and all that they had stood for were dead, she still could not say there was no God, she still felt that something went on which outwitted death and outlasted life. . . . And perhaps it was this that she was really going to America for, to find it again in the lives of Richard and Mahli and keep it somehow vicariously lighted in herself through them.

Now the great city of New York was in her sight for the first time, and again she thought that there must be something, *something,* beyond greed and restlessness, which led people to building up great towns and preparing for so much life. The city looked to her like a city of closely packed cathedrals, and she imagined that the streets must run like dark little aisles at their feet. And this was where Mahli and Richard belonged, probably they lived back in the heart of the magnificence somewhere, out of sight of the sea and the dividing rivers, protected forever by these looming towers. Heinrich's words about the barricades came into her mind for a moment, as she stood with her hand on the rail, and she thought perhaps some day all those many windows might be crenelles, the buildings fortresses. Perhaps she was slightly dizzy, as the boat ceased motion. For the buildings swayed a bit before her eyes, and for a moment looked less like cathedrals than like spears, like bayonets, marching in line over the heads of dead and living soldiers. . . .

***

"Mariedel, Mariedel!" Richard and Mahli, her dear Americans, were kissing her one moment and lightly weeping the next—they were unchanged in these seven years, Richard with his mild steady glare through his horn-rimmed spectacles, and Molly, tall and American as ever, with a gentle fringed bang to her eyebrows now, and her bright mouth painted redder than before, and her wonderful chic clothing that made her look like a mannequin. Mariedel stood dazed, allowing herself to be kissed and wept over—how easily happy people wept, either for joy or for sorrow!—and then stood with her hand through Mahli's while Richard did wonderful American things to find and get rid of her luggage. "This is a real reunion," said Richard, coming back, and speaking unconsciously a little louder to Mariedel as he always had, as Americans were always doing, as though foreigners must be slightly deaf, "a real reunion, and we ought to celebrate—in a real American *Café-Haus,* Mariedel?"

"In the Childs, in the Childs," said Mariedel eagerly remembering, "where you said you would some day show Heinrich and me, the very table where you sat and figured on paper napkins how you could marry and you forgot to leave out for the laundry, do you not remember, Richard and Mahli?"

"But—" began Mahli. They hesitated a bit, those dear Americans of hers, and Mariedel felt she guessed the reason. "No, no, you think I am sad, that it will make me sad, because of Heinrich, but it will make me gay—it is what I have come to America for," she begged them; "I want to see where Richard told Mahli, and Mahli told Richard, and about the laundry, and the lady making jack-flaps in the window—"

"Flap-jacks, you darling," said Mahli, hugging Mariedel again. And Richard said, "A real reunion, Molly, we might as well do it up brown," and Mariedel felt again their delicacy, their shyness with each other in her presence, because they didn't want to hurt her. She must explain it to them, how she had come all the way across an ocean to see them with each other. Richard said again, "What do you say, Molly?" and Molly, taking Mariedel's arm, cried, "Off for the reunion in Vienna!" So then everything was beginning to be all right again, and they found a taxi and Richard said solemnly to the driver, "Childs, on Fifth Avenue, where the best paper napkins are," and Mariedel sat between them holding both their hands and chattering briskly to put them at their ease about her and looking out at the strange streets and feeling thankful to God that she was here with them.

They came into the big clean restaurant, Mariedel dancing on her sea-legs, and because it was late afternoon it was fairly empty, and Richard and Mahli were able to find the same table in a corner that they had sat at years ago. "It is a reunion, a reunion," Richard kept saying, with his steady clear American eyes on his Molly—and Molly was beginning to look at him, and Mariedel felt happy that her Americans were remembering things and perfectly happy to be left out for the moment. "Only I am going to have a cocktail this time," said Mahli gayly, "just think, Mariedel, in those days one could not drink cocktails except in practically cellars, and now, right here in Childs. . . ." "I wish you would take just butter-cakes and coffee," said Mahli's Richard softly, "then it would be a real reunion. . . ." "Reunion, reunion, who's got the reunion," said Mahli merrily; and Mariedel knew it was an American joke of some kind and laughed in order to be one of them, and then saw that neither of them was laughing as Mahli turned to the waitress and re-peated firmly, "Yes, a Manhattan, please."

"Tell us, Mariedel," said Richard gently, "about your poor Heinrich, how terrible it must have been for you."

"No, no," cried Mariedel, "I do not want to talk about Heinrich, I want to talk about Richard and Mahli, I want to hear again how you say darrling to each other, and then there was something Richard used to say—"

"Oh, don't talk about *us*" cried Mahli, tipping her little velvet beret deeper over the fringe, "we want to hear all about Vienna, so terribly sad, awful about those beautiful houses and everything—"

"But I do not want to talk about all that," Mariedel explained to her Americans, "I want, I have come such a long way, just to see two people happy once more. Do you see, I have remembered so much, it gives me only joy to see you two happy, just as in *Wien* seven years ago.

. . . Always darrling this and darrling that—and that other word, Richard used to say—"

"I think I will have a cocktail too," said Richard suddenly. "How are the Manhattans, M—Beloved?"

"That is it, that is it—Beloved!" cried Mariedel, clapping her hands joyfully. "Ah, now it is like the old days! Heinrich and Mariedel, Richard and Mahli. . "

"The Manhattans are swell, darrling," said Mahli quietly. "Here's to you, Beloved," said Richard, lifting his little glass and staring at her through his spectacles. "To you, Mariedel darrling," said Mahli, but her eyes were returning Richard's gaze, and Mariedel could see that the two of them, Richard with his level eyes and Mahli with her red mouth made up for laughing were growing soft and misty again. Because this was where they had come, Mariedel thought happily (refusing herself to drink anything but coffee), this was where they had come and figured on paper napkins how they could make do, with Richard's little salary. It was not much like the Herrenhof, where Heinrich and Mariedel had come every night and figured on the marble tabletops how they could *not* make do—but it was lovely and clean and gay, and Richard was looking at his Mahli, not *quite* as Heinrich had ever been able to do, but surely as he had wanted to, as he had been meant to, if only so much misfortune, so much unsettledness. . . .

But her Americans had put down their glasses and remembered her again. "And what do you think of our skyline, *gnädiges* Fraülein," Richard was trying to say.

"Ah, do you not remember her, Richard," cried Mariedel, waving his nonsense away, "do you not remember her as she must have looked that night? In a blue sweater, you said—?"

"Yes," said Richard, nodding gravely. "Yes, she was wearing a bright blue sweater and a bright blue skirt, and it was summer and both of us had come out without our hats. She looked rather remarkably beautiful that night, if my memory doesn't play me tricks—"

"Though he couldn't have possibly seen me, Mariedel," said Mahli, "because he was so nervous he kept taking off his glasses and wiping them and doing tricks like making the cream stay on top of the coffee—"

"Whereas she, Mariedel," said Richard, "she was so calm and poised that she spilled most of hers all over that bright blue skirt."

"I did not, you fancy liar, it was you, you admitted it."

"Always a gentleman, Beloved."

"How silly we are, how boring to Mariedel," murmured Mahli.

"No, it is lovely," said Mariedel, "please, you have not come to the part about the laundry yet." She saw how the drinks were making them grow less shy before her, how each time they started speaking to her and ended by addressing one another as though they had no audience. "It was a terribly hot evening," she helped them out, "there was Donner *und* Blitzen," she prompted Richard. . . .

"and she pretended to be frightened"

"and we went on drinking coffee even though it was so hot because we didn't want to ever go home and end that evening"

"we sat through three shifts of waitresses, Beloved"

"I must have journeyed to the Ladies' Room four times"

"and when we'd checked through telephone bills— and were going to save by using candles instead of electricity—"

"then suddenly we discovered about the laundry, darrling"

"and Beloved do you remember I said something about how I wanted a dependable wife"

"and I was simply scared to death darrling, I almost burst out crying, I thought you were going to tell me I wouldn't do or something."

There was a mild diminuendo in their sweet gay American *Tristan,* and Mariedel saw that they both had tears, these Americans, as volatile as children—even Mahli with her bright red lips not made up for crying at all.

"And there was that frightened little moment after we had both said yes to each other when we thought that we would never again have anything to talk about"

"Oh, it was terrible, Mariedel," said Mahli, wiping her eyes, "we sat there and were afraid to look at one another—"

"and then—" said Richard.

"and then luckily we both started laughing at the same moment and that saved the day, darrling" "we confessed to each other, Beloved, how scared to death we were"

"and then we weren't any more, because we knew that—"

"because we thought—"

They were silent for a moment and Mariedel sat poised and expectant.

"We thought we could always laugh together in the bad moments," said Mahli softly.

"We nearly always did, Beloved."

"Only of course there are some things, darrling."

"Yes, there are some things, Molly."

There was a curious hiatus in their song now, coming, thought Mariedel, in the wrong place, just as they had been mounting to the allegro—and she sat perfectly still, feeling that perhaps they were going on with it silently, between themselves, in some other, private realms she mustn't enter. They looked at each other for a long time, and then looked away at the same moment. "It wasn't our fault," said Richard, setting down his glass. "No, it wasn't anybody's fault," said Molly, the tears rolling down past her bright red lips and falling into her empty cocktail. "Shall we have another drink, Molly?" said Richard, leaning across the table as though he were asking her something else. "No, I think not," said Molly, lifting her head and beginning to blink away her tears, "I think then nobody would be able to laugh at anything any more." And as Mariedel sat bewildered, out came

Molly's purse and from it a little red stick, with which Molly painted on another laughing mouth. "Heavens above," cried Molly gaily, "what awful fools Mariedel must think Americans are—and here we sit and sit with all of the sights ahead of us still, we must think what we would like to do this evening, Mariedel darrling—"

"Shall I—" began Richard, taking out his watch but looking at Molly instead.

"Yes, please, Richard, I think it would be better," said Molly smiling brightly through her new red lips.

"I guess you're right," said Richard, and to Mariedel's surprise he cheerfully whipped his watch back into his pocket again and rose and tossed his paper napkin on the table. "It's been a beautiful reunion, Mariedel, hasn't it?"

"You—you are going?" said Mariedel, feeling suddenly frightened and lonely.

"Why yes, I have to be going," said Richard easily; "but I'll see you again, Mariedel, for sure."

"You have to *go?*" said Mariedel, feeling stupid and shy.

"Yes, he has to go, Mariedel," said Mahli gravely. "Goodbye, darrling, it was a beautiful reunion."

"Goodbye, Beloved. Goodbye, Mariedel."

"But what is it," cried Mariedel, feeling as she had twenty years ago when her mother had opened the telegram from the War Office, black apprehensive despair and her limbs gone hollow, her heart beating like somebody else's heart—"what is it," she cried again, feeling she was a stupid Austrian girl, that perhaps her life, the death of Heinrich, everything, had unhinged her more than she knew.

"It wasn't anybody's fault, Mariedel," said Molly, putting her too-red lips to the empty cocktail glass. "It wasn't her fault and it wasn't mine," said Richard, standing now and putting his hands on both their shoulders—almost impersonal he was, Mariedel thought, as though he wished to comfort them, to apologize, for something none of them could help. "It was just as you used to say, Mariedel," said Molly, smiling and grave— and Mariedel could hear Heinrich telling her bleakly, through his bitten lips, that there was no God, that marriage did not ensure food, or peace, or even love—"here in America too—the times unsettled are."

Suddenly Mariedel was crying, crying as she had when the first thing went out of her life, for now the last thing was going too—and Molly with her red mouth not made up for crying, was crying too, and comforting her, as Richard walked away.

After the Party

First published in
Time: The Present, 1935.

Mrs. Colborne had given three cocktail parties a week in honor of various celebrities, ever since her nervous breakdown back in 1930. The doctor had told her then, when she was convalescing, that she must get interested in something; he suggested dancing (she felt she was too old), social work (but she shuddered, she had had dreadful experiences, really dreadful), writing a novel, going round the world, being psychoanalyzed in Vienna, studying economics in London, taking a course in sculpture, endowing a hospital, adopting a baby, breeding dogs, Christian Science (he was very broad), collecting early clocks, marrying again (oh dear no, Mrs. Colborne said, that was as bad as social work), starting a publishing house, running an interior decorating shop, moving to the country, or learning to hand-paint china. But Mrs. Colborne twitched her head, in that odd way that was part of her neurosis, to all of these suggestions; and at last they had settled that she should give parties, parties *for* people, in order that she should feel she had some contact with the world still.

They had talked over what kind of people Mrs. Colborne should give the parties for, and many interesting things, both about people and about parties, were revealed. For instance, Mrs. Colborne said, if she had musicians they would just come and stand about not talking and looking like Poles; you had to *push* musicians, Mrs. Colborne said, to make them go, at a party. If she had painters, they would line up in factions, the surrealists against the muralists or whatever you called that radical new crowd, and simply shout each other down. There were obvious difficulties with actors, and dancers were always hungry and homosexual; Mrs. Colborne thought earnestly for a while of establishing a salon for critics only, music critics, dramatic critics, book-reviewers, and thus correlating the arts—but there would be scarcely any turn-over that way, for most of the columnists she knew of had apparently been appointed for life and their sons seemed slated to inherit after them. Suddenly Mrs. Colborne brightened; there were the writers!

The writers would supply her with an everchanging list for guests of honor and guests of honor's friends. The author of a best-seller this Spring would be the author of a critical survey of Russia or the New Deal in the Fall; this would bring in an amusing variety of guests, as the famous writer's circle changed. Then too writers seemed more like other people than most types of professionals—lots of them made money, they weren't inclined to be too temperamental, and many of them came from quite good families. And finally, even the very stupidest writer was, from the nature of his profession, able to talk—and after all, you select a good caterer for the sandwiches, you hire waiters to mix and pass the cocktails, but it is still talk, good old-fashioned talk, that makes a party. Mrs. Colborne twitched her head in that funny way she had developed during her breakdown, and smiled at the doctor. She would get well, she would give parties; she would get well in *order* to give parties.

***

Everybody said that Mrs. Colborne made a marvelous recovery, considering. She would never be absolutely well, she must rest a great deal, and she could neither eat nor drink at her own parties. But by sheer effort of will she did manage to re-establish her life. And she had had a dreadful time, a really dreadful time, enough to drive anybody to a breakdown, and Mrs. Colborne had always been rather sensitive. Of course, if it hadn't been for *Henry* Colborne. . . . Mrs. Colborne had been an angel with him, a perfect martyr; and the funny part of it was that no one knew a thing about Henry Colborne, no one thought of him as queer, or cruel, or stupid, until *after* Mrs. Colborne left him. Then, of course, the whole thing came out.

All of Mrs. Colborne's friends were horribly shocked. Oh yes, said Mrs. Colborne bravely, she had always known that Henry was a *Socialist,* at heart—in principle; he had been inclined that way even when she first met him, when they were both at school. Wore old clothes, in those days, wouldn't take her to the best places to dine, professed to be ashamed of his father's wealth— and all that; but that, Mrs. Colborne said, was all right, it was Youth and it was even attractive. Later, when they were married, he insisted on certain things like living in an unconventional part of town (Gramercy Park) and drew the line at butlers, parrots, and things like Smoka- dors—but otherwise he was all right, he was all right at parties even though he wouldn't play bridge, and it turned out that the Socialists he picked up were really very presentable and gentlemanly and could be invited anywhere, just fellows like himself who had been to Harvard or, at worst, sons of New England clergymen. No, it was not the Socialism that Mrs. Colborne objected to, not in the least; she thought herself that it was what we were all drifting toward in the long run *anyhow,* the New Deal and the N.R.A. and after all the Republican Party was out, everyone was down on the bankers and about half the brokers had already committed suicide. No, no, *Socialism* was all right. It was particularly nice,

Mrs. Colborne said, for people who hadn't any children, who *couldn't* have any children (Mrs. Colborne had had to have a very sad operation in the first years of her marriage, the women of her family were very delicately complicated inside)—for then these childless couples could feel that they were doing something for the future of other people's children anyway.

No, it wasn't the Socialism, Mrs. Colborne said unwillingly; and gradually the whole story came out. Henry Colborne had grown increasingly moody ever since the event of their discharged chauffeur. Henry said he was sick of being driven about by a flunkey, it was *chi-chi* (as he termed everything from Aubusson carpets to remote control) to have a liveried ape at the wheel; there was no reason in the world why both of them couldn't learn to drive. Mrs. Colborne didn't mind in the least, most of her friends drove their own cars, and she really found it fun. So they fired the chauffeur (with a month's extra wages, and presents of old clothes for his whole family), the chauffeur gave them an ugly look and came back a month later to rob them. Fortunately he was caught, unfortunately it was discovered to be his second offense, and in the end he was given—despite Henry's efforts to get him off—several years in jail. Of course Henry had undertaken to support the chauffeur's family—but that was all right too, Mrs Colborne said, only fair indeed, since they were the victims of social injustice and all that. But Henry had begun to grow moody then.

He began to keep Mrs. Colborne up all night talking, and torturing her with tales he picked up, the Lord knows where, about the suffering and starvation of the city's poor. He seemed to derive a peculiar morbid relish from making these tales as harrowing as he could. Some of them Mrs. Colborne felt he rather exaggerated; others were, we all know too well, she said, lamentably true. But what could they do about it, Mrs. Colborne said, what *more* could they do about it, that is, than they were doing? They gave plenty of money away to anyone they heard about needing it, they supported the chauffeur's whole family, and they were already "carrying" members of their own who had never recovered from the War. Well? Mrs. Colborne asked him; what about Socialism? aren't we Socialists after all?

Socialism! Henry flung back at her. I'm talking about the working classes, do you think they're Socialists? have I ever brought a bricklayer in overalls home to dinner? I should hope not, Mrs. Colborne had said complacently; after all, we've all read that play of Shaw's about the lady that made her family wait on the servants one day every year and the servants were as miserable as the family, we all know those things don't work, they belong in the realm of Idealism. It was Barrie, not Shaw, who wrote that God-damned drivel, Henry had simply shouted at her, flung out of the house, and for the first time in their twenty years of married life spent the night away from her.

After that things went from bad to worse. He refused to accompany her places, forcing her to go to dinners by herself and to account for his embarrassing absences as best she could, and either maintained a disagreeable silence or shouted unpleasant things when they had guests at home. On one occasion he mortified her by refusing to dress for a welfare ball, and another time he insisted on coming to the opera early, before the overture even, because he said he was curious about the beginnings of operas, nobody had ever heard one and he half suspected that they hadn't any. Ridiculous things like that. Another night when they were coming home from the theater he sat on the little side-seat and left the window open allowing the night-air to blow down her neck, so that he could talk to the taxi-driver—and of all things, he asked him about his whole life, about a taxi-driver's pay, and if they had a union. Mrs. Colborne said of course the taxidriver looked at him queerly. But the worst thing was his shaking hands with a waiter one evening and calling him Comrade—Goodnight, Comrade, he said with the strangest smile—and after that (after the humiliation of seeing the waiter "indulge" a half-cracked customer), after that Mrs. Colborne frankly told Henry that she preferred not to go out with him at all.

Obviously they were headed for disaster. Mrs. Colborne began to feel shooting pains that she knew were not neuralgia, in the cords of her neck, at the back of her head. Henry said unfeelingly that the pains came from having been "stiff-necked" all her life and that he wouldn't be surprised if pretty soon her chin began to ache from holding it so high in the air. Then he fell to talking to her very earnestly, almost like a clergyman, about her *soul.* He said wasn't she tired and ashamed of the empty life they led. Empty! Mrs. Colborne tried to show him where he was wrong, tried to point out that they not only kept busier than many people but actually *did* more—she cited the chauffeur's family. It was not her fault, she said pathetically, that they had not had children; she had always wanted children—two. No, no, he kept saying, that wasn't what he meant; what he meant was, wasn't she tired of their living so easily and well when other people, *most* other people—and then he went on with his harrowing tales about the poor and the sick and the starving. When she put her hand to her heart one night (in the midst of one of his stories) and said quietly that she had a terrible pain there and did he think she ought to try psychoanalysis before she had another metabolism test, he said, listen, maybe what's hurting you is the same thing that's hurting me, my conscience.

But when the stock market fell in the Fall of '29, Henry seemed to take a turn for the better. He became more normal, Mrs. Colborne said. He worried to death, like anyone else. He stopped torturing her with his terrible stories, and seemed as eager as she to visit their friends and exchange information and hunches and advice. He figured all night, like everybody else, how to save their investments—and he was cleverer than most of their friends, in the end he saved nearly every penny both of her fortune and his own. Mrs Colborne said that despite the financial worry, she had a happier time then with Henry than she had had for over a year. This was because, although he drank pretty heavily that Winter, and his hair turned a little gray, he *did* seem normal again, as though he had got both feet on the ground once more. And Mrs. Colborne felt much better, she was able to get up for breakfast again, and the two of them had a happy time worrying and adding and subtracting together like any decent married people in that Winter. The second stock market break in the Spring sent, not Mrs. Colborne, but Henry himself, to bed with symptoms of the flu and nerves, and Mrs. Colborne's nerves and pains left her completely for three weeks, so that she could nurse Henry well again.

And then, then of all times, after their happy interlude, after Henry had saved an incredible amount of both their fortunes, came the tragedy. For Henry came out of his illness another man. He was very quiet and abstracted for a week or so, and one night said to her quite clearly that they must have a talk. He had been doing, Henry told Mrs. Colborne, a great deal of thinking during his depression illness. Of course, Mrs. Colborne said understandingly; one comes close to death and it does things to one; it changes one's whole horizon. Henry said yes, that was just what had happened to him: only that *he* was planning to change the horizon himself, change his whole way of life—and Mrs. Colborne said she asked him if he would like to adopt a couple of children.

Henry smiled quietly—afterward Mrs. Colborne said she thought there was something a little mad in that new quiet smile of his—and said, no, he couldn't afford two children, nor even one. Mrs. Colborne said that was very selfish of him, he wouldn't have to sacrifice anything to support two children. Henry said no, he couldn't afford even one child, or one anything—because, he said, with that mad smile, he was *giving away every cent of money he had in the world.*

Purely selfish, Henry went on that awful new smile—just to save his soul. He said that $500,000 was the new low for souls since the Depression, and his present friends wouldn't take a cent less than all he'd got. He was giving a small income to the ex-chauffeur's family, and sums outright to his brother, who had crashed with the market, and some of his father's cousins' children; that, he said, was pure malice on his part, for these people either hadn't got any souls or he (Henry) had no interest in what became of them. For himself, Henry said, he was keeping nothing, nothing at all; and Mrs. Colborne had her own money in her own name. As for the rest of his soul's price, Henry said, he was distributing it to defense and propaganda organs of—*the Communist Party.*

He had discovered, Henry went on to explain in that super-rational tone of one completely mad, that as long as one possessed money, one was primarily concerned with it; that he had only just discovered, through his illness, that he himself was not immune from this universal fact, and had only caught on to himself thoroughly with a contemplation of the past strange Winter, when all his ideals and principles and feelings had been subordinated to the passion of saving his stocks. That he had be-come at the end of the Winter a nervous invalid as a result filled him with nothing short of horror, and left him utterly convinced that his one way of salvation, or survival even, was to remove, permanently and irrevocably, every cent of temptation that he had so cleverly salvaged for himself. In the same way, Henry said, he had become disillusioned with the tactics of the Socialists, who hoped by compromise and persuasion to win over kindly converts like his former self to sacrifice portions of their incomes; he knew too much about his own class, Henry said, to believe in it; and hence he believed that for the larger good of humanity, that class must be wiped out once and for all, and by nothing short of revolution. The Socialists, he said, were a halfway house, a stepping-stone; the Revolutionists were the ultimate Party. And there was absolutely nothing she could do or say about it, Henry went on to Mrs. Colborne, for he would as soon die as continue another week in the life they had always lived.

Mrs. Colborne said she was sure that the origin of those pains in her throat was sitting there that dreadful evening and keeping herself from screaming. For she saw everything in her whole life crashing in little bits about her feet; it seemed to her that Henry was taking a quiet, mad pleasure in smashing her life before her eyes. She couldn't speak. She just sat there silently, gently shaking her head as though she were pleading with him, Oh no, Henry, no, no, no.

It seems he offered Mrs. Colborne a chance to "save her soul" too, and named the entire sum of her fortune as the only price. She should be flattered, he said, that her soul brought in so much, and that he thought enough of her not to allow it to be marked down. Mrs. Colborne said that she just went on sitting there helplessly shaking her head (that motion that became so strangely exaggerated during her breakdown later) and not knowing what to do or say to bring him to his senses. She said that he looked to her, with that quiet glow in his eyes, like a man utterly *possessed.*

Then, it seems, Henry abandoned all pretense of levity, and grew terrifyingly solemn. Look, Helene, he said, let me show you something; what is the newest article of clothing you have on, and what did it cost? Mrs. Colborne was so bewildered that she told him the truth: a crepe de chine petticoat trimmed with hand-made lace from France; it had cost twenty-seven dollars. Henry described the con-ditions under which the French peasants had made that lace, and said the reason for those conditions was simply and directly Helene's fault: because she would pay no more than twenty-seven dollars, some of which went to the United States customs, some to the wholesale importer, and considerable to the retail department store where she had bought it. The French peasants who had made it in the first place, Henry said, were now, thanks to Mrs. Colborne, miserably starving and living under thatched roofs through which the ice and sleet dripped in on their new-born babies. Nor was that all, Henry said (though Mrs. Colborne was sure she had turned pale as death and her heart was beating painfully), for they must not forget the woman behind the counter who sold the finished petticoat to her—undoubtedly either a middle-aged woman with varicose veins or a skinny little girl with pernicious anemia from undernourishment—who made at most seventeen dollars a week. Nor must they leave out, continued Henry with relish, the truck driver and his kid assistant who delivered the parcel to their Gramercy Park home, whose scant salaries also came out of that twenty seven dollars and robbed the original French peasants of still more—and meantime the peasants' eyes were giving out because it was such very fine work, and of course there was no insurance and no pension for blind and aged lace-makers—and for all this, said Henry, and much more, you, my dear, and I, are *criminally responsible.*

Mrs. Colborne's head shook mutely from side to side as though she were saying *No, No, No,* to some invisible ally.

Now all these people, Henry said, the French peasants and their friends the stokers on the boats which carried the imports, the truck driver and his friends the million other truck drivers, the sales-girl and her numberless colleagues—and hundreds of millions more for we have forgotten such tribes as the miners, said Henry, not to speak of the factory hands, the underpaid navy, and the great unemployed—are leaguing together to finish us off. Their class, Henry said, the class he and Mrs. Colborne so ably represented, was in the very small minority, and as soon as the important majority, what he called the working classes, got themselves together and organized and learned enough about fighting and methods of communication with each other all over the world, they were going to rise in a body and smash the handful of capitalists—ruthlessly, Henry said, and justly.

No, No, No, said Mrs. Colborne's poor aching, shaking head.

There were then, Henry said, two courses for members of the upper classes to pursue. Either they could hang on for as long as they could and go under when their time came; or they could become human and see that their own decency was identified with the welfare of the masses. For his part he was going to join the masses and fight his own class; he hated his own class, and his whole heart and brain and soul wanted to be in this fight to finish it off and end its centuries of barbaric domination. Of course, Henry said, he would be looked upon with suspicion by his new comrades for a time; but after all, he was giving them his money, his soul, and the rest of his life; and once he was without a checking-account the important differences between himself and them would be dissolved. Besides, he owed them a huge debt, an unpayable debt, for his forty years of capitalism, and a little mental unease was not too much interest to pay. To this life, Henry said with madly glowing eyes, he was looking forward happily; he felt that his life was only beginning. . . .

Here he broke off, Mrs. Colborne said, and turned to her again, earnestly pleading with her to change her way of living too. When the Revolution comes, Helene, he said, there will be guns pointed at all the things you love most in this City, the great department stores, the fine churches, the skyscraper apartment houses; you will hear their roar from the Battery to the Plaza, from the subway to the Bankers' Club on the top floor of the Equitable Building; the gutters on Fifth Avenue will run with blood; Washington Square Park which we see now strewn with the living unemployed, will be covered with the dead and dying of our own class; in the end the guns will be pointed at you. But right now, Helene, before those guns can be manufactured and distributed, before the working-classes dare to shoot, there are fingers pointing at you, pointing from all parts of the world, hun-dreds of thousands of them, fingers of French peasants pricked by their needles, bloodless fingers of rachitic babies, trembling fingers of beggars, fingers of factory hands, miners, all of them, Helene, lifting and pleading and in the end threatening, it will then be too late to turn the other cheek for the fingers will be on all sides, pointed at you. . . .

Mrs. Colborne heard no more. She had begun to scream, and her head, which had been shaking first in helplessness and then in anger, now shook in terror before the millions of pointing fingers which came at her suddenly out of the air, till the whole room, the whole world, became filled with them, and Mrs. Colborne was their sole target. She kept turning her head this way and that to escape them, but there was no escape, and although the fingers were disembodied and never touched her, she could feel their millions of sharp little pricks nevertheless all over the surface of her brain. What happened of course was very simple, the doctor said later; Mrs. Colborne being a person of great sensitivity and imagination, had temporarily taken over her husband's delusions and made them her own. By the time the doctor arrived, summoned at once by Henry, Mrs. Colborne had been carried to her bed and was lying there sweating and trembling, shaking her head weakly on the pillow at the many dim and angry fingers which had followed her up to her bedroom. When the doctor soothingly asked her if she could rest her head for a bit, Mrs. Colborne answered wearily, "No, for I must turn the other cheek."

Mrs. Colborne was in bed for three weeks turning the other cheek and was delirious on no other subject. From her sick-bed she continued to order the house quite properly, saw to it that the drapes were taken down and the summer curtains hung, dictated the correct complaints to erring butchers, florists, and second-floor maids, arranged with her lawyer for a divorce—but all the time spoke confidentially to the doctor and the nurses about the beggars who continued to point their fingers at her from the walls. At night the fingers stood out more clearly, and Mrs. Colborne's nurse cleverly turned round her schedule so that Mrs. Colborne slept during the safe, light day, and did her household figuring by night, when terror prevented her sleeping.

Gradually the delusion faded, the fingers receded; for a while they came only at night, and at last only when Mrs. Colborne was over-tired. She had stopped shaking her head in that frenzied way, though it still twitched a bit every now and then as if she suddenly remembered to turn the other cheek. But of course by now it was merely a tic, the doctor said, and was no more summoned by the delusions. Recovery was imminent, and after a restful trip to the mountains, Mrs. Colborne was so much better that the doctor told her it was now time to look for a new interest in life. Henry was gone,

one read his name in the papers occasionally as being arrested for picketing or speaking without a permit, and so there would be no real home to devote her time to. It was then that the doctor suggested dancing, social work, writing a novel, going round the world, being psychoanalyzed, studying economics, endowing a hospital, etcetera . . . and that finally, after much thought, it was settled that Mrs. Colborne should give cocktail parties, and after still more thought and consultation, parties for celebrated writers.

***

In the beginning Mrs. Colborne's parties were for the authors of articles in the liberal weeklies, or novelists of the *succès d'estime* rank at best, to whom she found it easy to obtain introductions; everybody knew somebody who wrote on the Plight of the Farmer or the latest medical discoveries or the lives of the Medicis. These early parties were not very good, and Mrs. Colborne was discouraged; there was not enough drinking, the women were "interesting looking" and correspondingly dull, and the men appeared to be present only on sufferance—those early parties broke up at seven at the first brave sign of anyone's leaving. But Mrs. Colborne was making contacts, even at these parties; among the guests that the dull article-writers suggested her asking there were always the names of half a dozen really celebrated writers, and of those half a dozen, three or four often accepted, and of the three or four who accepted, one was quite likely actually to come.

This celebrity Mrs. Colborne would quietly corner, let him talk himself out on the sale of his current book and the possibilities of the next one, and finally she would say, quietly, kindly, and firmly, "I am going to give a party for *you;* shall we say the twenty-second?" (She had her dates accurately in mind.) "You must mail me your list of guests by the twelfth, so that I can get out the invitations a week in advance; my secretary takes care of all that. You had better invite seventy-five people and I shall invite seventy-five more, for fifty people make a good party, and I have found that an average of one-third of the invited guests are able to come to a party." Then when the celebrity was leaving, Miss Rand the secretary (who had already been informed of all the details) bade him, not "goodbye," but "*auf wiedersehen* on the twenty-second," and shaking her finger at him admonished him not to let temperament get the better of him and postpone his turning in his list later than the twelfth. "Here, let me write it all down for you," Miss Rand would say humorously, "you authors, I guess I know you never remember a thing but your own ideas. And if you have any suggestions to make, you know, your favorite canapes or a little music or some special cocktails, just give me a ring some time before the twentieth, in the morning, between ten and twelve."

But the guests of honor seldom had suggestions to make, they always said they were content to leave the whole thing in Mrs. Colborne's hands, so all the parties were managed pretty much alike, except that now and then there was incidental music for a nation-wide best-seller, or an informal song or dance number for a prize-winner. There were always quantities of canapes, little sandwiches, nuts, ripe olives, and petits fours, and guests were always offered a choice of martinis and old-fashioneds.

Mrs. Colborne and Miss Rand had to run on a schedule, built up about the parties, in order to get everything done on time, and they made a great point of writing everything down and never slipping up on a detail. From ten to twelve every morning Miss Rand was at her desk tabulating guests and filing their little address cards with the dates on which they had attended parties—for they were careful to change the list of Mrs. Colborne's own guests so that the same people should not too often be meeting together; then there were a series of little cabalistic marks, understood only by Miss Rand and Mrs. Colborne, to remind them of each particular guest's characteristic behavior at parties—there were good mixers and poor ones, heavy drinkers and total abstainers, certain critics who should not be brought face to face with certain writers, couples who were too newly divorced to be asked to meet, and a set of single young ladies of no exact literary persuasion who could always be counted on to come and look smart and click glasses with gentlemen one didn't have to bother introducing them to. This file Miss Rand brought strictly up to date the morning after each party, based on the post-party discussion she and Mrs. Colborne held after the guests had gone home the night before, while Mrs. Colborne had her dinner in bed and Miss Rand on a table alongside. On mornings that there was to be a party, Mrs. Colborne stayed in bed until twelve, when Miss Rand brought the whole filing system up to her room and showed her the tentative lists she had drawn up for the coming parties; on non-party days, Mrs. Colborne was up and sat with Miss Rand, working with her. Both of them wrote and filed every suggestion that was ever made between them, and one of the index cards was called "Miscel." for Miscellaneous, and this section con-tained ideas found impracticable thus far, but filed for future use.

Eleven days before each party, Miss Rand telephoned the guest of honor if the guest of honor had not already telephoned her, and reminded him that his list was due tomorrow. Sometimes the prospective guest would say he'd been thinking it over, and after all why should there be a party given for *him,* who was he anyway, and besides most of his friends were out of town and he was terribly, terribly busy on his new book. In these cases Mrs. Colborne was called in, and gently encouraged the modest one, assuring him that in ten days it would all be over, Miss Rand had him down for the twenty-second and if he wanted to change the day maybe *that* could be done, but all the arrangements were made and Mrs. Colborne just wouldn't let him off. In the end the modest one always capitulated, explained how really he'd love a party given for him, but had just thought he wasn't important enough, and he'd send in his list tomorrow though he didn't think he could bring it up to seventy-five. Miss Rand and Mrs. Colborne would smile swiftly at each other. They had never lost a guest of honor.

Then twice more during the week Miss Rand telephoned the prospective guest on some pretext or other, just for the purpose of casually mentioning the date again, and urging him to come early; in the case of the modest capitulators she always added encouragingly, "Mrs. Colborne and I are so excited about your party; we're looking forward to it *particularly*," so that there might never be a last-minute lapse of memory or of courage. The system with caterers and liquor stores was equally perfect, and there was absolute harmony even with the men who brought folding-chairs and took them away again three times a week.

And so for four years before the particular party which is to be described, Mrs. Colborne's parties were a going concern. Everybody in New York had been to at least one of them, and to some persons they were a regular institution. The majority of publishers and critics had ceased to come because they would only meet for cocktails the same persons with whom they had been having lunch; but they generally sent a representative—an assistant or an editorial reader. Most of Mrs. Colborne's parties were neglected in the book columns, because there were so many of them; but there was mention of them in the cases of new arrivals in the world of fame or remarkably brilliant successes. It was in the former category—that of new arrivals—that this particular party was mentioned; and on Tuesday, the seventh of May, 1935, the top item in three literary chat columns read: "This afternoon Mrs. Helene Colborne will give a party for Miss Regina Sawyer, whose recent novel, *The Undecided,* has already won a place on the best-seller lists of New York City."

***

It was funny about Miss Regina Sawyer. She had come to one or two of Mrs. Colborne's parties in the past, her name appearing toward the end of some guest of honor's list—before she had published her novel, presumably while she was still working on it—and nobody had paid the slightest attention to her. She was quite small, Mrs. Colborne and Miss Rand remembered, and not bad-looking; but she dressed very inconspicuously, either in too-plain tweeds or a too-fancy and too-obvious "cocktail dress"—Miss Rand was not sure which. Miss Rand had approached her once and murmured something pleasant, and asked her to excuse her poor

memory but what (this was for the sake of the files)—
what did she do? Miss Sawyer had gulped at her cocktail, which she held along with a cigarette and a fancy
napkin in her left hand, and tried to dispose of a sand-
wich, a purse, and a pair of gloves in time to free her
right. Miss Rand remembered that Miss Sawyer had had
to clear her throat before answering—nobody had been
talking to her, and it seemed that she might be testing
her voice first to make sure of it—and then said, "I don't
do anything, really." Someone—the editor of one of the
smaller magazines—standing nearby had turned and
exclaimed kindly, "Why Regina Sawyer, you damned
little liar! She writes, Miss Rand, and very nicely too."
"Yes, I write," Miss Sawyer had said meekly. "Oh well,
then," Miss Rand had cast about vaguely for someone to
attach the nice little thing to, "then you *must* meet Mr.
Graham, Mr. *Judson* Graham—Mr. Graham, this is Miss
Sawyer whom we are expecting such wonderful things
from." Mr. Graham, widely known as a literary playboy,
had barely nodded, and Miss Rand had no other recollection of Miss Sawyer at the party. Mrs. Colborne was
not sure that she had ever spoken to her, though she
recalled a quiet and rather wistful face.

Then one day in the middle of April, almost a month
ago, Miss Rand had clapped her hands in surprise over
the morning book-review section, for there was a review
of "THE UNDECIDED, by Regina Sawyer, $2.50." "Well,
will you listen to this!" she exclaimed to Mrs. Colborne.

"Regina Sawyer . . . hmm hmm . . . vivid . . . hmm . . . portrayal New York intelligentsia . . . hmm hmm . . . promising newcomer . . . daring witty penetrating compassionate . . . hmm hmm . . . well, for goodness' *sake!*" she had cried to Mrs. Colborne. But Mrs. Colborne had scarcely listened, for she had reached the book-review section of the other morning paper and burst into exclamations herself: "Regina Sawyer . . . intellectual claptrap . . . hmm hmm . . . wordy nightmare . . . vicious and not very clever portrayals . . . hmm hmm . . . trite dull unimaginative cruel . . . hmm hmm. . . ." Miss Rand read on from her paper: "Prose perhaps a little crude, uneven. . ." Mrs. Colborne burst out over hers: "Prose, however, rhythmic and poetic ..." "Brilliant characterizations," read Miss Rand. "Characters so many puppets coldly illustrating thesis," read Mrs. Colborne. "Unfortunate that such a book will probably fail to achieve success," read Miss Rand. "Will probably sell widely because of specious air of 'truth-telling.'" Mrs. Colborne wound up triumphantly.

"Well, for goodness' *sake!*" they both exclaimed. "Little Regina Sawyer!"

After that they had scanned all the papers and clipped every mention of Miss Sawyer's name and waited to see if *The Undecided* would really catch on and sell. To their surprise the Sunday papers carried a two-column photograph of Miss Sawyer, and there was their neglected little mouse of an ex-guest looking as snappy and sporting as many an assured author of three best-sellers. Four days after publication Miss Rand found a publicity note stating that the first edition of Miss Sawyer's book was sold out and the second in preparation—and she immediately phoned the publishers and insisted that they dig her up a first for Mrs. Colborne. Mrs. Colborne and Miss Rand were very much excited and amused; and, really thrilled for the new little author, they held their breaths and read their clippings and waited to be sure.

Luckily the reviews were widely at variance with one another, someone started a controversy and Miss Sawyer responded immediately in an open letter somewhere—an interview appeared on Miss Sawyer's impression of the still-younger generation than herself—and gradually her name crept out of the literary columns and into the chatter columns as having attended parties here and there and there was even a vague rumor that Hollywood was Interested. Finally her name appeared toward the end of the city's best-sellers—she never made the provinces—and that Monday morning Mrs. Colborne and Miss Rand, who rather felt that they had discovered her, decided to give a party for Miss Sawyer.

"My dear Miss Sawyer:" Miss Rand wrote at Mrs. Colborne's dictation; "Miss Rand and I are so thrilled with your glorious success! May we offer our belated but nonetheless sincere congratulations? And I hope you will permit us a little secret pride, for we knew the celebrated author 'when' —and we always predicted great things for you among the literary 'stars!' We were both disappointed that you found so little time for us, but now we understand that you must have been working away on your splendid book! Paragraph. Now, Miss Rand and I have been wondering if you would allow us the privilege of giving a little party in your honor—we would be so pleased! You needn't go to a bit of trouble, I can imagine how rushed you must be these days!— just send us a little list of about seventy-five friends— or more if you wish—and we will attend to all the 'gory details.' Paragraph. Do let us know what date would be convenient for you. May I suggest the seventh or the tenth of May? Paragraph. Once more, we are so proud of you, dear Miss Sawyer! Most faithfully and cordially yours, Helene Colborne, per Fredrika Rand, sec'y."

***

The Regina Sawyer party was already in progress when Mrs. Colborne, who disliked the tension of the beginnings, came downstairs. Groups were already forming, and the waiters had begun to circulate with the cocktails among the early arrivals, who, as usual, consisted of interviewers, photographers, and critics' assistants, for whom it was more or less a business to be prompt. The guest of honor was just arriving, attended by Mr. Judson Graham and those two young men who looked just like him, wearing flowers in their button-holes—as

Mrs. Colborne herself swept down the stairs. Mrs. Colborne saw with relief that little Miss Sawyer had learned to dress at cocktail parties—she was wearing a strictly tailored suit that was anything but *pour le sport,* of a fine wine-velvet which belied the severity of the cut; a shoulder nest of three gardenias offset her smartly groomed hair, which curled in little clusters behind her ears—and which, Mrs. Colborne remembered, had been perfectly straight the year before. Miss Sawyer was laughing merrily and seemed to be holding all three of her escorts by the arm, and as Mrs. Colborne modestly approached to greet her it became clear that little Miss Sawyer had no recollection whatsoever of her hostess and also that she was a little bit tight.

"—but I never forget a face," Miss Rand was assuring a young gentleman who had what looked like a false black beard—as Miss Sawyer's procession tripped a little over the threshold, and Mrs. Colborne who had decided to remain incognito meekly sought an inconspicuous entrance behind them. "And here is our guest of honor!" exclaimed Miss Rand turning from the false beard and running with little cries to Miss Sawyer. "So *grand* to see you again, Miss Sawyer! Ah, Mr. Graham! so you have captured Miss Sawyer already, have you! Well, you will have to give her up for a time, everyone is *dying* to meet her."

Mrs. Colborne wandered quietly and contentedly through the growing little groups, and saw that more than the average fifty would soon be at the party. It had not been a mistake, after all, to give a party for Miss Regina Sawyer. Everything was going well; the folding-chairs lining the edge of the room had been properly pushed out of place and now reclined, properly unoccupied. The waiters skillfully made little paths through the standing groups, going away with empty glasses and quickly returning with fresh ones. The few critics who had come had retired comfortably to the alcove where the drinks and sandwiches were laid out upon a table, and were holding their usual tired, pleasant stag. The non-literary "extra girls," the helpful "party girls," who were oddly so much prettier than the average run of writing-girls, were smartly turned out and making themselves agreeable to the men, in particular the charming older men, and being pleasant about it when they were abandoned for the plain celebrities. Mr. Judson Graham was lying on a couch with his arms mildly embracing two middle-aged lady authors who chatted briskly over his knee with one another. Miss Regina Sawyer was doing beautifully, repeating her own jokes to guest after guest whom Miss Rand brought up, and raising her voice a little or laughing and gesturing gracefully when it seemed possible that someone was not recognizing her as guest of honor. Miss Sawyer was drinking steadily and kept up a stream of what seemed to be irresistible merriment, and Mrs. Colborne would have worried a little about her being intoxicated except for the thoughtful look Miss

Gramercy Park. She would soon be taking those heavy drapes down for the Summer, she thought, perhaps in time for Mr. Forsythe's party on the twenty-first, it would be nice to have the transparent gold net up by then; she must remember to speak to Miss Rand. Behind her the hum was pleasantly gathering as the crowd swelled and the drinks began to mellow all the voices. Ah, here were some more people climbing her steps from the street, strangers evidently, for they glanced hesitatingly at the number before coming along up. Mrs. Colborne let the Winter drape fall back in place and turned again to her party, to traverse it in her leisurely way from windows back toward the balcony again.

In one corner Miss Sawyer was posing for the photographers, and Mr. Judson Graham had roused himself to come and stand beside her. Miss Sawyer smiled and pointed her foot, and Mr. Judson Graham posed like a debonair poet, drawing her hand through his arm. Their friends came and stood laughing and drinking about them, until at last the photographers took them all in a group. The older critics had turned their backs on everybody and were standing and patiently drinking, and looked, Mrs. Colborne thought, rather like men who preferred to be playing poker when they were not shut up by themselves reading away at their new books. Mrs. Colborne was glad that she had not limited her parties to salons for critics only, for she thought them a serious-minded lot, excellent for the background of a party but less successful in the stellar role. She had reached the other end of her party by now, nodding composedly when she was nodded to, and graciously extending her hand when it was asked for, and now she slowly turned, and started on her pleasant ramble back toward the windows again—when Miss Rand dashed up and took her arm.

"Dear, it's going so *well!*" she whispered. "Miss Sawyer is a darling! And listen honey, you know the one with the black beard, there, the young one, well . . ." and here she whispered the result of some of her researches into Mrs. Colborne's ear. "And Mr. Kilpatrick, don't forget to speak to *him,* we've two more open dates in May. And Miss Beardsley, what do you think, dear? we might consider—perhaps in June. . . . And *Reckless Lady* is the name of his book, no dear, not Mr. Kilpatrick's, Mr. *Wallace's,* the young man with the black beard. . . ." Excitement had brought a flush to each of Miss Rand's hardy cheekbones and Mrs. Colborne thought affectionately how nice she looked. "I'll remember everything," she said obediently, "and Fredrika dear, I'm so glad you wore that, you look just lovely." They squeezed each other's hands and parted; their real fun would be afterward, when they would pick everybody to pieces over Mrs. Colborne's supper-in-bed.

Two of the "extra girls," who came to all the parties, danced up to Mrs. Colborne. "Such a *swell* party, Mrs. Colborne!" they said; "and Regina Sawyer's such a *duck.* My, she looks about eighteen!" and Mrs. Colborne, glancing down, saw that each of the "girls" before her must be thirty at least, though she had been thinking of them for the last four party years as twenty-five. "So nice to see you both again," said Mrs. Colborne kindly; "so nice of you girls to come to all my parties." "I may just have to run away early, Mrs Colborne," said one of them quickly, "I have a 'pressing engagement' for this eve—" "That's quite right, my dear," said Mrs. Colborne, "enjoy yourself while you still can." And she nodded to the "girls" and moved gently on.

And there was Mr. Wallace, momentarily free. Mrs. Colborne advanced and cut off his forward motion toward the fireplace. Mr. Wallace, apparently not seeing her, side-stepped mechanically to his right, and Mrs. Colborne side-stepped to her *left,* which brought them face to face. "Mr. Wallace, I *do* want to congratulate you," Mrs Colborne exclaimed, "on the success of *Reckless Lady.* And such a fine press as it got! Miss Rand and I were simply delighted!" Young Mr. Wallace murmured his thanks and said he wondered that he was recognized behind his new beard. "Miss Rand and I never forget a face," Mrs. Colborne assured him vivaciously; and then grew firm with him. "You must let us give *you* a party, Mr. Wallace. May we put you down for the twenty-fifth?" "But what have *I* done?" murmured the young man shyly. "Nonsense," said Mrs. Colborne crisply; "may I put you down for that date, may I, Mr. Wallace? Miss Rand will arrange everything. Come now," said Mrs. Colborne winningly, "it is only one afternoon."

I don't know which she is," said one of them, "but the story's killing. Regina says she's just like the head waiter at Tony's, you know, you bow if you happen to remember, but it doesn't really matter—" "And wasn't there something about the husband being an anarchist or something?" "I think so, and Reggie says the most heaven-sent *material,* but only God can make a plot—" The waiter moved on, and Mrs. Colborne said "Pardon me" to the stranger group, and managed to get past. There was Miss Beardsley, but she looked dull, Miss Rand had only said to *think* about Miss Beardsley, and Mrs. Colborne was aware of feeling rather tired, rather numb. Besides, the rest of May was taken, and in June perhaps she and Miss Rand might run up to the Mountains for a little rest. The city grew so warm in Spring, the room was quite stifling with the people and the smoke and the reflected afternoon sun, and Mrs. Colborne found herself leaning against the window again, thinking about the Summer drapes, and giving up Miss Beardsley altogether.

People were beginning to drift homeward now, and quite a number made their way to Mrs. Colborne to say goodbye. Mrs. Colborne felt wan and a little absent, but she brought her mind back with an effort, and remembered to sort them out cor-rectly: "Don't forget Mr. Forsythe's party on the twenty-first," and "You will be receiving an invitation to Mr. Wallace's party on the twenty-fifth" or "Mr. Kilpatrick's party on the twenty-eighth," and even, with a burst of initiative "Oh Miss

Undecided by Regina Sawyer which Miss Rand had left sticking out a little on the top shelf. Miss Sawyer was still standing merrily with Judson Graham beside her, bidding people goodbye and extending her hand now and then to be kissed, and Mrs. Colborne made her way smiling toward them.

"Miss Sawyer, my dear," said Mrs. Colborne gently, "if you would just autograph my book, I'd be so pleased! I know it is a bore, but I should love it so."

Miss Sawyer looked up brightly, recaptured her hand from a passing biographer of Cato. "Why, sure! I'd love to. Ah, a first edition! Aren't you lucky!" Mrs. Colborne piloted her gently to a little desk, where pen and ink were standing ready. "I hate to steal you from the guests, Miss Sawyer, but only for a minute." Little Miss Regina Sawyer, whose eyes were a trifle blood-shot now with liquor and laughing, dipped the pen politely into the inkwell and reverently turned the pages of her own book. Suddenly the pen dropped as Miss Sawyer was reading to herself. "Look at this, it's marvelous! Hey, look at this, Jud, you poor fool playboy. . . . Oh God, I'll never do anything like it again, never, never! It's got everything in it I ever saw or thought or felt. . . . Christ, will I ever do anything again? will anything ever mean so much again?" Tears were gleaming in Miss Sawyer's eyes. "God, finding my own book at a lousy party! it's like running into a mirror when you're naked, or seeing your mother suddenly when you're cockeyed drunk. . . .

"Reggie, pull yourself together!" Judson Graham stood over her, man-of-the-world with a flower in his button-hole. "We haven't time to stop for a crying jag now, honey, hurry up."

Regina Sawyer looked up again at Mrs. Colborne with her eyes brightly glazed. "Playboy takes care of me," she said; "year ago he wouldn't speak to me at parties. Now I'm a catch. Next year he won't speak to me either. What do you want me to write in this God-damned book? What name shall I put?"

Mrs. Colborne was about to tell her, but Judson Graham said angrily, "You drunken little idiot! It's Mrs. Colborne, your hostess. She's just cockeyed, Mrs. Colborne, don't mind her, of course she knows you."

"Mrs. Colborne! My God, of course," murmured Regina Sawyer blushing miserably. "Why my dear," said Mrs. Colborne soothingly, "that's perfectly all right! You've had a difficult afternoon, poor child! And Miss Rand tells me you've been perfectly fine about it."

Regina Sawyer bent over and wrote in haste, and Mrs. Colborne saw one tear roll down Miss Sawyer's cheek and fall on the fly-leaf of her book. "Thank you so much, my dear," said Mrs. Colborne, taking it up; "and—*now* the guest-book, if you *don't* mind?" and she drew out the Venetian leather folio which lived downstairs only during parties. "Thank you *so* much, dear," said Mrs. Colborne. "Thank *you* so much," murmured the frightened Miss Sawyer, "you must forgive me, I mean, you work and you work like hell on a book and all you know is that book and then suddenly—oh, you just go haywire, I suppose." Judson Graham was guiding her deftly toward the door. "And you must try and come to Mr. Forsythe's party on the twenty-first, both of you, the invitations have not yet gone out," said Mrs. Colborne in farewell. "Goodbye, goodbye, and thank you again, Miss Sawyer, you've been perfectly *fine.*"

Mrs. Colborne did not like the dwindling ends of parties any more than she did their beginnings, and feeling tired, feeling also a pleasant sense of accomplishment, another party gone and future parties set and to be planned at cheerful leisure, the guestbook signed again and a new autographed first edition, she slipped unobtrusively up to her bedroom. Let Miss Rand stand nodding in the hall, bidding the guests goodbye. Let the fine living-room slowly empty itself until only the furniture and the hired waiters remained. The party was over. Mrs. Colborne was needed no more.

In her room the bed had been turned down, waiting to receive her, her nightgown and bedjacket were laid out cordially across the pillow, and the windows were opened wide to the Spring twilight rising from the Park. Mrs. Colborne stepped slowly and contentedly across the carpet (the air was heavy and lush, inviting quiet movement) and sat at her little mahogany desk where the street lamp threw a beam across the blotter and the mother-of-pearl desk-set. She set down the guest-book and *The Undecided* and slowly drew out her memorandum book, Venetian leather like the guestbook. Very carefully she printed the dates for the new parties: May 21, 1935, Robert Forsythe; May 25, 1935, Julian Wallace; May 28, 1935, Richard Kilpatrick. Under the first day of June she wrote in pencil, very lightly, "Fitch-Beardsley, unsettled, confer F.R.—or should we go up to the Mountains?" she added dreamily, and laughed to see how funny the words looked on the business-like page, before she erased them neatly.

She really had taken care of everything, the book, the dates, the few necessary details—she must still place *The Undecided* on the shelves of autographed books, perhaps beside David Crane's book, the colors would harmonize—and it was certainly her time for undressing slowly and waiting in bed for her light dinner to come up, for Miss Rand. . . . But Mrs. Colborne felt she couldn't hurry. A pleasant apathy descended on her limbs, so that she did not move to press the lights, not even the little mother-of-pearl desk-lamp that Henry's mother had given her (*Henry!*) so many thousands of years ago. She sat there by the window, waiting to place Regina Sawyer's volume, and meantime holding it absently on her lap. She was mildly curious about the inscription, and tilted the book so that she could read it by the street-lamp: "To Mrs. Colborne, with my very best wishes, Regina Sawyer, May 7, 1935." Oh, how nice, thought Mrs. Colborne, the very same thing that Henrietta King had written in her *Preambles and Constitutionals*—and what was it David Crane had written to her? Which was David Crane's book? A moment ago she had seen it in the bookcase, but it was too dark now, and the air was too lush and mellow for one to want to move; presently Mrs. Colborne would rise and push the button and flood the room with light, and look into David Crane's book; he was a charming man, they had given him his party some time that past Winter, he had written a book on either Mexico or Lewis Carroll. Miss Rand would know.

But meantime Mrs. Colborne sat content in the window, Regina Sawyer's best-seller in her lap, watching the afternoon grow old and listening to the last sounds of the few lingering guests. Soon the folding-chair men would arrive, the waiters stack the glasses in the kitchen; her own servants would clean up; they would bring her supper on a tray. Soon Miss Rand, Fredrika Rand, would have given the last orders below-stairs, and would come and join her beloved friend and employer. Soon too the city Summer would be heavy upon them and perhaps they had better put off the Fitch-Beardsley party till the Fall and run away to the Mountains. They had better go soon, thought Mrs. Colborne, catching her breath in a sudden panic, soon, soon, everything had to be soon. For it was growing late. It was growing still. It would soon be too dark to see. She did want to find out, thought Mrs. Colborne, *before it was too late,* what David Crane had written to her in his book the Winter before. She did

For Better, For Worse

Delineator, January 1936

"When you cross back over this here bridge, Mrs. Mellor," said Bud, leveling his cowboy hat as they approached the courthouse, "you'll be a free gal—for better or for worse."

Mrs. Mellor's hand tightened on her lawyer's arm as they walked over the Truckee River. "If only I had a cowboy's peace of mind!" she said. "Oh, Mr. Harker—I'm simply trembling. If only I could have had it a closed case. Everybody in Reno will be there; they drop in at the courthouse the way people in the East attend the movies!"

"Let 'em have their show, Mrs. Mellor," the lawyer said. "It will be over soon. I had to advise you to have an open hearing, you know that; otherwise all the sleuth reporters would have been there to cook up stories— and your fiancé wouldn't have liked that a bit. And in a few hours you'll never have to see Reno again."

"That's true," she said. And she walked more slowly, for six weeks in any place makes it something of a home. "Unless," she laughed harshly, "unless I decide to get a divorce from Graham too."

She looked up at Harker, expecting an answer somehow. But ahead of them Bud was jauntily mounting the courthouse steps, and Mr. Harker held her arm loosely and impersonally, as befits a respectable lawyer conducting an attractive client to her trial.

She heard Bud's voice in a blur, drawling his testimony that he had seen her every day for forty-two days, six weeks of seven days each. When she herself took the chair beside the stout old judge dozing behind his bench, she was aware of the rows of faces staring at her, hoping for the worst. She was aware of them, but she did not see them; all she saw was the fine tanned face of John Harker, the wide western horizon in his forehead, as he faced her with his questions.

"And did he make scenes?" asked John Harker gently.

"Yes, he made jealous scenes," Mrs. Mellor answered mechanically. She smiled bitterly at the—the understatement. I will say anything, she had told John Harker, anything—but the truth. The truth she had withheld even from him; it was too terrible, too humiliating. The truth she had tried to hide from herself during these six short weeks between marriages. Only Graham—only Graham knew; knew too well, perhaps.

"And did he ever strike you?" said John Harker delicately, as though it hurt him to ask.

"Yes, he struck me," said Mrs. Mellor coldly. Struck her! If . . . her heart went cold with hate as she thought of Frank Mellor. She surveyed John Harker passionately now for some mark of understanding, but, facing the judge, his countenance expressed nothing but the calm certainty of his being a lawyer.

"And you are demanding no alimony?" came his steady voice, exactly as they had rehearsed it in his office, only then they had been drinking mint juleps made with corn, to make it easier.

"No alimony."

A moron could answer these questions, she thought, the answer incorporated tactfully in the form. No alimony! Why should she ask for alimony? Graham had more money than Frank had had. Graham made his money in the same way Frank did. Graham spent his money in the same way. Graham too. . . . While here in the West, she thought vaguely, and looked again into John Harker's eyes, at once shallow and deep, like the desert skyline, at once terribly near and far; but Mr. Harker was still sitting there looking like a lawyer.

"Has anyone any objections?"

Apparently a bell of habit had rung in the old judge's ears, for he came out with his question on time. No one spoke.

The thin man legally representing Frank rose in his place, was sworn in, said, "No objections," and sat down again.

Mrs. Mellor thought her audience must be furious! After all those jealous scenes, not to instruct his deputy to raise one objection! She thought too how Frank would have been amused if he could have seen the seediness of the little man who represented him for fifty dollars.

It was over. Mrs. Mellor found herself calm amongst the people who were rising to leave her show, or moving up closer for the next one. Mr. Harker perfunctorily congratulated her.

"Would you care for a drink, Mrs. Mellor, before your train?" he said courteously.

"Thank you, I would like that," said Mrs. Mellor; and they dispatched the cowboy to see to her trunks and settle them in the train.

They went straight to the Town House, out of sight of Virginia Street, to the very table where they had had their first drink forty-two days ago when he met her train. Over their very first mint julep, she remembered now, she had said she would tell anything but the truth. She wanted him to guess it now.

"Mint julep, darling?" the lawyer said.

"Of course, darling," Mrs. Mellor said.

They lifted their glasses gravely.

"It's been an awfully swell six weeks, honey," he said shakily.

"Swell," she said thoughtfully. "It's been—so terribly much more than that to me. I hope you don't mind that I've got you all mixed up with the desert and the horses, and the horizon, John. I'm in love with the lot of you. I've never felt alive before. Oh John, you don't know what my life is like at home—what hell I've been through." The tears came and stood in her eyes.

"Do you want to tell me, honey?" he said uneasily.

"Oh—I can't!" she said. "I can't. You wouldn't—you might not like me any more. Marriage!" said Mrs. Mellor, twenty minutes after her divorce.

"I've seen plenty of it," said John Harker wearily. "Out here in Reno, I would. And my own too—my own marriage. Oh, nothing terrible, as things go—but sometimes I think I'll go mad if I just go home and smell the lavender *eau de cologne* my wife has used for fifteen years. It's kind of pathetic, you know. She used it before we were married, and once I said I liked it, and she's used it ever since. On everything. Lavender soap, lavender talcum, lavender powder. . . . But I'm a selfish beast, talking to you like this, when you have real troubles. Worse than striking you, you said! Oh, my poor darling. . . ."

Unaccountably she was cheered by the recital of his petty woes. It was comforting to think of leaving him to go home to the hated scent of lavender. She thought with brief pleasure of the violet extract she used, an expensive flacon of which Graham had sent her in a traveling kit.

Graham. . . .

"Listen," she said rapidly. "I will tell you. The truth. Nothing but the truth." He looked up, startled. "I want to tell someone." She felt that cold hate filling her again for Frank Mellor. "John, Frank never struck me. Never. He never made scenes. He was a model husband. His secretary made a note of my birthdays on his date-pad. The florist telephoned him on all the holidays. The jeweler called him each year before our anniversary. He was a model husband." She began to laugh harshly. "Just as Graham will be."

"Listen," she said. "Do you know what he said when I told him I was going to leave him? He said, 'Very well, my dear.' Do you know what he said when I told him I was going to marry Graham? 'Better think twice, my dear, he plays a rotten hand of bridge.'"

"But don't you love Graham?" said John Harker, like a man stalling for time.

"Graham? He was cut from the same bolt of dry expensive asbestos cloth as Frank." Graham would lie awake nights too thinking of the stock market, or what a poor hand he had held, or how he had eaten too much of something.

She wondered fleetingly why she was changing from Frank to Graham. They were the same man. They were both financiers first, gentlemen second, and thirdly, near the bottom somewhere, almost men—but they never quite touched the bottom.

"My marriage with Graham will be the same thing," she said, "except that Graham takes rye and Frank drank Scotch." And then she sat there, frightened, for she found herself looking directly at John Harker, and knowing clearly that he was not a gentleman and that he was, decidedly, a man.

"Honey—"

But here the waiter interrupted with the information that there was just time to catch madam's train. Possibly no two people ever paid a check and left the Town House and hailed a cab and claimed baggage faster than did Mrs. Mellor and John Harker in the midst of their farewell. Mrs. Mellor was in a state of panic until the last suitcase—the little traveling bag that had been Graham's last gift—was stowed safely in her stateroom. Only then did she remember that she had been in a state of indecision—about something.

"I can't bear—" said John Harker, when the conductor yelled "All aboard!" and he took her in his arms and kissed her violently. If only she could get off the train, think things over, stay in John Harker's arms forever. If only Graham were not flying to Chicago to meet her. If only. . . . The conductor yelled "All aboard!" again, and John Harker dashed for the platform.

The train was making sounds of departure. Riotous parties of divorcees were clinging to the windows and shouting last goodbyes. Mrs. Mellor thought she would die when the train pulled out of sight of John.

He stood outside her window gravely. Their eyes stared, panic-stricken. Mrs. Mellor felt tears coming to her eyes and she held her handkerchief to them. The sudden scent of violet extract went to her head. Graham, Graham Winter—she was going home to become Mrs. Graham Winter as she had been Mrs. Frank Mellor; she would come home every day from tea some place, and bathe, and dress, and dash out to be looked at, in any kind of weather, in any kind of mood. As a matter of fact she was getting home in time for the MacAllister reception. . . . She managed a brilliant last smile just as the train began to pull out.

John Harker smiled back, sadness and relief mingling as he began mechanically to think of things he had to do. Brief Mrs. Archer's case—she was arriving tomorrow; what would she look like? And he walked slowly home, the scent of lavender already in his nostrils. But there would be a goodly smell of cooking too.

On Being Told That Her Second Husband Has Taken His First Lover

Story, April 1935

Well (you think in a sprightly voice) this is no surprise, at least *essentially.* So it's nice my dear, that you are always so clever; and sad my dear that you always need to be. Time was when a thing like this was a shock that fell heavily in the pit of your stomach and gave you indigestion all at once. But you can only feel a thing like this in its entirety the first time, after that it's a weaker repetition. Nowadays you go around automatically expecting the worst all the time, so that you can only be pleasantly surprised by the exceptions. Pretty nice to be so clever, Cornelia my gal, *pretty sad too.* Now when the message is shot out to you you've got a nice little lined glove like a catcher's mitt for it to fall into, more or less painlessly, more or less soundlessly. Oh sure, the details, falling like pepper into a fresh wound, sting a bit. And of course the confirmation, the *dead-certain* confirmation, of what you were clever enough to *know* and clever enough to keep away from knowing, does wrap you round in a sort of strait-jacket for a minute. . . . But no nausea comes.

No nausea. No sharp pain. A mild disgust, and a quick defensive rallying of your forces. Your wits are keyed to concert pitch, nothing can escape you, you are intensely self-conscious. You have utter and absolute control over all your nerves. You go right on lying there in his arms letting what must have gone rigid inside you with his words go rigid away inside your skin, so his arms can't sense the differ-ence, can't feel the animal flinch that maybe after all you couldn't avoid.

You observe the lines in his face, his weakness, his male pride which even in his moment of confession he cannot hide even from himself, and at the same time you are marking infinitesimal notes on your own emotions. Implacable logic comes and sits in your head. Your associative processes, like your wits, are functioning brilliantly, you are intensely, even thrillingly alive with the tingling call to battle in all your veins. Your past thoughts and observations, fragments from his conversation, kaleido-scopic pictures of his facial muscles scarcely noted at the time yet registered indelibly somewhere deep in the con-sciousness, stand out like well--framed entities of a jig-saw puzzle, only they cease now to be entities, and under your courageous and all-seeing eye they fit together and form a large bold map omitting nothing.

Oh, you could talk about the thing, in Proustian vein, forever. Show him where he was weak, analyze his emotions for him, tear him to pieces like a female lion. Time was, with Jimsie, (ah, *that* pain can still come, and it is not that Jimsie ever was more to you than Dill is now, it is because Jimsie was the first, and that pain was the first, his news was a blow the heart will never recover from—never) time was when you brilliantly talked, explaining away everything, for two whole days, while Jimsie stayed home from work to listen and neither of you so much as dressed nor saw another person but the boy from the delicatessen bringing sandwiches and cigarettes at intervals, and at last Vichy water when you fell to drinking. But you have learned a lesson. You know that you cannot handle these things as though you were giving a lecture course. No, no; no matter how much he acknowledges with his mind, there will be no satisfaction for you ultimately, and no sensitive revelations for him, unless you become at the same time an artist and an actress (or else of course an impulsive human being, but that is not possible.) Of course, you could go on forever, apparently relieving your mind of all its stored-up bitterness and grievances (some of them you never knew you had, some of them you had only against Jimsie and not against Dill at all), but a stream like that is futile and self-multiplying; you must be a highly selective artist,

Mrs. Dill Graham formerly-something-else; a gently restrained actress, *née* Cornelia North.

It is a delicate matter you have on your hands, my poor Cornelia, unless, that is, you choose to toss it down quickly with a drink and never look it in the eye again. But what's the use of doing that? Why make infidelity a painless operation and take from it its only possible lasting virtue, a possible binding closer together of the original two partners? Besides, there's something cheap in painlessness, something too modern-generationish. Go in for recriminations, gal, but on a modern scale; you can't of course go on lying there in his arms (and it's cowardice that keeps you so, even now) and mutter things about honor and weep, because you know too well that honor has nothing to do with it, and you don't feel in the least like weeping, in fact you couldn't manage it right now thanks. No, it has nothing to do with honor, it unfortunately has nothing to do with anything but human nature, and how can you take a man to task for that—not to mention *two* men?

He has the gall to ask you whether you feel "through" with him now. No, you answer, the thing has been going on right along and I've been happy enough—I'm not one to look back now that I know I've always had t.b. and say God how I have always suffered. "Well, but is it going to make any difference to you, from now on?" How in hell should I know? At the moment I have no desire but to keep my head above water and say funny things. And I can do it too, by God. (Like the time you wandered into the wrong room at a party and found him with his arms around that girl What's-her-name in no uncertain manner—ah, you put on a swell act that time, old girl! Just before being sick in the bathroom you managed a hearty laugh and said, O dear Lord, it looks so funny when you're not doing it yourself! How mad Dill was. But how he loved you for your wit. Still, if he had known about the mess in the bathroom which you so carefully cleaned up, *mightn't* he have loved you more? and *mightn't* you have prevented this other thing . . . ?) "Is it going to make a difference to you, Cornelia, now that you know?" "If you must be a gay deceiver, honey, for God's sake, be a *gay* one! My goodness, isn't adultery more fun than *that?*"

Suddenly you are filled with power which makes you light as air, which goes to your head like champagne the last night on shipboard. You have somehow got rid of something, somehow picked out his weakness in chiaroscuro. His triumph is smaller now than his guilt; his guilt you will reduce to sheepishness. I can do anything, my little man: now give me something *hard* to do. Besides, it occurs to you suddenly (elated as you are) that the thing is impossible. Simply and utterly impossible— it hasn't happened at all. Does he actually exist when he leaves your sight? Does he actually exist when. . . .

Ah careful there, Cornelia; the ice is thin that way, Mrs. D. Graham; watch your step dancing on those there *particular* eggs, Miss North—for the visual inner eye is a keen thing, a sharp sadist, a talented beast of an artist, an old devil of a perverted surgeon . . . delete that diagram, my dear, quick, before it stains the heart's plate permanently. . . .

And then you reason (philosophical now, the body gone cold in his cold hands, the mind gone cold in your own cold skull) it *is* impossible, elementally and fundamentally impossible—impossible on the level of real values. For you are YOU, therefore if he loves the real YOU he cannot *love* anybody else; and if, on the other hand, it is not the real YOU he has reached down and found to love, why then, the hell with him altogether—you don't want to be loved for what you have in common with other presentable women: for your decent hair, your fine teeth, your eyes, your neat little figger. No. You want to be loved, not really even for your wit, but for the whole tricky pattern of all these things and the mysterious something else besides which spells in the end YOU and you alone. So then, since he loves you in this way, Dill does (of that you are sure, both warmly and coldly), since he really *loves* you, since he loves the real YOU—what can it possibly matter if he touches her with his hands, not the real HER, and not with the real HIM, suppose he does say to her . . . laugh with her . . . kiss her. . . . Ah, ah, that way the ice is thin again, that way leads not to pain but to the terrible presentiment of pain. . . . Ah, cold philosophy! denying the body, consoling the brain! Philosophy is senility to the young, religion to the starving, a dictionary to a baby, a fine silk purse to a pig. . . .

To hell with philosophy, in short. "But what are you going to *do?*" he says, Dill says, and you discover that he too is lying without moving, as afraid as you that if a muscle twitches or a breath catches, something, or the whole of everything, will go smashing to small pieces in this life you share. What are you going to *do?* To *do?* Why, lie here, I suppose, for the rest of our married life, in your arms gone cold, in our bed gone cold, my heart gone cold as a philosopher's. What am I going to do, you think. It is a good question. One of the best questions, for there is never any answer to it.

Certainly, you think, you have a legalistic right to go out and get even. . . . But you did that once, you matched Jimsie amour for amour, and what happened? Why, the string between you wore out, it got like old elastic and finally, because it would never snap any more for deadness, each of you let go his end and wandered off, too empty to feel pain, too dead to feel anything. You merely destroyed something that way, Cornelia, you didn't even save your self-respect when that bank closed. No, that's painless dentistry again, remote control, the Machine Age, Watson and the reflex, the Modern Generation. To derive *full* value out of anything, one must pay the price in pain; full beauty consists of pain as well as joy—and halving the pain cuts the joy in two. Let us not compromise, you think strongly; God send me pain again, God let me feel.

"I mean, can you love me in spite of anything?" If I love you at all, you think, if there is such a thing as love at all, then I suppose it is in spite of anything. "Oh sure," you hear yourself saying like a girl scout, but it sounds like the kind of records your grandfather used to play on his gramophone. "And how about you, my gay deceiver, would you love me in spite of anything, Dill? Would you now?" Impossible, clearly, to speak without lilting; try a drop of pallid humor first thing in the morning, nothing like it to aid digestion, avoid those infidelity blues, that early-morning tremolo.

"Anything, *but no gents,*" he says, with fear piled up in his eyes and a sort of anticipatory hatred. "Don't ask me why, I don't *know* why, but it's different with a man."

He says and has said and will go on saying, *But no gents* for you, my girl, one gent and I am through. He will go on saying it until there has been one gent. (And the first is the only one that counts. After that, the elastic begins to stretch and go dead—we found that out between us, Jimsie and I.) Then it is a toss-up what he will do, when there has been one gent. But one thing is clear, Cornelia, you shrewd and calculating woman, one thing is clear: one gent, and you will have lost the large part of your power over him. For it is not true that men despise what they possess or what they have exclusive rights over; what is true is that they cannot love (in normal, masculine fashion) what they must share. No, there is no point to your going and doing likewise, not as long as there is any point to your relations with this man, this philandering second husband, this gay deceiver who tells the truth and looks so far from gay about it. As long as he can lie there with fear written on his face and say to you *But no gents,* you have a power which nothing can destroy. You gain thereby an integrity which exists not merely in his eyes, but which is actual, which is a fact. You become a whole person even in your sadness, while he stands before you, however male, a split one. He will know it, you will know it.

"The old Dolly Gray complex," you say. And evidently every man has the germs of it in him somewhere, the little woman waiting at home. It is even a little perverse that he can feel this way about you when he considers you were a bum (as he called it) out and out before he met you, ever since Jimsie in fact, and realizes that you were one on the very night he met you. But that's nice; that's what appeals to him; the very perversity of these strange facts: that you were a bastard (in his own language) and that now you sit at home and wait for him. He could not bear it if you were straight-out Dolly Gray, for he is a modern young man. But you have that whole rich background (rich! and supposing you have children and then grandchildren, would that story about falling asleep in a fraternity house with two "brothers" be the kind kids would like to hear from dear old Granny?)—but you have it, and he can never quite forgive you, and this is enough to tease him and please him for the rest of his life; you can never be quite Dolly Gray in his eyes be-cause you can never shake off your past and his memory of your complaisance (to put it mind, with your weighing-machine, for your tongue has ceased to give a damn, and your alimentary canal is working like a derrick without a soul). In fact the whole thing passes off rather like a fine English play, in which the husband has just murdered the child because he found out his wife had it by the butler, the wife is scheduled to murder the butler immediately after breakfast, and meantime the butler serves them an impeccable breakfast over an impeccable table with unimpeachable manners, and the husband and the wife delicately break their toast and wonder if the season will be a good one, if the Queen has got over her cold. Oh yes, yes, yes, it is all very nice, Dill flips over the pages of *The Times* (why is he wearing his good blue jacket and his natty gray trousers, he never starts that until May and here it is only April) and Cornelia does the wifely thing, she keeps his plate stacked with fresh toast and wipes the corners of her mouth (which she has rouged before breakfast, for a change) very nicely, with the edge of the fringed napkin (which belongs to the linen set they don't usually use when they are alone).

And it is all very nice (and a little bit formal), only that the house looks queerly different to you now, no longer quite your own, it no longer holds you as it held you yesterday. Yet there have been days when those four walls were so dear to you, too dear, times when they hemmed you in until you felt like a caged animal. Today you rather wish they pressed in closer. But the walls seem all made of doors today. Now the boredom that weighed pleasantly yesterday is gone. Why did you not whisper yesterday, while there was still time, why did you not shout it yesterday while you still had the voice— that that boredom was a good thing, let us preserve it, Dill, it is good, it is warm, it is real; it cannot be said today. No, no, and a good thing too, for this is life, life as it is spoken in the Twentieth Century, will you have a little toast dear? No? really not? then how about a second cup of coffee, well for heaven's sake, those politicians! when will they leave off cutting one another's throats?—all so very delicate and stilted, all so very fine and quiet, so civilized, so neat, the corpse inside in the bedroom but the play's the thing and let's not forget our very fine modern manners. (And why, with that impossibly gay suit, has he chosen that impossibly gay tie—a bow tie, does he think it's Spring?) but why in such a hurry, Dill, Dill darling—"You've left half your coffee, it's cold, Dill, let me pour you another cup? it's still hot." And you have the specious joy of seeing him stay against his will and drink his second cup of coffee, which he clearly doesn't want.

So he wipes his mouth and puts his fancy napkin down and stands there smiling at you quite politely. This is the moment for you to rise and casually murder the butler and come back and help your husband with his coat. But you can't make the grade. For you see it all suddenly, you see it there in his face, reluctant as he is to hurt you. He does have an actual existence outside of you, and he is anxious to leave you now and enter it. You see it in his face. It is clearer than any of the things you told yourself—and he cannot help revealing it to you. He will be lost to you the minute he walks out of your sight; he will be back, of course, but this time and forever after you will know that he has been away, clean away, on his own. You see it in his face, and your heart, which had sunk to the lowest bottom, suddenly sinks lower.

"Don't go yet." It is time to murder the butler, but you walk instead—or lilt, for you cannot trust yourself to walk—to your husband, and you begin a wretched game of opening up each button of his coat after he has fastened it. You go on playing the game together, both of you laughing, it may be a little ruefully. He lets you get all the buttons undone at last, and then when you press yourself against him like a very small girl suddenly, he puts his arms around you and holds you—oh *fairly* tight, you think, but you can feel his arms relaxing, you can feel goodbye in his fingertips. You indulge yourself anyway for a mad whirling second, you steal what he doesn't want to give you, the illusion of comfort against his apocryphal chest, the illusion that he is holding you so tightly that he will never let you go. And then you give up, quite nicely, and stand back surveying him with your head on one side. Very definitely you refrain from asking him why the Spring suit, the bow tie. Quite loudly you do not ask him what time he will be home.

He tells you, though, he tells you everything. "I'll be a little late," he says; "I've got to stop off someplace for a cocktail or something." I'll be a little late, he tells you, with his gay-deceiver's troubled eyes, with his blue serge coat and light gray pants, and with the tiny pause he gives his words, I'll be a little late because I've got to stop off for a cocktail or something—with my girl; because I'm helpless, Cornelia, helpless, caught in as strong a web as your misery makes for you. . . .

In a minute now the pain will go tearing and surging through the veils, drop the curtain on the polished comedy—but hold it for another moment. "Oh then," you say, reaching up, quite coy, quite gay, "you must let me fix your tie in a better bow, if you are stopping off someplace for a cocktail or something." Tweak, tweak, like an idiot, at his gay bow tie. "Which will you have, my darling, my blessing or my cake? And always remember, little one, that everything you do reflects on me," but this is bad, you realize, and turning with your hands raised in a rather silly gesture that is meant for mocking admiration, you wave him off, "There, there we are, now off with you in a cloud of dust."

B plus for that one, little sister, you tell yourself wearily, as you stand there hearing the door slam, and you wait there a minute but he doesn't come back, he isn't coming back, and if he were going to telephone you from the corner drug-store he would have done it by now, and you walk back past the laden table and you do not sweep the cups and saucers off the table, nor do you scream nor do you turn on the gas nor do you telephone the boy that used to take you dancing (though you think of all these things), nor do you fall in a heap sobbing on the empty bed (though that is what you thought you wanted to do)—you merely stand at the kitchen sink letting the hot water run to grow hotter, and you say to the cold walls reproachfully, "Oh Dill, Dill . . . oh Jimsie, Jimsie . . ." and when the doorbell rings at last you know that it is not Dill and not Jimsie but merely the man collecting last week's laundry.

Mr. Palmer's Party

The New Yorker, April 1935

"Well, we're all here then," said Mr. Palmer brightly. He rubbed his hands together genially and rocked from his toes to his heels. But his party went right on without looking up, Miss Field picking threads off handsome Mr. Sedley's coat, Mr. Palmer's own Agnes continuing disloyally to pass the cakes. Even in his own house, at his own parties, people were apt to forget that Mr. Palmer was in the room, and that would have been all right except that there were times when Mr. Palmer forgot it himself. He had only one way of reminding people (and himself) that he was there, and that was by clearing his throat. It was a grand, momentous process. It began with a low clucking in the back of his throat. Mrs. Palmer had once been able, at this point, to end it all merely by meeting his eyes with a clear and threatening gaze, but Mr. Palmer, after years of practice, had learned to combat Agnes by keeping his own eyes lowered throughout the preliminaries. By the time he arrived at the second stage, which was a series of crescendo staccatos like the rattle of movie machine-gun bullets, she was too late; he could even afford to lift his eyes and meet hers with a mild and righteous defiance. By this time, indeed, Mr. Palmer could stand back and watch how the increasing volume of his own voice went striking at corners of the room, like a billiard ball, knocking each of his guests skillfully into a pocket of silence. Now Miss Field sat brooding over Mr. Sedley's sleeve, Mr. Johnson paused in the middle of an anecdote, Agnes's hand bearing cakes was suspended in mid-air. Mr. Palmer's party sat respectfully at attention, as if it had been frozen in jelly. "So we might as well start," said Mr. Palmer merrily.

He suffered a moment of panic. Start what? Why had he said that? You didn't "start" a party. Besides, it *had* started, without him, and now he had stopped it. He darted his hand under his vest and let it rove furtively over his chest while he avoided looking at his wife. If only he could clear his throat again! But the process had spent itself. "I was just going to say," Mr. Palmer finished lamely, "that he, that Mr. Sedley, *looks* like somebody," and brought his hand out to the public gaze again, examining it minutely.

"Mr. P.," said Agnes, the cakes shaking bitterly in her hands, "can never rest until he has found who people look like."

"But doesn't he," said Mr. Palmer, anxiously, "doesn't he remind you a little, Aggie—"

"Not at all," said Mrs. Palmer shortly. "Can't I give you some more cake, Miss Field? Mr. Johnson? Mr. Sedley?"

"Goodness," said Mr. Sedley lightly, "are my ears burning! Is my conscience worrying! Help me, Miss Field!"

Miss Field fell to twisting a button on Mr. Sedley's sleeve, Mr. Johnson stuffed his mouth with cake and started over on his anecdote, and Mr. Palmer's party went on again nicely, in spite of him.

***

Mr. Palmer retired modestly and watched his guests with pride. All of them, he felt, belonged to him for the evening, whether they listened to him or not. He had made a stage for them, and in the sense that their coming together made a pattern which had never exactly happened before, he had created them. He had gone to the telephone and called eight times, first this one, then that, Mrs. Palmer standing anxiously beside him. Eight times he had said quizzically, "I wonder, could you come to my house on Thursday evening? I'm having some interesting people." After he had got through telephoning, Mr. Palmer had wondered guiltily just which were the interesting people and which the guests who had been asked to meet the interesting people. He had also been a little concerned lest he might have said "Wednesday" to some of them, and "Friday" to others, but here it was Thursday, and he had gone to the door eight times, in blissful gratitude for the coincidence that brought all of his guests to his home on one and the same evening. *And* an extra. The inclusion at his party of Mr. Sedley, a stranger, an uninvited guest, made Mr. Palmer's party almost a "function."

"All the same," Mr. Palmer started happily, in a burst of gratitude toward Mr. Sedley, and not even bothering with his process this time, "Mr. Sedley *does* put me in mind of someone."

"Aha," said Mr. Sedley, cowering melodramatically, "the bloodhounds are on my trail! Will you protect me, Miss Field?" Miss Field almost died laughing, falling into Mr. Sedley's arms.

"But doesn't he," said Mr. Palmer, addressing Agnes, "put you in mind, just a little bit—I don't say he has the expression, mind you—of that man on The Boat who made things out of wires? "

"As little as possible," said Mrs. Palmer coldly. "We are now going to play a word game that I cut out of the papers," said Mrs. Palmer hospitably, to her eager guests.

Mr. Palmer retired again and grew pensive. Mention of The Boat—which meant, of course, their honeymoon, their one flyer into the world one read about—always left Mrs. Palmer cold and Mr. Palmer sad and frustrated. Perhaps he had hoped that marriage with Agnes would make him grow tall, plant hairs on his chest, somehow improve his position in life. But the trip, The Boat, had made it plain that no such miracle would happen. And with the years, Agnes had merely grown discontentedly fat and Mr. Palmer had simply grown seedy. Not Agnes's fault. Oh, not at all. And not Mr. Palmer's, either. It was just life, somehow. He looked pitifully at Agnes. Her face was large and round and full, and her mouth was tragically small, like a fish's, a little, feeble hole of a mouth. Poor old Agnes! But his disease was on him again, the longing to fit things and people into place. Mr. Palmer started his coughing process again.

"Perhaps of the second mate, that time, Agnes," he said gently. "You remember, when he came on deck— that time on The Boat, Aggie? Doesn't he—"

"We are playing a word game," said Agnes. "You are interrupting. What was your second syllable, Mr. Johnson?"

"My goodness," said Mr. Sedley, laughing in his sophisticated way, "he'll be taking my fingerprints next! Don't pay any attention to our host, Miss Field," he said, and Mr. Palmer saw him touch her boldly on the knee. Now, there was a man, thought Mr. Palmer, feebly. There was a man. And because they all turned back to their game again, Mr. Sedley and Miss Field with their shoulders lightly meeting, Mr. Palmer went back to thinking of The Boat.

For an odd thing had happened on The Boat, and as the years went by it had come to be the only incident of the trip which kept reality. They had been lounging (just like the advertisements) over their morning broth one day, halfway to England. Suddenly a group of sailors closed in about a lifeboat, tore off the canvas covering, and dragged forth the gauntest figure of a man. His face was black, literally black, with starvation. His eyes were the eyes of a hunted dog. The second mate came leaping across the deck, and Mr. Palmer never forgot the study in contrasts as the officer stood questioning the ragged stowaway. The stowaway kept muttering through his blackened lips, "Where are we? How soon do we land? Where are we?" At last they took him away.

The incident seemed like a concrete symbol of Mr. Palmer's whole existence. In his mind, all people were forever afterward catalogued accordingly: either they were stowaways or they were lucky second mates. Dreamily he catalogued the people at his party: Mr. Divine, who had held the same job for thirty years, was a stowaway like Mr. Palmer himself; Mr. Johnson was on the fence; Mr. Sedley and Miss Field were clearly second mates. All at once, the remembered episode became plain as day to him—the second mate standing in his handsome arrogance, his hand on the stowaway's shoulder; Mr. Sedley now, touching Miss Field upon the knee! Mr. Palmer coughed convincingly.

"By gad," he broke out recklessly, in the very teeth of Agnes's anger, "he *does* remind me! You must remember,

Aggie. Don't you remember that morning on The Boat? We were drinking our broth, and the second mate—"

"Well now, Miss Field," said Mr. Sedley smoothly. "What say we trot? Speak up for me, Johnson," Mr. Sedley said gaily, "and tell Miss Field I'm safe to go home with. Before our host," he said, and turned and stared at Mr. Palmer with so clever a simulation of anger that Mr. Palmer would have sworn he was that second mate, "before our host accuses me of being a stowaway or something."

And Agnes darted at her husband a look of hate, for now all their guests were rising, laughing, and protesting that they *must* be trotting; it was late (though it was barely midnight), and any minute, they cried, struggling into their coats and hats, Mr. Palmer might remember who *they* looked like. Agnes held out the platter of cakes as if she were pleading for alms, Mr. Palmer pretended to refuse to give them their coats and threatened them with some of his California wine, but it was all over. Miss Field picked a last thread off Mr. Sedley's sleeve, Mr. Johnson said, "Age before beauty," ushering Mr. Divine out the door, and Mr. Palmer's party was definitely at an end.

A Life in the Day of a Writer

Story, November 1935

O shining stupor, O glowing idiocy, O crowded vacuum, O privileged pregnancy, he prayed, morosely pounding X's on his typewriter, I am a writer if I never write another line, I am alive if I never step out of this room again; Christ, oh, Christ, the problem is not to stretch a feeling, it is to reduce a feeling, *all* feeling, all thought, all ecstasy, tangled and tumbled in the empty crowded head of a writer, to one clear sentence, one clear form, and still preserve the hugeness, the hurtfulness, the enormity, the unbearable all-at-once-ness, of being alive and knowing it too. . . .

He had been at it for three hours, an elbow planted on either side of his deaf-mute typewriter, staring like a passionate moron round the walls that framed his life—for a whole night had passed, he had nothing or everything to say, and he awoke each morning in terror of his typewriter until he had roused it and used it and mastered it, he was always afraid it might be dead forever—when the *telephone* screamed like an angry siren across his nerves. It was like being startled out of sleep; like being caught making faces at yourself in the mirror—by an editor or a book-critic; like being called to account again by your wife. His hand on the telephone, a million short miles in time and space from his writing-desk, he discovered that he was shaking. He had spoken to no one all the morning since Louise—shouting that she could put up with being the wife of a non-best-seller, or even the wife of a chronic drunk with a fetish for carrying away coat-hangers for souvenirs, but not, by God, the duenna of a conceited, adolescent flirt—had slammed the door and gone off cursing to her office. Voices are a proof of life, he explained gently to the angry telephone, and I have not for three hours heard my own; supposing I have lost it? Courage, my self! he said, as he stupidly lifted the receiver and started when nothing jumped out at him. All at once he heard his own voice, unnaturally loud, a little hoarse. *I wish to report a fire,* he wanted to say, but he said instead, roaring it: *Hello.* The answering Hello sunshine came from an immeasurable distance, from America, perhaps, or the twentieth century—a rescue party! but he had grown, in three long hours, so used to his solitary island! And though he was a writer and said to be gifted with a fine imagination, it was beyond his uttermost power to imagine that this voice addressing him was really a voice, that since it was a voice it must belong to a person, especially to the person identifying herself as Louise.

Ho, Louise! he said, going through with it for the purpose of establishing his sanity, at least in her ears if not actually in his own: he spoke courteously as though her voice were a voice, as though it did belong to her, as though she really were his wife; *now, darling, don't go on with*—But then he discovered that she was not going on with anything but being a wife, a voice, an instrument of irrelevant torture. *How goes the work,* she said kindly. What in hell did she think he was, a half-witted baby playing with paper-dolls? *Oh, fine, just fine,* he answered deprecatingly. (I'm a writer if I never write another line, he said fiercely to his typewriter, which burst out laughing.) *Well, look,* she was saying, *Freddie called up* (who in hell was Freddie?), and then her voice went on, making explanations, and it seemed that he was to put away his paper-dolls and meet her at five at Freddie's, because Freddie was giving a cocktail party. *Cocktail party,* he said obediently; *wife; five.* Cocktail party, eh—and a dim bell sounded in his brain, for he remembered cocktail parties from some other world, the world of yesterday; a cocktail party meant reprieve from typewriters, rescue from desert islands; and it might also mean Betsey—he cocked a debonair eye at his typewriter to see if it was jealous—Betsey, who, along with half a dozen coat-hangers, had been the cause of this morning's quarrel! *Yes, your wife for a change,* came the off-stage tinkle over the telephone again; *and you might try taking her home for a change too, instead of someone else's—and by the way, my treasure, don't bring those coat-hangers with you, Freddie has plenty of his own.—Right you are, my pet,* he said, feeling smart and cheap and ordinary again, r*ight you are, my lamb-pie, my song of songs, ace of spades, queen of hearts, capital of Wisconsin, darling of the Vienna press—* But she had got off, somewhere about Wisconsin.

He looked, a little self-conscious, about his now twice-empty room; aha, my prison, my lonely four-walled island, someone has seen the smoke from my fire at last, someone has spied the waving of my shirttails; at five o'clock today, he said, thumbing his nose at his typewriter, the rescue plane will swoop down to pick me up, see, and for all you know, my black-faced Underwood, my noiseless, portable, publisher's stooge, my conscience, my slave, my master, my mistress—for all you know it may lead to that elegant creature Betsey, whom my rather plump Louise considers a bit too much on the thin side . . . ah, but my good wife is a bit short-sighted there, she doesn't look on the *other* side, the bright side, the sunny side, the side that boasts the little, hidden ripples that it takes imagination, courage, to express; the little hiding ripples that the male eye can't stop looking for. . . .

He seated himself again before his typewriter, like an embarrassed schoolboy.

Black anger descended upon him. It was easy enough for her, for Louise, to put out a hand to her telephone where it sat waiting on her office desk, and ring him up and order him to report at a cocktail party—Louise, who sat in a room all day sur-rounded matter-of-factly by people and their voices and her own voice. But for him it was gravely another matter. Her ring summoned him out of his own world—what if he hadn't written a line all morning except a complicated series of coat-hanger designs in the shape of X's—and because he couldn't really make the crossing, it left him feeling a little ashamed, a little found-out, caught with his pants down, so to speak—and a little terrified, too, to be reminded again that he was not "like other people." He was still shaking. She had no right, damn it, no damn right, to disturb him with that sharp malicious ringing, to present him with the bugbear, the insult, the indignity, of a cocktail party—she, who was proud enough of him in public (Bertram Kyle, author of *Fifty Thousand Lives,* that rather brilliant book), although at home she was inclined to regard him, as his family had when he refused to study banking, as something of a sissy.

Still, when you have accepted an invitation to a party for the afternoon, you have that to think about, to hold over your typewriter's head, you can think of how you will lock it up at half-past four and shave and shower and go out with a collar and a tie around your neck to show people that you can look, talk, drink, like any of them, like the worst of them. But a party! Christ, the faces, the crowds of white faces (like the white keys of the typewriter I had before you, my fine Underwood), and worst of all, the voices. . . . The party became abnormally enlarged in his mind, as though it would take every ounce of ingenious conniving—not to speak of courage!—to get to it at all; and as he fell face downward on his typewriter, he gave more thought to the party than even the party's host was likely to do, Freddie, whoever the devil "Freddie" was. . . .

O degrading torture, lying on the smug reproachful keys with nothing to convey to them. He remembered how he had once been afraid of every woman he met until he kissed her, beat her, held her captive in his arms; but this typewriter was a thing to master every day, it was a virgin every morning. If I were Thomas Wolfe, he thought, I should start right off: O country of my birth and land I have left behind me, what can I, a youth with insatiable appetite, do to express what there is in me of everlasting hunger, loneliness, nakedness, a hunger that feeds upon hunger and a loneliness that grows in proportion to the hours I lend to strangers. . . . If I were Saroyan I should not hesitate either: But I am young, young and hungry (thank God), and why must I listen to the rules the old men make or the rich ones, this is not a story, it is a life, a simple setting down in words of what I see of men upon this earth. No, no, I am not Saroyan (thank God), I am not Thomas Wolfe either, and I am also not Louise's boss (ah, *there's* a man!). And I cannot write an essay; I am a natural liar, I prefer a jumbled order to chronology, and poetry to logic; I don't like facts, I like to imagine their implications. O to get back, get back, to the pre-telephone stupor, the happy mingled pregnancy, the clear confusion of myself only with myself. . . .

And so Bertram Kyle opened up his notebooks. He felt again that the story he had outlined so clearly there, of the "lousy guy" whom everyone thought was lousy including himself, but who was so only because of a simple happening in his childhood, might be a fine story; but it was one he could not do today. Nor could he do the story (which had occurred to him on a train to Washington) of the old lady, prospective grandmother, who went mad thinking it was her own child to be born. Nor could he do the story—partly because he did not know it yet—which would begin: "He lived alone with a wife who had died and two children who had left him." Perhaps, he thought bitterly, he could never do those stories, for in the eagerness of begetting them he had told them to Louise; too often when he told her a story it was finished then, it was dead, like killing his lust by confiding an infidelity.

And so, desperately, he turned to those thoughtful little flaps in the backs of his notebooks, into which he poured the findings in his pockets each night; out came old menus, the torn-off backs of matchbooks, hotel stationery that he had begged of waiters, ticket-stubs, a time-table, a theater program, and odd unrecognizable scraps of paper he had picked up anywhere. The writing on these was born of drinking sometimes; of loneliness in the midst of laughing people; of a need to assert himself, perhaps, a desire to remind himself—that he was a writer; but more than anything, he thought, for the sheer love of grasping a pencil and scratching with it on a scrap of paper. "If I were a blind man I should carry a typewriter before me on a tray suspended from my neck by two blue ribbons; I think I *am* blind"—he had written that on a tablecloth once, and Louise was very bored.

"It is always later than you think, said the sundial finding itself in the shade"—from the back of an old match-box, and undoubtedly the relic of an evening on which he had strained to be smart. A night-club menu: "Dear Saroyan: But take a day off from your writing, *mon vieux,* or your writing will get to be a habit. . . ." Another menu—and he remembered the evening well, he could still recall the look of tolerance growing into anger on Louise's face as he wrote and wrote and went on writing: "Nostalgia, a nostalgia for all the other nostalgic nights on which nothing would suffice . . . a thing of boredom, of content, of restlessness, *velleities,* in which the sweetness of another person is irrelevant and intolerable, and indifference or even cruelty hurt in the same way . . . linking up with gray days in child-hood when among bewilderingly many things to do one wanted to do none of them, and gray evenings with Louise when everything of the adult gamut of things to do would be the same thing. . . ." (At that point Lou-ise had reached down to her anger and said, "All right, sunshine, we come to a place I loathe because you like to see naked women and then, when they come on, you don't even watch them; I wouldn't complain if you were Harold Bell Wright or something. . . .") "In order to make friends," he discovered from another match-box, "one need not talk seriously, any more than one needs to make love in French"—and that, he recalled tenderly, was plagiarized from a letter he had written to a very young girl, Betsey's predecessor in his fringe flir-tations. "A man's underlying motives are made up of his thwarted, or unrealized, ambitions," "The war between men and women consists of left-overs from their unsat-isfactory mating." "But the blinking of the eye"—this on a concert program—"must go on; perhaps one catches the half-face of the player and sees, despite the fren-zied waving of his head, a thing smaller than his play-ing, but perhaps the important, the vital thing: like the heart-beat, at once greater and smaller than the thing it accompanies. . . ." "We are not so honest as the best of our writing, for to be wholly honest is to be brave, braver than any of us dares to be with another human being, especially with a woman." *At bottom one is really grave.*

He was pulled up short by that last sentence, which was the only one of the lot that made sense. "At bottom one is really grave."

Suddenly he raised his head and stared wildly round the room. He was terrified, he was elated. Here was his whole life, in these four walls. This year he had a large room with a very high ceiling; he works better in a big room, Louise told people who came in. Last year he had worked in a very small room with a low ceiling; he works better, Louise used to tell people, in a small place. He worked better at night, he worked better in the daytime, he worked better in the country, better in the city, in the winter, in the summer. . . . But he was frightened. Here he was all alone with his life until five o'clock in the afternoon. Other people (Louise) went out in the morning, left their life behind them somewhere, or else filed it away in offices and desks; he imagined that Louise only remembered her life and took it up again in the late afternoon when she said good night to her boss and started off for home—or a cocktail party. But he had to live with his life, and work with it; he couldn't leave it alone and it couldn't leave him alone, not for a minute— except when he was drunk, and that, he said, smugly surveying the scattered coat-hangers, relic of last night's debauch, that is why a writer drinks so much. Hell, he thought, proud, I'm living a life, my own whole life, right here in this room each day; I can still feel the pain I felt last night when I was living part of it and Louise said

... and I can still feel the joy I felt last week when Betsey said ... and I can feel the numbness and the excitement of too many Scotch-and-sodas, of too perfect dancing, of too many smooth-faced, slick-haired women; I can remember saying *Listen—listen* to anyone who would or would not, and the truth of it is I had nothing to say anyway because I had too much to say. . . . Hell, he thought, my coat-hangers lie on the floor where I flung them at three this morning when Louise persuaded me that it was better not to sleep in my clothes again, I have not hung up my black suit, I have not emptied yesterday's waste-basket nor last week's ashtrays (nor my head of its thirty years' fine accumulation) . . . everything in my room and in my head is testimony to the one important fact, that I am alive, alive as hell, and all I have to do is wait till the whole reeling sum of things adds itself up or boils itself down, to a story. . . .

There seemed now to be hunger in his belly, and it was a fact that he had not eaten since breakfast and then only of Louise's anger. But the turmoil in his insides was not, he felt, pure hunger. It came from sitting plunged in symbols of his life, it came because he did not merely have to live with his life each day, but he had to give birth to it over again every morning. Of course, he thought with a fierce joy, I am hungry. I am ravenously hungry, and I have no appetite, I am parched but I am not thirsty, I am dead tired and wide awake and passionately, violently alive.

But he lifted his elbows now from his typewriter, he looked straight before him, and he could feel between his eyes a curious knot, not pain exactly, but tension, as though all of him were focused on the forefront of his brain, as though his head were a packed box wanting to burst. It was for this moment that, thirty years before, he had been born; for this moment that he had tossed peanuts to an elephant when he was a child; that he had by a miracle escaped pneumonia, dropping from an air-plane, death by drowning, concussion from football accidents; that he had fallen desperately and permanently in love with a woman in a yellow hat whose car had been held up by traffic, and whom he never saw again; that he had paused at sight of the blue in Chartres Cathedral and wept, and a moment later slapped angrily at a mosquito; that he had met and married Louise, met and coveted Kitty Braithwaite, Margery, Connie, Sylvia, Elinor, Betsey; for this moment that he had been born and lived, for this moment that he was being born again.

His fingers grew light. The room was changing. Everything in it was integrating; pieces of his life came together like the odd-shaped bits of a puzzle-map, forming a pattern as one assembles fruits and flowers for a still-life. Listen, there is a name. Bettina Gregory. Bettina is a thin girl, wiry, her curves so slight as to be ripples, so hidden that the male eye cannot stop searching for them; she drinks too much; she is nicer when she is sober, a little shy, but less approachable.

Bettina Gregory. She is the kind of girl who almost cares about changing the social order, almost cares about people, almost is *at bottom really grave.* She is the kind of girl who would be at a cocktail party when someone named Fr—named Gerry—would call up and say he couldn't come because he was prosecuting a taxi-driver who had robbed him of four dollars. She is the kind of girl who would then toss off another drink and think it funny to take old Carl along up to the night-court to watch old Gerry prosecute a taxi-man. She is the kind of girl who will somehow collect coat-hangers (I give you my coat-hangers, Betsey-Bettina, Bertram Kyle almost shouted in his joy) and who will then go lilting and looping into the night-court armed to the teeth with coat-hangers and defense mechanisms, who will mock at the whores that have been rounded up, leer at the taxi-driver, ogle the red-faced detective, mimic the rather sheepish Gerry—all the time mocking, leering, ogling, mimicking—nothing but herself. Frankly we are just three people, she explains to the detective, with an arm about Gerry and Carl, who love each other veddy veddy much. She must pretend to be drunker than she is, because she is bitterly and deeply ashamed; she must wave with her coat-hangers and put on a show because she knows it is a rotten show and she cannot stop it. It is not merely the liquor she has drunk; it is the wrong books she has read, the Noel Coward plays she has gone to, the fact that there is a drought in the Middle West, that there was a war when she was a child, that there will be another when she has a child, that she and Carl have something between them but it is not enough, that she is sorry for the taxi-driver and ashamed of being sorry, that *at bottom she is almost grave.* In the end, Bertram Kyle said to anybody or nobody, in the end I think. . . .

But there was no reason any more to think. His fingers were clicking, clicking, somehow it developed that Gerry had muddled things because he was drunk so that the taxi-man must go to jail pending special sessions, and then Bettina and Gerry and Carl take the detective out to a bar someplace; explaining frankly to waiters that they are just four people who love each other veddy veddy much . . . and, perhaps because they all hate themselves so veddy veddy much, Carl and Gerry let Bettina carry them all off in her car for a three-day spree which means that Gerry misses the subpoena and the taxi-driver spends a week in jail, earning himself a fine prison record because he stole four dollars to which Carl and Gerry and Bettina think him wholly and earnestly entitled, and perhaps in the end they give the four dollars to the Communist party, or perhaps they just buy another round of drinks, or perhaps they throw it in the river, or perhaps they frankly throw themselves. . . .

And is this all, Bertram Kyle, all that will come out today of your living a life by yourself, of your having been born thirty years ago and tossed peanuts to elephants, wept at the Chartres window, slapped at mosquitoes, survived the hells and heavens of adolescence to be born again, today—is this all, this one short story which leaves out so much of life? But neither can a painter crowd all the world's rivers and mountains and railroad tracks onto one canvas, yet if his picture is any good at all it is good because he has seen those rivers and mountains and puts down all that he knows and all that he has felt about them, even if his painting is of a bowl of flowers and a curtain. . . . And here, thought that thin layer of consciousness which went on as an undercurrent to his fingers' steady tapping, here is my lust for Betsey, my repentance for Louise, my endless gratitude to the woman who wore a yellow hat, my defeatism, my optimism, the fact that I was born when I was, all of my last night's living and much that has gone before. . . .

The room grew clouded with the late afternoon and the cigarettes that he forgot to smoke. His fingers went faster, they ached like the limbs of a tired lover and they wove with delicacy and precision because the story had grown so real to him that it was physical. He knew that his shoulders were hunched, that his feet were cramped, that if he turned his desk about he would have a better light—but all the time he was tearing out sheet after sheet and, with an odd accuracy that was not his own at any other time, inserting the next ones with rapidity and ease, he typed almost perfectly, he made few mistakes in spelling, punctuation, or the choice of words, and he swung into a rhythm that was at once uniquely his and yet quite new to him.

Now each idea as he pounded it out on his flying machine gave birth to three others, and he had to lean over and make little notes with a pencil on little pieces of paper that later on he would figure out and add together and stick in all the gaping stretches of his story. He rediscovered the miracle of something on page twelve tying up with something on page seven which he had not understood when he wrote it, the miracle of watching a shapeless thing come out and in the very act of coming take its own inevitable shape. He could feel his story growing out of the front of his head, under his moving fingers, beneath his searching eye . . . his heart was beating as fast as the keys of his typewriter, he wished that his typewriter were also an easel, a violin, a sculptor's tools, a boat he could sail, a plane he could fly, a woman he could love, he wished it were something he could not only bend over in his passion but lift in his exultation, he wished it could sing for him and paint for him and breathe for him.

And all at once his head swims, he is in a fog, sitting is no longer endurable to him, and he must get up, blind, not looking at his words, and walk about the room, the big room, the small room, whether it is night or day or summer or winter, he must get up and walk it off. . . . *Listen, non-writers, I am not boasting when I tell you that writing is not a sublimation of living, but living is a pretty feeble substitute for art. Listen, non-writers, this is passion. I am trembling, I am weak, I am strong, pardon me a moment while I go and make love to the world, it may be indecent, it may be mad—but as I stalk about the room now I am not a man and I am not a woman, I am Bettina Gregory and Gerry and the taxi-driver and all the whores and cops and stooges in the night-court, I am every one of the keys of my typewriter, I am the clean white pages and the word-sprawled used ones, I am the sunlight on my own walls—rip off your dress, life, tear off your clothes, world, let me come closer; for listen: I am a sated, tired, happy writer, and I have to make love to the world.*

Sometimes it was night when this happened and then he must go to bed because even a writer needs sleep, but at those times he went to bed and then lay there stark and wide awake with plots weaving like tunes in his head and characters leaping like mad chess-men, and words, words and their miraculous combinations, floating about on the ceiling above him and burying themselves in the pillow beneath him till he thought that he would never sleep and knew that he was made . . . till Louise sometimes cried out that she could not sleep beside him, knowing him to be lying there only on sufferance, twitching with his limbs like a mad-man in the dark. . . .

Louise! For it was not night, it was late afternoon, with the dark of coming night stealing in to remind him, to remind him that if he were ever again to make the break from his life's world back to sanity, back to normalcy and Louise, he must make it now, while he remembered to; he must leave this room, stale with his much-lived life, his weary typewriter, he must shake off his ecstasy and his bewilderment, his passion, his love, his hate, his glorious rebirth and his sated daily death— and go to meet Louise; go to a cocktail party. . . .

He was shocked and terrified when he met his own face in the mirror because it was not a face, it was a pair of haggard, gleaming eyes, and because like Rip Van Winkle he seemed to have grown heavy with age and yet light with a terrible youth. He managed some-how to get by without letting the elevator man know that he was crazy, that he was afraid of him because he was a face and a voice, because he seemed to be look-ing at him queerly. On the street Bettina appeared and walked beside him, waving her drunken coat-hangers and announcing, "Frankly there is nothing like a coat-hanger," while Gerry leaned across him rather bitterly to say, "If I hear you say frankly again, Bettina, frankly I shall kill you." But they walked along, all of them, very gay and friendly, despite the taxi-driver's slight hostil-ity, and then at the corner they were joined by Carl with the detective's arm about him, and Carl was saying to anybody and nobody that they passed—"Frankly we are veddy veddy mad." And they came at last to Freddie's house, and there Bertram Kyle stood for a moment, deserted by Bettina and Carl and Gerry—even the detective was gone—hiding behind a collar and a tie and frankly panic-stricken. The door opens, he enters mechanically—good God, is it a massacre, a revolution, is it the night-court, a nightmare . . . ?

But he pushed in very bravely and began to reel toward all his friends. "Hello, I'm cockeyed!" he roared at random. "Hell, I've been floating for forty days, where's a coat-hanger, Freddie, frankly, if there's anything I'm nuts about it's coat-hangers, and frankly have you seen my friends, some people I asked along, Bettina Gregory, Gerry, and a detective?" He saw Louise, ominous and tolerant, placing her hands in disgust on her soft hips at sight of him. Frankly, he shouted at her, frankly, Louise, I am just three or four people who love you veddy veddy much, and where's a drink, my pearl, my pet, my bird, my cage, my night-court, my nightmare—for frankly I need a little drink to sober down. . . .

A Hollywood Gallery (The Old Man, The Old Man's Wife, Brick)

Michigan Quarterly Review, 1979

THE OLD MAN

He was only thirty-five and a dynamo of nervous energy and nervous ambition. Having reached the top at such an early age, he could afford to be a great man, and he was a great man. In his field he had the most money and the best talents at his command; he knew how to use them, how to retain his own executive power, and how to get, after tireless persistence, exactly what he wanted out of them. Having achieved everything he wanted, yet by no means having sated either his ambitions or his imagination, he was almost free of obsessions. His prejudices were the natural result of what went on most closely about him, because his interests were confined to his work and he was never curious enough to investigate outside of his immediate field, either in politics, literature, or anything else.

He was a perfectionist and a deep lover of his profession. He loved it partly because in itself it was successful; partly because it moved so many millions of people that he honestly believed it to be important industrially, and tremendously in-fluential; and he loved it because he had grown up with it from the bottom and knew every phase of the work, knew every bootblack on the lot, loved every corner and cranny and idiosyncrasy and professional joke about it, and was never bored.

Like a professional general in war-time, he thought the picture industry was great enough to sacrifice lives to. Presumably he would have sacrificed his own; if he held his own in greater esteem than those of ordinary camera-men, it was (besides a man's natural selfishness) because his own life was of more value to the profession; a cameraman can easily be replaced.

He wept at accidents to his men in taking pictures; but it glorified the picture for him, that blood had been shed, a life had been lost. Thereafter, in holy gratitude, he spent his money and spent his men and spent himself in ruthlessly drawing an "epic" out of tired brains and bodies, and he would shoot over the same dangerous shipwreck in the same dangerous spot of water until, whether another cameraman was lost or not, he achieved the scene he had dreamed and demanded.

He was easy and informal with his people, but he remained consciously and pleasurably and indisputably the boss. He was a little nicer to men far below him than to those immediately his inferiors. On one occasion, while a close assistant of his was delivering a serious opinion of some length in a conference, the boss suddenly disappeared. They all waited. After five minutes they called the secretary and asked where he had gone. She said he had gone to the barber-shop, and would be back if he had time.

He had something of the over-lord feeling at seeing his employees at a party. He loved to see them liking each other and going out together; he wanted his unit to be happy and congenial—partly because they worked together more efficiently, but also because it gave him a feeling of power and kindliness. And the employees in turn enjoyed seeing his pleasure, and like children smiled and winked at their boss, and actually—even persons older than he—got a kick out of it. Only those officially directly below him could be angered at his arrogance or condescension. In many ways he was psychologically a fine boss.

He loved wasting money on a picture, wasting it in quantities, just as he loved wasting the brains of his writers. He did not regard either as waste; they were necessary to build up a "great" picture, and the more expense, both of money and brains, the "greater" the picture must be.

Just what his reaction was to the great god Audience it was hard to tell. Sometimes he spoke of the Audience as though it were a fool; sometimes as though it were the measuring rod of real values. Sometimes he seemed to adore it, sometimes to despise it. He was always deeply conscious of it; identified with it yet was apart from it, superior to it yet catering to it—almost as though it were his conscience.

He was sentimental by nature, but practical enough never to let his sentimentality interfere with business interests. If a picture made him cry, he cried; but if he thought the Audience would not cry, he cut out the scene from himself and from the reel and let it run on colder stuff.

You could imagine that the Old Man, born in poverty, in city near-slums, of clean, ambitious, humbly patriotic parents—must have been a precocious and attractive child. Since he was extremely bright in the early years at school, it was perhaps never discovered that his waning interest in studies later on was due to the fact that he had more memory and spontaneity than penetration or depth. His parents, mistaking this early precocity as did his adoring teachers at public school, hoped he would be something unusual, something artistic; and he was reared accordingly with a reverence for "the arts"—also revered and disproportionately misunderstood by his parents, who thought a rhyme was as much as you could ask. This accounted perhaps in his professional career for his mingled attitude toward his writers; in spite of himself he respected and feared them (having discovered secretly that he himself could not have been a writer), and yet he despised them a little for working for him, working for money, when they could with their gifts have stayed home and worked for themselves. He at once admired their business acumen in selecting salaried work, and—almost unconsciously—deplored their lack of idealism. He couldn't help admiring most those writers who refused to be tempted by Hollywood; and for one of these he would go to any price. In a way he considered himself by hiring writers a patron of the arts. In a way he considered himself the greatest artist of them all because he could dictate to writers, make the last decisions on their work; and it took him, he considered, to lend that practical twist that made it possible for thousands to attend and appreciate works of art on the screen.

On the subject (again) of audience reaction—The Old Man had become, without knowing it, the concentration of Audience himself. He had "catered" for so long to their tastes that now those tastes were actually his own. He might beg his writers for a little sentimentality for the masses, but actually he wanted it for himself. He loved it. He, like many of his rival producers, deliberately and consciously set out to "make a propaganda picture"; if he made an anti-labor picture one day and an anti-lynching picture the next, it was because both of them represented his own inner feelings and convictions. In feeling the pulse of Audience, he had really only to take his own temperature.

This means in the last analysis that though he was himself the important source of much national (and even international) propaganda, he was also the victim (unconsciously, as were his own victims) of a more basic propaganda: the newspapers, the opinions of his bankers, the state of his investments under a democratic president, etc. The difference between his propaganda aims and those of other producers and big shots, seemed to be his *sincerity;* though bred of the elements of self-interest, his aims somehow took deep root inside him, and he came to believe in them. His politics appeared to him ultimate verities, rather than opportunistic tactics. Essentially a "good" and "honest" man himself, he could understand only the "honest" motives in most other capitalists, and genuinely thought his rich friends and richer bankers good and well-meaning citizens.

In his reactions to the Guild, all The Old Man's characteristics came into the open. He did not use threats or cheap bribes with his employees; only occasionally did he slip up and use stock sentimental arguments (such as the one about "our duty to the widows and orphans among our stockholders, whose stewards we are")— and even then, judging from his character, it seemed possible that he genuinely meant them. Because he quite naturally associated the success of his beloved industry with the success of his own class, its rulers, it seems that he honestly believed that the aim of the writers was to "destroy" that industry. He believed that if the "power" were even to be shared by the underlings (writers, directors, actors), ruin was spelled for pictures. When he said (to his credit it must be pointed out that he used this argument rather to his peers than to his employees) that the challenges and criticisms of the writers' guild hurt him, he meant it. This belonged to his role of paternalistic and kindly boss; it was really terrible to him that his children would band together and make a Guild against him and his kind. He remarked to a fellow-producer that if the writers' criticisms were correct, then either he or the writers ought to resign from the whole business. Because money was to him an ultimate value, he could not concede that the writers desired anything except money. The thought of "strikes" and "unions" not only belittled the writers in his mind, but belittled himself; if they became common workers, then he became the boss of common workers, rather than the archbishop of high- minded artists. He took their action as personal offense. It is noteworthy that he did not immediately afterward boost the scabs in the scabs' guild, and that he remained a gentleman in his tactics—he refused the open and ass-licking invitation to join in heckling the one guild-member present in a conference, and rebuked the scabs with a quiet his, for she becomes the vessel of his all, his ambitions, and constantly, pathetically, and bravely dresses her soul to suit his "ideal"—built up and become his own through years of created movie attitudes.

Re the Guilds again: When he reminded his writers of their humble, sometimes slum beginnings—what had happened to his memory? Did he really forget his own origin (which, nevertheless, when it was convenient, he could describe with senti-mental pride)? When he accused his writers of being "nouveau riche," of their unaccustomed money going to their heads and making them greedy—just what was his opinion at that moment of himself and his fellow-producers? Was he the victim of amnesia? Did he unconsciously succeed in burying his past except when it was needed? Or was he, by denying it, hoping to wipe it out? (I, for one, don't know).

He built a house on the beach. The following points about it are things no one can explain, nor has anyone dared ask him about them: Evidently he does not believe in sea breezes, for all his windows are permanently closed, and a ventilator system (price $30,000 to install) imports air from the San Fernando Valley. Apparently he also does not care for sea bathing, for his swimming pool, built on the sand and defying the ocean by a few yards, contains fresh water—the temperature alterable of course, and usually warm. Also it appears that he does not care for the ocean's sound effect, so his entire house has been soundproofed to shut out the smallest crashing of a wave. And finally, strange as it seems, he must have a horror of the view of the sea, for the front of his house is carefully guarded by a high woven fence which permits not the slightest glimpse of so much as a dash of spray. Civilization can go no further. Yet one feels that if a writer presented him with a script containing such a civilized house, The Old Man would wrinkle up his nose, shake his head, and declare that there was no human interest in farce.

THE OLD MAN'S WIFE

The Old Man married Mary after she had made her first hit picture under his tutelage. He "made" Mary carefully before he married her—created her in his sentimental image of the ideal movie American sister-sweetheart-wife-mother. Not only was she a heroine in his eyes, but she had to wait to become that same heroine in the eyes of the whole American audience, before he could marry her. She came along, either at the end of silent pictures or at the beginning of talkies, just when the Old Man figured that the audiences were tired of flashy heroines. Mary was "sweet," quite naturally; she had a soft, rather poorly carrying voice; she was essentially feminine and submissive, and yet healthily spirited and defiant toward the male on the proper occasions. She was less of an actress than a real human woman, with the accident of beauty which screened well. Sensing the Audience's—i.e., his own—need of a modern Mary Pickford, of a woman who despite youth would remind men of their mothers, who would rouse their protective rather than their passionate impulses, the Old Man built Mary mainly by letting her be herself in public.

Every step of their married life was molded gently on picture ideals. He was chivalrous, he remembered anniversaries and birthdays (with the aid of a competent secretary), he made expensive presents. He was a charming father to their children; a charming lover and escort to Mary. Mary would have been happy to have seen the charm relaxed; would have been more convinced of his love if he had occasionally lost his temper or appeared at breakfast with his hair tousled. She would have been terribly happy to have been allowed to relax herself, not to force herself back into training immediately after each child was born, and act in another picture. In fact, though she never admitted it to him or anyone else, she would have loved never to act in another picture again. But her success was most of what he loved her for; he had nothing really to talk about to a woman except her beauty, and beauty to him was stock-in-trade. He would never let her relax. When she was forty, she visualized how he would change her roles, and let her be the epitome of American womanhood at forty.

Basically he did not model her pictures on their own life, but rather modeled their own life on the pictures. Poor Mary! She was intuitive enough to sense everything that was going on, but not strong enough to oppose it. She knew that even his devotion to her, even his fidelity, was partially the result of his constantly taking part in a mental moving-picture. He might not have loved their children if they had not all been picturesque or beautiful. His private and his public life of course were retroactive, and sometimes even Mary was taken in and made happy by the semblance of reality in their home life; only she knew it was not complete.

After his marriage to Mary, his whole attitude toward women changed. He really ceased to be a Don Juan, and began to look at all attractive women rather tenderly, as potential mothers, as faithful wives to someone, as patriotic and self-sacrificing examples of American womanhood. Having himself mounted them on this pedestal and told them how to behave, he was a good enough and disinterested enough artist to look at them and admire them, forgetting his own creative efforts, and content to kneel at the foot of the pedestal along with the humbler males for whose benefit he had raised them. Mary was too real to enjoy pedestal life, but too much in love to squirm and spoil the effect.

Occasionally Mary did have a flare-up and lose her temper—always tastefully. But her husband was too gentle and considerate for her brief revolt to bring her any comfort; he assumed that woman's delicacy had occasionally to be paid for, would have preferred to have staged Mary's rare tantrums himself, but on the whole was grateful to her training and her voice for sparing him the ordeals his own poverty-stricken mother had often imposed on his exasperated and overworked father. Her mother-in-law, ensconced in an "ideal" widow's retreat not far from their own home, merely served to double the effect of Mary's husband. For Anna shared all her son's idealism, and instead of freely loving and quarreling with her daughter-in-law, she remained her son's version of the "ideal" mother-in- law/grandmother. The difference between her and Mary was that Anna loved her role and at bottom was the realer actress.

BRICK

His total physical disregard for himself (unfortunately paralleled in other fields by general sloppiness, absentness, inefficiency) leads either to disgust or to a feeling of maternal compassion. Oddly, when you see him (through negligence) go about for months with a bit of court plaster on his glasses instead of having them mended, you think—how his mother would hate to see him now, ruining his eyesight needlessly like that. He has forgotten the need for vegetables long ago, and his skin shows it. His pants hang sloppily over a shapeless belly. He lacks even normal human vanity. His personal habits are disgusting and lax—and for all that he seems to have a definite charm (not sexual, but something inexplicable) for women, especially bourgeois women—at least for half of them, the other half loathing him to the point of promoting him to a grievance and an issue.

Nobody knows exactly where he came from or where he worked last, and this seems to please him. Indeed, the parts of which he is the sum total are a mystery even to the imagination. He seems totally dissociated from any past whatsoever, of background, family, education, a native city, childhood friends, early traditions. His peculiar personality seems entirely a product of his own, not any result of heredity or environment. You would think he had never had parents, except when you look at his broken glasses and feel he has a mother worrying somewhere. He has used so many names that perhaps he himself has forgotten his original name; you feel he may some day choose it for an alias, and it will fit him as illy as all his other names do, for really he *has* no name. Similarly he is neither young nor old, neither Jewish nor non-Jewish—that is, in his traits and characteristics.

He has odd bits of information on assorted and irrelevant subjects. One doesn't know whether they are samples dropped out of a truly rich and varied education, or just scraps picked up from other people's backyards. His language is equally mys-terious—he has a variety of vocabularies, sophisticated, literary, communistic, slangy, pedantic—yet none of them peculiarly his own, none of them springing from natural and accustomed association. His accent—well, you might say he was the person in the world who came nearest to having no accent at all. Whatever it is, it is impossible to place him from it, either socially or geographically. His accent and pronunciation are equally individual without being conspicuous—but never those of a worker, a professional, a "native" of anywhere, never suggestive of any particular trade, any particular background. He seems to have sloughed off all distinguishing traits that are the normal product of a community or a life, and seems to have developed others that are inimitable, impossible to analyze; he seems to have *accumulated* absolutely nothing; his character is the result of last-minute orders, as his clothing is the result of last-minute dressing.

Sexually he is again a mystery. As I said he had no accent, so he seems to have no sex. Yet this is impossible. Perhaps it is sublimated in his work—yet his work lacks the passionate fervor of a sublimator. He can certainly tell a pretty girl from a plain one, and is quite capable of a sort of heavy coyness, also of a genuine and sweet gallantry, yet it seems to have no end in view, and is complete in itself. One feels he would look different if with drums beating and red flags waving at all. He got in touch with the closest known sympathizers in Hollywood, through them made the acquaintance of weaker sympathizers, and through them met up with the quite casual people who had never thought about things one way or another. For some reason, everyone accepted him quite nonchalantly—and wherever he went some little seed was fertilized, and pretty soon there was a genuine, if loosely organized, "field" actually blooming in Hollywood. Though one would have guessed that he was not the man for the job, he evidently was. In a quiet way, his elusive personality and cryptic character fascinated people. And then he had a tolerance which did not make the rich people ashamed of their swimming pools or finger bowls or canapes—he enjoyed them too frankly himself. Whether this tolerance was a result of studied policy, or policy dictated from headquarters, or whether it was just laxness on Brick's part, or whether it was even his secret love of luxury and a sign that he was getting spoiled—I don't know myself.

But it's true his tastes, though never his table manners, were "raised" to a more expensive level. He enjoyed cigars (and looked very funny smoking them), turned down beer for scotch and soda. Still his sloppiness persisted. He spilled his cigar ashes over an Aubusson with the same carelessness that he must have used in party offices. There was something both good and bad about this, something both loveable and unlovable.

Quite naturally, he drifted toward the richest of his sympathizers, or the most famous of them. Never— absolutely never—a sycophant, still he found their houses more pleasant than those of the earnest middle classes, he found their names more fun to roll on his tongue, perhaps he even preferred their meals. There was some purpose to this tendency, since these were the people who had the most money and the most influence, but his close friends did begin to suspect that a curious kind of snobbishness had entered into Brick. At the same time that he lavished tolerance on his richest converts, he exercised a severer discipline on his humbler ones; and in some cases abandoned or neglected the latter altogether. When taken to task for this, he replied naively that the "aristocrats" of the bourgeoisie were better people, more earnest, helpful, conscientious, interested, than those modest souls who had neither the personality nor the money to be flashy. This sentence got him into plenty of trouble. It led to some of his friends declaring that he had "gone Hollywood"; and people worried and raised quizzical eyebrows when he was heard addressing women indiscriminately as "honey" and "darling" in true Hollywood fashion.

Brick arrived in town and in no time had formed committees (Scottsboro, Mooney, Fair Play in General) composed largely of people from New York, people tired of parties, wives whose husbands worked at night, and actresses whose profiles were slipping. To make the

Mooney Committee for instance over into a Committee against Fascism was not too difficult; eventually his committees were merged, and merged under a name so general that reds would think it liberal, and liberals would know it was red.

Brick's corruption, under the capable hands of Vernon who put an end to the psychoanalytic post-mortems and came in with a clean economic interpretation, became an example rather than a disillusionment. People were enchanted to have intimately known an adventurer, a victim, a Nietzschean, to have had him at their tables, or loaned him towels. When he died in Spain he left a letter—a letter which would have been marked down as cheaply and laughably dramatic had he lived, but which was hallowed for his readers by the aura of a martyred death. All right, he was dramatic, possibly he even enjoyed his last gasp. But some of us go through life with long noses, others with hunchbacks, and we may allow an occasional pose of "divided personality" to a martyr. (Note: written before his actual death, which occurred in Spain some months later and made fact of this fiction.)

The perfidy discovered, a new character was built for Brick. But no matter what you did with him, he remained a phony. Even those who credited him with the dignity of a divided personality, felt that he must have affected it.

Who shall say today that Brick was not a great man—whatever his name, his character, the title of his psychosis? He it was who started the first committees, gave the first Scottsboro affair at the Trocadero, won signatures to telegrams which had hitherto been signed only to gambling checks. He it was who joined husbands and wives on the verge of a separation due to boredom, he it was who parted husbands and wives who had thought they loved. Let us say that he was only a cipher playing a necessary historic role; maybe the god of historical necessity withdrew him at the end because "his usefulness was outworn." But what a fascinating cipher! What a brilliant imitation of a complex human being! What a mixture of corruption and courageous idealism, of non-comprehension with crystal-clear understanding, what filth of body with what cleanness of vision! Brick, I hope they let you into the soviet heavens because I can think of far honester people who accomplished less than you, in your whirlwind career in Hollywood and Spain!

***

It was hard to tell what Brick fell in love with, when he fell in love with Eleanor. He was in love with the feel of his feet on her lawn, with the rich, subdued notes of the bell when he rang at her door; with the deference of the maid who admitted him; with the nonchalant manner in which everyone took a bath every day as a matter of course instead of as a chore; with the fact that Eleanor, even working in the garden, smelled as though she were at a party. His love was a love of all the senses, perhaps omitting the conventional sexual. The voices fell like velvet on his ears; the scents mingled like aphrodisiac in his nostrils; his finger-tips were constantly lulled by the touch of everything; his eyes feasted voluptuously, never having their fill of a thing like a dark-red carpet melting into blue chintz drapes. The meals were perpetual manna; and the colors, the softnesses fed some other appetite in him that grew to be insatiable.

It was living in a play, to be part of a group that rose languorously at a given moment and drifted, still talking, into the candle-lit dining room; he loved every instant of the simple ceremonies which were unconsciously observed, the waiting for the hostess before unfurling the fresh, large napkins; the tentative dallying with demi-tasse cups till the hostess gave the signal, the soundlessness of pushing back the chairs when the guests rose at last and returned to the living room for liqueurs. He learned not to call for scotch-and-soda till an hour after dinner; he learned to smoke cigars; he learned to sit gently upright instead of slouching into the sofa. But he never learned to accept these things without a full, aching consciousness of every smallest part of them, without a return on his side of overpowering love for the smallest flower in the curtain, the faintest breath of scent wafted to him from this fine, high world.

As for Eleanor, she felt attraction and repulsion at once for Brick. Had he been a man of her own class she wouldn't have spoken to him a second time. But as it was, his presence in her house was exotic. She thought he was truly a great man, and was endlessly fascinated by the combination of reverence and maternal solicitude in which she held him. There were times when she thought the end must surely come; and then she would be swept by a repellent tenderness, almost nauseating to swallow, because his glasses were still fixed with adhesive, or he needed a new tooth in the side of his jaw. But it was an interlude in her real life, she was always aware of that. She would either go back to the plane she had lived on, or she would make some adjustment to a new one. But she could always visualize the period when Brick had stayed in her house as a thing that happened to her in the past, when she was young—even while it was happening, she was telling about it in the future.

Nothing in a sense, ever happened between them. When Brick came to her and told her she must hide him, that he would be completely safe and unsuspected in her house, Eleanor had both feared and hoped that consummation was imminent. Even as she dreaded it, she prepared for it. But the inevitable never seemed to happen with Brick; he was guided by no rules, not even by instinct as other people had instinct. Perhaps only some small thing kept him back, like a terror of himself climbing into those silk sheets on Eleanor's bed. But it became a habit with them to visit in each other's bedrooms, clad in pyjamas and bathrobes, and then to bid each other casually good-night.

The relation, tenuous as it was, permitted her to dine and dance with other men, but kept her from anything deeper, as though she were remaining faithful to Brick. After one of these dates she would return, dash into his bedroom all fresh and glowing, and in a way would taunt him with his loss. But he was never taunted; he was fascinated; like a father he wanted every detail of her evening—where they had dined, what they had eaten—and sometimes she even suspected that if she hinted at more he would sit up in his bed, breathless with vicarious excitement, and ask for the details of that. Yet something drew them together, to a point; by an unspoken wish, they became as intimate as two people could become, without being lovers; they never touched each other save casually, to adjust a lapel or pull down a skirt; but even their glances became a physical exchange on some level all their own, and satisfying. Their highest consummation was a joke which could send them sprawling all over each other with laughter; and close to him Eleanor could count the things that repelled her like the pores in his skin without hating them, and Brick could breathe in her scent without fear of violating it.

She loved his never taking money from her, yet it was one of the first things that led her to suspicion after it was roused. Where did he get his money? Not only did he always have car-fare and lunch money for his mysterious trips "downtown," but he had bought little things lately, or had at least appeared with new things—shirts, a tie, a character, a split personality. She was to tell him he must leave her house at once; they had already told him he must leave town.

She went home, building up in her mind how she would upbraid him, how she would put two and two together, how she would tell him that she was disillusioned now not only with him but with everything he represented. She was so filled with hate that she promised herself she would tear down all his disciples in the town, end the wave of liberalism in Hollywood. And she would tell him. . . . Driving into the garage, she was suddenly smitten by the fear that he might have killed himself, or might have run away. She ran desperately into the house to save him, if it were not too late. The maid told her he had been called on the telephone and had gone out, saying he would be back at six o'clock. He would never come back! She despised him again. . . . At six o'clock he returned. With shining eyes he told her he had been transferred; he was to do secret duty in the South. He must leave tonight. It was of the utmost importance. . . .

Eleanor found she could say nothing to him. As though she were attending a man who was going to be executed, she helped him pack, asked no embarrassing questions, behaved in every way as though she believed him, and believed in him. And in a curious way she did. And she found she was not disillusioned in his cause, she believed in it even more; for he was the symbol and the proof of it. He had merely turned out to be a victim, instead of a leader. When she learned that he had gone to Spain, she knew everything about him. Knew that his work in Califor-nia had been an attempt to rehabilitate himself, to regain his lost standing. It failed. Now he had gone to Spain, and she knew he was hoping to be killed, to exonerate himself, no longer in the eyes of his party, but in his own eyes. She wondered if his mother, who-ever she was, wherever she was, knew about her son.

Afterword

"She had done it as a girl"
by Paula Rabinowitz

Tess Slesinger's stories—arch and insightful, playful and poignant—are modernist gems, almost forgotten since they first appeared in the 1930s, first collected then and reissued in the 1970s. Now almost 50 years since that resurrection, they have been brought together to mark this *Time: The Present.*

Born to Upper West Side middle-class Jewish parents on July 16,1905, Tess Slesinger was not yet 20 when *The New Yorker* was first published in February 1925.[1] In many respects, she represented its target audience. A graduate of Columbia School of Journalism, she was smart, ironic, knowing, urbane, in short, modern. The magazine's brand of writing—satirical and witty—fitted her, or she fitted herself to it. In his brief "Announcing a New Weekly Magazine" framed in the familiar border and declared in the typeface still in use, Harold Ross reveals *The New Yorker's* style and content: "a reflection in word and picture of metropolitan life...human. Its general tenor will be one of gaiety, wit and satire. It will not be what is commonly called radical or highbrow. It will be what is commonly called sophisticated." Concerned with the "goings and doings of the village of New York... *The New Yorker* will be the magazine which is not edited for the old lady in Dubuque. It will not be concerned with what she is thinking about." It "is a magazine avowedly published for the metropolitan audience..."[2] And within the space of a few years, she was writing the kinds of pieces found in its pages—and those of other national magazines, both high-brow and radical.

At 29, she published her first and, tragically, only novel, the 1934 quasi-*roman* à clef, *The Unpossessed,* which was celebrated as the "American novel of a generation victimized by its own unconventional ideas," according to the cover blurb on its first paperback reissue by Avon Books in. In the mid-1960s, its glimpse of New York Depression-era bohemia rhymed with the Beats and emerging counter-culture and student rebellions against Jim Crow racism in the South and the exploding war being waged in Vietnam. Here was a past as prologue.

A generation later, in 1984 (during the campaign for Ronald Reagan's second presidential term, battles over NEA funding for queer and feminist artists, and the

Hyde Amendment's restrictions on federal funding for family planning), *The Unpossessed* was reissued again by Feminist Press as part of its Novel of the Thirties series (the series introduced by Alice Kessler-Harris and Feminist Press co-founder Paul Lauter) with an afterword by Janet Sharistanian. This time, what stood out was the overt discussion of young middle-class women's sexuality and its explicit description of a woman's decision to have an abortion—a feminist foreshadowing.

By 2002, New York Review Books, the book publishing off-shoot of that 1960s radical heir to *The New Yorker* as a sophisticated literary and news magazine, had again brought it back for a new audience bristling under the Bush-Cheney-Rumsfeld doctrine of perpetual war on terror in the wake of the 9/11 attack on Manhattan's iconic Twin Towers, with an introduction by Elizabeth Hardwick. Its importance as a political critique was somewhat diminished by its presentation as another in the endless saga of New York Stories from Walt Whitman to Hart Crane to Jules Dassin's 1948 film, *Naked City,* to Jonathan Lethem's 1999 novel, *Motherless Brooklyn* and so on. In his review of this edition, Morris Dickstein called *The Unpossessed* "the *Big Chill* of the *Menorah Journal* circle, though etched in satire and sardonic affection rather than nostalgia."[3]

It seems every generation after the 1930s must reinvent its intellectual and political fervor and strive to understand the decade's artistic productions beyond the Cold War confines that had framed them as hopelessly dull social realism tainted by a disgraced or dangerous politics that whitewashed Stalin's crimes and thus easily dismissed by the New Critics in and out of the academy. But the literature of the 1930s, like the art, movies, and music of the period, was never bound by its later simplistic caricature.

Two years before Avon's first paperback edition of *The Unpossessed,* the pulp publisher had resurrected another radical novel from 1934, Henry Roth's *Call It Sleep,* like Slesinger's novel, lauded upon its publication but neglected until 1960 when an obscure press, Pageant, brought out a new hardcover edition, sparking a rediscovery with essays by noted critics Meyer Levin, Maxwell Geismar, Leslie Fiedler, Alfred Kazin among them, and cementing the novel in the canon of immigrant literature. Though stylistically very different, both novels, the first written by authors in their late twenties, explore the psychologies of characters forged in the dual crucibles of the rejection of Orthodox Judaism in the face of modern society and the invention of modern American Jewishness . Roth and Slesinger needed Freud as much as Marx to explore the contradictions found in this new American identity—one developed both in the cramped poverty of the Lower East Side Yiddish ghetto and—another world apart—in the expansive river view apartments of the secular Jewish Upper West Side.

Neither Slesinger nor Roth could withstand the hot-house world of New York literary radicals after pub-lishing their first signature novels. Both fled New York City and its internecine left-wing politics with its pro-liferation of little magazines and diverging party lines. Roth retreated from writing for more than fifty years, holding a number of regular jobs and ultimately raising ducks on a farm in Maine. Slesinger, divorced her first husband Herbert Solow in Reno in 1932 and left a few years later for Hollywood to work for MGM, where she embarked on a career as a screenwriter married screen-writer and producer Frank Davis, had two children and became immersed in various left-wing causes and con-tinued writing short essays, stories and sketches—some published, others still in drafts when she died.[4]

"*The Unpossessed,* with its narrative structured around aspects of marriage, friendship, and adultery, is above all, a study of group dynamics," explains Alan Wald.[5] And these group dynamics unravel in the dual plots involving the efforts of left-wing professor Bruno Leonard and his "Black Sheep" to form new kinds of heterosexual couples, on the one hand, and produce a radical cultural magazine, on the other. Both story lines converge at the fundraising party for the Hunger Marchers and the nascent little magazine thrown by the mother of one of Bruno's acolytes.

Parties need parties. And a number of the selections in this volume, "Mrs. Palmer's Party," "After the Party,"

"The Friedmans' Annie" among them, explicitly unpack the preparations, events and aftermaths of various New York parties. These quasi-public yet highly domestic affairs lay bare the class dynamics, ethnic tensions and gender politics running through the sheltered world of supposedly sophisticated bourgeois New Yorkers. Jerre Mangione recalled a party given by the "young and beautiful" Tess Slesinger for William Saroyan shortly after *The Unpossessed* was published: "I had never met her but came to the party at Saroyan's invitation, arriving late after a great deal of liquor had been consumed. At the door Tess Slesinger greeted me with the salutation, 'Come right in, sir. Will you have me? Or would you prefer a martini?' ... I could only gulp and blush, and settle for a drink."[6] Slesinger's spoofs of upper-crust New Yorkers' attempts to cultivate "radical chic" anticipate by more than a quarter century Tom Wolfe's skewering of Felicia and Leonard Bernstein's notorious fundraising party for the Black Panthers first published in *New York* magazine in June 1970.[7]

Her unfinished Hollywood novel was equally savage. "A cocktail party held to benefit Tom Mooney is captured through a scrap of overheard conversation," notes Sharistanian: "'This is a swell party, I got here at four. By 4:30 I had adopted a Spanish orphan, by 5 I was supporting the New Masses'."[8] Elizabeth Hardwick dedicates most of her introduction to *The Unpossessed* to delighting in Slesinger's seamless glide through the conversation of those attending the fundraising bash at the Middletons. "In the staccato brilliance of the party scene more than two dozen voices and human shapes appear in a raucous mingling...The pages have the reckless exuberance of the open bar, the dance floor, the plentiful harvest of the buffet table, the tribal company, each in its vanity, language, armor, and folly."[9] Slesinger knew these drunken festivities not only as fodder for sarcasm but as a host herself. She was an artifact.

In *Part of Our Time,* his 1955 excavation of the 1930s, Murray Kempton called *The Unpossessed* "almost our only surviving document on a group of intellectuals who were drawn to the Communists early in the thirties and left them very soon."[10] But it is a novel and thus both more and less than a document, better understood as an archive waiting to be mined. For many, it was a lifesaver.

Tess Slesinger's writings literally gave me my grownup life.

I first read her when my friend and colleague, Charlotte Nekola, discovered *The Unpossessed* in the card catalogue of the University of Michigan library. The dusty copy was not available in the stacks. It was in storage: "almost forgotten," as Kempton had called it.[11] Charlotte was taking a course on the literature of the 1930swith Professor Cecil Eby. This being the late 1970s, there had been no women on the syllabus and according to her professor, no women wrote about the

Spanish Civil War or the Depression. An absurd decla-
ration—considering Josephine Herbst and Martha Gellhorn among others—but not atypical for the time.[12] As
burgeoning feminist scholars, we were in the throes of
feminist archaeology, digging up the remains of the forgotten and almost forgotten, lost and despised "damn'd
mob of scribbling women" so abhorrent to Nathaniel
Hawthorne and the much later architects of the emerging postwar American literary canon, who also ignored
many 1930s writers no matter their gender.

Slesinger's voice was a revelation: smart, sassy,
just nasty enough. But her subject, a radical magazine's internal fights and the different ways that men
and women experienced politics and culture, was at
the heart of our lives. *We* were members of the editorial
collective of a journal of "feminist art and literature,"
we were inventing Women's Studies, *we* were leading
graduate-student union organizing, *we* were living with
testy art-y leftie men. And perhaps most amazing, considering this was just a few years after *Roe v. Wade, The
Unpossessed* concluded with "Missis Flinders," a long
section on one woman's abortion—an abortion which
she chose to have for personal and political, not medical, reasons.[13] It was as if our avenging angel had been
hiding on the shelves awaiting us. We went on to com-
pile a 300+ page anthology of radical women's writings
from the 1930s.[14] I ended up writing my dissertation
(and subsequent first book) on the dozens of novels I

uncovered while researching our collection. *The Unpossessed* figured as a crucial emblem of these works.[15]

Lionel Trilling, a friend of Slesinger and her husband Herbert Solow's from the heady days when Solow co-edited *The Menorah Journal* with Elliot Cohen, explains how the group around the magazine—those lovingly mocked in her 1934 novel—were seeking "fame through literary achievement," even as they were also ashamed of this crass desire. Slesinger got there first and he speculates about the "difficult situation" this would have created for a man, one even more fraught "for a woman. And it wasn't only as a woman that Tess had done what men wanted to do and hadn't done. She had done it as a girl." Slesinger was 29 when the novel first appeared and had already published some of the short stories and pieces collected here in *Menorah Journal,* which gave her her first break. By the time *The Unpossessed* appeared, she was also publishing in the slicks, including *Story Magazine, Scribner's, Pagany, Vanity Fair,* and *The New Yorker.*

She was hardly a girl. But her pose as a girl (or Trilling's perception of her as such) seems to have been cemented, in part, by her "*persona*...daughterly...her expectation of being loved, indulged, forgiven, of having permission to be spirited and even naughty."[16] Hers was, in the words of the "Publisher's Note" to the reissue of her 1935 short story collection, "a wholly feminine voice—compelling, shooting off insights, sure of its tone, searching after the feeling behind appearances, and everywhere finding it."[17] Slesinger's ability to chart "the interaction between character and *milieu*, the ways place and profession impinge on personality," as Sharistanian notes, were the hallmark of her socially aware psychological or psychologically astute social portraits.[18] She understood the uncanny asymmetries unbalancing all human interactions—between children and parents, friends and lovers and spouses, boys and girls, mena and women. She was, after all, the daughter of Augusta Slesinger, a psychoanalyst who worked in various child welfare bureaus in New York and helped found the New School for Social Research.[19]

Like so many of the writers of the 1930s, she grew up with the century. She was in her twenties during the 1920s, living the ideal of the free woman, the flapper, the wild girl who could dance, like Joan Crawford in *Our Dancing Daughters* (1928), given literary shape by F. Scott Fitzgerald's frivolous Daisy Buchanan in *The Great Gatsby* or Christopher Isherwood's louche Sally Bowles in *Goodbye to Berlin.* She was a precursor of the Jewish American princess—sassy, self-loathing and socially aware, like her eventual friend Dorothy Parker. (Who could not want to devour a story entitled "On Being Told That Her Second Husband Has Taken His First Lover"?) But the Great Depression, colliding with her thirties, brought a new awareness to this generation as poverty, hunger and war loomed across the globe and the political choices starkly divided between communism and fascism. This is the gist of her tour-de-force *Vanity Fair* story "Memoirs of an Ex-Flapper."[20]

It is tempting to dismiss Trilling's casual sexism—his infuriating references to "Tess" as a "girl"—so predominant at the time (at both times!). However, Slesinger's astute ability to tap into her girlness, her girlhood, enabled her keen dissection of the mores of her class. Henry James hinted that modern America was best represented as a girl in *Daisy Miller* at the end of the 19th century, dispelling the rough boys—Huck Finn, Ishmael—as emblems of modernity. Attuned to her times, Slesinger could both represent and be this girl. In many ways, Trilling perceptively realized how her pose enabled her prose.

This comes out most clearly in the story "White on Black," which literally enters the classroom and inspects the double standard of middle-class white liberals when it comes to race. A poignant sketch about two Black siblings enrolled in the mostly white private school, the story exposes tokenism as another form of class and racial prejudices and divests the Ethical Culture Society and its school of its ethics. The story's title indicates how much well-meaning white authors frame Black experiences solely within white people's needs and fears, as Toni Morrison argued in *Playing in the Dark.* The brother and sister from Harlem, first popular with the other white students in the early grades, are gradually excluded from their insular world outside. Eventually, as adolescence adds another complexity to the groups' interactions—sexuality—the boy stops coming to class and his sister remains—without friends. The white students rationalize their marginalizing the pair: they would be uncomfortable--after all, they just don't fit in.

Slesinger's awareness of the nuances of gestures and eye contacts are manifest in her acute ear. Attentive to discerning speech patterns and accents when rendering them as dialogue (as in "Kleine Fraue"), she makes clear, through syntax, that "The Times So Unsettled Are." This story, which combines a number of themes vital to Slesinger, reveals the self-absorbed romance of two American newlyweds on honeymoon in Vienna as Hitlerism rises in Germany and National Socialism encroaches on Austria. The Americans can escape Europe's impending horrors, but their Austrian friends are stuck. These unsettled Austrians' relationship survives "the times," Mariedel's euphemism for the Depression, but in the meantime, the Americans' marriage has disintegrated, further unsettling the fantasies of the Europeans that these naïve Americans are immune to tragedy. In New York, trouble looms at home and youthful love cannot survive its pressures.

Mothers and their testy relationships to grown daughters is another recurring theme of Slesinger's work. In "Mother to Dinner," her first published story from 1929, a young wife frets about her planned dinner with her mother and husband. The chaos she foresees as slights and arguments are bound to develop between the two people she most loves are foreshadowed by the impending thunderstorm darkening the sky outside her apartment windows as she procrastinates making dinner. Mothers (and mothers-in-law) loomed large in American popular culture. W.C. Fields and the Marx Brothers constantly mocked the battle axes—Margaret Dumont playing the foil to Groucho in countless movies—who bankrolled them and thus reined in these errant men, nurturing the men's comedy at the women's expense, literally and figuratively. These female stuffed shirts held the purse strings, but they were necessary and often they had lovely daughters, too.

Generational and gendered miscommunications trouble relationships, especially for the middle-class daughter seeking another kind of life than that of her mother, a life of intellectual talk of art and politics beyond the ladies' lunch set. "Deception had begun with her engagement," thinks Katherine in "Mother to Dinner." "One had to keep one's eyes constantly glowing, however terrifiedly they looked at the approaching cliff, one's words constantly gay and effervescent, lest one's mother look searchingly at the prospective bride and say, But are you sure, Darling, absolutely *sure?* Of course one was not sure. One was suspended..."[21] The effort to align with a husband who dismisses her mother splinters Katherine's marriage, but so do the questions her mother raises. As a reviewer noted of Slesinger's volume of short stories, "No one has done better with the female psychology in the throes of frustrated maternity."[22] With a mother trained as a lay analyst, how could Tess Slesinger not be attuned to womb envy? Janet Sharistanian claimed that "Mrs. Slesinger never forgave her daughter for this parable of conflict between the maternal and the masculine."[23]

There is no way to reconcile past and present, to be sure, when the times so unsettled are. Writing to Alan Wald in the 1970s, Sidney Hook claimed that Slesinger "never understood a word about the political discussions that raged around her...the political isms were something her 'obsessed husband and his old friends' were concerned about—a concern which affected her life. She ended up hating them...she was a political innocent until the day of her death."[24] This harsh assessment was likely motivated by Slesinger's later embrace of a more conventional communism than that of the anti-Stalinist leftists surrounding the Menorah group. But it is also a telling reminder of how little this group of zealous Jewish intellectuals, so attuned to workers' struggles, resisted seeing women's oppressive social, economic and political status during the 1930s (and after) or so it appeared to Slesinger's many jaded narrators.

One of the reasons Slesinger's fiction has resonated across generations is her keen sense that behind the "political discussions that raged" was a rage against women and their tiresome bodies and needy emotions. Heterosexuality and its discontents and the subtleties of the homoerotic connections between women and some men fueled her work; but sexism was an unrecognized ism among her New York intellectual set.[25]

Like so much of Slesinger's writing, the stories collected here toggle between a mood of pathos and one of satire. Her wit, a double-edged sword that for the most part served her well, was the source of frequent comment by literary critics. Novelist Robert Cantwell, writing in the *New Outlook* found *The Unpossessed* to manifest "a tireless wit...an apparently unlimited skepticism." He went on to praise how the novel "fluctuates between being good and being brilliant. The language in which these people are dissected is sharp, sometimes very witty, always full of unexpected little twists, a mocking reference to some conventional literary pose."[26] Like almost all of Slesinger's readers, he was dazzled by her prose, by her pose, of mockery and wit. Her sharp, dissecting wit may have been a defensive as well as offensive move. The following year, when *Time: The Present* appeared, some reviewers were tiring of her reliance on it: "At her best Miss Slesinger is very good indeed," concluded Marie Syrkin, "particularly when her wit is curbed by her deep understanding instead of riding roughshod over it."[27]

The Unpossessed, a fresh and welcome takedown of sanctimonious intellectual poseurs, garnered critical acclaim and popular sales. For a mid-Depression first novel, its sales in the thousands was impressive. Cantwell cited as context that between 1929 and 1931, sales of books in the United States plummeted from over 45 million copies to under 19 million. Novelists were reduced to writing book reviews (Slesinger for *The Saturday Review of Literature*) to make ends meet.

The title of *Time: The Present,* the 1935 collection of Slesinger's stories, emphasizes the currency of the issues encapsulated in each tale—and the problems of modern life, then and now, were financial, romantic, existential—how to live a decent life in fundamentally awful times. Many of the stories found here only fleetingly glance at the times writ large, instead circling back to the domestic realm and focusing on the small details of daily life—shopping at the butcher, setting the table, arranging an extravagant bunch of flowers, ending a friendship—yet History looms both within the household and beyond. A lively use of chiasmus in her titles—most vividly "A Life in the Day of a Writer" but even "White on Black"—point to Slesinger's interest in reversals, in beginnings and endings, of marriages, love affairs, friendships, jobs and writing. It's difficult to find a way into and out of that blank sheet, whether it is another person or a new work, and Slesinger's ability to go behind the scenes—of a marriage, a party, or the stage—is among the charms of the seemingly effortless fabulation she achieves through her character studies.

Commenting on the screenplay of *A Tree Grows in Brooklyn,* Judith Smith surmises that "Slesinger's literary interest may explain the film's sharpened focus on the marital discord between Katie and Johnny as well as the Freudian psychological terms with which it frames the tensions between the couple's memory of romance and the economic pressures that divide them."[28] Class intrudes into every home.

In "The Friedmans' Annie," for instance, the self-indulgent Mrs. Friedman convinces Annie, her German maid, that she should eschew a potential marriage with a fellow German immigrant and remain her loyal servant. Mrs. Friedman bribes her with cast-off evening gowns; she promises that someone better will come along in the future, while exploiting Annie in the present. Annie's devotion to her middle-class Jewish mistress belies her fantasy that the bond the two women have will overcome class (and ethnic) divisions. Annie cannot see that to Mrs. Friedman, she will never be more than a valuable possession.

The title of the story "Jobs in the Sky," plays on the refrain of Joe Hill's labor ballad, "The Preacher and the Slave": "There'll pie in the sky when I die." Here, false consciousness slowly dissolves as it dawns on Joey Andrews that he too will be canned on Christmas Eve, like Miss Paley and many others, now that the holiday rush is over at the department store where he had snagged a job in the book department. Slesinger's acute eye and ear are on amazing display in this tale of "the Commercial World." She typecasts salespeople and customers alike, gleaning clues from the titles perused and purchased about personality and status. Miss Paley, with her varicose veins, is a has-been, too fussy, too outré, for the work. But Joey loses out because he is "young and life holds many opportunities," as Miss Summers, the floor manager, reminds him when she hands him his pink slip after a grueling day. Competition for sales is the lifeblood of the commercial world, of capitalism, and whether books or workers, commodities are exchangeable, expendable. And there is always a good reason for dumping a commodity when there's a surplus. That's business, then and now.

Slesinger conveys the hectic pace of the Christmas rush through a series of biting scenes as each of the salespeople makes pitches to potential customers and then scurries to write up a sales slip documenting the purchase. The successful old-timers, making commission as well as wages, can size up a potential buyer in a heartbeat and move in for the kill. Anyone who has served the people—in sales, in restaurants, driving cabs, cleaning houses—learns this skill quickly or else is doomed to the unemployment line. And Slesinger knows it too.

That Slesinger zeros in on the psychology of workers, dissecting the mini-class struggles accompanying any encounter with the public as a mirror of the larger class dynamics within a capitalist economy is partly due to what Trilling dismissingly called her "bright controlled subjectivity of a feminine prose manner inaugurated by Katherine Mansfield, given authority by Virginia Woolf, and used...with a happy acerbity of wit superadded."[29] But it is precisely in detailing the relationships of the service economy, what we call after Maurizio Lazzarato "immaterial labor,"[30] and what Marx and Engels could not see as labor because it apparently was not productive (despite it including the reproduction of labor itself in the form of motherhood), that Slesinger speaks to our current economy, a feminized one in which women form the majority of the working class, both paid and unpaid, in the United States and much of the world.

Slesinger's stance (or at least the voice she employs in her fiction and later film scripts) as thoroughly modern discerns how urban spaces—taxicabs and automats and department stores and clerical offices—encase a new kind of labor, one that incorporates the intellectual into its functioning either as client or as worker. In this, she is nodding as Trilling noted, to Virginia Woolf's casting of the department store as the penultimate location for Orlando's time travel, as the now female poet, rushes to purchase the various items on display. By the end, the century-leaping Orlando travels up and down the elevator from floor to floor in search of "boy's boots, bath salts, sardines." And also, "sheets for a double bed." Her vertical movement matched in the final scene where she disgorges her manuscript,

Theodore Dreiser, so clearly Trilling missed something crucial about what weighs on the "controlled subjectivity of a feminine prose manner" in modern times: that is, while the proletarian novels of the 1930s were detailing the physical and psychic traumas and triumphs of factory labor and union organizing, Slesinger and many others were tracking the transition from a producing economy to one of consumption, from what was deemed a man's job to woman's work.

Hollywood also found the department store a fitting site for expressing modern times: Charlie Chaplin roller skating around its upper floors in *Modern Times* (1936); George Raft and Sylvia Sydney rehabilitating themselves as sales clerks in Fritz Lang's *You and Me* (1938); Joan Crawford batting her eyelashes at Norma Shearer's (aka, "The Old Man's Wife") husband at the perfume counter in *The Women* (1939).[36] Its displays of material goods in the midst of the Depression drew audiences as much as the stars who wandered the aisles buying and selling—a waste of time. These movies allegorized Hollywood as visual inventories of consumable objects—sexy and unattainable. By the time these films were made, Tess Slesinger was also in Hollywood working as a successful screenwriter.

Beginning with the adaptation of Pearl S. Buck's novel *The Good Earth,* she and Davis co-penned typical Hollywood fare such as *Are Husbands Necessary?* (1942) and her final film, *A Tree Grows in Brooklyn* (1945, nominated for an Academy Award). They also co-wrote the screenplay for the feminist underground classic *Dance, Girl, Dance* (1939), directed by queer icon Dorothy Arzner and starring Lucille Ball and Maureen O'Hara. Slesinger's wry, sly humor was superbly suited to the veiled double entendres floating through movie dialogue during the era of the Hays Code. In Hollywood, Slesinger immersed herself in California left-wing circles more closely aligned with the Communist Party than were her New York Anti-Stalinist comrades. She was a well-paid script writer and political activist whose life was cut short just as her career blossomed.

Her "Hollywood Gallery" comprises sketches of various studio types and was meant to serve as the basis for a second novel.[37] Those included here are loosely based on Irving Thalberg and Norma Shearer but others investigate people in all walks of Hollywood life, including "Brick,"[38] modelled on the communist organizer who led the Marxist study group held at Slesinger and Davis's home—later identified by Frank Davis as Stanley Lawrence when he testified before the House Un-American Activities Committee in 1955.[39]

Written in the 1930s and 1940s but only published as fragments in 1979, these sketches join the many Hollywood novels—Fitzgerald's *Love of the Last Tycoon* (1941), John Dos Passos's *The Big Money* (1936), Budd Schulberg's *What Makes Sammy Run?* (1941), Horace McCoy's *I*

Should Have Stayed Home (1938), Nathanael West's *Day of the Locusts* (1939), Aldous Huxley's A*fter Many a Summer Dies the Swan* (1939), Martin M. Goldsmith's *Detour: An Extraordinary Tale* (1939), as well as behind-the-scenes films from Busby Berkeley's chorus girl sagas (*Golddiggers of 1933, Footlight Parade* (1933) among them) to Billy Wilder's *Sunset Boulevard* (1950) and many more written by men—to find in Hollywoodland a metaphor for America and its emerging celebrity culture.

But none of these quite approaches what goes on in Arzner's *Dance, Girl, Dance.*

Slesinger's obituary in *Variety* describes her as being "Called to Hollywood by Metro ... after publication of two successful books,"[40] and this slippery word *called*—as a vocation or by a telephone—would have delighted her sense of irony. In Arzner's film, the question of a calling, as nun or call girl, as prima ballerina or burlesque queen, conventional poles of womanhood so prevalent in that "so often graceless thing, a novel of feminine protest," is turned on its head as it is the audience that gets called out on the inherent sexism of calling for females to perform for men's pleasure.[41]

The calling out occurs at a crucial moment towards the end of the film, which has positioned Maureen O'Hara as the good girl aspiring to follow in the footsteps of the émigré ballet mistress who is run over while crossing the street leaving her company without its head, and her opposite, Lucille Ball, known as

"Bubbles," who becomes the burlesque dancer Tiger Lily White. Ultimately, O'Hara takes a job as the straight stooge for Ball's sex queen; her role to elicit jeers from the leering men in the audience awaiting Ball's appearance. So, when O'Hara stops the show and turns on the audience, breaking the fourth wall of the stage and the screen to castigate the audience members for a demeaning interest in the women's bodies and gestures rather than see their performances as professionals, necessary for them to earn a living, she moves beyond the backstage to confront the system of voyeurism on which Hollywood is based.

In many ways, this gesture of female solidarity and defiance of an entertainment industry that bartered women's bodies, often by pitting them against one another, allegorized the reasons Slesinger gave for remaining in the Screen Writers Guild despite being pressured to resign from it by her boss Irving Thalberg, who told her that she "owed her living [to the studio] and that I had been a starving writer before they took me on... and that the Guild was an enemy of the motion picture industry and I couldn't be loyal to both," as she testified before the National Labor Relations Board Los Angeles hearing in October 1937.[42] Her loyalty was to those professionals who made movies, not the big shots who ran the works.

Tess Slesinger continued to write screenplays, but to some degree *Dance, Girl, Dance* hints at an unfulfilled turn in her career, toward political activism and work on another biting novel. During the late 1930s and early 1940s, she was engaged with the left-wing causes swirling around Hollywood. In addition to the Screen Writer's Guild, she was a board member of the California League of Women Shoppers,[43] an active supporter of the Hollywood Anti-Nazi League, a fundraiser for the Republican cause in the Spanish Civil War, an advocate for Tom Mooney and the Scottsboro boys. Her early support of the Screen Writers Guild helped ensure its success when it had negotiated its first certified contract through collective bargaining in 1941.

The party's not yet over, but it is winding down. The year before the release of *Dance, Girl, Dance,* the Nazi-Soviet Nonaggression Pact was signed by Hitler and Stalin throwing many allied with the Communist left (especially Jews) into turmoil. Tess Slesinger died on February 21, 1945, at age 39, coincidentally 20 years to the day after the first issue of *The New Yorker* appeared. Frank continued writing and producing for film and television, his last credit being a remake of their film version of *A Tree Grows in Brooklyn.* And almost three decades after Slesinger's death, their son, Peter Davis, directed the essential antiwar film about Vietnam *Hearts and Minds* (1974), a milestone in political documentary filmmaking that won the Academy Award for Best Documentary in 1975. Until her death, Slesinger continued to write for California left-wing journals and craft scripts to subtly foreground a social critique;[44] but her illness curtailed her efforts to finish a second novel. The times so unsettled were—and still are.

Notes

I wish to thank Charlotte Nekola, Jani Scandura and Alan Wald for their keen suggestions for improving my essay.

Endnotes

1.   For a brief overview of Slesinger's biography see my entry on her in *The Shalvi-Hyman Encyclopedia of Jewish Women.* https://jwa.org/encyclopedia/article/slesinger-tess

2.   The original brief is on view from the collection of the New York Public Library at the "Treasures" exhibit, Fall 2021.

3.   Morris Dickstein, "Womb versus World," *Bookforum* June/July/August/ September 2006 https://www.bookforum.com/print/1302/womb-versus-world-564

4.   Clearly, unlike Roth who retreated to rural life according to his obituary by Richard E. Nichols "Henry Roth, 89, Who Wrote of

Immigrant Child's Life in 'Call It Sleep' is Dead," *New York Times* (October 15, 1995): 41, Slesinger remained an active member of New York's intellectual scene, for a few years living in Greenwich Village and having a brief affair with Max Eastman. Like so many modern women, she had been "reno-vated." For more on the commodification of the divorce industry and its contribution to a new kind of American woman during the 1930s, see "Reno: The Divorce Factory" in Jani Scandura, *Down in the Dumps: Place, Modernity, American Depression* (Durham, NC: Duke University Press, 2008), pp 30-69.

5.   Alan M. Wald, *The New York Intellectuals: The Rise and Decline of the Anti-Stalinist Left from the 1930s to the 1980s.* [1987]. Thirtieth Anniversary Edition (Chapel Hill: University of North Carolina Press, 2017), 69. Wald first explored the story of the New York intellectuals through his interest in Tess Slesinger, whose novel he found in the University of California Berkeley stacks as a graduate student in 1971, in "The Menorah Group Moves Left," *Jewish Social Studies* 38 (Summer-Fall 1976): 289-320. Email message to author from Alan Wald, November 9, 2021.

6.   Jerre Mangione, *An Ethnic at Large: A Memoir of America in the Thirties and Forties* (New York: Putnam, 1978), p. 159.

7.   Historian Alice Echols is currently researching how Wolfe's antipathy towards the limousine liberals of the Upper East Side began at Yale University, when he wrote his PhD dissertation in the American Studies program on the League of American Writers.

8.   Janet Sharistanian, "Tess Slesinger's Hollywood Sketches," *Michigan Quarterly Review* 18:3 (1979): 429-39, 433. Citing Hy Kraft, Jonathan Miles, the biographer of Otto Katz, who was known in Hollywood as Rudolf Breda and helped organize the Hollywood

Anti-Nazi League, mentions that "Tess Slesinger, left-wing satirist and Paramount scriptwriter, gave an informal party of Breda, who was on top form. There was a 'charged air of mystery and danger' about him." Jonathan Miles, *The Dangerous Otto Katz: The Many Lives of a Soviet Spy* (New York: Bloomsbury, 2010), pp. 155-56.

9. Elizabeth Hardwick, "Introduction," *The Unpossessed* (New York: New York Review Books, 2002), xii.

10. Murray Kempton, *Part of Our Time: Some Ruin and Monuments of the Thirties* [1955] (New York: NYRB, 2004), 122. Lionel Trilling who hung out with the *Menorah Journal* crowd, even attending Tess Slesinger and Herbert Solow's 1928 wedding at the Ethical Culture Society center on Central Park West where Tess had attended school, adamantly rejected Kempton's use of the term "document," but methinks he doth protest too much...in part because the document was a reigning aesthetic of the 1930s and because Slesinger so carefully limns outlines to be filled in by those in the know. In some sense, this is the hallmark of a document which guides an interpretation but never provides the complete picture of the event, person, place, etc.

11. Kempton. p. 121

12. Herbst's collection, *The Starched Blue Sky of Spain* and Gellhorn's reporting for *The New Yorker,* beginning with "Madrid to Morada," (16 July 1937) https://www.newyorker.com/magazine/1937/07/24/madrid-to-morata were only some examples of women writing about Spain. For more details, see Noël Valis, "'From the Face of My Memory': American Women Journalists in the Spanish Civil War," *The Volunteer* (27 February 2018). https://albavolunteer.org/2018/02/from-the-face-of-my-memory-american-women-journalists-in-the-spanish-civil-war/ . For dozens of

authors, see Charlotte Nekola and Paula Rabinowitz,eds. *Writing Red: An Anthology of American Women Writers, 1930-1940* [1987] Chicago: Haymarket Press, 2022.

13. "Missis Flinders," the novel's final section first appeared in *Story* in 1932. In her "Afterword," to *The Unpossessed* (New York: Feminist Press, 1984), p. 385, Janet Sharistanian quotes the editors of Story who selected it for reprinting in their tenth anniversary issue as one of the ten best published among more than 1000 over the previous decade: it "cross-sectioned the mind of a woman foregoing motherhood. It had been rejected all over American, and when it appeared in *Story,* it was the first story with its subject matter ever to appear in a magazine of general circulation." *Story Magazine* (May-June 1941): 28. Abortion had appeared earlier in some American women's novels—Ursula Parrott's *Ex-Wife* (1929) and Edith Wharton's *Summer* (1917) among them—but this was a story in a mass circulation magazine with a far wider readership than a novel, even a popular one, might glean.

14. *Writing Red* (New York: Feminist Press, 1987) includes Slesinger's story "The Mouse-Trap," about sexual harassment (before it was so named) at the workplace and labor organizing, pp. 106-124.

15. Paula Rabinowitz, *Labor and Desire: Women's Revolutionary Fiction in Depression America* (Chapel Hill: University of North Carolina Press, 1991), chapter 4: "Grotesque Creatures: The Female Intellectual as Subject," pp. 137-172.

16. Lionel Trilling, "Afterword," *The Unpossessed* by Tess Slesinger [1934] (New York: Avon Books, 1966), p. 314.

17. Publisher's Note to Tess Slesinger, *On Being Told That Her Second Husband Has Taken His First Lover and Other Stories* (New York: Quadrangle Books, 1971), p. ix.

18.   Sharistanian, "Tess Slesinger's Hollywood Sketches," p. 436.

19.   Myrna Dunham, "Ambivalent Times: The Short Fiction of Tess Slesinger," MA Thesis, Iowa State University, 1983, p. 1. See also, Sharistanian, "Afterword," p. 359-61 for more biographical information on Augusta Singer Slesinger.

20.   In the 1993 film *Shadowlands,* about the relationship between left-wing American writer Joy Davidman and Oxford Don and novelist C.S. Lewis, Debra Winger, who plays Davidman, explains to Lewis (Anthony Hopkins) that in the 1930s is you weren't a communist, then you were a fascist.

21.   Slesinger, *On Being Told...,* p. 109. This volume, like the present one, was a reissue of *Time: The Present* and dedicated "To My Mother and Father."

22.   Marie Syrkin, rev. of *Time: The Present* in *Jewish Frontier* (November 1935): 24-25, 24.

23.   Sharistanian, "Afterword," p. 364.

24.   Wald, p. 40.

25.   I made this point in *Labor and Desire,* p. 149.

26.   Robert Cantwell, "Outlook Book Choice of the Month," rev. of *The Unpossessed* in *New Outlook* 163: 6 (1934): 52-57, pp. 52, 57. A few years later, Cantwell (along with Herbert Solow) would help Whittaker Chambers secure a job at *Time* magazine after he had ceased serving as a courier between State Department employees and the Soviet Union. See Allen Weinstein and Alexander Vassiliev, *The Haunted Wood: Soviet Espionage in American—the Stalin Era* (New York: Modern Library, 1999), pp. 46-47. Lionel Trilling's novel, *The Middle of the Journey* [1947] about disillusioned 1930s

leftists and their paths away from communism fictionalizes Chambers odd odyssey within a complex tale that is not an exact record perhaps explaining his reluctance to see *The Unpossessed* as a document, see "Introduction" (New York: Penguin Modern Classics, 1977), vii. Such were the interlocking connections among left-wing intellectuals during the 1930s and 1940s, which resurfaced in the 1960s and 1970s.

27.   Syrkin, p. 25.

28.   Judith Smith, *Visions of Belonging: Family Stories, Popular Culture, and Postwar Democracy, 1940-1960* (New York: Columbia University Press, 2004), p. 63. Moreover, Sharistanian notes that despite Tess being doted upon by her parents and older brothers, there was tension, class tensions among them, between her parents. Theirs was not a happy marriage: "Because of the sharp difference in their personalities, because Augusta Slesinger enjoyed steady professional success while Anthony Slesinger's status in the public world was insecure, and because Anthony was doing unpalatable work in what had been his father-in-law's [garment] business, there was considerable tension in their relationship," "Afterword," p. 361.

29.   Trilling, "Afterword," p. 330.

30.   Maurizio *Lazzarato [1996]. "Immaterial Labor." In Paolo Virno and Michael Hardt, eds. Radical Thought in Italy: A Potential Politics. (Minneapolis: University of Minnesota Press, 2006), pp. 142–157.*

31.   Virginia Woolf, *Orlando: A Biography* [1928] (New York: Harvest/Harcourt Brace Jovanovich, 1956), pp. 300-301. Michael North, *What is the Present?* (Princeton: Princeton University Press, 2018) dissects how the concept of the present enables an engagement with not only modern times, but time writ large.

32.   For more on the modern novel and department stores, see Rachel Bowlby, *Just Looking: Consumer Culture in Dreiser, Gissing, and Zola* (London: Routlege, 1985).

33.   Theodore Dreiser, *Sister Carrie* [1900] (New York: New American Library/Signet Classic, 2000), p.21.

34.   Kate Chopin, "A Pair of Silk Stockings." [1897]. In *The Complete Works,* ed. Per Seyersted (Baton Rouge: Louisiana State University Press, 1969) I: 500-504. In "Sheer Luxury: Kate Chopin's 'A Pair of Silk Stockings'," Cristina Giorcelli argues that by eschewing her responsibilities as a mother who should have spent her money on her children and buying herself accessories: new black stockings and boots (which she displays by lifting her skirt to cross the street) and kid gloves, "little" Mrs. Sommers enters the modern world through the "dream" of her self-indulgence as a purchaser not only of accessories but of "high-priced magazines" and "a tasty bite" at a restaurant and a matinee seat at a theater. In *Habits of Being 2: Exchanging Clothes* ed. Cristina Giorcelli and Paula Rabinowitz (Minneapolis: University of Minnesota Press, 2012), pp.78-96. Patricia Highsmith's *The Price of Salt* (1952) places the start of the romance between Therese, working the toy department and Carol.

35.   Trilling, p. 330.

36.   These mid- to late-1930s films' location had already been the setting for a remarkable example of left-wing Chinese popular modernist cinema, *Cosmetics Market* (dir. Zhang Shichuan, 1933) Chinese title: 脂粉市场. Aleksander Sedzielarz brought this film to my attention in Chapter 4 of his dissertation, "The Revolutionary Task of Cinema: Modernism and Mass Culture in Shanghai and Buenos Aires," PhD. Dissertation, University of Minnesota, 2019,

entitled "Bullets, Bodies, and Beauty: Leftist Sound Cinema and the Militant Modernism of Xia Yan," pp. 239-243.

37.   See Sharistanian "Tess Slesinger's Hollywood Sketches," pp. 429-39.

38.   Tess Slesinger, "Brick," in "A Hollywood Gallery," *Michigan Quarterly Review* 18:3 (1979): 446-54.

39.   Testimony of Frank Davis, Hearings by the Committee on Un-American Activities, Communist Activities in Los Angeles, #2522, 84th Congress, First Session, 13 October, 1955, released 30 December 1955.

40.   Obituary for Tess Slesinger, *Variety* 157: 12 (February 28, 1945), p. 46. The newspaper of Tinseltown claimed she arrived in Hollywood in 1937; but they got the date wrong. She came to Hollywood in 1935.

41.   Trilling, p.331.

42.   Quoted in Shirley Biaggi, "Forgive me for Dying," *The Antioch Review* 35 (Spring-Summer 1977): 224-36, 233.

43.   California Legislature, "Report of the Joint Fact-Finding Committee on Un-American Activities," 1943, lists Tess Slesinger as among its "directors and sponsors," p. 102.

44.   According to Sharistanian, "One of Slesinger's more interesting unproduced scripts...was based on the life of Elizabeth Blackwell, the first woman doctor in the United States." "Afterword," p. 384.

Time: The Present
Selected Stories of Tess Slesinger

First published in this edition by Boiler House Press, 2022
Part of UEA Publishing Project
Time: The Present: Selected Stories of Tess Slesinger copyright ©
Tess Slesinger 1935, renewed 1962
Introduction copyright © Vivian Gornick, 2022
Afterword copyright © Paula Rabinowitz, 2022

Proofreading by Clare Kernie

Cover Design and Typesetting by Louise Aspinall
Typeset in Arnhem Pro
Printed by Ingram Book Group
Distributed by NBN International

ISBN: 978-1-913861-58-2

9 781913 861582